# The Last to Know

# THE LAST TO KNOW

## Candida Crewe

C

Century · London

Published by Century in 1998

1 3 5 7 9 10 8 6 4 2

First published in the United Kingdom in 1998 by Century
Random House UK Limited
20 Vauxhall Bridge Road, London SW1V 2SA

Random House Australia (Pty) Limited
20 Alfred Street, Milsons Point, Sydney,
New South Wales 2061, Australia

Random House New Zealand Limited
18 Poland Road, Glenfield
Auckland 10, New Zealand

Random House South Africa (Pty) Limited
Endulini, 5a Jubilee Road, Parktown 2193, South Africa

Random House UK Limited Reg. No. 954009

A CIP catalogue record for this book is available from the British Library

Papers by Random House UK Limited are natural, recyclable products made
from wood grown in sustainable forests. The manufacturing processes conform
to the environmental regulations of the country of origin

ISBN 0 7126 7574 4

Typeset by SX Composing DTP, Rayleigh, Essex

Printed and bound in Great Britain by
Mackays of Chatham PLC, Chatham, Kent

For my mother and father

# Acknowledgements

With many thanks to the Authors' Foundation for their generous award which helped considerably during the writing of this novel.

Also thanks to:
Elizabeth Bennett, Dr Annette Steele, Dr Heather Elliott and Sue Stone.

# 1

It's the sound of flapping, soft feather and delicate bone, going like a dying man's convulsions. Haunts me. I used to know a woman with a phobia about dolls. The rigid limbs, she told me, with their shocking pinkness; and those uniform roots springing glistening hair. They said if she went to have it cured, her fears would only come out in something else, more inconvenient perhaps, like buttons or wasps. Myself, I have a thing about birds. The claws, the juttering eyes, and of course that sound.

My name is Sylvia Black. I'm married to Kim. I'm as ordinary as ordinary can be, quite dull really. The only unusual aspect of me is my fear of birds in general, pigeons in particular. Luckily we're far away from Trafalgar Square, spot of all my nightmares. It's a phobia I can hold in check if I keep my wits about me. The children had guinea pigs, never budgerigars, and if I'm shopping in the city centre I tend to avoid St Giles. The pigeons congregate there round the church, in hellish numbers. The street where I work is OK. The pigeons ignore it. It's a quiet street. Nothing there to appeal to Oxford's tourists and the attractive detritus they like to leave in their wake – crusts of sandwiches, unforgiven sausage rolls. As far as I'm concerned, this is one of the perks of the job: it's a virtually pigeon-free location.

I'm a Court Welfare Officer. It sounds like I'm the person who hands out the tea to those awaiting their cases, the one who shows them to the relevant courtrooms. In fact what I do is help disaffected couples sort out their wrangles over the children, and then make appropriate recommendations to the judge regarding residence and contact. There's nothing I haven't seen. It's a job which can break your heart on a daily basis if you don't watch out; only the unspoken rule of the profession is your heart must stay intact.

Mine is holding out due to the love and support of my family. I have emotional days, but it's the family which keeps me strong. Kim and I will have been married for twenty-three years next

1

month, and I think I can safely say he's never been unfaithful to me, although I believe women who state that uncategorically are fools. The only person you are with twenty-four hours a day is yourself, so actually the only person you know for absolute certain who's remained forever faithful is yourself. Even so I'd stake a pretty large bet Kim has never strayed. He thrives on familiarity, the comforts of home. He's a man who has his own place on the sofa, won't even let me puff up the cushions because his indentation in them represents the security of permanence.

We live in east Oxford, off the Cowley Road in a street called Divinity Road. Victorian terraced houses. Kim is a GP. He and his partners, Sam, Clive and Abigail, are based at a practice in Cowley. Kim loves his work but is almost permanently exhausted. Of an evening he likes to have a quiet time in with me, reading a book, watching television, catching up on the weekend papers' motoring sections. I couldn't care less about cars myself, as long as they don't give out on me, but he maintains this modest little obsession of his, sometimes even buys car magazines, studies them with as much attention as he studies the *British Medical Journal*. I don't feel excluded by this, nor am I irritated by it. It's just another manifestation of his passionate nature. He's a passionate man.

We have two children. Our son, Jack Black, is twenty-two. He left school at sixteen and looked for a job for three years. Now he's working as an assistant chef in one of the university colleges. He started out last year as a kitchen porter and worked his way up. These days he's chopping carrots for stews and cottage pies, and apples for the crumbles. His fingers fairly race with a knife. He lives at home but his hours are such we rarely see him. Sometimes, when I come down in the night to get a drink of water, I catch him in the white light of the fridge, a silhouette against the milk cartons and hazelnut yogurts. It's always, 'Oh, hi, Mum, just got in, fixing myself a sandwich, starving, have we run out of cheddar?' It's Kim's voice he's got, and in the dark I'm thrown. At once I hear my husband as a young man again, same voice as that which asked me to marry him; and I also hear my child as an adult. I still can't get used to the idea that I, as a woman, have given birth to a man, a man what's more who no longer has the soft skin and rounded contours of a boy, but whose

2

outline is now defined by perfectly natural but nonetheless curious muscles and angles – sinewy forearms, pointed Adam's apple; who has ambitions, that are quite literally none of my business; and to whom girls no doubt give compliments which I both do and don't want to hear. Jack intends to graduate to a restaurant, get a house, a car, almost certainly a wife, probably kids, though I'd never press him. I have no doubt he will achieve all these things.

His sister Mackenzie, four years his junior, is at college in Northern Ireland. She wants to be a physiotherapist. I admire her desire to help people in a way I never could, to tend to limps and bruises, to fashion back into working order dead-bird flesh and bone. You wouldn't want to be squeamish in a job like that. Kim and I have our reasons to be proud, content.

So who am I, Sylvia Black, to dictate to broken families what should happen to them?

Sometimes, when I'm sitting in our kitchen, with its soothing tones and reliable features like a pen on a string near the phone and cushions tied onto the chairs with ribbons, I ask myself this question. Like this evening. Who am I, with my little nuclear creation of a family, to know what's best for mothers and fathers and children at war? Who am I?

It is November. The sky fell dark at four o'clock but the artificial street lamps obscure the stars, and it's a wistful moon. When I drove home the wipers were working overtime smoothing the amber rain from the windscreen. I inched in the traffic along the Cowley Road away from my gruelling day, but it was still with me.

Still is. I had, first thing, a family conference, something which has a habit of lingering in the mind. It's when I meet a couple and their kids for the first time, an introduction to them and their circumstances which goes on for an hour and a half.

I popped into my office to knock back a cup of coffee, gather papers, collect my thoughts for a few moments before the intense session ahead of me. I'd left the window open last night. My room is small and was cold as a morgue. I sat with my coat on at my desk, clutched the polystyrene cup, and sniffed my raspberry-coloured nose into the coffee steam. I couldn't move, just stared at the leaflets and postcards on my notice board – *Domestic*

*Violence: The Enemy Within*; Van Gogh's *Sunflowers*. I've not managed to warm up yet.

With loose documents under my arm, I rushed to the Family Room a few doors along from my office. It has no windows, but it does have a skylight and that carpet, popular in office buildings, of bile-green tiles with a hairy texture which spooks the skin. It has armchairs, and a low table covered with blunt wax crayons the colours of a dreamcoat. A children's plastic postbox of a reassuring red stands in the corner, its dark slit shaped into a smile. Surrounding it are a number of stuffed toys with faces designed for maximum appeal.

The Winstons, having been shown in by our receptionist, were waiting for me. They were talking in low voices as if not really allowed. I did the usual greetings, trying to make them feel at ease ('I'm Sylvia but please call me Sylvie, everyone does').

I met Mum, whose name is Sally Winston. She was wearing purple leggings and white trainers, and for the first hour couldn't look the rest of us in the eye. With her were her ex-husband, Richard, and her parents, Glenn and Joy, who are seeking residence of their six-year-old granddaughter.

'If they gang up on me, I'm out of here,' Sally said almost immediately, staring at the floor and shifting her weight in her seat.

'We're not here to gang up on you, Sally,' Joy reasoned. Joy had a kindly face, folds of her neck a hanging of faded, dusty pink velvet like the Lord Mayor's curtains; grey hair tinged with blue as faintly as recycled glass is tinged with green. She was palpably tired, exhausted out of retirement by having to be a young mother again, only old.

'It's a takeover bid, that's what it is,' groaned Sally.

If people ask me about my job, I say the best way to describe it is I'm a sort of emotional funambulist. Remember as a child going to stay at a friend's house, needing to pee in the night; having that out of proportion fear about waking anyone, walking down the passage, bladder stinging fit to burst, yet desperately trying not to make a single creak because one's life depended on it? It's the same in that Family Room, I'm treading so I don't make even one fateful creak, but I've still got to find my way.

'All right, Sally,' I said, voice soft. 'Let's start at the begin-

4

ning, because I've only the sketchiest details of the situation.
You've got Flora for the weekends only, is that right? And your
mum and dad have her during the week because that way she's
closer to school?'

'I lost my licence.'

'So it seems the most practical arrangement then?' I ask,
looking at her while writing notes at the same time. Body
language is all-important. You look at people to gain their trust,
obviously. It didn't take me long to learn that; in fact, I like to
think I knew it instinctively. Took me a long time, mind you, to
learn to write without looking. Even now, seven years a CWO, I
often find I can't read back my own handwriting, could be squid-
ink noodles. 'Best for Flora to be with your parents during the
week?'

'Drink-driving.' Sally still fixed her gaze away from us, now at
the floor; now at the postbox, whose smile proved not to be infectious.

'Drinking's the main problem,' her father commented quietly,
folding his arms on his belly, and leaning back into the armchair,
his patterned jersey merging with the herringbone upholstery.

'When I'm depressed, I drink. It's a problem when I drink but
not the rest of the time. But it seems to be a problem for my
family all of the time. It's what's brought us here, drink. It's
everything.'

'The problem started,' Joy told the room, 'when she came on
the bus to pick Flora up, Fridays, and she was drunk. Flora
knows. Soon as Sally came into view, she'd start creating.'

'Yeah, but as soon as she was out of sight of the bungalow, it
was over. All it was was a drama performance. She's six going on
thirty-six. I never have any problem with her. Take bedtime.
They're too soft,' Sally said, kicking her crossed leg in her
parents' direction but still not looking at them. 'She can manipu-
late them, and what good's that for a kid if she knows she can do
that?'

'It's different styles of parenting maybe?' I asked.

You have to be so damn careful all the time, I guess that's
partly what I'm paid for. Tact and discretion, absence of prejudice. You're not just treading on creaky floorboards, you're
treading on ones that are quite likely to crack underfoot any

5

minute, have you fall through. It's imperative never to judge, or at least to be seen to judge. Times I think someone's a real shit or a complete bitch, unreasonable and selfish to a degree, but they must never know that. You always read about those who work in highly responsible jobs, moving billions round the international money markets, giving out under the strain, succumbing to heart attacks and what have you, at all of thirty-two. I'd say dealing with the delicate lace of a child's welfare and formative years, arguably having a hand in the eventual pattern and design, is an altogether more serious affair, if less noisy, conspicuous, pin-striped. We go about our invisible, less splish-splash business – who's ever heard of a CWO? – and while I can attest to the fact it, too, has its especial highs, my God, it also has its own stresses. I'm not meant to take it home with me but, honestly, could I call myself a human being if I didn't? Sometimes the faces of those I'm trying to help, and voices, stay with me for the nights as well as the days; cause me to turn in my sleep so my pillow is twisted in the morning, its case troubled with wrinkles; and my neck, over-wrought, is positively bleating to be relieved of its aching pains.

The Winston family have the faces and voices of ordinary people, no memorable features, would blend into a crowd like crumbs into a lardy cake. It's just a sweet old couple with liver pâté colouring, raw egg-white eyes, gnarled hands, comfort shoes, and sensible knitwear. I have the nasty feeling that if there were a shocking homicide, the police would be hard pressed to issue descriptions which would be distinct enough to jog a single person's recollection. Perhaps Joy's Germoline-pink anorak with its detailed braid the length of the zipper and round the cuffs might just yield something in someone's mind. As for Sally, there's her purple leggings. And cheeks and eyes, puffed up by long-term, conspicuous sadness. Her face belies her thirty-one years, has aged beyond its time. Then there's her ex-husband, Richard, quiet Richard, can't be twenty-nine if he's a day, who would blend into any crowd. A modest character, only speaks when he is spoken to; the sort who just wants the easy life, and has the face and voice to show for it – diffident expression, mumbled whispers. He leans his head against the crayon-infested wall behind his chair, perhaps out of habit, perhaps to hide his youthful bald patch. He has got a leather jacket, a brown, blouson one; what he's not got is attitude, and she, Sally, clearly still loves him for it.

In that Family Room, with its improbable props – the smiling postbox and a stuffed laughing lion – I learn the things that the Winstons – and many more besides – spend their existence otherwise trying to conceal. And those private things I have the privilege of hearing sharply bring into relief the fact that their lives are far from plain and simple. I suppose I'm a hypocrite, because while I believe I'm as ordinary as they come and always will be, every day I am being educated in such a way as to know there's no such thing as an ordinary person. It's a patronising perception, one cherished by those who think their lives are full of glamour and incident and intrigue and variety. Perhaps they make the luxurious distinction between themselves and 'ordinary' people, because it bestows upon them a sort of status, lends a sense of purpose to their own vacuous and usually materialistic existence. Well, I'm one of their 'ordinary' people, with a semi-detached house, and a wholly attached husband, two point nought kids, a dab hand with a duster, and a phobia about flapping.

As I say, these 'ordinary' people, the Winstons, have the extraordinary power to come home with me, even though they're not here. In the womb of my kitchen, I can hear the melancholy requiem of their blighted voices and sorrows.

'They're not parenting her,' Sally's saying, 'they're grandparenting her, and there's a difference.'

'Bugger the different styles of parenting, Sally,' Glenn snaps, ''Scuse my French, Sylvia. Whatever the rights and wrongs of all this different parenting malarkey, the bottom line is drink, that's the crux of the problem here.'

At this point, it's my own voice, asking Flora's father, who hasn't said a word, what he thought, would he be seeing her at all?

'I can a bit at the moment,' Richard replies, 'but I've taken a new job in Nantwich. I'll be coming most weekends to visit, but it mightn't be possible every one.'

'Does that arrangement suit you, Sally?'

'Yeah, Richard and me, we're best friends.'

Richard was the diplomat of the family, respectful to his ex-parents-in-law; loyal to his ex-wife; torn; loyal to his child.

Sally is choked. We can all see her eyes beginning to glisten, tears gathering at the rims and whites turning that crying red of a glacé cherry. Watching her, I remember that thing, as a kid, when Mum used to tick me off, I'd feel the coal-like lump pressing in the throat trying to push out the tears. I was damned if I was going to let her see me cry. I couldn't speak, used to suck in my lips and grip them in my teeth until they bled, anything to keep the flow in check. Sometimes, although practically about to burst, I could just about hold myself together, then afterwards rush away and be alone. Other times, the collapse would come in front of her, a huge heaving gasp followed by shaking sobs, and the sense of failure would be grotesque.

I can see the same, unbearable, childlike struggle in Sally; and almost feel the hot headache smacking her brow. She's staring at the ceiling, unblinking, lips downturned like a bad luck horse-shoe. That level of dignity always moves me. They say people like Sally, with alcohol or drugs problems, lose their dignity. It's a view I find disappointing. The greater the vulnerability, the more remarkable and affecting the leap to dignity.

I pass Sally a box of tissues, and she sniffs with relief, a minus-cule act of charity giving her leave at last to let go.

'I just want her back with me weekdays,' she groans, and pauses to cry. 'That's it. I've got so much competition against me it's unbelievable.'

'We don't really want to bring up another child,' ventures Joy. 'But while she's not got any money, and still drinking . . .' Her words are petering out.

'At the end of the day the judge will decide,' Glenn says, taking over.

I can see Sally becoming angrier, louder. 'They always threaten me with the judge, the courts. Crap. She's my daughter. I'm not giving up my legal rights.'

'If the judge ruled against her,' Joy tells me, 'she said she'd kill herself and her father could dance on her grave and tell himself, "I did that."'

It's ordinarily, irredeemably sad.

Kim's not back yet. I switch on the telly which hangs from a metal arm above the kitchen table, but I don't look at it or hear it.

8

I lean against the oven and wonder what might be in the house I could knock up for our supper. My feet are cold. I pour myself a glass of wine. I need it after my morning, and my afternoon in court. A couple of clients of mine, Paul and Marie, were shouting blue murder at each other before we went in. Times like that, I am the referee, only minus the black shorts and the whistle. They were ready to hit each other over something trivial. Paul bringing their sons back to Marie in T-shirts covered with choc-ice and Ribena. Before I started this job, I always wondered what couples meant when they said they argued about the tiniest things. Kim and I don't argue much, and if we do you'll never catch us at it over the toothpaste cap. When we have a go at each other, it's about money, or our jobs, or sex. It's good to get straight to the point because it means you can sort out the real issue. But I suppose it's easier to flip out over the small things. The other day I read about a husband who caught his wife in bed with another man and never said a word. A few days later they were eating their lunch and she wouldn't pass him the mustard. So he stabbed her in the throat with a fish-knife.

I'm looking forward to Kim getting home. Company. We always have a good chat in the evenings. We've been apart just a few hours but every night we've these news bulletins for each other.

I hear about the trials and tribulations of his patients – a finger mangled here, a benign lump rumbled there. I tell him about my fellow Court Welfare Officers. Giving no surnames, I also tell him about my cases. He says listening to me on each one is like shaking a kaleidoscope afresh, the colours and patterns of human nature, how its configurations fall and form, are infinite and compelling.

Some might say it's strange we like to keep our own company, and still have so much to talk about after all these years. I like to call it marriage. Optimistic, maybe, but when there's no talk, what is there left but the husk of a marriage? In my particular line of work I'm sifting through the husks most days. Paul, who I was with this afternoon and who's demanding weekends with his children, is typical. Last time the three of us had a meeting, he said he found it easier to talk to his ferret than to his wife. I remember, when he told me that, Marie rolled her eyes to the heavens, but they were bleary eyes, and in that moment the parched scroll of their marriage unfolded right there in front of me, I suddenly got a glimpse of the whole. He swung his crossed leg with a sing-song indifference; his mind had moved on, the pink hurt in her eyes to him just a background irritant like an intermittent car alarm. As if terrified of being blown away, she clutched the arms of the chair. I'm the mother of your children, were her words, we should be together as a family. She was a woman who for all the world wanted to be the one he chose to speak to, to come back to. And the more she tried to draw him out, the more he resorted to whoever else, a mistress, an animal, almost anything but her. You clutter saucepans, he accused, face turned away, pincered profile, and you're an inadequate mother, let the children watch too many cartoons, drink too many fizzy drinks, and wear a shade of green that don't suit them. I listen, and in common with Kim, am constantly astonished by the variety of human misery I happen upon in the course of any working week. Each family unhappy after its own fashion. Each one a salutary lesson how to try not to be. I am reminded every day, can never forget, and for that, I am a lucky soul.

Kim's key in the lock, a comforting shiver of metal against metal. I'm sitting in the kitchen, haven't turned on the lights. There is only the lightning-sky flickering of the television, and grease-splattered glow from the oven in which some fish is baking for our supper. I call out otherwise he won't know I'm here, I'll give him a fright.

Felty tread in the hall.

'Where are you, my love? What're you sitting in the dark for?'

His face appears round the door, smiles. He has a big face with a small double chin which, when he laughs, wobbles just enough for me to notice. I want it to stay there; it's him, my Kim, he wouldn't be the same without it. 'I haven't been home long,' I say. 'Catching my breath.'

'Family conference today?' He taps the plastic switch with his knuckles not his forefinger. It's one of his many funny ways. The kitchen, which I keep show-room clean, seems warmer in the yellowy light thrown out by the long bulbs hidden behind the well-tailored cupboards which are my pride and joy. I amaze myself sometimes with the excitement I can glean from something so inherently dreary as kitchen units. Perhaps it's an inanimate refuge from my catalogues of animated sadness.

'Was it ever,' I reply.

He joins me at the table, puts his hand on my immodest knee, keeps it there, a wholesome presence. 'Yet another completely new twist on family relations?' Close-up, Kim smells as ever he does when he arrives home after a long day. It's a unique mixture – surgery clinical and husband's very own. You couldn't bottle it.

'A complicated one, yes. Grandparents seeking residence because of the mother's drink problem.'

'Child misses its mum?'

'Oh, yes. Except when she's drunk. When she's been on a binge she falls so fast asleep the kid can't wake her. She's only six.'

'The mother admit she's an alcoholic?'

'Up to a point. Denies it's a major problem, reckons she can cope.'

'Father around at all?'

'He was there, sympathetic, anxious to do his best, not much part of the picture though. I suspect she's still in love with him. She held her hand out to him when she was really crying at the end; kept repeating and repeating that she felt this terrible sense of loss. Her husband as well as her child.'

'Not good, not good at all.'

'Well, it's going to take some sorting. Fancy a glass of wine? Or there should be some beer in the fridge.' I move to reach for one or the other, but Kim keeps his hand on my knee.

'No rush,' he says. 'Pass us the remote there, my love, the seven o'clock must be about to start.'

Kim's one of those people, they're a breed, who's always frantic to catch the news. Of an evening he's quite happy to watch the six o'clock, the seven o'clock, and the nine and ten o'clock. Two of them is just about sufficient, but if he can only catch one I can see him getting really quite fidgety. That's one of the reasons he doesn't like to go out to eat much with friends. It's not just that he loves me so much he doesn't need for others' company! I tell him in another life he should have been a newscaster. He refers to them all by their first names as it is. I think he'd be rather good at it. He'd love being surrounded by the news every minute of his working day.

I used to ask him why he was so bothered to see all the bulletins. 'The world's a big place,' he would say, 'important things are happening every second, not just conveniently in time for six o'clock! There could be a new war breaking out, or a plane crash, a deadly disease discovered, or a military coup, anything.'

Me, I'm someone who could wait to read about it in the paper the next morning, though it was never any use my putting this to Kim.

'But then you'll have had a *whole night* not knowing about something.'

I like that, that unjaded quest for knowledge of what's going on in the world, that desire for a greater understanding, an overview. I fear I am more parochial, happy to learn about the world within my own little world. Certainly there's enough in the Oxfordshire area I cover for a lifetime's study. Perhaps that's why I don't feel that hankering others do, constantly to travel. It's all here, everything to be learnt about life, on my one square inch of canvas.

I envy Kim's sort of blanket altruism. Not always, obviously, but sometimes he sends bouquets of flowers to bereaved families of children who have died, or money to a fund for single mothers when he hears their benefits have been cut. There's all manner of things on the news that anger or move him. And much though he enjoys his own comforts, he can't just sit in his cushion indentations on the sofa, me lovingly by his side, and do nothing. It's one of the reasons he's a doctor. Some would say he's a soft touch, but it's one of the reasons you love a person, if they have so much love for mankind in general. His fascination with my work is not just about what his Sylvie is up to, it's also about the plights of those I come into contact with. His infinite curiosity and concern may mean my having to sit through the news five times every night – that's if you include *Newsnight* – but we do jabber our heads off in between. And it may mean that I sometimes have dreams that we're making love and the news jingle keeps starting up and stopping, and we have to keep interrupting ourselves for the duration of the headlines (when I first recounted that one to him, we cracked up laughing); but the principle behind it is right and good. A long time ago I stopped asking him, Why?

So Kim is absorbed, and I potter; chop vegetables for our

supper with rather less dexterity than my son can do it. The faces of my day appear before me willy-nilly reminding me that I have notes to make about one couple, the need to call a mum to arrange a home visit tomorrow. Also I must buy butter and light bulbs and mustn't forget I've got to go for a smear on Thursday; and that piece I read in the paper this morning about divorce really pissed me off, I want to remind myself to ask Kim what he thought. There's a citrus pain in my chest which is stabbing on and off like strobe lighting, only for a few seconds, perhaps a minute, then it's gone. Isn't it funny how from time to time we all – I imagine – have these insignificant sensations, barely register as pain; they've gone before we've even had time to voice them. I could say to Kim, interrupting the item on class sizes, 'Kim, there's this weird sort of stabbing in my chest,' but it'd be gone before I'd finished the sentence, and the very voicing of it would be bestowing on it an importance, even an existence, it didn't have. And Kim would laugh and warn me against overexerting myself, or else he'd be all misplaced concern. No, it's private. Daily, hourly, you judge these things with your spouse, make little internal adjustments, gauge when to speak up, when to leave off. I think I fancy a bath. After a news.

When I see the early news, I'm all concentration, but it's a mishmash of thoughts I have during Kim's second, third, and fourth viewings. He and I are comfortable with being miles away from each other, whether in each other's presence or not, because we are still together. I've always said to the kids, rather be alone than lonely in an unhappy marriage because loneliness is all the more critical when you're lonely and not alone. I see that all the time with my clients, as loud as scarlet, and it's more debilitating than the sense of outrage and injustice, the resentment, the hurt, the anger, even the hatred I see most days. The loneliness within marriage is upper case Hell. I think of the woman, Marie, whose Paul was more at one with his ferret. I am chilled; loneliness flaps like the sound of eternal wings so close to the ear as to make one recoil and forever crick one's neck.

Have I cheese enough for Jack? I check the fridge. He'll be home at around midnight. Perhaps. If he doesn't go on to a club after work, end up with a girl. All Jack's girls have the same zebra crossing of white midriff between black stripes of Lycra miniskirt and stunted T-shirt. They have silver rings pierced into their belly buttons. They wouldn't want to snag them on something. The blood would be terrible. Jack says he likes the novelty, but he must be lonely with all these girls. Kim says why doesn't he just stick to the one, they're interchangeable, so what's the difference? The advantage being Jack could get to know her. It's not a suggestion which goes down a treat.

'Can't be bothered to watch the rest,' Kim says when the first commercial break comes on.

'No?' I ask, concentrating on taking the supper out of the oven to check its progress.

He stands up and puts his arms around me. His breath wisps the hairs of my neck. Its pattern is as individual as a fingerprint. It's with me like my own heartbeat, I know it that well. 'What're we having?'

'Haddock in milk.' I can feel his not large but nonetheless convex stomach against me. It fits into the small of my back, is warm there.

'Smells nice.' His neck curves round my own the better to see the contents of the dish. 'Looks good too.'

'Like an egg on top of your bit?'

'That'd be specially nice. Thanks.' He's always been apprecia-tive, Kim. Even of the smallest things. I'm thinking of all the domestic detail that doesn't pass him by. My buying and cooking the simplest of suppers; clean sheets; cold beer in the fridge, a vase of tulips on the pine dresser. I do these things, he notices them, so I carry on doing them. While we both work full-time, it's never a question of him doing them. I don't mind. It just so happens I'm better at them and it suits us. We've an old-fash-ioned marriage. Reactionary. Or, looked at another way, it's just my way of showing a bit of thoughtful human kindness to the person I love, regardless of sex, and all those loaded issues of feminism. I stick my neck out when I say I actively enjoy the menial, I suppose wifely tasks. Mackenzie freaks. Sees me as some kind of enslaved zombie I think's the phrase she uses. But I find them therapeutic, pleasing, satisfying. Whether he noticed or not, I would probably carry on doing them out of habit, perhaps, or good manners, but the resentment might well start to encrust me. Most men fail to understand the most basic truth: that the

14

majority of women are actually asking for very little. A word or two here of gratitude, there of affection; and not just as the password to open the legs. Thereafter a few signs as well, a bit of declaration. You'd have thought it was the easiest thing in the world. Yet so many men neglect to fulfil even these negligible expectations. The one who does is a rare creature.

'Anything for pudding?' he asks, arms still round my waist.

'Oh, if you want, of course. I didn't make anything, I didn't think you'd . . . There's fruit?'

Kim shakes his head.

'I'm sure there's some cheesecake in the freezer, if you'd like that.'

'What I'd really like is some ice-cream. Would you mind if I was to nip out quickly? Have I got time?'

'Sure.'

'Any preferences?'

'You choose.'

'All right, I'll surprise you,' he says. I think he kisses the back of my neck but am distracted by the hot dish in my hands. His lips are as quiet and soft as the oven glove.

'This won't be ready for ten minutes or so.' The fish is not quite done enough, not yet how we both like it. By the time I shove it back in the oven and stab the carrots in the saucepan, the front door has made its reliable click, and Kim is gone.

I am busying myself with fetching a couple of plates out of the cupboard, laying the table in a haphazard sort of way. We don't stand on ceremony, never been great ones for formality. Perhaps I am humming but the noise is dampened by the steam from the stove. This is my favourite time. Anticipating our supper together. I'm wanting to ask Kim's wise advice about the Winstons. He has a better instinct, often, than me. Frequently, if I disagree with him at the beginning of one of my case studies, I've come round to his point of view by the end of the eight weeks. I joke that if he fails as a newscaster in the next life, he should try the probation service.

I pour myself another glass of wine, have a sip as I drain the carrots. Steam goes haywire, I can feel my hair turning into an instant frizz, what the hell. Did I check the cheese for Jack? I peer into the fridge. Fool me, I did. There's enough blinking cheese there to feed a whole army of young sons with bottomless pits for stomachs. Register the fact. Kim's taking his time, isn't he? I glance at my watch, only take in the time subliminally. I look at it again, see it isn't even two minutes later. I didn't notice what time he left. Maybe it's not been so long, or Barnett's is closed.

The carrots safely cradled in the sieve, I sit down on my favourite chair opposite the telly and the big slide glass door overlooking the small terrace outside. I can't see the terrace or the garden beyond. Opaque rain dawdles on the black window. It's cosy inside this apricot kitchen, the kernel of our family life. In the corner are a pair of Jack's trainers, stinking like a wet dog, but a welcome reminder of his presence, I'm thankful he's here still. There on the dresser, colourful mugs; a pile of bills, junk mail, notepaper covered in scrawl, all to be dealt with; old school photographs of the kids, their faces pudgier and pinker, their eyes wider; a bowl with several unwanted oranges and a pride of leopard-skin bananas. Kim's address book by the phone, not exactly overflowing with entries – the plumber, an old aunt, a few people he met when he was a medical student and who remain his closest friends. He's not a great one for picking up the phone just for the sake of a chat, so he tends to rely on me to keep up with our friends, make any social arrangements we might have. Of course, he enjoys it when we do see them. I'm not saying we have this great social life, only that, left to him, we would hardly ever see anyone at all. He's often said to me he's happiest just us, family, really, he's quite content with that. I suppose it's a bit redundant that address book of his.

I kick off my shallow leather shoes and they tap onto the tile-look lino. I rub my stockinged toes. They have warmed up but they throb with aches which come every few seconds like mini contractions, I wonder how that is. Maybe Kim'll know the medical explanation. Bunions, and I'm only forty-two! When Kim was seducing me he told me I had pretty feet. Other men might have said beautiful eyes, but Kim's always prided himself on avoiding a cliché. Pretty feet sounded more sincere, I'll give him that. Just as I'm resting them on another chair, they're less than pretty these days, distort all my shoes, the phone rings. It's Mackenzie. Frantic hellos. We're weekly dictated to by small change. 'How much you got? Shall I call you back?'

'I've got 40p, s'alright. How are you? Dad?'

'He's great, he's out at the moment buying ice-cream, would you believe it?' I can hear Mackenzie's smiling. 'He'll be back any minute. I know he'll kick himself that he missed you.'

Kim has a special relationship with Mackenzie. They're very similar. She's got his dark hair, his not so elegant feet, his concern about the world. They've a repartee, same interests, shared jokes.

I can hear muffled voices and music in the background and imagine her in some corridor newly polished with aerosol roses or lemons, fellow students lolling around drinking beer out of plastic pint glasses, smoke all about like an overcast day. I see her in her black jeans, sloppy jersey, hair messily dragged back into an approximation of a ponytail, expression on her face one of hesitant confidence as acquaintances pass by, her smiles quick, silver-fish flickers. She sounds robust enough but I can detect a certain diffidence, her voice is low, she doesn't want to be heard. She's always had an underlay of shyness, Mackenzie. She has friends, of course, hangs out, has a good time, but she's not the life and soul of the party. Mackenzie's the quieter type, mysterious I suppose. Her work is going to involve loads of old people. I think that's part of the attraction with her. She feels more at ease with them and, while she's stretching their withered limbs this way and that, she'll derive enormous pleasure from listening to their reminiscences, however rambling and inco-herent. Oral histories about people's lives and pasts fascinate her. Kim says she should have been a sociologist or historian, but physiotherapy's just the thing. To be actively helpful and a listener at the same time.

Course Jack has his own theories. Says she wants to be a physio because whenever she goes to bed with her young boyfriends and grapples with their limbs it's going to be like the holiday of a lifetime. Cheeky bugger. She's not like these forth-right girls he goes to bed with. They're unbelievable, they're off the starting blocks before he's even reached the stadium. He's told me some stories. I'm not boasting, I'm not making out my son's got the physical attributes of some sort of Greek god, and they're all clamouring. It does seem, though, that any young man who stands still long enough will have any number of this new

17

breed of girls moving in on him, though moving's not an adequate description. It's more a full-on leap-frog. He hasn't the time to wink at them, let alone give the glad eye, and they've done it all for him. Occasionally they don't even want to know his name, such niceties seen as a waste of bloody time. Course, Jack's not exactly complaining, but I see it as rather emasculating, a modern perversion of the nature of things. I'm glad Mackenzie maintains a more old-fashioned restraint.

I am tingling with questions – the course, her room, boyfriends, the lot. But hold my tongue. Just ask if she's having a good time.

'Yeah, Mum, 's wild.'

'Enjoying the work?'

'Yeah, it's OK. It was cutting up dead bodies today.'

'Kidding?'

'Serious.'

'I couldn't handle that. I'd be sick.'

'Nah, it was a laugh. The formaldehyde makes your eyes water a bit like onions, otherwise it's fine. Tell Dad I've a funny story for him about it.'

'He's still not home yet, but when he does. How much more money you got? He should be back any second now.' I look at my watch again. It's about twelve minutes since I last did. 'I wonder where he is?'

'Who's Jack playing around with this week, poor unsuspecting wretch?'

'Probably couldn't find the right flavour in Barnett's and's now trailing round the whole of Oxford for another shop still open that has it, I reckon.'

'I'm running out here, only 8p. Send love to Dad and Jack for us, will you? I'll call again next week, right?'

'Lots of love . . .' The line goes dead before I've time to tell her to take care.

Again, I glance at my watch. The ache in my bunions is throbbing along with the second hand. I estimate Kim's been gone about thirty-five minutes. He must be very serious about this icecream. Long hard day at work. Famished. Fair enough.

I go to the oven, turn it right down. The dial makes a clicking sound, more seconds ticking by. The small shard of anxiety alights upon all manner of time-keepers.

I fire the remote at the telly. Slightly at a loose end, to be honest. Starving. Some crap sitcom with flimsy jokes that have been doing the rounds since about 1956. The kitchen on it's just like mine. It's a programme which makes me feel more ordinary than ever. Only I hope I'm not like the harridan wife with her boot-face and down-trodden fleecy slippers. I've a pair of silvery mules. I'd like to put them on and give her wimpy husband a good kick up the hole. Mute button, and a sip of wine. Nothing to do but to wait. I wish I smoked. I sit on my white chair, notice a chip, it could do with a lick of paint. Or I might just Tippex it.

Mackenzie sounded happy, I think. You never know, of course, about your children. There's me, going on about her old-fashioned reticence. Maybe that's closer to how I perhaps wish I had been before I married Kim; closer to what I like to think about her than to the real truth. Just because she doesn't hold up a room with loud-mouthed chatter and bedeck her stomach with jewels, doesn't mean she's not having her 'fun' as my mother used to call it. Kim couldn't have had an accident, could he? No, Dad always said women invariably assume when their husband's five minutes late he's had a car crash, funeral already playing up in front of their eyes. This is more than five minutes. It's the quest for ice-cream. He's worse than me. No, he's not had an accident. Anyway, he'd have walked.

My mother always talked about having to have one's fun before getting married. Fun was her way of saying sex with several different partners. I hate those priggish euphemisms. Just like couples who tell you they're 'trying for a baby'. What they're actually trying to do is prevent a picture instantly forming in your mind of them having been going at it like rabbits for months on end.

Unless someone ran him over. I should be so lucky, ha! Come on, Sylvie, that's hardly likely. You're being neurotic. Statistics are against anything having gone wrong. Hurry up, sweetheart, your supper's going to be ruined, and I'm hungry.

What was I saying? Oh yes, about my mother. She's unbelievable. She's lived in Oxford all her life. She worked as a secretary in a big house on the top of Headington Hill which has a turret on the end, and is now bedsits and student accommodation. It was owned in those days by her boss, a professor at the university, who lived there with his family. My father came to see him one morning with architectural plans for some extension, and that's how they met. Restraint was never her most conspicuous forte. She got pregnant with my brother in about five minutes flat, and went in for a little cattle-prodding in order to stun Dad up the aisle. To this day, I'm not sure why she was so keen to get married. My father – a cautious man, likes to take things slowly – always loved her, but she was always the flighty sort, not a great one for abiding by any given convention. I suppose she became a wife after her own fashion. She gave up her job, and while Dad was working his arse off trying to establish his tiny architectural firm, she'd leave us with our grandmother. Time out from us meant she could go and do what she was best at, namely meeting men in bars. Life's an opportunity not to be missed was her motto. She can say.

My mother's that thing I've vowed I'd never be with my lot: inconsistent. Not just with Dad; with us too. Blows hot and cold. So one minute she was all over you with love and hugs and these high-pitched kisses right up close to your ear – no wonder my brother and sister and I are all half deaf – and the next it was this temper: she hated your guts, wished she'd never had kids, did we know how we'd ruined her life, she'd been beautiful once, men had wanted her, not any more, and it was all down to us, she was exhausted. It was really hard. I think Simone and Patrick suffered more than me. I just determined that stability was everything. Of course I'd have my fair share of 'experience' – I was taught by example, wasn't I, they forget to mention the sins of the mothers – but I'd only ever settle with someone who was fun, but solid, loving, and dependable too, and likely to stick around.

She'd disappear for hours on end, out enjoying herself, and Dad would come home from work to find us either with Granny or on our own. We lived in a terraced house in Walton Street, which wasn't so posh in those days. He'd try to have us laughing but his face gave him away, was potato-peel bleak. An hour and five minutes. Now I am getting worried. What on earth can he be doing? The haddock has had it.

Bugger the haddock. Anyway, I'm not hungry anymore, in fact I feel slightly nauseous. The thought of food! Perhaps he fancied

20

a bit of fresh air, lost track of the time. But it's so unlike Kim. He's the type who, when we go on holiday, gets to the airport three days before the flight. Once he swaddled himself into such a false sense of security – browsing through all the papers and magazines, ordering Heathrow's full English breakfast (which is always rather tired-looking but which he can never bear to miss), lingering in the duty free, wobbling on about the merits of this whisky over that – he missed the damn thing, didn't he. Jack and Mackenzie laughed so much they had to lie down for half an hour.

I'm not enjoying this worrying all alone. It makes me wonder, am I going mad? Has he actually been out the house five minutes, is my watch conspiring to deceive me, or have I just mislaid my clutch on reality? I remember at school I'd sometimes turn up for class a few moments early, before anyone else, and for a few seconds, it was only a fleeting thing, I'd ask myself, is this really Tuesday? It is a Geography double period, isn't it? Am I reading Room 3D correctly on my timetable? Should I really be here? Does everyone know something I don't? Am I Sylvia Thomas?

Then one of my year, Dora or Elizabeth or someone, would come in, slump herself down at the desk beside me, go hi, the automatic assumption being that this was where we were meant to be and I was who I was, and everything was ordinarily, gut-achingly boring and normal. I'd privately sigh with relief, reality hadn't gone AWOL.

I pick up the phone, call Dora. We've been best friends since we were ten. She's the chief pharmacist at the city centre Boots and has a suitably understanding way with her.

'Have I got you in the middle of your supper?' I ask.

'No, no, you're all right, we've finished. You OK? You don't sound it.'

Hearing Dora's voice is the aural equivalent of drinking Horlicks. 'It's only Kim's been gone for over an hour and it's beginning to really worry me. He just popped out for something at Barnett's. Should've taken him a couple of minutes, five at the most, not an hour and a half.'

'Oh God,' she says, dismissively. She's great that way, Dora, you can depend on her to be immediately comforting. 'He's just bumped into a friend, or something, and they've gone to the pub.'

'What friend?' I ask. 'Unlike him.'

'He'll be back soon. There's always some obvious explanation. Did you see if he took the car?'

'What, to Barnett's?'

'I'll hold, you go and have a look.'

'Hang on then,' I say. I put the receiver on Kim's table mat and rush to the front door. I open it, half expecting, hoping, to get a fright with him looming in the porch. No fright. Our car, a small Rover, is parked outside the house directly opposite. There's no mistaking it's ours, I can see the crumpled route atlas on the back shelf. Anyway, nobody else in our street has the same sea-green metallic. Shivering, I hasten back to the phone.

'It's still there,' I tell Dora. 'Where the bloody hell do you think he is? Said he was going for ice-cream. It doesn't take this long to buy ice-cream, for God's sake. I'm getting worried now. Sick.'

'He's all right, my love.'

I don't hear her. 'I wish Jack was here.'

'Will I come round? I can be there in a second.'

'That's a bore for you. My hands are sweating. God.'

'I'm coming now, Sylvie, OK, right now, just get my coat on. Give me five minutes.'

'You sure? This is horrible. What's going on in his head? I mean, he must know this is driving me round the bend. Could've rung or something.'

Dora is true to her word. I kiss her at the door, smell the violet scent that's her trademark, pull her inside.

'No news, it's nearly an hour and a half. I'm that near calling the police.'

Dora sits me down at the kitchen table, goes through some questions with me: what he said before he left, how long he said he'd be, had we had a row?

'No, definitely not.'

'There was no bad atmosphere?'

'Come on, you know us, how often in a blue moon is there a bad atmosphere? Even if there was, he wouldn't just sod off for two hours.'

'Perhaps you're forgetting he said he had to do something?'

'That's very sweet of you to say so, but I just know he didn't, I know it. He was looking forward to supper, said so.' I'm leaning on the table, head so heavily in my hands my elbows are boring into the table, hurting. My fingers are pulling my hair so my wrinkled brow is superficially smoothed of worry. Feel hot, sick, cold, shivery, instant flu. Lukewarm sweat drips down my sides.

'Have you had anything to eat yourself?' Dora asks, her arm round my shoulders.

'Joking.' My stomach feels vacuum tight, like a car airbag awaiting an accident. Dora squeezes me for a moment. 'Haven't seen you in this before,' I say, feeling the sleeve of the lilac jumper she's wearing.

'New. M & S. Saturday.'

'Right.' I pause, distracted. ''S nice. I could do with a new . . . Cup of tea, Jesus, a drink?' I stand up to get the bottle out of the fridge. 'You could do with one, me dragging you over here when you were expecting a quiet night in.'

'You sit down, I'll do that. You know, he'll walk through that door any minute now, don't you? You'll see.'

'Well, I bloody well hope he will. He's already missed the nine o'clock news. Doesn't augur very well for the rest of the evening!' I laugh, if you can call it a laugh. 'If he's not back soon he won't make the ten o'clock either and, oh God, then he'll be in a poor way. I'm holding out for that, the ten o'clock. He won't be wanting to miss that. Not if he can help it. Surely?'

# 2

When Kim Black closed the front door, he felt the cold against him as if he were pressing his cheeks up to a redundant radiator. He wondered, briefly, if he should take the car to the shop but fancied instead the air, the idea of his blood starting to race.

He walked fast down the steep hill of his familiar street. The small terraced houses stood in shadows, illuminated only by far-apart street lamps, boiled-sweet orange, and the single, cobwebby bulbs in the dim little porches. There were a few lights on in the windows, but curtains muffled their glare. A door slammed, a dog barked twice, otherwise silence. Kim was aware he was alone in the cold. He thought of his neighbours scorching their shins in front of sparky bar-heaters; kids shovelling down steaming baked beans on toast; icy couples moving closer to each other on their sofas, overcoming perennial disaffection, winterly craving the warmth of flesh and intimacy. It would be a bit of a foolish person, he thought, out on a perishing night such as this, but he was quite a happy fool. He liked monitoring his ghostly breath on the charcoal air; liked the elastic band twang of cold snapping at the tips of his ears; liked the momentary fantasy that he was the only person out in the city, everyone else cowering in front of the solicitous flicker of their television sets, including Sylvie.

He came to the main road at the end of the street. Cars swished by, but still no pedestrians. He walked towards the small parade of shops to the left, among them a newsagent, a gloomy late-night supermarket, a butcher and, rather improbably, a bridal shop. Kim had often speculated how such an establishment had survived so long. How many people, when nipping down the road to do a spot of shopping, think, 'a paper, a pound of pota-toes, a couple of chops and, of course, a wedding dress, the very thing!'? He and Sylvie had lived in Divinity Road for seventeen years, and in all that time he had never once seen a single person enter or leave the place. Tonight there was an even more elabo-rate dress in the window than usual. It was blue-white in the low night-time display lighting, and extravagantly shiny. The puffy skirt and sleeves with all their elaborate bows and tucks made it look like one of those outsize cakes made specially for slapstick folk to jump out of. How glad he was that Sylvie, on their wedding day, had worn nothing so immodest.

The late-night supermarket was the only place still open. Outside it were various plastic crates showing off the last few examples of mid-life crisis fruit. A metal sign advertising a jaded Walls ice-cream swung in the wind, rustily croaking against its little stand. It reminded Kim of what he had come for. He stepped inside onto the shop's cream and pale blue lino tiles. The floor was grubby, and there was a smell about the place of stale dog-biscuits, sour milk which had long ago leaked into the inaccessible crevices of ageing refrigerators, wounded Bombay mix, and the limp cardboard of frozen, ready-made meals.

Kim began slowly wandering along the aisle. Although he had come for one specific thing, all the choice before him made him feel put-upon. He hurried to the end of the shop to the freezer counters full of frozen gateaux and Lean Cuisines. A tub of superior ice-cream was what he was after, none of this synthetic raspberry ripple nonsense stuffed with BSE-giving properties. Sylvie was keen on quasi home-made varieties in tubs with the type of gold piping fashionable on Elizabethan dresses. He glanced through the icy steam to try and spot the one she liked most. It wasn't there, nor even any of her favourite brand. Dispiriting business. Kim did up the buttons of his overcoat. He was tired after a particularly long day. His patients had been especially needy. His fault. When he was feeling buoyant, their indigence was exactly what he was there to serve, enjoyed serving; and when not, it acted as the very aspect of his job which most burdened and depressed him. Some days – not many, but enough to have had him worrying recently – he hadn't the energy to care any longer. This was not good. Once a doctor no longer cares for or about his patients, he is no longer a doctor. A frightening thought. He knew himself well enough; it would come at him when he was exhausted, unbidden, like those unspeakable thoughts one can't control, of doing something utterly uncharacteristic and bad, like jumping under a train or killing someone. The idea that he couldn't give a toss about patients, about people, undermined everything he stood for and threatened to upset the very fabric of his life. That was what he was, after all, Doctor Black. It was his identity, his *raison d'être*.

The ice-creams with their chocolate chips and cappuccino hints rose up before his eyes to confuse him. They weren't right. He didn't want any of them, and hadn't the energy to try and choose one. He longed just to sit down.

He walked back towards the entrance, looking at the ever-friendly proprietor with a guilty smile as if to apologise for leaving empty-handed. He made his way out, no plan in mind. The small wall between the shops and the pavement presented itself. Kim automatically sat down on it, his back to the super-market. He folded his arms against the cold, and thought about the cold. It didn't bother him much. Used to it. When you've been brought up in a farmhouse with no heating, and a father who favours hoarding logs over burning them, you soon learn to be immune.

The red bricks Kim was sitting on felt strangely sharp through his trousers, as if they were trying to puncture his thighs. He shifted, things weren't much better, but it didn't occur to him to move on. Cars were whisking past and he was enjoying watching them, guessing their make by the shape of the approaching head-lights. A silly private game, but a compelling one. He didn't want to pull away from it just yet. A few minutes longer, then he'd think where to try next for Sylvie's ice-cream.

He once had a patient who was tormented by her private games and superstitions. Jacqueline Wright, that was her name. Rather dashing cheekbones, he remembered. Whenever she turned round, she had told him, she'd have to turn back the other way, to correct herself, as it were; and whenever she walked up a number of stairs, she 'wouldn't feel right' till she had walked back down that very same number. Her whole life had been taken over by these curious inner rituals. No question of a social life, or boyfriends, or anything like that. What a dismal waste of such forlorn beauty. He had referred her to the local psychiatric hospital, the Warneford, never heard of her again or knew if she was cured of her unusual strain of obsessive-compulsive disorder. Perhaps she had finished treatment and moved away; perhaps he was becoming obsessive, on a wall in the Cowley Road, playing

26

car-spotting. Or could it be it was just a bit of fun?

It was amazing how the different shapes of the headlights lent such different characters to the faces of all the different cars. The sloping shape of the Citroëns' eyes gave them a rather sly look. The heavy-lidded appearance of the Mazdas' were rather glamorous and aloof, like a sixties fashion model, and seemed to belie the car's somewhat vulgar image. Kim tried to catch a glimpse inside the windows to see if their drivers were at all like them. Why not? Dog-owners resemble their pets.

He smiled at the thought, even chuckled to himself. And what, he said to himself, would be the biological theory for that, I'd like to know. Do physiognomies synchronise along the same lines as menstruating women?

Kim carried on watching the road from his vantage point. He was unaware of time passing or, now, of the cold. An elderly couple shuffled by and eyed him suspiciously. Concentrating on keeping his score in mind, he ignored them, didn't offer any reassuring platitudes – 'I'm just waiting for a friend.' His whole life was reassuring platitudes. Brute realities juggled so as not too much to wobble over-burdened sensibilities. Not, 'You're going to be dead in six months,' but, 'You've got six months to live.' The doctor's specialised fudging of absolute truth.

After the old couple, two youths sauntered by with a lopsided swagger so exaggerated it put Kim in mind of an orthopaedic condition. They had cans of beer in their hands and trousers so loose the low-slung waists threatened to drop away from their non-existent backsides. They spoke loudly, didn't notice him, and he stayed put, unruffled and content in the cold.

Kim thought he ought to get going, Sylvie might be starting to wonder where he was, but he was enjoying himself. Just a little longer, he whispered out loud, and turned his attention from the cars to the passers-by. He speculated about a young mother with a sleeping child. She had about her an air which seemed to pulsate with loneliness, but Kim couldn't bet on it. It might have just been the freezing air, or the rattling on the pavement of the small plastic wheels which managed to shake the whole pushchair, and in turn shook her. He wondered where she might be going to at this time of night although he had rather lost track of what this time of night was. Perhaps she had just been visiting the child's father and was hastening back home to her mum, except she didn't appear to be hastening. She was in no hurry. Reluctant steps. The other way round, could be, going back to a volatile fellow she only wished she could stop herself from loving.

He watched her making modest headway along the pavement. The heralding bell of the gloomy supermarket sounded and its door closed. Kim turned, and to his surprise saw that the crates of fruit had been taken inside. He hadn't heard them being moved. The owner was searching for the right key on his extensive ring, about to lock up.

'Were you wanting something?' he asked.

'No, no, you're closing,' Kim faced the man but didn't stand up.

'Sure? It's all right, if you're not long.'

'No, I'm fine, thank you.' He couldn't remember what he wanted but was grateful that the man was being so accommodating. A rare quality these days, he thought sadly, stranger to stranger.

'Freezing. Coldest yet, I reckon.' The shop owner turned the key in his lock and walked towards Kim's wall.

'Oh, yes?' Kim said.

'Best be getting home.'

'Early start, have you?'

'It's the getting up in the dark, you know?'

'Oh, I do. Sometimes it's actively painful, physical pain,' he said, thinking about those nights when he was on call.

'Yes, yes.' The man's laughter was in recognition, his visible breath a jerky accompaniment.

'You'd gladly die rather than get up that very moment.'

'I have that most mornings, even though I've been doing it thirty years,' the shopkeeper told him. 'Have to earn a crust.'

'Indeed, alas.' Kim smiled, and the man shivered, pulled his collar closer round his neck. 'I mustn't keep you, let you catch your death.'

'Well, nice talking, see you soon. Good night.' The man moved off.

Kim settled back to guessing cars, his mind wholly preoccupied with his score. There was a moment, during a brief lull in the traffic, when he wondered about his boyish game, even

28

laughed at himself a little. Then another car approached and the serious mental debate – a Golf or a Polo – once again overtook him.

After how long he didn't know, Kim became aware that his fingers were aching with cold, he could no longer feel his feet, and inner lurches of hunger were becoming ever more acute. When he tapped his feet on the pavement to encourage the blood to return, he felt only those deadening vibrations characteristic of walking in clogs. He glanced along the main road and could make out, a few hundred yards away, the familiar red and white neon sign outside the Taj Mahal which he passed every day on his way to and from work. Suddenly he yearned for warmth, and decided the thing he most wanted in the world was to eat a huge curry. The desire came over him like a bulimic's incontrovertible craving to binge on French bread and Dairy Milk. Suddenly the idea of haddock in milk didn't seem adequate, somehow. He sighed. Sylvie would understand. He would ring her and ask her to join him. Excellent plan, he told himself with a wide grin. Without further ado, he set off with feverish, clomping steps.

Kim bowed into the door with the feigned nonchalance and slightly shameful discretion employed by a besuited man crossing the dingy threshold of a prostitute. Inside, the restaurant had a powerfully irresistible smell. Kim could instantly feel the spicy fugginess warmly caress his complexion. It was as if a soft beautician was giving him a facial using chicken tikka flavour aromatherapy oils and creams . Even as he breathed he could taste the tempting atmosphere on his tongue. A waiter approached him, and before Kim could ask where he might find the restaurant's payphone, he showed him to a small table. He sat down with a sigh and leant his head against one of the faded posters on the wall of an Indian sunset, silhouette of an elephant in the foreground. He'd call in a minute, when he'd ordered a drink. For the moment he didn't feel like moving his legs.

The place was dark and empty but for a middle-aged couple. Both man and wife (or lover), probably in their mid-forties, stared at the maps of brightly coloured food on their big plates, as absorbed by them as they might be by an atlas. They spoke to each other in whispers, perhaps afraid to talk normally in a place so quiet.

29

Kim ordered some beer. Sylvie, admirably economical, was bound to tell him that coming to an Indian was a waste of good haddock. He wondered how he might get round that one. The waiter brought some poppadoms and offered to take Kim's coat but Kim decided to keep it on until he had thawed out. He read the menu slowly. As he did so the intense atmosphere seemed to seep into his very clothes like cigarette smoke, and weigh him down heavily onto his soft seat. Even the sound of poppadoms crunching in his mouth, their sharp zip on his tongue, did not shake him from his sleepy hunger and warm daze. Lazily he unwrapped his pink linen napkin over his knees and wondered if he wasn't some sad bastard for being in a restaurant on his own. Well, he was waiting for someone or, rather, would be when he had rung her to let her know that he was.

The waiter interrupted his thought by asking if he was ready to order. He wasn't, but realised he could hold out no longer. He would order for both of them, then ring Sylvie. It would be a *fait accompli* she would be unable to resist, some lovely curry all ready and waiting for her by the time she arrived. He would promise her that, the following evening, he would make kedgeree out of the haddock. Kim looked at the leather-bound menu. It had an encylopaedia of entries. He knew what he wanted without looking far, but felt he was too tired, wasn't in a position to guess, from all the tempting choices, what his wife might like. Perhaps he would be better off waiting for her, but he couldn't wait. If he told the waiter he was in a hurry, the food would come quickly, he could call Sylvie and scoff it down on his own before rushing home. She wouldn't mind, she was a tolerant woman. It wasn't often he ate out alone, after all. Or at least not since his days as a medical student, before he met Sylvie, when he probably was a sad bastard. Then he'd occasionally have a solitary, distinctly unmedically aware, breakfast in the early morning sandwich bar round the corner from Queens. Smokey Joe's, it was called, the best in Belfast. More recently, whenever he had spotted a lone diner in a restaurant he had had a patronising tendency to think he or she was rather an admirable sad bastard to butch it out in the face of a thousand pitying stares. Especially, he remembered, the solitary figure of a woman he had seen the other day when out on one of his rare lunches with a friend. She had ordered two heavy courses, followed then by a rich sticky toffee pudding, intravenous cream. Desperately lonely, he had concluded. Not just desperately hungry. How arrogant of me, he now thought. Am I lonely here?

The waiter looked at him oddly, and recommended a particularly hot curry.

'I'm a creature of habit, I'm afraid, always have the same thing.' He placed his order for a milder dish, and asked the waiter where he might find the telephone.

'It's out of order, I'm afraid.'

'Oh, don't worry,' Kim said, guiltily relieved. He couldn't really face getting up, fishing for ten pence pieces, descending into some dingy basement. 'But please could I have the food as quickly as possible, then, because I'm in rather a hurry?'

'If it's a local call, sir, you're welcome to use our main line.'

'Thanks, but never mind. If the food's quick, perhaps there's no need.'

His nan bread, orange curry and yellow rice arrived, accompanied by ladies' fingers. Of all the names for food, this had always struck Kim as the most romantic, alluring, sinister. He shed his coat from his shoulders and arms but kept it wrapped round his waist and legs. He ate slowly, as if carefully labelling and filing every mouthful. The textures and colours and tastes delighted and overwhelmed him to the point that he could think of nothing else but the sheer pleasure of filling his demanding belly. When the time came, and his plates were cleared away, he didn't want to leave, but the restaurant was becoming crowded. Two women were hovering just inside the door waiting for a table. They kept looking at Kim hopefully, each privately trying to divine whether he was the type to swig three quarters of a glass of beer in one go, or more likely to linger over every sip. Their sweet expressions seemed to indicate their dread that he might be a pudding man. Sensitive and obliging, Kim finished quickly and paid the bill with his Switch card. When he stood to put his coat fully back on, they both appeared to be so grateful that he was pleased he had made the effort to hurry for them. One of the women even thanked him as she took his place at the table.

The cold, even harsher now it was so late, struck Kim again the moment he stepped outside. Not even all the hot curry inside him could protect him from it. To walk briskly, that's the main thing, he said to himself, and started off towards the nearest telephone box, regardless of the fact it was in the opposite direction to his house, and regardless of the rain. He had two immediate concerns – to let Sylvie know that he was on his way home, and just to get warm.

That was why he began walking towards the city centre. The first telephone was occupied. Kim peered inside. A woman of about thirty was leaning against the telephone itself, heavily ensconced in conversation. On the shelf beside her was a pile of coins the height of counters stacked on a gaming table. Kim's heart sank. The woman noticed him. Her doing so gave rise to the faint hope in him that, due to some common humanity, she might begin to wind up. Vain hope. He waited for a few minutes, but the woman just stared at him and shamelessly carried on gabbling and pushing those coins in. Were Kim the sort to harbour an aggressive imagination, he might have let it run wild now with the thought of flinging open the door and clobbering her over the head with a copy of the Yellow Pages. Instead, he tutted quietly and began to go in search of another telephone.

Soon he was cursing the inadequate provision of public telephones in Britain. In America, he knew, stomping onwards, there are a gaggle of them on every block.

The next call box stank of dank piss, but it was free. Shivering, Kim fumbled in his pockets for some coins. He drew from them a ten pound note and a frivolity of useless coppers. 'Shit,' he shouted at himself furiously, and barged out of the door. 'Shit.' The street was empty, there was no one about who might be able to give him 10p in exchange for all his 1p and 2p bits. He marched on, hoping to come across an accommodating fellow pedestrian. Of course, now that he didn't have the right change for any of them, he seemed to pass a positive platoon of telephone boxes.

Sooner than he knew it, he had reached the Plain and was crossing Magdalen Bridge, which, but for a stray car now and again, was deserted. The downpour could be heard hitting the water of the Cherwell. The pale beauty of Magdalen Tower against the wet, black sky was like a widow in mourning. The very sight of it pushed and tugged at Kim in the way usually only a piece of music can so wantonly and unashamedly budge and shift the emotions. This was another Oxford. Not his Oxford. His Oxford, in general terms, was the astonishingly violent provincial town with one of the highest rates of homelessness in the country; and, more specifically, a not-so-temporary prefab structure in Cowley which acted as his surgery and the city's lightning conductor to every possible feeling of pain, misery and despair. A serious case of disaffection between image and reality. The thought made Kim angry, but going past the buildings along the High Street lent also a sense of elation which made him forget about telephones. Normally, when Kim was in the centre of town, it was because he was hurrying in his car to the shops or dashing to tend to a patient. Rarely did he walk the city's streets late at night, merely for the sake of walking, of keeping warm, no real notion in his mind of hastening from A to B. When he was no longer freezing, he even allowed himself to stop and stare up at the gargoyles. Grotesque, Bedlam faces they were, peering down at him, some with hollow eyes and strawberry noses, like alcoholics down the ages; some like his patients; others with contorted, murderous expressions. How many times had he driven or dashed past these compelling, mythical creatures and not given them a second glance, let alone begun to make their acquaintance? Now he stood beneath them, eyes darting from one to the other, wondering that they didn't shout abuse. Certainly, with the rain spluttering down on his upturned face, they appeared to spit at him. But in fact they were pretty helpless in their evil intent, Kim thought, grounded by their own inertia, and humiliated by the pigeon shit which had once splattered wetly on their sunken or pointed foreheads but had long ago dried into a grey crust like a seedier form of lichen, now soggy. Kim craned his neck and snarled back at them, trying to ape their own fearsome sneers. He fancied their stony faces were just for him. Did this reveal some deep-rooted self-hatred and paranoia in him? Bollocks to that. It was as innocent a game as guessing cars.

He moved on and cut through Catte Street to the Radcliffe Camera. Without caring that he might catch a chill even though he was wearing his thick coat, he stood on the sodden grass and contemplated in peace the building's beauty. This was something he had never really done before. His was a case, he thought, of for the most part taking his surroundings for granted, however spoiling they were. As well as, to some extent, an inability to believe in the myth. Tonight he was ready to embrace the myth, resplendent as it was in its floodlit state. He walked a few steps back, the better to view the full extent of the building in front of him. After a few minutes, the cold began to invade his body all the more. He turned in a circle looking all about him. His desire to stay, staring at All Souls, St Mary's Church and the Bodleian Library as well as the Radcliffe Camera, outweighed any dull practical considerations like retreating from the rain, like finding someone prepared to swap him a 10p so he could go into a call box and ring his wife. Anyway, he thought, it was almost getting too late to ring her now. The haddock would be crisp, and she might have lost even her eternal patience. What a fool he was for not having forced himself to move his arse and ring her earlier, especially when the waiter had offered him the restaurant's phone. What on earth would he say to her this late on? She'd ask him why he hadn't come back all this time, and what would he say? There was no ice-cream.

Kim stared on at the stunning view surrounding him. After a while, twenty minutes or so, an elderly man hurried by and wished him good night. He was gone before Kim had time to respond, let alone ask for 10p, but he had made him aware that it was late and it was a curious thing to be standing about in the open on such a night as this. So he strolled off. He turned in the direction of home, left into the High Street, but suddenly stopped for no reason to look at some antique engagement rings in a dark shop window. It was like the place where he had bought Sylvie's in Belfast. Fusty-looking and intriguing. As he made his way again, towards Queen's College, he thought he might start singing. A cyclist with a ludicrous luminous mackintosh in the shape of a tent swished by. His wheels sprayed Kim's shoes so that his socks started to squish with sogginess at every step. Just as he reached a bus stop, a large vehicle drew up close and flung open its doors at him with alarming gusto, like an old aunt given to extravagant welcomes. A relief of hot, dry air billowed over Kim.

'Are you coming, mate, or not?' the driver asked.

34

Kim, standing at the open door, noticed the man's white shirt with a flourish of red logo on the breast pocket saying Thames Valley Services. He looked from side to side, up and down the street, somewhat hesitant.

'Well are you? Is it London you want? We're the slow coach, stop at High Wycombe and that. There'll be an express coming along in a minute.'

'I'm not in a hurry.'

'You might not be, mate, but the rest of us haven't got all night.'

Kim stepped up inside.

'Single six pounds; eight for a return.'

Kim didn't reply.

'Come on. Make your mind up time. What'll it be?'

'Single, I think, yes, a single, please. Thanks.' It was far too warm to step outside again. Kim gave the man his tenner. As the coach moved off, he took the jerky ticket from the machine, and his change. He wobbled to the back seat. There were only three other passengers dotted about. He wanted to sit completely alone to dry off and to relish being in a sanctuary of joyous heat.

# 3

Although we have the television's volume on low, I can hear *Newsnight* starting. It is half past ten. I already know that, intimately. I paged him an hour ago, and he still hasn't rung me. I have been keeping a dedicated eye on my watch, seeing the long hand move – it's not often you see that – but the programme's opening music is like Pavlov's bell. On cue, I leave Dora's side, withdraw my hot hand from hers, and rush up to the bathroom to be sick.

Up close, I notice, the cold lavatory bowl appears to yawn like a bored, pasty-faced monster, the water at the bottom of its throat kept in place by a delicate vein of limescale. I retch. Little comes up because I haven't eaten since lunchtime but my body convulses, as if undergoing electric shock treatment, beyond my control.

Inside my head, though, things are weirdly calm.

Seeing as it is a crisis.

Dora has slunk into the bathroom, silently. I know because I can feel the hot potato warmth of her hand on my shoulder blade. The convulsions try to kick it off but I want it to stay there. Her being so close to me, I can smell and picture violets, and will myself into a daydream. It lasts the fraction of a second but is a luxury when you don't wish to contemplate the tragedy.

'Never you worry,' she is whispering. 'He'll be back in a minute, I promise.'

Bless her, she keeps saying that. It's a rash promise, Dora, I say in my head. I beg to differ, see. I've a feeling Kim is not coming home.

I can tell you that right now. He's gone for good. Dead, or other. That's the end of it. Him. Us.

'I did get in some cheddar for Jack, didn't I?' I ask, still kneeling at the lavatory and doubled up over it, my arm clutching the convex curve of its bowl, like it might hug a lover's middle-aged spread, for comfort.

'What, my love?'

'Only, otherwise he'll be a bit pissed off,' I tell her, before sitting up straight, wiping a fang of sweating hair from my brow. 'He has to have his midnight sandwich.' The catastrophe is too mammoth to fathom. You know how a chicken doesn't realise it's dead and carries on running round for a bit. I want to ask Dora how much her new sweater cost. Banality, as a balm, is very underrated.

Dora asks me how I'm feeling and suggests she takes me to lie down on my bed. I am feeling better. I tell her I want to go out in the car looking for him. She says firmly that that would be pointless. I disagree. It's the obvious thing to do, search the nearby streets at least.

'It'd be like looking for needle in a haystack,' she says.

'But it might make me feel better that I was doing something!'

'I'll come with you, love, if you think so, of course, but where would we begin?'

I take her point. He's not going to be walking the streets now, looking for ice-cream. He's not here because he's gone, or been taken, somewhere – whether it be a mistress's love nest, a hospital, or a kidnapper's hideaway. I can't honestly imagine he's wandering just for the hell of it, hoping I might come across him by chance in the car and give him a lift home.

I allow Dora to steer me into Kim's and my white bedroom. It is simple, with a white iron bed, an old pine wardrobe and chest of drawers, all from the farm where Kim grew up. It has that inimitable smell of new carpet, my rose talcum powder, and one of Kim's stocking presents to me, an orange he and Mackenzie had spiked all over with cloves to keep away the moths. An ageing print of Bacchus hangs above his bedside table. It is faintly water-stained which reminds me of the night the roof leaked, water dripped from the ceiling and pulsated down the walls like a doll's tears. Kim slept with a bucket on his stomach. He refused just to move the bed out of the way. Said it'd be giving in to the leak. I teased him, and Mackenzie, who must have been about five at the time, was woken by our laughter.

Kim's towelling dressing gown is hanging in place at the front of the wardrobe. It is so inert. I think of him in it, *Martin Chuzzlewit* precariously propped upon its soft navy folds, as he lies across the bed, still, but full of warmth and life. Now, as Dora makes me comfortable with pillows, I look at its scrawny shoulders and empty sleeves and pity it. His slippers, by the door, have fleece inside but an air of coldness.

'I think,' Dora starts. She is easing the bedclothes over me. Her pretty, rounded face is pinched, perhaps with concentration. As ever she is wearing blue mascara. It becomes her air-force blue eyes. She sits at my knees and holds my hand. Her chunky engagement ring rests on my knuckles, and suddenly a picture of her wedding day plumps itself in my mind. She wore a white wet-look mini-dress, thigh-boots, floppy hat, and lipstick to match. Roy had a shirt with a collar which pointed halfway to his shoulders. How astonishing the past.

In a few years' time I will surely draw upon my mental picture of this present scene here with Dora – which, though modest, will be a beacon in the memory – and every time I do, Kim's slippers will seem so old-fashioned; the inoffensive Horlicks-colour of the carpet such an unusual choice; Dora's hand so smoothly young. Only the nausea I feel now, and am bound to do so whenever I look back at this moment, won't seem strange. For I fear this curdled-cream gag in my stomach and throat might never shift or dim.

'You think it's time to call the police?' I ask her.

Dora pulls in her lower lip so she only has half a mouth. 'Oh no, but maybe Jack, see if Kim's gone round to the college?'

'He hasn't.'

'You never know, and while there's a chance—'

'No, I think we should call the police.'

'It's too early for that, Sylvie, surely. Someone has to be gone twenty-four hours before they take any notice.'

As Dora talks, I become aware of the sound of rain outside. Normally it is a sound I cherish. I think particularly of being in the Family Room at work, dark afternoons, lights on, the rain trying to savage the skylight, me reassuring children who are melancholy that we won't get wet in here, we're all all right in here. I also think of it as we can hear it in this bedroom, throwing itself against our windows; Kim and I with the lights out, the reflection of the street lamp on the ceiling, dribbling; us manoeuvring my rounded stomach into the small of his back, dry, warm, safe, together smug against its sound.

Tonight, though, with my worry about Kim, it has a wearying quality. I imagine, if he is out, the drops worming themselves beneath his collar, chilling his damp neck; nagging at his eyes and, could be, icing his fingers to a possible tub of ice-cream. Kim doesn't like the rain except, he says, when he's in bed, away from it, with me. When he was a child he used to have to help out his dad on the farm. The rain always soaked his thick jerseys, and the sodden wool, rank as a wet sheep, would rub at his neck and wrists, his chest and waist, chafing his skin with each movement. The itching was so acute he would scratch and scratch himself to distraction and his father, David, would mock him. One day, when Kim was fifteen, David bought him one of those tuppenny hats, the polythene kind which fan out from the size of a Christmas stamp, last just the once, and were popular back then, with old ladies. He took it as a joke, but David made him wear it out in the fields. Kim still reels from the humiliation he felt in front of his brothers and the other farm lads. He's told me more than once, 'I can still hear them laughing.'

'Perhaps I should ring Roy, tell him I won't be home till Kim comes back,' Dora is saying. I'm half-listening but, my ears, acutely tuned by worry, suddenly hear a key in the front door. Of course, it's him.

All thoughts of a few moments ago, that he wasn't coming back, were only in place temporarily.

Funny how the mind works. Sometimes, when I'm driving to work, or having a bath, say, it begins to hit upon terrible thoughts, a sort of negative daydream, if you like, of my husband and children being wiped out in an accident. The entire scenario – my reading the paper at home, still merrily unaware; a policewoman knocking on our door asking me if my name is Mrs Black and might she step inside; her hopeless expression; the drive to the morgue to identify the bodies; the sight of Kim's umbrella in the hall when I arrive home alone, Jack's half-drunk chocolate milk in the fridge, Mackenzie's wide-eyed photograph on the dresser; my unearthly howling. I have the power to put a stop to it, but I find myself allowing it to unfold for a few minutes longer than is entirely healthy, almost enjoying it like a session eating too many custard tarts. I hate myself for it, but wonder if I am the only one who every so often indulges in such dubious dreams? And on those rare occasions in my life – like tonight – when tragedy really does potentially present itself, I am mortified to discover that, at first, I don't wholeheartedly recoil from it. Rather, with my imaginings of the worst, it's as if I even make tentative steps towards it, almost embrace it. It could be a defence mechanism, a way of preparing myself for a horrible outcome, but I don't think entirely so. A singular, perverted quirk of human nature seems to be that the stench of beckoning despair holds for us a kind of gross curiosity, as compelling in its own way as our more wholesome quest for love.

Naturally, I am out of bed, practically shoving poor Dora out the way, and down the stairs before I even register my actions. I am not angry with Kim. I just want to ask what happened that took him so long. My instinct is to grab and clutch him to me so damn tight that I squeeze all the rain out of him.

'Oh, hi, seen a ghost or something?' Jack asks, nonchalantly shrugging off his jacket. He smells as he always does, but maddeningly tonight, of cooking – garlic and caramel, bad combination. 'You look pretty rough, Mum.'

'Where's Dad?'

'How should I know?'

'He's not with you?' Dora asks him, coming down the stairs.

'He went to buy ice-cream,' I tell him pleadingly.

'Right,' says Jack and shuffles off towards the kitchen.

'No,' I say, following him, 'that was about seven o'clock, earlier even. Look at the time now.' Not trusting myself to stand without falling over, I sit down at the table while Dora makes us all a cup of tea and Jack invades the bread bin. I am shivering, feverish.

'Not like him, I admit. Waylaid I expect. Easy enough.'

'There's not many places you can get waylaid round here, Jack, where there's not a phone at least,' Dora says.

'Waylaid, and not inclined to ring. He'd either have rung or be back by now. He's not coming home.'

When I say this, my friend lets out a gentle, kindly sigh as if to say, 'You know that's nonsense, Sylvie,' and Jack carries on spreading a duvet of butter over his soft mattress of bread. Perhaps he didn't hear my murmuring, ears ruined by years of

Smashing Pumpkins and their like on the Walkman. Or he thinks his mother is being hysterical and deems it better to ignore her.

'I'm telling you.'

'Come off it, Mum. His bleeper went off, some emergency. Usual stuff. Calm.'

'He's not on call tonight.'

'It's late, OK. The head's playing tricks. He might've forgotten to tell you he was, or you might have forgotten he told you. Have you seen his bleeper lying around?'

'No.'

'There we go, then. He must have it with him.'

'She paged him,' Dora says quietly, 'and he's not responded to her message.'

'Listen, Mum, he's probably attending to an emergency. Fancy a sandwich? Might make you feel better. Peanut butter?' Jack helpfully already has his knife in the jar.

'She feels sick as a dog.'

'I'm sorry,' he says. 'Didn't realise.'

He puts his hand on my shoulder, knife still in his hand, gob of peanut butter round the end of it. A small amount catches a wisp of my hair, clings on. I don't care, but Jack pulls it off between his thumb and forefinger and wipes it on his jeans which came out of the wash this morning. I think, I myself would never knowingly wipe peanut butter on my trousers. Usually I'm strangely impressed by that sort of abandon. Tonight it grates painfully.

'Perhaps you should go to bed, like. Then you'll wake up in the morning to find he's right there beside you, you were worrying about nothing all along. Listening, Mum? Yeah?'

'Look, am I the only one taking this seriously?' I ask him tetchily. 'Am I going mad, overreacting or something?'

'No, but it's just not very likely that there's anything other than a harmless explanation.'

'It's not like your father. I don't understand you, Jack. How can you be so bloody calm?' Irritation seethes in my voice as obviously as interference on a radio wave.

'Because I know Dad,' Jack explains patiently, 'I know he's responsible, and he'd've rung if he could. As we speak, he's probably saving someone's life and reckons putting in a call to you can

41

wait. It's not unheard of, Mum, in an emergency, that he literally can't call because it's all hands on pumping someone's chest. To be honest with you, I feel it's too early to start worrying that he's been abducted or something. If he's not back by morning, then I will start. Please don't worry. Trust him, all right? You know he'd call if he could.'

He has a good nature, Jack. Breezy enough, but kind to his mum really. Doesn't like to see me distressed.

'He's right,' Dora tells me gently. 'At least try and get some sleep.'

She, an ever-comforting presence, moves to take my mug and accompany me back upstairs. I give Jack a kiss. His bristles at this time of night are minuscule but sharp as a doormat's. I still expect his cheek to be as soft as a girl's. That it is not is both pleasing and sad. His breath is a mottled mixture of peanut butter and blackcurrant jam. Detail has a way of intruding, even on despair. I wonder, briefly, why he has eschewed cheese, but don't bother to ask as I might have done any other night. This doesn't have the feel about it of any other night.

Making my way to my room, I settle down to more pressing speculation and wonderment. Where is Kim now, right this minute, now? I ask Dora this, and she answers with admirable optimism. This late in the day she can come up with no fewer than three possible explanations, each one as mundane as the last and plausible enough, I suppose. She is amazing. I smile graciously but don't believe any of them.

'Roy'll be wondering where you are,' I tell her, lifting my bedside telephone to my ear just to make sure the line isn't dead. Naturally, it is purring, as ever. I tell Dora to make her way and reassure her that I will be fine even though it's not strictly true. She offers to stay the night. When I tell her no, she clutches my shoulders and leaves quietly.

Left alone in my room, in bed, I am at a loose end. I am as certain as instinct that my husband of over twenty years has gone for good. To list how I feel: gagging nausea; a deep, uncontrollable trembling; sweat that, even as it emerges, does so cold; a tight headache stretched across my forehead, as perfect a fit as an elasticated mattress cover; the cool realisation that in an ideal world my broken heart would just stop and I would be dead.

I rock my feet from side to side in a vaguely satisfying rhythm, flesh against the wax-soft sheets, just so as to have one nice sensation, however small. For the moment my book won't do. I couldn't concentrate on it if someone were to slap each word of it in my face. I am only just capable of dialling the number of our local hospital. After a long wait they tell me that nobody of Kim's name has been admitted. 'Sorry, love,' the receptionist says, and I realise I'm crying. Sometimes, right circumstances, just a 'love' can push you over. I blot my eyes on the top sheet, and when I stop the wheezing sobs, I phone the police. I know he's been gone nothing like twenty-four hours yet. Bugger that. I'm going to make them take notice, damn well do something.

It is a desultory call. The man on the end of the line calls me Madam and is wearily kind. There is mild surprise it is not a minor or an adolescent who's gone. He tells me he is sure my husband will return, that he's most likely gone off for a few drinks with friends. He gets me to tell him exactly how and when he left.

'Did he have a vehicle with him as far as you know?'

Policemen have a peculiar, formal language of their own. You don't really ever hear normal people saying vehicle.

I tell him all I can, there's not much. I tell him that our car is still parked out in the street, what we were watching on the telly, how he doesn't like to miss all the news. I tell him what was cooking for our supper, haddock in milk, he specified he wanted an egg even; how it was Kim's own suggestion to go and get ice-cream to complete the meal. He must have left at about twenty past seven, I say, because he'd just turned off *Channel 4 News* during the first ad break, so he's been gone over five hours. I don't know whether or not he's got his pager with him; certainly he hasn't responded to my message. Perhaps he left it at work, as he sometimes does when he's not on call. The policeman takes this all down as far as I can tell from his slow responses and repetitions, and then logs Kim's details.

'Build?'

'Medium,' I say unhelpfully. 'Though he's bigger than he was.'

'Who isn't, madam? Years of roast dinners begin to take their toll on the best of us.'

43

Age, height, colour of hair and eyes. God, what colour are his eyes? I can't remember. Rising panic, as if this is real betrayal, such as could pull the carpet from under our more than two decades together. How can I fail with this, such basic information about him? I've looked into his eyes often enough, lovingly. What the hell colour are they? Not brown, but not blue exactly either. A sort of blue-green, I think, but with brown speckles like on a free-range egg.

'Clothes. What was he wearing, do you know?'

I blank. 'Trousers, I think,' I say stupidly.

'Yes, madam, what sort would that be?'

'Black, yes, not jeans, but cut like jeans. That tough brushed cotton, what's it called? Got them from a catalogue. Moleskin.'

'On top?'

'He always wears his big long coat in the rain. Black.'

'Any distinguishing features? Tattoos? Body-piercing?'

'No tattoos, no. Or body-piercing.'

'Don't cry, Mrs Black.'

I am crying because the fact of Kim's not having come home is no longer within the contained realm of these walls, the little-bothered head of Jack, and my domestically anxious mind. Now that I have rung the hospital and the police, and they have asked me questions, Kim is not just late or waylaid. His missing is official, and the stamp of officialdom, though I couldn't hold off from it a moment longer, has the dread tone of a bar in a requiem.

'As I say, madam, the vast majority of people who don't come home when expected are back before you know it.' It is a cheery voice that doesn't convince. I hear it again suddenly. 'And he's not been gone long. Nothing to worry about. The rain'll have him home in a trice, you'll see.'

Well, that's a crass bloody remark if ever I heard one. I know Kim doesn't like it, but what's the frigging rain got to do with it when he's been gone this long? Platitudes serve their purpose, I'm sure, but times like this they grate, like the sound of a damp finger tugging over the surface of a birthday balloon.

There he is, the policeman with his platitudes, sitting in probably a rather deserted office this time of night, half-drunk polystyrene cup of white coffee precariously balanced on the mess of papers strewn across his desk, jaundiced fag-end inert in the stagnant liquid; tie and collar beginning to feel tighter; vaguely keen to get this bleak woman off the line, though she is worthy of one of his inner sighs of 'poor soul', like half a dozen others he comes across in any given day; glance at the heavy watch warmly embedded in the black hairs of his freckled wrist; it's a sex on night tonight, he can feel it. There he is, with this picture of his lovely cosy adorable wife drowsily stirring in her sentimental duvet as he treads softly into their pink bedroom, crunching her closed eyes tighter together as he snaps on the bedside lamp, her hand clawing at the pubescent curves of the buttoned bed-head as if warming it on the coal-glow velour and, in the nick of time before he lowers his jittery, junket-coloured body on top of her, her dutifully lifting her thick, pink be-sprigged nightdress over a ready hip which no longer shows much evidence of a bone but is as beautiful in its new way as ever; basically asleep, dependably drooping open her legs in unconscious anticipation, smiling. There he is, coming out on cue to this Mrs Black, his latest 'poor soul', with his only semi-attentive platitude, meanwhile his groin twitching and raring at his Fuzzy Felt composition of domestic warmth.

'We can't open a report until somebody sees you. The details I've taken of your husband are just for local detection purposes, so officers can be on the lookout tonight for someone fitting his description. Then, in the morning, if in the unlikely event that he hasn't returned home, I'll see to it that one of our officers visits you at home or you pop down to the station and a report is made first thing. We can take it from there.'

'Can't I see someone tonight and make one now?'

'I think we should leave it just a little bit longer, madam. It's still a little soon. As I say, it's usually the case that people have gone somewhere and had a few drinks too many, but they roll up sooner or later.'

'My husband's not like that.'

'I'm afraid that's what they all say. We've no way of telling. Best leave it till morning, eh?'

'I'm frightened he might not come back, so surely it's better to start looking for him before he gets too far.'

'It might seem like that, I know. The hours pass so slowly

45

when you're worried. It's highly unlikely he's not coming back, highly unlikely I assure you. Had you had a domestic dispute at all, madam?'

'Not at all. As I told you, we were about to have supper together. He'd just nipped out, two seconds down the road, to buy ice-cream. Listen, every minute we're talking, someone could be out looking for him.'

I probably sound terse; poor man's doing his best, but it doesn't feel like halfway good enough. I envy him. A few minutes more of this shift, and he can knock off, slip into his car, switch on the device in the driver's seat which warms his bottom, hasten home, and cover himself with his duvet and his wife in the time it takes to make a piece of toast. From his comfortable position, it's easy enough for him to feel concern. Concern functions on auto-pilot in the face of others' raw, white turmoil and distress, and makes one feel good in a passive sort of way. His line of work, he probably feels concern rather a lot. I do myself. Feel it most days, in fact, at work, and nights, when I'm sitting with my good husband watching the news bulletins conveniently packaged within the neat little box in my easy-tone kitchen.

The man tells me, politely, to hang up now and someone will ring back in the morning. I obey. The telephone receiver makes a quiet but deadening clunk as I replace it. Now what? How to fill anxious time? It's weighing me down but there's no shrugging it off. The awareness of its aged pulse is a form of imaginative torture. I want to get in the car and drive in circles round the city, a crazed kerb-crawler scouring the streets for a result, for any sign of my Kim. Activity at least. But Dora has told me it'd be mad to do that. Although her special brand of common sense currently eludes me, deep down, something stops me from leaping from my bed and taking flight into the night. In the city, one man is such a tiny, slippery object, he's like a contact lens lost on the floor of a vast and crowded restaurant.

I double-check that the telephone receiver is properly placed on its perch and turn out the light. That uses up about eight seconds. The room is not dark because the street lamp pollutes it with its barley-sugar light. The odd sombre shapes on the ceiling and of the furniture are familiar yet strange tonight. I lie back, rigid, so alert to every sound and movement outside my door. I can hear the pop of the bathroom light as Jack goes in there to clean his teeth. On the pavement beneath my window are quick, high-heeled footsteps. A telephone trills dimly in a house opposite.

I do not fall asleep. The black elastic night stretches as if to breaking point.

I lost my virginity to a man called Stephen who had eyes the colour of a nutty blemish on a pear. I was sixteen and he was thirty-three. It was a laugh, of sorts.

We met at a nightclub. It was a grimy place, in a forgotten part of Oxford, on a bit of wasteland down near the station. The walls and floors were all black and sticky with spilt drink. My friends and I used to go there on Friday and Saturday nights and all make out to each other we were having a good time. Stephen was a friend of a friend. He wore copper bracelets which jangled as he moved, and a grubby piece of string round his neck, no key on it, just there. He smelt of cloves and bought me a bottle of beer. He said he was self-employed, in the music business, which sounded lofty enough, managing fledgling bands. I questioned him as to what time he got up in the mornings, don't ask me why.

'Fact is, I'm more of a nocturnal person, Sylvie,' he shouted above the noise of the sound system. When he talked he used my name a great deal. It was either just a more evolved use of 'um', or a calculated move to give the impression of an intimacy between us, created on fast forward. I was young; I chose to believe the latter.

'Because you have to go out to gigs every night, stay up so late?'

'Partly, Sylvie, but it's more to do with my phobia about pigeons. Days aren't good for me. I can't go out much. Bound to come across a pigeon in the street somewhere, however much you try to avoid the ones where they like to hang out most. Nights are no problem, Sylvie. They all've pissed off somewhere, to sleep I guess, I don't like to speculate too closely. Nights I'm a free man.'

I couldn't believe that here I was talking to someone with the same affliction as me, couldn't believe there was an official word for it, that it had already been dignified as a recognised condition. Before I met Stephen, I had thought I was the only person in the world daft enough to have a thing about pigeons. I'd presumed I was a freak. Sometimes when I was out of doors with family and friends they would see me duck if a pigeon came in to land too close to me. If I accidentally let out a giveaway yelp, they'd laugh, but very soon forget about it. When I was left shaking, I'd pretend it was the cold. I devised so many methods of covering my shame. You can exercise deception like a muscle and, sure enough, steadily the use of it comes ever more naturally to you.

I'd never dared breathe a word of my dread fear of birds to a soul, and here was a virtual stranger, a perfectly ordinary-looking bloke, nothing freakish about him, breezily telling me he'd designed a whole way of life round his terror of them. To my mind, he was heroically open about it. Later that night, in his bedsit bed with him, virginity just lost and copper bracelets calm at last, I found the courage to admit my own dread fear of birds.

'Oh, you have it too, do you, Sylvie? Yeah, well, it's quite a common one,' he told me, holding me tighter so I couldn't mistake the warmth of empathy. 'Like snakes or spiders.'

'I know some people don't like snakes and spiders much,' I told him, 'but do they give them the shakes and make them sweat and retch?'

'Course. That's what phobias do. Nothing to be ashamed of. Just have to learn to live with it really. It's hard for my uncle. He's a phobia about visitors. Whenever anyone rings his doorbell, he has to cower under his kitchen table. Pigeons are a bit easier to avoid, I guess. Personally, Sylvie, I don't find the nocturnal life much of a problem. Suits me in many ways or, rather, I make sure it does. Bit of a bore for the bank and the post office and that, otherwise it's fine.' He pulled on his post-coital cigarette and shrugged, and I was overwhelmed by the extent of his cool.

I am remembering Stephen because it is six o'clock in the morning and I am whiling away my Kim-less dawn with thoughts of those in my life who have let me down.

I went out with Stephen for two or three months. The squalor of his bedsit, far from acting as a repellent, was a fetching turn-on to my peculiar teenage sensibility or, as I see it now, derangement. The bathroom was damp and reeked of stale flannels and towels that had never been given a chance to dry. The bath itself, in unflushed pink, served as a cat-litter and its bottom was patterned with the yellow-stained map of where the cat had oft-times hazarded to shit. Stephen was not a sentimental soul, but he was a passionate defender of his cat. He loved it, logically really, as the natural enemy of the pigeon. I recall the detail of his purple carpet, dank, and stained with coffee, booze, cat's piss, and more besides; his spluttering ashtrays; his cold plates with encrustations of old food reminiscent of suppurating sores; his leprous bedclothes. All these things were glamour on an unprece-dented scale. Stephen had that magic combination – cool and sensitivity. I fell in love with him, after a teenage fashion.

So it was I skipped school for a while in order to stay up with Stephen through the nights and sleep during the day. My mum either didn't notice or didn't care, deflected by her own detailed personal life. Stephen's singular solution to the pigeon problem seemed perfect for me too.

At first, during my brief sojourn with him, I began to wonder if we night-birds weren't some sort of alternative, apocalyptic population. It was an idea I relished. While we were cut off from the rest, we had different habits and feelings and desires. Thoughts of being slightly superior to daytime folk, above commonplace considerations or needs. His arrangement had started out as a practical one, to avoid pigeons, but quickly became something else, a vacuous little rebellion. Our smugness was the same as that of people who congratulate themselves on always being late, or for being above breakfast. We wallowed in letting go of our feel for basic things, like planting a potato in the sun; walking in the city without being frazzled by headlights; thirsting for a down-to-earth daytime drink (namely one without any alcoholic content); seeing the colours of grass and letter boxes, of sand and chocolate, of hats and cow parsley, untainted by artificial light. It was more mysterious, and certainly smarter, to be a creature of the night.

But I soon discovered that never seeing daylight was depressing. While I might be the type who's always secretly liked that time of year when the nights draw in – I never was a summer person – as the weeks went by, it became harder and harder to reconcile myself to a totally dark existence. The novelty wore off. Baths at three in the morning, the water with its echoing sound. Night streets, blissfully innocent of pigeons, but also bereft of people and ordinary life. Oh, there was real life of course, people peeing in doorways and throwing up extravagantly on the pavements, shouting, fighting, laughing, dancing. What I soon realised I missed was the very ordinariness of daytime occurrences – a bright smile from the woman in the butcher's; bumping into a mate on the bus; weekend elevenses in a café; watching a joke pink sunset flirt with Oxford's impossibly beautiful skyline; seeing a dog being stroked by a kid in a pushchair; reading a paper when it was less than fifteen hours old. I began to yearn for the merrier periods in school with friends, and my regular shopping trips with my sister Simone. She and I often used to go down to Oxford together, have a bag of chips, then fling ourselves into the crowds and hit the shops. Our visits to Miss Selfridge and its like were more for the Saturday crack in the communal changing rooms – shrieks of laughter and cigarettes – than for the purchase of cheap spotty skirts and fun furry jumpers. I began to hanker after food that my gran was so good at cooking but which I wouldn't have had a stomach for except in the day – roast chicken and bread sauce, hot chocolate pudding with cream. When Stephen and I got going, which was usually around eight o'clock in the evening, we wanted to go out to parties and gigs, didn't remotely fancy cooking. So we lived instead off petrol station sandwiches and sausage rolls, crisps, Flake bars, and flapjacks.

I was quick to gather that if you only ever emerge at night, the atmosphere on the streets regresses in the mind from one of excitement and adventure to one that is as lonely and eerie as an off-season amusement arcade.

'I don't think you can handle it,' he told me one night after a party as we were walking back to his place in Jericho at five in the morning. I was stumbling with fatigue. 'I don't want to be with someone who can't handle it.'

I hate that expression, handle. Maddeningly, I have a very visual mind and it makes me think of a saucepan.

'What do you mean?' I said desperately, feeling I was on his way out. 'Being with you, staying up nights to avoid pigeons, it's the perfect way to be. I'm just a bit tired tonight, that's all.'

'It's your problem, not mine. I'm well sorted. If you can't hack the nocturnal existence, fine by me. Perhaps you should be in school, living normal hours.' As he was starting to reverse the intimacy, he left off the Sylvies.

'Normal hours means I have to be haunted by pigeons,' I remember protesting. 'I don't want to go back to that. You can't wish that on me. Not after all we've talked about. Besides, how would I get to see you?'

'It'd be difficult, I agree.'

'What are you saying?'

'Perhaps it's not healthy, us feeding each other's pigeon fears.'

'But who else are you ever going to meet who could understand you like I do?' I hadn't learnt at that stage that begging's not a safe bet. 'Who's going to know exactly how it feels when you're woken at dawn by cooing in the eaves, and why it makes you break down in tears? Good luck to you finding another woman who's not going to think you're the wettest man that ever walked the earth.'

'The fact is, my personal life could do with some down-sizing right now.'

Looking back, from the perspective of a year or two, I can only say the modern way of rejection, the language, can be disappointing.

Anyway, it was over that night. Now I suspect my not being able to 'handle' living by night and our phobia duet was just an excuse Stephen used, he never really loved me. I shall never know. Certainly, men are even more feeble about telling you they don't love you than they are about telling you they do. Can't bring themselves to come to the point. They couch the truth in meaningless terms, sidestep it with all the deft ingenuity of a clubber dancing round her handbag. Perhaps it's because they don't want to hurt you. Perhaps it's because they are cowards.

Stephen later married a girl with a penchant for amphetamines and a phobia about traffic. I'm staring at the illuminated figures of my radio-alarm clock. It is six twenty-three in the morning. The happy couple are probably just getting ready for bed.

In the sombre light of dawn I shift my eyes to the phone again. I have been staring at its black outline for much of the night, imagining the little device inside its plastic covering which causes it to ring, though it's not ringing now. I'm willing it to make its sound but it is as steadfastly dormant as a spent volcano. When it

51

eventually erupts, I fear what comes out will be explosive.

If it's time to do anything it's time to get up and wake Jack. I've waited these past long hours till such time as it's halfway reasonable to interrupt his sleep. Maybe, somewhere deep down in me, lurks a pebble of hope that Kim is fine really. Otherwise what was it that stopped me from barging into Jack's room a hundred times during the night?

I manoeuvre myself out of bed and stagger giddily from my room to his door, thin nightdress sticking to me in clumps like damp ribbons of pasta. I knock a few times before I can hear him grunting.

'What's going on?'

'Can I come in?'

'What's the time? Fuck it. You've done it now. All right.'

Fuck his grumpiness. I go into his room. It smells of boiled vegetable night breath. I am crying. Can't help myself, although I don't like to do so in front of my children. It embarrasses and distresses them.

Jack is twisted up in his duvet and a long-sleeved T-shirt; one slim calf is exposed. He's rubbing his face awake. The rings round his morning eyes are the colour of moulded purple grapes.

'This better be good, Mum, I'm knackered.' He levers himself up against a squashed pillow and lolls against the headboard uncertainly. I sit on his bed. 'You crying?'

'What d'you mean, it better be good? What d'you think it is? Dad's still not back.'

'Still?' He pauses. 'Oh, Mum, I'm sorry. Did you have any sleep? Don't cry, Mum, no need to cry. Whatever's happened it's going to be OK, yeah? We'll find him.'

When he was about thirteen I started to grieve for the son that was, Jack as a child. The tenderness had flown. The milky neck had given way to fledgling bristle, and he had begun no longer just to love me but to judge me. Whereas he used to confide in me, to weep openly in the face of pain or danger, to seek out maternal caresses, he began only coming close in order to pick at me like a sharp fingernail at a too-sealed envelope. For a while, he hated me, then he tolerated me, and these days I am a friend of sorts, the kind who provides him reliably with toothpaste and Jaffa Cakes, and occasionally with mirth.

Times such as this, fleeting moments, I glimpse that tender side of Jack again. It never left, just has been, since adolescence and perhaps necessarily, closed up awhile. Right this minute, as I catch it, the magnificent roll of a sheep's eye in headlights, it reduces me further into such a state of weeping as he doesn't know where to put himself.

'Oh, Mum.' His morning eyes are pleading, his hands as hesitant a burden for him as for an actor in amateur dramatics. Eventually they throw manly caution to the wind and clasp me, even brave my matted hair with a rhythmic rubbing. 'You've got yourself in such a state.'

'Maybe he took off to go and visit Mackenzie? But why? What if he's dead? He could have been killed in an accident, murdered. I mean, why wouldn't he have rung me?'

'No, I promise,' Jack's saying softly. 'Dad's not dead. That's daft. He's only been gone a few hours and your mind's going crazy with explanations. I understand your anxiety, course I do, but there'll be a good reason. You know Dad.'

'How can I be so sure anymore? I think I do, but, well, this. Tell me you don't know anything I don't know.' My head buried in my son's chest, all I can see close up is the microscopic knitting weave of his T-shirt.

'What like? He's shagging another—' He stopped. 'He's got some other woman somewhere? Mum. Please. Dad?'

'No, not that necessarily. Anything. Has he told you he's been depressed or wanted to have a bit of time away or something?'

'Nah. Dad's not like that.'

'You never know though, do you? You hear of those men who live with their wives four days a week. The other three, when they say they're off working, they're living with a whole second family, wife hasn't the faintest clue. Years it can go on. You think you know someone.'

'Come off it, Mum,' Jack says, holding me tighter to him, 'what other mad thoughts have you been coming up with in the night?'

'Anything's possible.'

'Yeah, just not very likely.'

'I'm telling you I've got this feeling he's not coming back, for whatever reason.'

53

'For what reason?'

'Something's happened.'

'Come on.' Jack holds me up, continues to keep his gentle grip on me. 'You've got to stop crying. It'll do your head in. Let's go downstairs, get a cup of tea.' He stands me up. 'You're shivering. Where's your dressing gown?'

'I don't know. I'm not cold.'

'I don't care, you're shaking. Have mine.' He lets go of me very carefully. Even as he reaches for his towelling dressing gown hanging at the back of his door, he holds his breath and keeps one hand out in my direction, as if I might collapse any second like an edifice of playing cards.

Jack is a thoughtful, kind man. That's all I ever hoped for, if I had a son, to bring him up so he would be a good and kind man. He has his singular way with midriff girls, I know, but he is young, and he is not cruel.

Together we go down the stairs. In the kitchen he makes some tea. I opt to take it without milk or sugar. I sit at the table, desolate. Jacks pours himself a bowl of Frosties. It's a wonder he can face food. We don't say anything to one another for a few minutes. As he eats, the crunching sound seems three times as loud as on normal mornings.

'I'm not going into work today,' I tell him.

'That's a bad idea. It'll be much worse for you, sitting here, waiting. I'm not going out till lunchtime. I can tell Dad to ring you when he gets in.' He is standing, lower back leaning against the kitchen units, talking and spooning the cereal into his mouth at the same time. A drop of milk slaloms down his unshaven chin and he catches it with his tongue.

'No, I'm telling you, I'm staying right here. How can you be so sure he will get in? The police'll be coming round at some point. I rang them last night.' My mental picture of the man I spoke to instantly presents itself to me again. I hope he had a nicer night than me. 'They're calling back this morning.'

'Well, that's good, but can you work on some of your reports or something here? Otherwise you'll drive yourself up the wall.'

'Jack, my love, I can't do anything till your father walks back through that door.' I pick up my tea. 'Or the phone goes with some kind of proper explanation. I'm not moving. However long

54

it takes.'

Jack nods, and clatters his bowl into the sink. 'I'll stay with you.'

'I'm OK,' I say automatically. I'm not.

'I think you should go back to bed for a little while, try to relax a bit if not sleep. It's still really early.'

He steps forward to help me up, his hands almost sentimental in their gentle movements. I am reduced to tears once more, wildly grateful for this simple gesture of filial gallantry in the face of my impending despair. He guides me back to bed and tactfully leaves me be. I lie back staring at one invisible amoeba on the ceiling for three and three quarter hours. Across my mind thousands of thoughts dart into life only to be abandoned as rapidly as feverish doodles across a page.

At twenty-five to eleven my bedside telephone finally explodes.

# 4

The bluster and bombast of the coach's gears and brakes as it manoeuvred its way through the arched entrance and into its individual bay ruthlessly roused Kim from sleep. As he opened his eyes to the station's punishing lighting his head was lolling worryingly close to the window. Several times on the journey it had dropped sideways and bumped hard against the glass but Kim hadn't woken enough to change position. Now his neck ached so badly on one side that it was a strain to hold his head upright. He rubbed it as vigorously as he could, then walked down the coach's aisle and stepped onto a ribbed concrete covered in oil-stained bruises.

What now?

Kim felt far too sleepy to walk anywhere. He looked about him. Several coaches were parked without their lights on. A couple of stray folk waited at the closed door of one of them, hugging themselves against the cold. Their breath hair-sprayed the air. Otherwise there was no one else about. Kim shivered. The see-through waiting room seemed to beckon. He pushed open its heavy glass door. Its handle, a long red tube, was like a cutting from the outside of the Pompidou Centre. Corporate modernism, Kim thought, has even pervaded trusty old Victoria Coach Station.

Once inside, he didn't sit down immediately because it took him some time to select one of the perfect metal-doily seats on offer. They were fixed together in rows and nailed to the black rubber floor. Kim felt all the indecisiveness of the cinema-goer who arrives early for a film, spoilt for choice. Eventually he sat down at the very back because he thought he might be able to lean his head against the wall. He tried, but it was a cruel design, just too far to reach. Kim was reminded of those modern semi-detached seats on Underground platforms – each one with its own hard, bum-moulded curves – which had replaced the good old-fashioned bench. He had often wondered at the petty-minded sadism of the

56

man so bent on torturing the homeless he had invented this alternative seating specifically, it seemed, to render an innocent and much-needed lie-down by a footsore tramp all but impossible.

From where he was, Kim could see a row of public telephone boxes. He had change from the coach driver so he could quite easily ring Sylvie. He contemplated doing so, but something held him back. He told himself that it was that he feared that he might wake her, God knows what time of night it was, and that he would ring her at a decent hour – wait until at least a few moments after her alarm clock would have gone off. Of course, deep down he knew he was making excuses, feebly procrastinating, because the truth was, the night was wearing on and it was becoming more and more difficult to think of something to tell her. There was nothing to tell her.

The waiting room was an uninteresting space. The uncomfortable seats and the litter were about its only features. Beneath Kim's feet was a spread-eagled front page of the *Sun*, and beside it a plastic sandwich triangle. The speciality sanitary towel in place to absorb mayonnaise and crumbs was still sticking to its bottom, but the sandwich itself had long ago bolted. Old, flattened gobs of chewing gum infected the ground like plague-disfigured flesh.

There were few people for company. A woman in a squeaky coat, her back to him, tried to settle in a front seat. It was either the puny metal arms, or life itself, which dissatisfied her. A man lay slumped across an end seat in the row behind her as if he had been dropped from the ceiling. His legs were wide apart but uninvitingly so: faded-jeans crotch with a fleshly peplum of stomach for all to marvel at. His arms dangled, one over the back, another over the side, and his mouth was way open. Kim thought maybe he was dreaming of saying 'Aah' to his dentist. A young couple sat near him. The girl with a ring in her nostril could have been one of Jack's friends. She had her head on her fellow's sweatshirt chest, her hand in her sleep clutching his arm in a blood-stopping grip. The youth, whose Adam's apple seemed poised to burst through the tenuous skin of his throat, just stared ahead of him, giving nothing away. His feet, trussed up in Princess and the Pea trainers, moved up and down, jiggling perhaps with the frustration of waiting, or impatience for the end of the affair.

Kim slept a while, felt like ten minutes, could have been two hours, there was no way of knowing. When he woke up again he didn't mistake where he was. The litter and the dramatis personae remained the same, but for the addition of an upside down Pepsi paper cup on the seat next to him (what sort of curious person, he asked himself, except for someone with the territorial needs of a micturating dog, would feel the urge to upend his discarded cup specially, so it seemed, to make sticky the seat for the next man?); and an elderly man whose face was a galaxy of starburst blood vessels. The backs of his hands, which were holding onto his cheeks, were the dry patterned texture of off-colour honeycomb. For a troubled moment Kim thought he recognised the sad appeal, evident in the man's eyes, for some life-denied affection by another living creature. Wasn't it one of his patients? He stared at the man, who chewed an invisible cud, trying to determine if it was or not. Then, slowly and with some relief, he remembered that his melancholy patient had died some weeks ago from complications to the bowel, but apparently his almost palpable brand of loneliness was all about. Kim was a lucky man. No lack of affection for him. He could afford to sit and hampster-wheel away his time asking himself what these others were doing here in the terminal of a lonely night. What were they called? What did they do? Where had they come from? Where were they going? These were questions he might have applied to himself, but he had become too busy wrestling with luxurious speculation about them to examine matters closer to home. And it passed a happy hour or so.

The calm in the waiting room disintegrated when a coach-load of early-morning arrivals wheezed and chattered through it on their way from the concourse to the main exit. It suggested to Kim that the bustle of the morning might be upon him. The notion of dawn, etiolated out of significance by the shrill lighting of the coach station, was nonetheless heartening. He hadn't been bothered by time since long before he left Oxford but now he glanced at the clock, and then the blinking information screen to check the departures. Several were listed. The 6.13 to Inverness caught his eye. It was the furthest destination displayed, and the one he decided to take. Perchance to sleep.

Kim went to find a place to buy some regulation sandwiches, a

58

chocolate bar, some crisps, a bottle of water, and a couple of news-papers for the journey. Although he had thirty-five minutes to wait, he was still telling himself that it was as yet much too early to ring home. He was convincing himself it was better to put off the call till the coach stopped for petrol, or even until Inverness. He could surprise her then. Guess where I am? She would be amazed. What on earth for? she'd ask. He had the whole journey ahead of him to work out the answer to that one. When he rang her, he'd be prepared. So he strolled out to the numbered spot where his coach was waiting. There were already a few people in their seats, already tucking into their packets of food.

Kim took off his overcoat and folded it up in a cushion on the seat beside him, a woollen appeal to fellow passengers who might threaten to invade his temporary nest kindly to reconsider and choose to sit elsewhere. He laid out his picnic on top of it by way of an added hint that he was absolutely serious about wishing to keep himself to himself. Not that he was a man who didn't like the company of strangers. Quite the opposite, in fact. Unlike most people, the thought of being buttonholed by a bore on a train or aeroplane didn't fill him with dread because he was of the – what his family and friends considered singular but admirable – view that no human being is dull. On this coach journey, though, he just wanted to sleep.

His papers he placed in the string vest pouch in front of him, then he folded his arms, rested his head on the faintly suspect antimacassar, and closed his eyes. For a short while he listened to people boarding the coach, fussing with their bags and settling down. After a time he was aware of a smell scorching his nostrils. It had been let out of a crisp bag a few rows back. It was a combi-nation of what could only be described as cheese-fragranced spray-on deodorant, chemical onions and pub burps, and it inspired in Kim a sort of comic resentment. This was what he called snack abuse and it was of the most offensive kind. His feel-ings towards the innocent crisp-muncher might have been quite violent had he not been a gentle man. He waved his hands in front of his face and shook his head rapidly to try and disperse the tainted air, but it clung onto him like the contoured pack-aging round supermarket bacon rashers. He held his breath for a moment, then breathed in through his mouth, but the smell just plumped itself on his tongue. For a moment he wondered why he was embarking on this journey, what explanation he might come up with for Sylvie but, before he could come up with an answer, he had fallen asleep and was dreaming.

He woke on the rainy motorway briefly, caught a glimpse of an eternal tarmac through his smudged window, and a bleary sign to Leicester, the white letters of which appeared to tie-dye into their turquoise background. He read a headline on the front page of his *Guardian*, and opened his bar of chocolate. He felt guilty enough eating anything when he himself had not long before harboured such bitterness towards the person with the crisps. But he was hungry and believed a Snickers bar, though an improbable break-fast, would have a more easy-going smell for his fellow passengers than that of his own plain crisps or his potentially psychotic Peking Duck and spring onion sandwich. He unwrapped the chocolate as quietly as he could and kept his mouth purposefully closed as he chewed. Soon the breathy, death-throe squawks of a nearby Walkman lulled Kim back to sleep. His paper slid down his knees, its fold lodging at his feet between the small sleepers of his shoelaces.

When he next woke, he had no idea where he was. The coach was still cruising along in the rain, its wheels making a monoto-nous hiss against the motorway surface, but there appeared to be more passengers in the seats around him. He hadn't been aware of stopping let alone of people getting on. Nor had he been aware of the start of the film on the video up at the front, playing out its Technicolored violence for all it was worth. An unusually deep sleep for him. So many years of both having young children and being on call had made Kim's sleep a tenuous thing. He couldn't remember the last time he had dreamed in his own bed. It wasn't that he was an insomniac, just that he had taught himself to sleep in such a gossamer way as to reduce the nausea he felt during those first few moments of his regular rude awakenings. His neck ached again but he was full of joy. It was a luxury for him to be able to let go, not have to think about the driving, the route, even the outcome of his journey.

When Kim opened his eyes he found himself in pitch black,

60

slumped sideways and face-downwards between the back of the seat next to his and the inadequate pillow of his rolled-up coat. One unshaven cheek was velcroed to the carpet-material seat covering, the other indented into the packet of his now distinctly under-the-weather sandwich. His mouth tasted like a cowpat, his head and hips ached, and pins and needles fizzed and sparked as if the insides of his thighs were being sprayed with furniture polish. He creaked himself upright.

The coach had parked in a bus station. There were no clues as to which one it was except for the fact that everyone was queuing to get off. Kim stretched and yawned and weakly stood up to shake his beleaguered legs. He asked a woman in the aisle where they were.

'Inverness.'

Thanking her, he shook out his coat, put it on, and stuffed his sandwich and bottle of water in the pockets. The air outside was damp, but he was glad of the real thing as opposed to the dry stuffiness of the coach which had been regurgitated out through a mechanical system which fancied itself as a blow-dryer.

Inverness bus station was made up of an expanse of concrete, puddles, a number of covered stops, and half a dozen single-decker buses from a bygone age in a grimy cream and orange livery. One of them had the word Culloden written above its windscreen. Kim stopped still in front of it. Culloden.

'Sixteenth April 1746,' he said to himself automatically, cata-pulted as he was straight back to the parrot-remembered date of the famous battle which he had learnt about at school. He could see in his mind his own childish illustration in his exercise book of the exposed moor and the thousands of tiny figures headed either side by Charles Edward Stuart and the Duke of Cumberland, whom he drew with unpleasant lines for eyes. He found that, thinking about it now, he still felt as he had as an eight-year-old, on the side of the heavily outnumbered Scots who were defeated in less than an hour. Finding himself close to the spot which had so captured his imagination in his indistinct past, his spirits lifted. It surprised him that he could gain such a vicar-ious warmth from that long-gone boy and his long-gone inspira-tion on this chilly, solitary evening, in this place which was so strange to him. He walked with a more certain step than he had when getting off the coach, and made his way towards the information and ticket office, perhaps even smiling.

The office had a blue and cream tiled floor covered in a watercolour of brown footprints brought in from outside puddles. A Formica bar ran the length of the room. Behind it, and beneath a curling National Express poster, stood a woman with a fat book containing page upon page of timetables. For her passengers they represented a certain promise but, for her, ever set in dull black print on flimsy paper, they were unlikely to graduate to reality. She was giving a pedantic passenger, with an English accent and an ill-judged hat, every possible variation on the Inverness to Glasgow theme, and back. It took nearly twenty minutes before he decided that he did, after all, want to go to Newcastle, and she had to start all over again.

Kim sat on a chair which was vomiting bile-coloured foam from a split in its plastic seat. There were three other people waiting. He pretended to browse through some leaflets on the windowsill all about the saver fare from Inverness to Paris, but was actually listening intently to the conversation going on at the counter. A girl of about eighteen, another who looked like one of Jack's progressive girlfriends – they were everywhere it seemed – was sitting near him. She was making it abundantly clear to Kim and everyone else in the room, by the act of chewing her gum noisily, humphing and sighing, that she resented having to waste her time waiting for this man in his silly hat, the most boring person on earth, while he sorted out his pathetic little version of a life. Kim had often marvelled at the intolerance of youth. Had he ever been like that? Admittedly, when the traffic was stopping him from reaching an emergency quickly, or one patient with nothing more than a severe case of hypochondria was preventing him from seeing to his more serious cases, then he felt impatience. But not intolerance. It didn't marry with his view that there was a good reason for everything. It was hard to believe he had ever experienced intolerance, feeling as he did these days, so sanguine. Even his beloved Mackenzie, shy though she was, and something of a reactionary compared to her brother's bedfellows, had been known to betray surprising intolerance. Jack was not an intolerant soul, but that was only a side-effect of that other famously youthful characteristic which he had in spades, namely nonchalance. If you were young, Kim thought, you were either one or the other and, in some improbable cases, both. As for himself, he was brought up on a farm. No time for intolerance, and no room for it either. You'd be on a losing wicket if you were the intolerant type, he mused, and a sheep farmer. Not a good combination.

For the next quarter of an hour or so, Kim learnt about all the coaches to Newcastle, the ones which changed in Edinburgh, and those which went direct. He learnt about the man's genteel courtesy, the woman's admirable resistance to the girl's increasingly manifest aggravation – he even felt he detected in her voice a slowing up, specially to incense her more and teach her to be so bloody impertinent – and he learnt exactly where lay the threshold of the girl's intolerance.

'And what about the return journeys from Newcastle?' the man with the hat asked the woman behind the counter. 'I think I'd like to come back on Tuesday. Or maybe Sunday.'

With which question the girl did a record humph and charged out of the door while lighting a livid cigarette and thrice shouting fuck. The room was left more startled than offended by such an elaborate sitcom of anger. While always puzzled by intolerance, Kim was used to outbursts of raw emotion. In a doctor's surgery it splatters about the place with the sure regularity of the spray from a smart hosepipe over a summer lawn. The woman behind the counter briefly looked after the girl as if, in her capacity of dealing with a ridiculous public, she was used to a bit of volatility here and there. She was only mildly anxious, perhaps, that such a slam to the door might have cracked its glass. Meanwhile, the man in the hat was the only one who didn't seem to notice that anything was amiss, and continued doggedly to press the woman for her vital information. The middle-aged couple waiting opposite Kim shrugged together, as if to say nothing more judgemental than, 'Whoops, there she goes.' And Kim just observed them all with genuine glee, thinking, God I love humanity.

Five minutes later, and with a now only mildly cross cigarette in her hand, the girl returned more quietly than she had left. After all, Kim concluded, she still needed the coach times she had been there for in the first place. She sat down on another stomach-upset chair beside Kim's, and he smiled at her because he admired her, having lost her wick, for facing up to all of them again, but also just to see how she would respond. He knew that a stranger's innocent smile was uplifting. Certainly, on those occasions when a face in a crowd had looked at him and smiled, unbidden, for no more significant reason, perhaps, than an acknowledgement of sharing that specific moment together, two absolute strangers, his day had been made. She smiled back. Her eyes had a shine like Minstrels. Had he been of Jack's age and inclination, he supposed his smile and hers in return would have been a less innocent thing.

'Still at it, is he?' she asked him, glancing at her unwitting tormentor of a few moments before, but with a forgiving voice now, almost unrecognisable from those earlier fucks. 'Fancy a cigarette?' she asked, proffering her packet of Benson & Hedges in Kim's direction. Between her beringed fingers he could make out the Government health warning. 'Most doctors don't smoke,' it read.

Kim was one of them, but it annoyed him anyway, the thought of some pious bureaucrat making up such a slogan to force people to feel guilty about their freedom of choice. He was probably friends with the man behind the individual seats on Underground platforms. Kim was about to take the girl up on her offer out of sheer bloody-mindedness, but then remembered he hated cigarettes, so changed his mind.

'I don't, but thanks all the same,' he said, in a voice which expressed appreciation for her small gesture of generosity.

When the man had eventually acquired enough coach details to keep him in journeys to and from Newcastle for a lifetime, the girl, in what appeared to be gratitude that there was someone who was still willing to smile at and talk civilly to her, offered Kim her place in the queue.

'I'm in no hurry,' he told her, 'no hurry at all.'

'You sure, mate? Thanks.' She took her turn with the woman at the counter and asked what time the next coach to London was due to leave. When she had taken down the time and paid for a single ticket – running away? there's a story there, thought Kim, then again, when is there ever not a story? – and it was his turn, he enquired after a B & B that was close and cheap.

64

'How much do you want to spend?' the woman asked, broad accent, soft voice. She had creases above her mouth like a tiny, neatly sewn pleat. Close up Kim could smell she was wearing a cream like Ponds or Nivea. He had smelt it in the surgery, and the bathroom at home.

'Little as possible. Fifteen quid?'

'There's Mrs Lawson's Guest House at £18.50 a single. Will that do? It's very nice. Comfortable. TV and kettle in the room.'

'Could I walk from here?'

'It's only ten minutes or so.' The woman leant beneath her counter to bring out a leaflet with the room rates and a small map. She drew a helpful circle round the spot marking Mrs Lawson's with her blue biro. Kim thanked her for her help and went out. There was a drizzle as light as a mobile of midges.

Leaving the bus station he turned left towards the centre of the town. He walked alongside a mini department store with clothes in its window which, despite their nightclub colours, managed to look limp and cheerless. Passing another shop he saw hundreds of Scottish souvenirs on display – shortbread in tartan tins, tea towels illustrated with castles and the Loch Ness monster, trolls in kilts and sporrans. Seeing them, Kim became aware for the first time that he was many miles from home. He reluctantly went towards the nearest call box. The heavy door opened with a creak; its concrete floor was dubiously dank. He lifted the grubby receiver. It was cold against his ear, but the line hummed welcomingly. Kim hesitated. He felt guilty and hungry and, shivering, decided to walk on towards the B & B where he could call her from the warmth of his room. The more he put it off, the harder it was going to be, but he couldn't face doing it quite yet. With any luck, thawed out and a bit of food inside him, he might find inspiration.

He came to the station and its hotel. He gazed up at its lofty facade and felt a compulsion to go inside. There was no doubting why. As a child he had once travelled on the night train to Scotland; he had no idea where in Scotland, just Scotland. (Funny, he thought, looking back, how children are often made to make do with very general information, as if detail might sicken them like so many chocolate biscuits, but it is very detail, about every aspect of life, which they always crave.) The family –

his parents and two older brothers – were on one of their rare holidays. They'd breakfast at a station hotel. He had never forgotten it. The hotel, he remembered, had had wide red carpets such as he had never seen, with a black design, and a huge stair-case with bannisters so thick it was as if they had been made to slide down. The reception desk had a brass bell which a man in a green jacket had slapped with his palm, bringing instantly to attention a younger man in a red coat and pillar-box hat. Kim, who hardly ever left the farm except to go to the local school, had wanted to trill with the excitement of it all, but was subdued by the whispering atmosphere of gentility and reserve. They had gone into a dining room which was dark in a way that had seemed to belie the vast windows. Right across the ceiling were ornate decorations, like topsy-turvy icing, which Kim condemned in retrospect as Victoriana run wild, but at the time had been worried sick might drip on his head. The tables were covered with white linen cloths, and pale green china. A few elderly guests ate in silence, their spoons metallically echoing against their porridge bowls as if in protest at the overall oppression. Kim, who must have been no more than seven, thought it was the most astonishing place he had ever seen. What struck him most, he could remember to this day, were the four baby jam jars clus-tered on a plate with a silver teaspoon – marmalade, strawberry, blackcurrant, and apricot – each with a gold lid and a tiny tartan label saying Preserve. When he had sat down in a wide uphol-stered chair, he had gasped so loudly at their very existence that his mother had had to say, 'Hush.' Such things he hadn't known till then, and they seemed to him too perfect to be real. When his father popped open the marmalade he had felt a grip on his throat. He had watched him take up a scallop of butter from a special dish and casually spread it and the marmalade on his toast. Full of resentful disillusion, Kim had stared at his every slow mouthful.

'You can have the others, I'm sure the waiters won't mind,' his mother had said at the end of breakfast.

'What, you mean for keeps?' Kim had not been able to believe his good fortune. He had put them in his pocket so fast it was as if he were testing for a placement with Fagin. Before she could change her mind. And, back at home for years afterwards, he never opened them, just kept them on a shelf in his bedroom and regularly thumbed the dust off their lids.

Thinking about the rest of that Scottish trip now, he was a blank. He was sure his parents had taken him and his brothers on from that charged breakfast, to some B & B, and presumably for walks across moors and round lochs, but he didn't remember any of that. All he could recall of the holiday was that station hotel, the little quartet of miniature jams, and the fact that his father had ruined it all for him by so callously eating the marmalade.

Of course, he had to go into the Inverness station hotel, now that it had confronted him, to see if it were the same one. Besides, he was hungry and wanted to eat his sandwich away from the grey drizzle. It seemed as good a place as any. He tapped up the stone steps and went inside.

In the reception was an enlarged menu in a brass free-standing frame, and a careful arrangement of a mahogany coffee table and two upholstered chairs, in red and gilt. They had a look about them of having been made not for sitting on but just for looking at, appreciatively, a fact which made Kim want to plonk himself down on one of them immediately. Although the staircase was wide and grand, and a quiet air of respectability pervaded the atmosphere, the lay-out was different from the station hotel he remembered. It was not the same place. There appeared to be no separate dining room. Tables for two with pale pink cloths were dotted about the bottom of the stairs between palm court-style plants. At almost all of them sat an elderly widow having a flaccid omelette supper with another elderly widow. Same against-the-odds curls, same caution-to-the-wind necks, same grey-hooded eyes betraying a fierce fidelity to memories. Wedding rings firmly entrenched in padded fingers as if grown into them like new tissue around broken bone; still married in all but flesh to husbands long passed on.

Kim thought of Sylvie, pictured the ring on her finger, the one he had found for her on Royal Avenue. He remembered so well the day he had gone to buy it, two and a half years or so after they had met in south Belfast. Almost from the moment he saw Sylvie – pale face, long dark hair, and fringe teasing such melancholy eyes – at that otherwise unappealing party, he had been in no doubt that he was in love with her and wanted to be married to her for ever. Simple enough (and he had been proved right: never a moment of regret since). Naturally, for the shy boy he was in those days, going about the proposal was a less certain business. Their second meeting had taken place by chance – or so he thought till she admitted some years later, much to his amusement, that she'd planned it – in Smokey Joe's. It was after that that he had begun the slog of saving up for the engagement ring. He lived off spaghetti hoops and didn't light the fire in his room for nearly three years (except when she came round), and checked the balance of all the money he had so carefully saved up since the age of twelve – the pocket, birthday, and Christmas money he had never spent but had always kept for something special – but unspecific – in the future. Sylvie's engagement ring was going to be that special thing. When the day came to take the plunge, he borrowed a suit from a friend because he thought the jeweller mightn't take him seriously, a young man in scruffy jeans rolling up and asking to look at diamonds. Then he went to the post office to withdraw, without a moment's hesitation, his entire life savings.

He had never been in a jeweller's shop in his life. It had smelt of pipe smoke and dusty display velvet warmed by dusty light bulbs. Voices were sombre. At first he had looked at the modern rings, three stones all in a row, and each one as small as a red corpuscle. A more measly show for over two and a half years of spaghetti hoops he hadn't been able to imagine. Just as he had been about to leave the shop, mortified with disappointment and without a clue where else to look, the cobwebby jeweller, who had an egg-like bald patch in his nest of dark hair, had produced his selection of old rings. 'Most people don't care for what they see as second-hand, but we keep a few; they're less expensive and a hundred times nicer on the whole,' he'd said. Kim's eyes had lit up as they fell upon a stunningly simple ring – which turned out to be Georgian – with diamonds set in the form of a child's drawing of a flower. His heart had lurched with the excitement of happening upon the perfect one. He had handed over the hundred pound notes – which had taken so much gathering – sweating from top to toe. Twenty-three years on, Sylvie had never once taken it off, even during her swelling pregnancies. Now Kim wondered, glancing at the station hotel widows, if, thirty or forty years hence, were he to die before Sylvie (as all those life-expectancy tables predicted he would), she would be as faithful to her husband's memory as these old birds were to theirs. Would she, like them, keep the ring on her finger fiercely for ever? Perhaps he should wish that, after he had gone, she would make a new life for herself, even meet a new companion to see out her final years, but it was not so. It was too awful to imagine, Sylvie and another man.

Kim walked on by, towards the back of the building where he found the Ladies/Gents and telephones, near a pair of double doors leading into the kitchens. He went into one of the two telephone booths which was decorated with striped green wallpaper, and had a built-in seat like a Victorian lavatory. He sat down, and the first thing he did was to eat his packet of crisps while reading the doodles on a wood-chip shelf stacked with directories, and a Scottish Tourist Board leaflet about a castle which was stuck in a crevice behind the ashtray. It was a comfortable and quiet place to be, hidden away, and his crisps weren't bothering anyone. He had already decided he wasn't going to ring Sylvie till he got to Mrs Lawson's, even if it did make him feel guilty in the meantime.

He stayed in the phone booth for twenty minutes or so, all the while staring about him, leafing through a six-year-old Yellow Pages, filling his mind with Refrigeration Engineers and Woodworm; distracting himself. While he was eating his snack, he managed to forget about the telephone itself and so deflected from his conscience the notion that he might make his call sooner rather than later. Under Pest Controllers he spotted a huge advertisement with a picture of a pigeon. It put him in mind of Sylvie, but still he wasn't tempted to ring. His quick-flap thought was what a bad illustration it was, that he could do better even though he couldn't draw for toffee. Then he flicked on to Roofing Services, and back to Banqueting and Function, wishing he had a book with him. Martin Chuzzlewit and Mark Tapley had just been about to make their way back on board ship to England following their disastrous trip to America. What had been about to become of them?

What was to become of him in this dead-ash telephone booth in the intestines of the Inverness station hotel? Suddenly he felt very hot and isolated. Being so alone in the booth, no one on earth, not even Sylvie, knowing he was there, was something he had been enjoying only a few moments before. Now it became a sensation which troubled him, even made him tremble very slightly. A minute shiver darted up his neck like a small, swift ladder up a pair of tights. He quickly opened the door of the booth and sat down instead on the banquette outside it. Doing so, he panted, as if for air.

'I will call her later,' he told himself, wiping his brow, and opening his beleaguered Peking Duck sandwich, now doughy and defeated, as done in by life as the widows in the foyer. He vaguely asked himself if someone might object to his eating it there, but couldn't believe for a moment they would. Anyway, hunger over-took him still and he wasn't doing anyone any harm. As he began chewing, a young chef in gingham trousers whistled past him and into the kitchens, and either didn't see Kim and his sandwich, or didn't care if he did. Kim had just enough time to recognise the same Jackson Pollock design on the lad's white jacket as he had so often seen on Jack's. Splattered tomato, egg, chocolate, spinach, God knows what. It amazed him any ingredients ever made it on to the plates in these places.

'What do you do in those kitchens of yours?' he remembered asking his son on numerous occasions. 'Throw the food at each other?'

Kim was smiling to himself when the chef shot out of the doors again, followed by a young woman with sun-lamp legs, short skirt, a faux blazer with brass buttons, and a supercilious expression. She clutched a clip-board to her bosom.

'Excuse me, Michael,' she shouted at the chef. 'Can I have a word?' There was an officious tone to her voice. She issued some instruction to him. Kim, who had polished off one half of his sandwich, hastily pushed the other up the sleeve of his coat. It was an instinctive thing.

'Can I help you, sir?' the woman asked, turning unexpectedly towards him. She placed her left leg straight out to the side, dug a high-heel into the carpet and pointed her toe in the air. It was undoubtedly a stance she had perfected to lend the air of authority appropriate to her position. Kim supposed she was a manageress and very pleased about it too.

70

'No thank you, I'm fine, thank you.' Kim had had to posit a mouthful of sandwich into his cheeks, so his words sounded muffled and he was aware of being at something of a disadvantage.

'Are you a guest at the hotel, sir?'

'No, no, sadly not.' Why the 'sadly', he asked himself? He squirmed to realise he was being obsequious.

'Well, might I ask you what you're doing here, sir, if you don't mind?'

The woman had a way about her of giving the appearance of consummate politeness, but actually being as rude as hell.

'I'm just waiting for a call.' Kim, whose words were still muffled by bread and duck between his teeth and his cheek, was about to indicate the booth with his arm, but felt the damp sandwich pressing at his cuff. He nodded his head in its direction instead.

'Those phones don't take incoming calls. Sir.'

'They don't?'

'I suggest you use one of the ones on the station platform.'

'But I've just asked someone to call me back.'

The woman looked at Kim with a contempt which was apparent even through her icing of make-up, and from between her royal blue insects of mascara. He estimated she must have been all but twenty-six. Only a few years older than Mackenzie, for God's sake. The foot of hers which was pointing in the air was now swaying slowly to and fro as if she was asking for it to be amputated.

'Do you like the carpet here, sir?' she asked, sweeping her hand in an arch above the floor. It was a tartan carpet, in bright greens and blues, and evidently new.

Kim blinked with astonishment at the question. 'I'm sorry?'

'The carpet.'

He hadn't misunderstood her. 'Yes, very nice,' he said, wondering what on earth she was getting at.

'Yes, well, we have to pay for nice things like this carpet, and that means making a profit. People can't get the benefit of a nice carpet such as this without in some way contributing to those all-important profits. Understand? So, if you will forgive me, I suggest once more that you go and make your telephone calls elsewhere, not in this hotel, which can't afford to have its carpets worn down under the feet of just anyone who decides he or she fancies them. I'll show you the way out.'

Back on the street, Kim found himself literally out of breath with indignation. He had to sit on a stone bollard at the entrance to the hotel's forecourt to allow the incident fully to sink in. It was uncomfortable but he was so cross he didn't care.

'The bitch, the bitch! How dare she?' he kept saying, only just under his breath. But he knew he was more angry with himself than with the woman, for having let her get away with it. While he could understand, grudgingly, that a hotel couldn't welcome everyone in from the cold who had no intention of checking into a room or buying overpriced food and drinks, nothing could excuse her tone and that attitude. To give him a lecture about the economics of the frigging carpet! Was it possible? And he had taken it. To think of it, to think of how he been so submissive in the face of her phony corporate authority, and of how almost every last detail of his dignity had been compromised, enraged him. He felt frustrated and helpless.

'I'm a doctor, for fuck's sake!' he spat. 'A doctor.'

Suddenly he stopped and was still. After some moments, he put his hands up to his cheeks and chin, and held them there, as if to take them away would be to risk his falling apart. Then he was still once more, completely still.

Kim Black was born in 1953 in Herefordshire. His mother came from Ludlow, the daughter of a butcher. His father, David, was a sheep farmer. David had lived all his life on a small farm near the borders of Wales and Shropshire which he inherited in his early twenties. The house was made of rough stone and had a view over hills without another building in sight. When Kim was growing up there the modest rooms were painted white, the floorboards were bare and dusty, the plain wooden furniture was functional, the china cracked. No money had been spent on the place since Kim's paternal grandmother had moved in as a young wife of eighteen, but it was well lived in. There were dogs' hairs on every surface, and cardboard boxes filled with old newspapers and tools and shoes and toys lined the length of the hall. The larder always seemed to boast a tall churn brimming with creamy milk, shelves with packets of rice and flour, jars of sugar, plates of cheddar cheese covered in muslin, a cold fat-globule roast lamb, a half eaten blackberry and apple crumble, vast tins of Heinz baked beans and Bird's custard, and under-size apples with sweet-smelling flesh and the first showing of liver spots around their peel. In the bathroom there were always towels in damp pats on the floor, and sprinklings of talcum powder across the black plastic lavatory seat. The two bedrooms were simple – iron beds, no curtains, bare floorboards – but untidy. Kim shared a bedroom with his two brothers, Mark and Craig. Mark and Craig shared a bed. The sheets and pillows seemed to be twisted and compacted like nightmares, but smelt of warm bread. Their parents' room had the advantage of an iron fireplace, but crows nested in its chimney making sinister scuffles. Faith refused to allow David to clear them out and certainly never let him light it. One February night, in one of his deep winter moods, Kim's father lost his temper with his mother. Frustrated that he couldn't find the words to express his anger, instead of shouting at her he struck a match to the fire's decorative coals. She couldn't put it out in time. Smoke choked the room and emanated into the passage and the rest of the house. Meanwhile, she heard the desperate squawks of the crows, and the blistering of their feathers and flesh, same sinister sound as pork crackling in the range. At breakfast the following morning she was crying. Kim, aged about nine, was so anxious to comfort her he couldn't eat. As usual, his father made sure his cereal was luxuriating in cream and tucked in. It was only when he had gone out into the fields that she described to Kim and his brothers what had happened, in haunting detail. May it was before their father apologised to her and asked her to forgive him.

David Black was a lean man, with arm and chest muscles as defined as those of any back-street boxer in the peak of health. When Kim looked at family photographs he was always surprised by how his father's face, even when he was still in his thirties, already had the look about it of having been duffed up well and good by the weather. And, for as long as Kim could remember, the expressions across it were as changing as an open landscape. Kim reckoned he could see the seasons on his father's features. In winter his pallor was grey, his brow cold and cross. Then it was that he retreated into himself, found it hard to talk to his family, seemed only to step up his perennial communication with his working dogs. He was not a cruel man really. In summer, his complexion changed, browned by the sun, and with it his very disposition would shift. Gradually, with the lighter mornings, he would talk more and more at breakfast and throughout the day. By the end of May, the hesitant smiles of spring would graduate into full-blown laughter. With his father's change of spirits, Kim, from a very young age, was able to detect his mother's shoulders either tightening with tension, or loosening with relief, depending on the time of year. He was sure the bread she made in summer came out less heavy than its winter counterpart. Nothing to do with her menstrual cycle, as some old wives might maintain, but instead a symptom of a devoted and close allegiance to her husband's seasonal metamorphosis.

When Kim went away to Belfast, in 1971, to study medicine at Queens University, the thing that most struck him about city life was that people were relatively impervious to the seasons. His father was so finely attuned to them he became with them a different man. Kim liked to believe it was the summer which drew out, from a temporary winter self, his true nature. Only it could as easily have been the other way round.

His father had always fascinated him. While Kim believed that on the whole men are made up of a mosaic of different characteristics, David Black was made up of just a few, but could embrace the whole spectrum of each. It seemed extraordinary to his son that there could be found, under the same roof, as it were, such extremes of the same trait. There was, for example, his father's exceptional energy and ability for physical hard work; and his unusual laziness for paperwork of any kind. There was his profound parsimony (the family had to use up pencils till the wood was spent and they were practically down to their lead tip, and was made to keep a bar of soap to within the very slither of its existence); and his flagrant extravagance (at breakfast he would anaesthetise his and everyone else's Weetabix with cream, and at night – because he was too lazy to turn them out – he would leave lights on all over the house). He was both rash and cowardly; arrogant and lacking in confidence; boastful and understated;

74

selfish and selfless. Never in his life had Kim encountered anyone so inconsistent, nor did he believe he ever would.

As Kim grew older and more open with his mother and brothers, they used to marvel at the phenomenon together. When he was a junior doctor in Belfast, he came across a case study in the *British Medical Journal* about an American woman with an estimated forty-seven different personalities. He cut it out and sent it to his mother with a humorous letter saying, 'I think at last I might have discovered Dad's condition!'

His mother, although miraculously compatible with her changeling husband, was a more reliable character. Her name, Faith, was an entirely appropriate one.

Kim had never met a man who, when asked to describe his own mother, hadn't said that she was beautiful. Whether he loved her or loathed her, in his eyes at least, her beauty was never in question. Kim was no exception. But he did wonder if this belief in maternal beauty wasn't an absolute prerequisite of filial perception. Mackenzie was of what Jack called 'the hippy conviction', that all mothers were beautiful; it was an intrinsic part of motherhood. Kim had often tried to go along with his daughter's more magnanimous view of the world, but wasn't quite so sure.

Anyway, he certainly believed his mother was. She had brown hair which she always wore in an untidy bun. On those rare occasions when Kim had caught a glimpse of her hair free, he had gasped at how long and thick it was, how it transformed the very shape of her face, and how it made her look even softer and more feminine than usual. Her eyes seemed darker, her skin even paler. He had once told her how pretty it was and asked her to wear it down all the time. 'What,' she had laughed, 'and get it caught in the barbed wire all the time like the sheep?' She always wore dungarees over thick jerseys the colour of porridge or heather, and filthy, heavy boots. Sometimes, like everyone else on the farm, she smelt of grassy sheep shit, rat poison and damp dogs, but mainly her scent was of yeast from her bread-making, damp logs and treacle. She had the nipped-in waist, curvaceous bottom and rounded hips of a forties matinée starlet, but did not give off the same disingenuous air of pouting hopelessness. She worked hard and long both with her husband and looking after him.

Kim felt that his parents had a happy marriage of sorts. They had an understanding. They didn't talk to each other much, except in the summer when David became more loquacious, but neither of them could have survived for more than an hour or two without the other. On the mornings when she went to the local market, he was on edge and crotchety and did not regain his better temper until she came home. It was a wonder to Kim that they could seemingly communicate so little, and love each other so unstintingly.

He always vowed that whenever he had a wife, he would communicate with her a lot as well as love her so unstintingly.

Eventually, no feeling in his bum, Kim moved off from the bollard towards the B & B recommended to him by the woman in the bus station.

He rang the bell of a terraced house with a pebble-dash facade the colour of cold dishwater. A woman with an all-in-one bosom welcomed him with captivating enthusiasm. She was very fat and so might have looked older than her years, but she had a pretty face, carefully but not overly made up in a way that hinted at self-respect as opposed to vanity. She was dressed in a smart ankle-length skirt, and a black satin-feel blouse with pink and yellow splodges which Kim took to be blowsy roses. Her hall was clean and frilly, with a spongy pink carpet and nightdress curtains.

She introduced herself as, 'Liz Lawson, the proprietress of this humble establishment', and asked him how long he would be staying. Her accent was broad Scots; any broader and it might have been hard to understand. But Kim had conquered some of the more impenetrable Belfast dialects, so Mrs Lawson's was relatively easy. 'I think you'll like your room,' she told him before he could answer, 'I'll give you number nine, which is my favourite. It has a nice view of the gardens at the back.' She invited him to sit with her at a small table at the bottom of the stairs to fill in a registration form.

'We serve breakfast between seven and nine, cooked or continental, and we have a bar and telly room in there which we find a lot of our residents enjoy.' She pointed out the door on the right, then turned back to Kim.

Kim was listening but staring at the registration form which asked for his name and address. He was confronted with direct thoughts of home, his present circumstances, and what he was doing. What was he doing? he asked himself, panicking suddenly. What would he tell Sylvie when he rang from upstairs? What should he write in the space provided?

'You look as though you could do with a nice long bath, love,' Mrs Lawson was saying. 'There's plenty of really hot water. Listen, I'll take you up now, you can fill this in later.' She took the form from underneath Kim's poised pen.

He followed her upstairs, clutching at the orangey-pine bannisters, but feeling a huge sense of relief. He could postpone any questions until later. She opened his door. Sure enough there was a kettle, just as the woman at the bus station had promised. But there wasn't a phone.

'No phones in the rooms?' he asked Mrs Lawson politely.

'This is a B & B,' came the reply, rather offended. 'We've a payphone downstairs.'

'Oh,' he muttered, 'I'd been hoping to make a call from my room.'

'I'm sorry.'

'No, please, not your fault,' he said quickly. 'Silly of me. I'd left it a bit late anyway. It's a good excuse to put it off a while longer.'

'Well, you're welcome to use the downstairs one any time. It's there for the guests.'

'Lovely,' he told her. 'Thank you.' Mrs Lawson went to the door, on her way out. 'Perhaps I'll leave it till the morning,' he added. The guilt was still throbbing away inside, but right now all he wanted was to have a bath so hot it would lobster his body and melt his mind.

# 5

It is the police on the line.

Has my husband still not shown up? Might they come round some time within the next two hours?

I'm not doing anything.

When I put the phone down, I suppose I ought to get out of bed and get dressed, although the incentive is not immediately obvious to me. I don't care if policemen see me in my dressing gown, they've seen worse. Until Kim comes home, if he ever does, I am ill, and wish to stay right where I am. Maybe I'm hoping the sheets and blankets can mummify me, even to a limited extent, from pain.

I am considering not budging when there's a knock on the door. 'Mum?' Jack, sounding a little more anxious than he was at dawn. 'You awake? I brought you some tea.'

'Come in.'

'You look shit,' he tells me gently, sitting on the end of the bed and handing me the mug. He is clean-shaven and dressed. 'And you feel worse, right?'

I nod, with my finger to my mouth. I bite it as a stopper against the crying. 'The police are coming soon,' I murmur. 'Doesn't feel like soon enough.'

'I'll stay with you.'

'What about work?'

'I'll get Andy to do my shift. I did one of his at the weekend. Did you call the office?'

'Uh uh.'

'They'll be wondering where you are. Mum, you must.'

I tell him I can't face talking to anyone, and he rings them for me. He then telephones his colleague, and Dora. For all his strength and sweetness, Jack is agitated. He doesn't say so, he just mentions he thinks I ought to get up and dressed. A childlike worry is revealing itself. That his mother might not be all courage and control, because it is in the nature of mothers to be so. When

78

she is upset or weak or afraid, the natural order of things is displaced and all those around her are unsettled. I can see on Jack's face an almost pleading expression to persuade me out of bed, as if if I stay here everything in our world will destruct. I fear it already has.

'Come on. What would you like to wear? Here's your green skirt.' He goes over to the chair by the window. 'Or would you prefer your jeans? They look nice on you.'

'Today I don't care about looking nice.'

'No.' His voice is quiet, apologetic. 'Well, anyway, how about this jumper with them. Least they'll be warm, eh?'

I cannot refuse my Jack. Slowly, I set aside the bedclothes and tentatively put my feet to the floor. He lays my jeans and jersey on the bed, holds my hand while I stand up, and without another word leaves the room. A while later, dressed, I join him in the kitchen. He is eating a second, mid-morning breakfast. Normally I worry he will overdose on Frosties. We don't talk much. We both recognise that the room for conjecture is bottomless, we could speculate and speculate, but that it would all be pointless. For as long as we don't know the truth, to voice what it might be is a waste of breath. Could be one of a million truths. So, sensibly, we sit in virtual silence. Perhaps less sensibly, we sit and hope. Although I know Kim's not coming home I'm allowed a smidgen of hope. It's overrated: helps about as much as a luke-warm hot water bottle over a stomach cramp. But it's better than nothing.

Two policemen arrive around lunchtime. I take them into our sitting room. They are big. One of them, with a grey-singed beard, I didn't catch his name, has to bend his head to go through the door. I wonder if he is the one I spoke to last night, but his voice is not the same. He and his younger colleague, PC Simmons, have no-messing black boots. Their footprints in the carpet appear to snuff out the life of the resilient pile. Their radios spasmodically splutter with crackles and screeches, like recorded torture, which they ignore. They talk on in the way mothers can often conduct grown-up conversations beside their screaming children. It's hard for others to bear. I am too polite and distressed to ask them to reduce the volume.

The older man starts by telling me that, unfortunately, before anything else, he is obliged to search the premises.

'What for?' Jack asks, almost as if he feels guilty. He is clearly taken by surprise and affronted, as am I.

'I am sorry, sir, but it's normal procedure.' He speaks with careful deliberation. 'We have to look into, and discount, every possibility.'

The word possibility suddenly takes on a resonance beyond its normal, modest boundaries. I bite my lip to deflect my mind from the policeman's positive vista of possibility. As I do so, I am aware of the inside walls of my nostrils beginning to sting, as the sure advent of more tears. I slump into the armchair by the unlit fire. It is Jack who takes them on their grisly tour. I can hear the taps of their boots on the kitchen lino, the swish of the patio door, voices in the garden. They come back inside, tread heavily on the stairs, and make their way slowly round the three bedrooms and the bathroom above my head. I imagine them looking in the cupboards expecting, literally, to happen upon a skeleton, almost disappointed to find only a forlorn skirt or two, a greying blouse, three pairs of put-upon shoes. They troop back down again, peer behind the *Wonderland* door under the stairs behind which we keep brooms, mops, dusters, cleaning fluids, nails, plugs, old newspapers, other such unsinister basics.

The two men join me again. I indicate that they should sit down. The bearded policeman settles on the sofa with the quiet tact of the undertaker. His face is familiar. I suppose I must have come across him when I was working in Child Protection, before I went into Court Welfare, but I don't bother to mention it. The other man hovers by the window. He is awkward, smiling politely. Someone might be shining a torch behind his downy ears; you can see the blood in them. His semolina complexion and crew cut make him look all of fifteen. Jack appears with cups of tea and a plate of milk chocolate digestives. He turns on the gas of the pretend-coal fire.

The older man's knees are wide enough for him comfortably to balance his mug on one of them. He takes a biscuit and rests it on the other. It is he who asks the questions, all the same ones I was asked last night on the phone, and more besides. He lays his note-book on the sofa arm to take notes, leans towards it with great

80

care so as not to upset his knees.

'You say he didn't take a vehicle with him? That's a pity in a way because that's something we could've put on the national computer immediately, a vehicle's something easier to trace, you see. But it might suggest that, if he's on his own, he's not gone very far afield, which is good.' He pauses to ponder his next question, takes a sip of his tea.

'Now you'll excuse me if this sounds rather obvious – it's amazing what people don't think of, understandably so when they're worried – but have you rung the surgery this morning to see if he's turned up there? Or spoken to any family members or friends who might have seen him?'

'My mum's not really wanted to talk to anybody,' Jack tells him.

'Fair enough, madam.'

'No point. I mean, if my husband was all right he'd've rung me.'

'But I gave one of his partners a bell early this morning,' Jack reveals. 'No sign. He said he'd ring the minute he heard anything. I also phoned a couple of his friends. Nothing.'

I didn't realise Jack had done this. I am indignant and appreciative at the same time. I'm still sitting on the armchair, staring into the fire so hard it's drying out my eyeballs. My son is standing above me. Without looking away from the flames, I take his hand.

'Madam,' the policeman asks, 'if you'll excuse me, would you say your husband was a steady person?'

I don't answer immediately because I have first to register what he's asking. When applied to Kim, it is such a wholly inappropriate question that in any other circumstances I would laugh at it. 'I should say so, very,' I tell him after a few moments.

'No debts that you knew of at all which might have been unduly concerning him?'

'We've always fretted about money, we have our worries, but nothing out of the ordinary, no.'

'They were very open about everything, weren't you, Mum? I mean, they never didn't talk about their finances to each other, even in front of us, my sister and me; they never hid anything.'

'That's good. And can we safely say there was no depression that you were aware of?'

81

I shake my head, and he jots down a note. These questions coming at me seem so wide of the mark. Yet the very fact that I can answer them so emphatically spawns numerous doubts which dart through me like a school of minnows. Pushed much further I fear my whole system of beliefs will be at risk of disintegrating. My insides are curdling. I begin to tremble.

'No chance that he might have just been out on the lash with a few friends?'

Again, I shake my head.

'Truly, Mrs Black, is there anywhere you think he could have gone? I mean, in your heart of hearts? No one he could have been staying over with? No possibility he could have been out visiting?'

'No,' Jack said, defensively.

You always have a picture of the other woman, don't you? It's hazy admittedly, like that of a character in a novel, necessarily sketchily drawn. You have the basics, size, colouring, but there's a good deal of ghostly indistinction surrounding the detail, the exact set of the eyes, the precise lines of the nose and mouth, the true contours of the breast and hips. My picture of Kim's other woman is an impossible but all too real amalgam. She is partly what I know to be his type, a type inspired by his mother, and one not so far removed from me. So presumably she has dark hair, dullish blue eyes, curves, pale skin, and with any luck something of a sense of humour. But she is partly, also, what I admire in a woman, that preposterous ideal which I have come to believe, after years of officious brain-washing, is the only sort of woman any man can ever desire. She is of course as far along the evolutionary scale from me as it is conceivable for two women to be, given that they both have heads and limbs and wombs and bellies and breasts. So it is that my Kim's other woman has sun-bleached blonde hair, a Caramac complexion, legs up to her nostrils, costume-jewellery eyes, breasts as toned as rubber, the sex appeal of Brigitte Bardot, the wit of Dorothy Parker, the cool of Françoise Sagan, the intellect of Simone de Beauvoir. I could go on. Would she be the sort to give Kim a second glance? That's not the point. The point is, she exists in the imagination, an ever present threat. The fact that she is an over the top figment of it, and I know that damn well, does not detract from her poisoning power.

Sometimes I see her. She is the girl in some student café on Oxford High Street, wearing construction site boots, leaving half her sandwich, smoking cigarettes, ever pushing her laughable hair from her lilac, night-before eyes. She is my forty-year-old sexual peak client from north Oxford who's denying her ex-husband contact with his children while having contact herself with most of the middle-aged married men south of Kidlington. She is the bubbly young midwife attached to Kim's surgery, who laughs whenever he opens his mouth, and who all the fathers think is quite the most reassuring soul to be near when their partners are in the throes of labour. She is the thirtysomething patient who calls him Doctor just a little too reverently. She is the actress who appears wildly but memorably in that flabbergasting film we saw the other night about love and despair and madness.

She is all these creatures. And yet she is none of them because, as I rightly know, she doesn't exist. The irony is that the true stuff of nightmares isn't this splashy type of woman at all but is, more likely, the woman I never see. She is the woman with hips even slightly wider than mine, bottom definitely bigger, mousier hair, droopier tits; she is the woman who goes for no-comment clothes in low-key colours, and is so terribly shy she has to be cajoled into speaking at all. She is the girl others bullied at school because she was so out-of-the ordinary ordinary, so middle of the road, all she did was show up their bleak extremities. If she were a food, she wouldn't be one to be eaten of its own accord, but would be instead a mild, almost invisible ingredient that exists purely to fit in with others, a ricotta, say, or cornflour. If she were a house, she'd be one of an infinite row beside a motorway, which millions pass each day into and out of town, but to which they never extend a second thought let alone a thought to stop by. She is the ultimate forget-me girl, and I overlook her as a risky prospect, because perhaps I don't notice that she utters a sincere hello, or has a mysteriously sweet way of saying goodbye. I'm unobservant, and fatally patronise or dismiss the beguiling form of her simple smile, the unassuming beauty of her outwardly unstartling eyes. Yet she's the very one he cannot forget.

Before I met Kim, I had friends and lovers who were very sculptures in untrustworthiness. When I met Kim, it took a little while to get to know him, but soon I felt confident enough to throw caution to the wind. If ever there was another person on this earth, other than myself, that I could trust, then surely it was he. All our time together, I could allow myself to indulge my fears with negative infidelity fantasies, but I never, in my heart of hearts, as the policeman would have it, thought that Kim was having an affair with any woman, any Amalgam, or any Forget-me. I don't think I do now, even though as the bearded man asks his fecund question, a surreal woman begins provocatively to dance before my eyes. I cannot tell if she's tall or petite, if she's rounded or gamine, if she's blonde or dark. All I know is this minute she's haunting me. For trying to catch a closer look at her elusive form, I cannot answer what's asked of me although the policeman is waiting for a response from my lips even now.

'No,' Jack says again.

'Very good. Fair enough.' The man takes a bite of his biscuit and writes something more in his notebook.

I can guess roughly to what effect, to what sceptical effect. I sniff, and look a bit tearful I imagine. Kim's other woman won't go away, seems to want this moment particularly to mock me. It is with a struggle that I pummel her down and push her out of my head. With or without her, naturally the terror of loss remains. I can feel the younger policeman's eyes upon me, as if he is transfixed in the presence of such bloodless pain. His diplomatic colleague switches to a less delicate line of questioning.

'Do you know the name of the shop where he was going to buy the ice-cream?' Out of politeness he is looking at me, though I know by now he's probably expecting all the answers to come from Jack. 'Was it Barnett's down the road? Helpful man in there, we can start by asking him if he saw Dr Black at all.'

I'm not really listening. Not so long ago, I read about a Jewish woman from Byelorussia who spoke fluent German. She was captured in occupied France in the War with forged papers that were so good they passed for real. Nevertheless, the Gestapo officer who personally supervised her torture still suspected his prisoner could understand his language. She was interrogated for many hours but she refused to let on. Eventually the man barked an order, in German, for her to be shot. Even then she did not flinch. Thwarted in his attempt to break her, he let her live.

When she returned to her cell, unrecognisable due to the abundance of her wounds and the extent of the damage to her head and body, her fellow prisoners said they had not heard her screams. She said that that was because she had not screamed. So practised was she at suffering, that she had devised a method mentally to distance herself from pain.

Often I have thought of that story, and how that miraculous woman must have had a unique gift to have been able to blank out to that degree. Certainly, for the majority of us who only ever encounter pain at its most prosaic, we cannot even manage the breeziest reduction of it without recourse to outside aid, in the form of a fleet of drugs and counsellors. These modern cushions were not ever so. It is hard not to think of that woman who, through sheer will, found the means to do it all alone.

'Obviously, we'll start by going to see the gentleman in Barnett's, Mrs Black, and his colleague at the surgery of course, a Dr Samuel Cohen, isn't it? Talking, also, to family and friends. We'll be wanting to investigate every avenue.'

I notice some biscuit crumbs have landed in his beard. As he witters on kindly and I am quietly weeping, I become fascinated to see if they are going to fall onto his knees. The words 'thorough search of the area' seep through to me. So many times when watching the news with Kim, there has been footage of police all in a line, crawling through brushy grass, searching, searching. This year alone there was that little boy on a beach in Cornwall; the teenage girl on a camping site in Derbyshire; the woman out walking her dog in a village in Kent; the prostitute from the streets of Sheffield. All there one minute, gone the next. Endless missing. Mainly younger people, but not always, not by any means.

You read those articles, you do, about people – let's face it, men – who say they're just popping out to buy a packet of fags and who never come back. It's become a bit of a standing joke, hasn't it? 'Don't you push it too far, Jane,' people say or, 'Don't you deny him sex too long, Kate,' – 'Cos one day he'll just pop out for a packet of fags and never come back!' Ha, ha, ha.

I've heard the banter amongst my colleagues at work. I've joined in. As recently as a few months ago, I remember Peggy coming in one morning, just before a case conference meeting it was, and setting us all off.

'You'll never guess what Martin said to me last night?' she said. 'The two of us were having a laugh. "One day I'm just going to pop out to buy myself a packet of fags and never come back." I said right back to him, "I should be so lucky!"'

Roars of laughter in the corridor.

' "Then you'll really miss me!" he said.'

Shrieks of, ' "Then you'll really miss me!" '

'So I said to him, "Not bloody likely!" I said it straight out!'

It doesn't translate, but we were all doubled up. We must have been in a particularly good mood that morning. Even Gerald, who has a tenuous sense of humour at the best of times, thought it was funny. Joy was cackling like a witch: 'That's brilliant, that is, "I should be so lucky." '

'You be careful, though, Peg,' one of us said, still laughing, could've been me, 'he might just say it one day and the wind is changing.'

Ice-cream not fags, that's the only difference; and the fact that Peggy's husband Martin was only joking.

I am aware of the policeman rising to his feet and placing his empty mug on the low table in front of him.

'Of course, madam,' he is saying, 'we will do everything in our power to find your husband, you can count on us for that, and we will keep well in touch. If in the highly unlikely event that he has disappeared—'

'Could he have been attacked or abducted; killed?' I ask, mainly because I want official reassurance.

'As I say madam, it's highly unlikely. But if he doesn't show in the next few hours, there is a special helpline which I know a lot of people have found very comforting in cases such as these. Perhaps it's too soon for that yet, but it's worth thinking about.'

I just about manage to thank him. Jack follows him and PC Simmons to the front door.

'Ah, before we go,' I can hear the older policeman saying in the hall, 'we mustn't forget to take a photo with us of your dad. Would either you or Mum have one available? We'd take care to give it back, it's just it'd be very helpful with our inquiries.'

Jack tells him to hang on a minute and comes back into the

sitting room. I haven't moved. My fingers are splayed and stiff, propping up my forehead. I nod towards the cupboard under the bookshelves where there's a cardboard box of snaps I've been meaning for years to stick in an album. Jack pulls it out hastily and starts rifling through it. I can't look.

It was taking a leap, from mere private anxiety to something altogether more serious, when I plucked up the courage to ring the police in the first place. Since then it's all been talk with them, and a few notes jotted down, and that seemed official enough. But now handing over a photograph of Kim is to shift the situation into another league again, to make it publicly urgent.

I've seen those bleary snaps blown up into posters, underneath them 'Missing' writ large in grabby pink letters. Sometimes, in the background, telling hints of a life, just like a stranger's choice of groceries in a supermarket basket. Perhaps a shelving unit can be made out, with a red box-file and a potted plant; or a bar can be seen, with a Mexican hat and pairs of castanets dangling in front of its exotically coloured bottles. The faces themselves are often hard to make out – complexions cake-mixture fluffy and yellowing, with foetus-black eyes, wine-splodge lips. But their holidayish smiles are all gone now. They remain just past, tenuous truths transposed onto fading memories, as bleached out as the images across unreliable photographic paper.

Jack empties the box onto the carpet and pushes the pictures about. 'You don't mind if I give them this one?' he asks me. 'It'll do, won't it?'

I cover my fingers over my eyes and without peeping through them tell him I'm sure, if he thinks so, it will be fine.

'I think it was taken on that holiday in Devon, what, four years ago? It's clear enough,' he's saying, 'and a good likeness. Not looking so young that nobody would recognise him.'

I can hear him getting up and taking it out to the policemen, followed by their quick goodbyes and the click of the lock. Jack comes back to me and sits on the other armchair. As I take my hands from my face and turn towards him, I can see out of the corner of my eye the haphazard pile of photographs he has left spread across the carpet. I am scared to look at it. Some of the pictures go way back to when Kim and I first met. There's a whole mishmash in there, more than twenty-five years together. What I consider to be the whole of my better life, effectively. I look upon my life as the contents of two entirely separate crates: before meeting Kim, and after. The years in the first crate didn't add up to much. They were not immeasurably bad, but nor were they good. Whenever I've thought about them, since that turning-point day of 13 May 1972, it's always, always, been favourably to compare the present with the past. Perhaps until now.

By the age of eighteen I'd had enough of my mum's gadding about and, in 1971, had left home in Oxford to do my degree in Social Sciences at Queens in Belfast. I needed to be far away, in a place she was unlikely to visit. It turned out to be a good choice. Like most English people, my mother knew nothing about Northern Ireland and the Troubles, just enough to know, unarguably as far as she was concerned, that it was a little Vietnam raging in one of England's outlying and untended allotments. When I told her I was going there, not that I knew she cared, she cried, 'You'll be killed in a bomb!' When she failed to change my mind, she told me that she would never visit me. I said that that would suit me just fine.

How can I have loved Belfast so? – but love it I did. After the refined character of Oxford, even though my life was far removed from its cliché of dreaming spires, Belfast was remarkable to me, being as it was virtually devoid of anything resembling a middle class. There were no restaurants to speak of, except the odd Belfast Bap emporium which sold nothing but a dusty can of Fanta and their inimitable speciality: fried potato in a squidgy sandwich of fat bun. The one in Dublin Road was bombed, on average, about once every three months. There was a sort of collective cold turkey amongst the citizens of Belfast till each refurbishment was complete. Over the years the Government must have had to sink more money into that little takeaway than into the replacement for the *Belgrano*.

Shops consisted of several branches of Sean Grahame's bookmaker's, and stores that were darkened within by the rolls of patterned carpets leaning against their outside windows. Grocers knew of oranges and bread, but few luxuries besides. Adverts on telly were straight-up, no messing – a stills picture in three colours of a pack of sausages, with the words, 'Buy McCormack's sizzlers 'cos they are good'. I remember the catchily optimistic jingle for a brand of biscuits: 'Kimberley Maccano's, the coconut cream, for someone you love, you love some*one*.' That was Belfast for you, through and through.

Belfast. It was the rawest city I ever knew – weather, architecture, bent of activity. In the residential areas, the gloomy terraced houses, permanently dampened by rain, were dried-blood red. The centre was dominated by a majestic City Hall, and an illiberal rubble. Boys born and living two miles up the Antrim Road might not so much as glimpse the heart of their home town until, as defiant teenagers, they took the first 45 bus in. Learner drivers, who all their lives had not travelled outside the city's perimeters, had heart attacks if they happened to stray into a part of it which had pavements painted and decorated in stripes that were not their colours. Yet for a people so fizzing with bigoted hatred, the majority of 'ordinary' citizens were imbued with a warmth and spirit of hospitality that was singular to a degree that I, as an outsider, had never witnessed before. The outsider in Belfast is always struck by its friendliness; they always remark upon it, so much so it's become a sort of cliché. I was no exception. I loved the city – and I love it still – for that, and because it remains forever the place I met my Kim.

I lived in a tiny house in Rathcoole Street off the Lisburn Road. There was textured wallpaper throughout and, in the sitting room, a low-slung fifties-type fireplace made with creamy tiles high on the effect of mother-of-pearl. I shared with two friends on the course. We were out to get our degrees but also to have a good time. I'd learned what I thought was the way to go about having a good time from my mother, even though she had never seemed particularly happy in her gadding. Like her, I had various assignations with men, numerous, some might say. I met them on the course, or in the pub. Some were Northern Irish (they seemed, temporarily anyway, to appreciate the easy-going ways of English girls), some not; some were friends, some not. I managed to be indifferent to most of them after we had become lovers, as most of them regressed to indifference towards me. Today I can't even remember some of their faces or names. I think they were all strange men.

But I can remember so many couches – a semicircular-shaped one upholstered in red velour, tea-stains, and cigarette burns; a hard monstrosity in bobbly herringbone tweed, not unlike the one in the Family Room at work; a fifties-style three-seater covered in itchy orange hessian and boasting a taut mini-skirt round its base which revealed squat black legs with brass-button feet; a squashy cushioned two-some of a worn olive chintz blooming with faded yellow roses and elaborate antimacassars; a leather number, colour of condensed milk, with seams puckered like flesh folds and stretch-marks on aged inner thighs.

Only a few of the men I encountered on them spring to mind. The widowed man in a tower block flat whose wife had found its aspect an all-too easy jump onto the M1 to Dublin; the young fellow with a mass of hair round his head like an unchecked box hedge, but with a chest as smooth as a compact disc; the bloke, Catholic I seem to suppose, who had yet fully to explore his sexuality and insisted on my wearing a pyjama top else he couldn't do the business; the clever-clogs who turned the death of his father to his advantage, using it as his special and sensitive way of scoring a sympathy fuck or two.

English, Irish, Catholic, Protestant, they had so much in common, there was no sectarianism about their methods of blossoming one into bed. They all said similarly flattering things, which didn't wash necessarily, but which on balance still seemed to do the trick. Not that I was taken in by most of them. Sometimes I said yes out of politeness – extrication seemed too wearisome by half – or because I had just finished a cup of tea and had nothing better to do until supper. Occasionally I said no because at that moment I fancied instead a piece of carrot cake or a bout of watching *Candid Camera* on the telly; or no just to see the particular brand of thwarted expression on that particular face. I recall one settee – Indian cotton throw a poor guard against torn brocade seats with cartoon-broken springs – man on it, now nameless and faceless, reciting by rote his repertoire of lines that on past occasions – same settee, different sucker for it – had proved so winning. He held me to him as he spoke. I had an apple in my hand and was saying to myself with each twist of its stalk not, 'He loves me, he loves me not,' but, 'I'll do it, I'll do it not'. Can men know, for all the spuriousness of their bedding words, on what capricious grounds sometimes lies the success or failure of their stabs at seduction? Petals off a daisy.

It was on 13 May 1972 that I met Kim, in an area of the city called Stranmillis. Predictably enough, at a party. It was the usual sort of party for those days – about two hundred people in a house both the size and temperature of a boiler room, shouting at each other's nostrils, gyrating on a cheap lagered floor, throwing up behind the radiators.

Kim's and my introduction was not the formal sort. Rather, we were forced together by the push of the crowd, found ourselves face to face squashing up full-on against one another, slightly but rhythmically swaying with the throng, but unable to move apart. Wrong person, and I would have felt distinctly uncomfortable, if not actively turned off by the situation; I would have clamoured to move away. Right person. They were perhaps the most erotic moments of my life.

Can you credit it? Not one of the more clichéd accoutrements of eroticism was present, just a room choking with lowest-common-denominator booze, eye-watering smoke, migraine music, worker-bee bodies. It was all due to him.

I have pinned those moments down like butterflies in a boffin's collection. They are more delicately suspended and balanced, more perfectly preserved than any mere pressed flower, which in comparison would appear faded and crushed. I can see a young man's clean-shaven complexion; the kindly eyes, still only decorated with smile lines, yet to contract life's wrinkles; the almost effeminate curl of his lips; the slump of fringe over the side of his forehead. I can feel, in detail, through his jeans and T-shirt, the set of his body. I can conjure up the smell on his breath and his neck, of alcohol, of cigarettes, and him. When did a stranger's personalised whiff of drink and smoke ever seem so alluring?

He was smiling and smiling at me. Soon we were being manoeuvred by the ebb of the crowd towards a narrowly unpopulated bit of wall. Nothing for it but to start to talk. Less well preserved in my mind than the sight and the smell and the feel of him then is what we talked about, other than, presumably, telling each other our names. Whatever it was, it wasn't for long because just as the mass of party-goers had thrust us together, in classic tradition, so they wrenched us apart. Although Kim and I were

91

happily dry-mounted to each other, someone contrived to shove his or her way between us with head-down determination towards the window. He or she was in turn followed by more, and so started a slipstream. Kim and I were parted. I was unceremoniously bustled into the corridor, suddenly edgy about being forcibly clammed to alien bums and shoulder blades and tits, and about losing track of Kim. It made me breathless and panicky. But before I knew it, I was lost in the current and out of the front door. Among other shadowed and languorous figures slumped on the path and commemorative stamp of lawn, I found my flat-mates, Siobhan and Jodie. They said they weren't prepared to brave the crush again and had had enough, were going home. They told me I was white as a sheet. I said I wasn't ready to leave yet but they urged me to go with them. 'You'll suffocate if you go back in,' they warned, and all I thought of was how worried I was for Kim.

Turned out, usefully enough, that he was a friend of Jodie's, and by hook and by wily female crook, I managed to see him again. She took me to Smokey Joe's, a coffee house in University Road, where she knew he used to hang out. We went along a couple of times before we spotted him. We left it to Kim to approach and join us. Jodie generously didn't forget to tell him what a nice surprise it was to bump into him there.

So it was not at the party but at a boisterous and steamy greasy spoon, over eggs and chips and beans and lovely milky tea, that I learnt that Kim came from a farming family in Herefordshire; that he was in Belfast to study medicine with a view to becoming a junior doctor in one of the city's hospitals; and that he was nothing like the normal run of men I used to get to know.

One of the first things that struck me about him was that he was completely unfashionable. In mid-seventies Belfast the man who went abroad without a luxuriant pair of sideburns was something of a peculiarity. (The clean-shaven British soldiers were the only exceptions, but they didn't count.) So was the man who didn't don the ubiquitous short flared trousers which enjoyed flapping about the ankles like a bird's enfeebled wings. Kim stood out because he favoured a face innocent of hair and the kind of drainpipes he had probably always worn, practical and farming-friendly. These were signs of what might have been a steadfast refusal to bow to the flock, or alternatively might have been a total lack of awareness surrounding the pressures to conform. Either way, I was impressed.

Another notable thing about Kim was the quiet way he spoke. The Belfast accent, while I had grown accustomed to it, can be a fearsome, if perversely beautiful, thing. If in the south of Ireland people appear to have feathers for tongues, some of their counterparts in the north have, more, the guttural throats of the parrot or cockatoo. Speaking as they mostly do there, fast and furiously, they can sometimes appear to be engaging in a series of elongated squawks. Although Kim, too, had a pronounced regional accent, it was an altogether less urgent type. With the lilting quality of its intonation, it verged on the Welsh, but at the same time remained recognisably English. It came as a surprise later to gather that this soft, unassuming voice of his could express so fervently his passion and quasi-obsession, which was, of course, for medicine.

Over that very first session in a steaming Smokey Joe's, with the smell all about us of heart-attack breakfasts, and cutlery and china that had almost burnt in the dishwasher, we asked of each other the question all English people in the city used to be asked, and which certainly broke the ice – why had we come to Belfast?

It was, of course, a time when outsiders had to have good reason to be there. I'm not saying they had to be desperate, but clearly the seventies wasn't the era trivially to choose the city as one's assumed home.

Kim, like me, had wanted to be in a place as far as possible from home. Belfast was excellent for studying medicine but, for obvious reasons, less over-subscribed than Edinburgh, say, or London. I will never forget how he admitted that day he was likely to gain wider medical experience in the casualty departments of Belfast's hospitals than anywhere else in the country. When he spoke of wanting to treat victims of bombs and shootings and so-called punishment beatings, he had none of the bravado about him of the usual war groupies, like a few correspondents and aid workers who are ill-disposed to enjoy their jobs for entirely altruistic reasons. I can remember how almost apologetically Kim appeared to pour, from a gammy-spouted bottle, the ketchup on his eggs. 'I know that sounds cynical,' he said. But I could tell, over our chips and beans, that coming from him, it wasn't. Since then, I've had over twenty years for it to be confirmed in my mind that Kim is a dedicated doctor, and not in the least a cynical man.

After that opening breakfast, we had several meetings, he and I, in Smokey Joe's, occasionally with other friends, more often on our own. Proximity to him played havoc with my appetite. Often I couldn't manage so much as a mouthful of fried egg and was only able to stomach perhaps one chip or two. I used to smoke cigarettes and order things to drink instead. As well as cups of tea, I used to have milk or concentrate orange juice from catering glasses that were short and scratched. Sometimes, as I held them to my mouth, my hand would shake, responding wantonly to the sheer flurry of lust and nerves inside me. But the hard chairs, though I sat on them for many a long hour, seemed more comfortable than any one of those varied Belfast couches which I had previously come to know.

From our talks it was clear that Kim had never wanted to become a farmer. He and his brothers had been made to work on the farm before and after school and throughout the holidays. David Black had always just assumed that his three sons would continue the family tradition. But from a young age Kim had felt resentful of this paternal expectation and had determined never to fulfil it. He did not know which came first, the resentment or the desire to become a doctor. There have been times over the years, especially when he's been exhausted and so sceptical of his enjoyment of his job, when he's worried that it wasn't so much a love of medicine which prompted him to choose his profession, as a loathing for farming – anything not to go into farming. I was always able categorically to reassure him that this was not the case. Kim is a born doctor.

For a start, he is a good listener. From those early days it was apparent that he had a natural inquisitiveness about others (which I think goes a good long way to explaining his passion for the news). In Smokey Joe's he used to ask me questions. Well, that was something of a departure for me. The men who had made passes at me on couches either hadn't talked much, using grunts for cool, or had given me the benefit of full-blown exclusives about themselves. Few of them seemed to realise that a little jot of curiosity can be so very winning. Had the man, for instance, who went on and on about the death of his father, perhaps asked me a question or two about my own, he would have discovered how much more sympathy I might have felt for him, and how much sooner he might have achieved his goal.

With Kim at last I found there was an equality of curiosity. For our first few meetings we exchanged anecdotes and talked about our families, our pasts. He wanted to hear all about mine. I think I first had the notion he might be close to falling in love with me when he allowed me to describe the treacle pudding my grandmother used to make. What other man, you might think, but a sop would have put up with that? But Kim was no sop. He seemed simply to relish such details as others would have scorned. If I mentioned a favourite pink and white dress I had worn on my fifth birthday, he'd ask, what sort of pink? If I referred in passing to some prank at school, to an argument with my sister, he'd ask what kind of prank, what caused the argument? That's why he's such a good doctor. He likes to get to the bottom of things, not because he's plain pedantic or nosy; it's as if he wants to leave no stone of human nature unturned and that the answers genuinely enthral him. Of course, his patients love it. They can spot a true listener when they see one.

But it wasn't a one-sided thing. He was equally as happy to answer questions, to the extent that I presumed to ask those I mightn't have dared ask of somebody else for fear of earning their contempt – the lay-out of his house, the names of the stories read to him by his mother, the petty cruelties of day-to-day life on the farm, his brothers' taunts, his first introduction to a dead body. So it was I soon began to form a vivid picture of his background and upbringing. This is something you rarely gather, even from close friends. So much of their childhoods, especially if you meet them later in life, remain a mystery. We may know some of the broad strokes – number of siblings, where they lived, whether or not their parents divorced – but there is so much they never proffer and we never learn. We are very casual with our pasts. How little of them we bother either to reveal or ask after. Perhaps all pasts are necessarily dreary, unless proved to be populated with those things which excite professionals and supposedly make them more interesting than the norm – adventures abroad, sexual abuse, precocious talent. These are the only kind of pasts which give rise to a more widespread stir. These are the pasts which are examined by shrinks, are wrought into biographies, or made into movies. The so-called ordinary past is for private reflection only. If it ever does inspire the attention of another, it is usually that of the individual in love with its subject, but even then it is not guaranteed an airing. If you were never abused, or an inquisitive type never fell in love with you, you could go through a whole life and no one might ever ask even simple things, like where exactly you were born, what was the wallpaper pattern on your childhood bedroom wall, did you prefer pear-drops or sherbet lemons? But it is surely these seeming trifles, every bit as much as the broad strokes, which reveal so much about the true nature of a particular character.

In meeting Kim and, to an extent, having children, I have had the privilege of a tiny handful of folk expressing a wish to hear a detail or two of my un-newsworthy past, of wanting to know the detailed me. If it has not gone so far as to put my life on the map, it has at least enabled it to become, if fleetingly, a mildly diverting tale for the amusement of a few. I hope I can say that, through loving Kim, asking him about his past and showing in it a genuine interest, I have contributed to lending his life, too, a modest sense of purpose.

Kim and I, we soon graduated from revelatory lunchtime breakfasts at Smokey Joe's to revelatory drinks in either the Club Bar opposite, or one of two pubs popular with students, the Botanic or the Eglantine (known respectively and not very winningly, as the Bot and the Egg). It was there we carried on our discussions, in the self-conscious but nonetheless alluring privacy of the bars' darker corners. I seem to remember we spoke earnestly, in the way students are wont to do, about politics and the meaning of life, but we found that pints of beer also encour-aged us to set free further finer details about ourselves. After one such session, buoyed up by all our important talk, we decided to walk home. Passing the heavy, almost haunting hulk of Queens on our way towards the Lisburn Road, Kim told me, for the first time, that he loved me. It was 16 June 1972. A Friday.

He said he didn't want to take me back to his digs or mine. Too many people about. So he took me to a big, derelict house in Adelaide Park, laid out his jacket under a big, derelict tree in the garden. The grass was dank and the ground unforgiving. Pieces of twig nipped at us through the thin material of our summer clothes, and then bit into our naked skin. I'm sure we got birdshit in our hair. We could certainly hear the hideous howl of a neighbourhood cat. Perhaps, with the seedy yawn of a far-off bomb, we could even smell hatred on the heat of another troubled night. Yet the wanting spot we had chosen was better than any couch I'd ever known, in the whole of Belfast, and elsewhere.

'Don't worry, Mum, I'm putting them back in the box. You don't have to look at them.'

I don't want to look at them, but there's part of me that can't resist glancing at Jack's quick hands as he gathers up the uncertain piles of photographs and dumps them back where they belong. Some spill onto the floor again. Each random snap that I glimpse serves as a tiny tile in the incomplete mosaic of the family's shared past. I see Jack in smart uniform on his first day at school, boyish thin legs poking out of his shorts with knees knobbly as a horse's; magnificent grin. I see Mackenzie circa 1985 in a pink towelling top with a hood, sitting on the bonnet of a new second-hand car. I see a picnic devoid of faces – just the lay-out of tartan rug, hard-boiled eggs in grey-knickers colour Tupperware, anonymous sandy ankles. I see studio-lit me in front of a stippled background with a graduation mortar board, pudgy smile, impossible perm.

I see Kim, *so young*, with his bare forearm shielding his eyes from the sun, but you can see he is talking and smiling. He is leaning against a window which I recognise as Smokey Joe's because of the tell-tale facade and the luminous cardboard cut-outs in the shape of stars pronouncing the price of chips and beans and a bacon sandwich. I can date the photograph precisely – 17 June 1972 – and almost to the very moment I took it. We were leaving together, after one of our breakfasts, a memorable breakfast. He has slung over his shoulder the very jacket which he had laid out a few hours before to protect us from the damp grass. I fancy I can detect a tiny twig still in his hair, and I can hear him talking. I know what he was saying.

It's not so hard to remember.

# 6

Kim had slept well but not late. He was used to early mornings. He had got up slowly. He had washed his face but, because there had been no razor, had been unable to shave and so didn't feel entirely spruce. In an ideal world he would have put on a clean set of clothes. The only ones he had, had crumpled and softened to his shape, and were on the cusp of smelling a day or so too personal. Not that he cared all that much. He felt so well, even though he was still half-asleep. He went downstairs wondering if it was the clean Scottish air.

Mrs Lawson greeted him with a fittingly merry good morning and asked him to call her Liz. He thanked her and said, very quietly, 'I'm Kim.' She showed him into the modest dining room at the front of the house which overlooked the road, and made various suggestions for his breakfast. He knew what he wanted. Liz went into the kitchen.

He sat at a small table. His legs were a little long beneath it, he felt a bit squashed as if in an aeroplane and was at some pains to arrange his knees. As he tried to do so the cups shivered and clinked in dispute with their carefully laid saucers. Eventually he sat still, if a bit lopsided. He didn't want to read the newspaper that had been left on the sideboard. Instead he folded his arms and stared out of the window, watching stray figures get into their cars and drive away, dispersing the blackbirds. His thoughts were of nothing much, inconsequential speculations about where that man in the Ford Escort was going, whether this woman loved her husband as much as she evidently relished her Fiat Bravo. After some minutes Liz snapped open the hatch joining the two rooms, then walked round back into the dining room so as to collect the plate she had put on the dividing shelf. She laid it triumphantly on the broderie anglaise tablecloth in front of her new guest. He stared at the sumptuous breakfast, his eyes almost as wide as the yolks on his two fried eggs. There were grilled tomatoes, two sausages, mushrooms, bacon, even a slice or two of deep purple black pudding. When they were first married, Kim mused, Sylvie used to make him a full breakfast about three times a week. No longer. Not that she was unwilling – far from it, she was the ever-spoiling wife – just it was a habit they had snuffed out in the eighties when cholesterol had become fashionable. For the same reason as he had stopped smoking – of all people, he grudgingly supposed, doctors really had no excuse – Kim didn't feel a GP should eat too many fatty foods and fry-ups when he daily told his patients they were doing them harm. Still, some days, he could make an exception.

Liz had also placed a basket beside his cup of coffee and jug of milk. It contained a stack of toast, and a clutch of miniature jams which prompted in him almost as much excitement as a previous selection once had. She asked if everything was to his satisfaction.

'Yes, thank you, very much,' he replied.

'You have a beautiful accent, you know. Where would that be?'

'There's probably a trace of Belfast thrown in there some-where. I spent a lot of time there.'

'Yes, but it's mostly English, isn't it?'

'I'm from Herefordshire, originally.'

'Not anymore?'

'Not anymore.'

'Can I get you anything else?' she asked, eagerly eyeing the table, and straightening the basket of toast. 'Goodness, butter, you have no butter!' Her banana-coloured fringe took fright as she sped away to right her oversight. She returned as quickly as she had disappeared with a saucer of butter fashioned into stiff, neat curls, ribbed like those which have been sculptured across the head of a shop window mannequin.

While others might have been irritated by such a zealous pres-ence, Kim was enjoying her company. Liz had a warmth and sweetness about her which made him feel very much at home. He wondered if she had many guests. He wondered if there was still a Mr Lawson.

'Have you had any breakfast yourself?' he asked her.

'Oh, no, I don't eat breakfast.' She tapped her large stomach by way of a tacit explanation. She was wearing a tight bright yellow skirt and an almost blue-white silky shirt which fell from her bosom in such a way as to conceal the shapeliness of her entire middle body.

'What nonsense! Have a piece of toast. There's too much here for me.' Kim leant over and pulled a chair out for her. Her green eyes landed on the toast, looked to the chair, to Kim, and then back to the toast, as if making some kind of calculation. She sat down saying that she shouldn't really. Kim held out the basket to her. She took a slice and buttered it daintily. Between each bite she dabbed her mouth with a napkin. Her nail polish was the colour of Kim's grilled tomatoes, only slightly richer. The fingers themselves were laden with rings.

'Breakfast's the most important meal of the day,' Kim said cutting up a sausage and dappling it in egg yolk.

'My doctor's told me as much,' Liz nodded. 'He's torn between telling me to breakfast like a king and lose weight.'

Kim smiled. 'Have you had the B&B long?' he asked, changing the subject.

'Only a couple of years. Since my husband left. We were living in Nairn. Tradespark Estate. I'd not done this type of thing before; only catering work in hotels in Aviemore, not running a place. But I had to get off the estate. Family reasons. When Nick was around, it was all right them all about me and not talking to me. Not after he'd gone, though. Then I'd had enough.'

'Why weren't your family talking to you? If you don't mind my asking.'

'Because they were racists, the lot of them. I married an Englishman. From that day to this they've not spoken a word, though my mum and dad lived in the next street to where I did, my sister and brother-in-law only two streets away, and my brother and his wife just a couple of streets on from that. We'd bump into each other on the pavement, or spot each other on the bus, and they'd cut me dead, the lot of them. It's a wonder they found the energy to keep it up for eighteen years, but find it they did.' Her Scottish accent was broadened by indignation.

'Did you try to make them see sense?'

'For a while. Didn't work. No point. A bigot's not one for changing, that's why he's a bigot.'

'I suppose. You weren't very upset by them though?'

'I was in love with my husband and the kids. Everything else

100

was not so important.' So saying, Liz helped herself to another piece of toast. On that one she permitted herself the odd spot of marmalade. 'I tried not to let it bother me. I could ignore them every bit as much as they could ignore me. It's a game everyone can play.'

'Sounds like they got their just desserts. Still, it must've been something for you to be forced to sever links with your entire family.'

'All my nephews and nieces, too. Mine isn't a family to do things by halves. Their loss. Nick was worth more to me than the lot of them put together. As I say, it only really did my head in when he went. They must have been laughing off the sides of their faces. But even then they weren't prepared to let bygones be bygones. I suppose I hadn't the strength to cope with it alone.'

'No.'

'I'm still in love with my husband. Every day I pray and hope he'll see the error of his ways, although I know I'm probably wasting my time. I still can't believe it, him gone. Classic case, it was. Younger woman. Need I say more? But I realise that while I'm waiting for him, I have to stay away from my family. And, of course, waiting, I have to keep myself busy. Helps pass the time.' Her voice was beginning to sound brighter. 'That's why I decided to put my course in catering to good use.'

'You've done that all right,' Kim complimented her, setting his knife and fork down on a completely clean plate.

'It nearly killed me setting this place up, getting the money together.' Liz dabbed her lipstick with her napkin. 'It was a big risk, but I'm the type who likes to live life close to the edge, else what's the point? You get to a ripe old age and you're just covered in a mildew of regretting.'

Kim pondered her words but said nothing.

She changed the subject. 'You don't get a full breakfast at home then? I find a lot of the businessmen who come here lap up the opportunity of a nice big fry because they've only usually time to grab a coffee, and a piece of toast if they're lucky. I like to treat them to the works. A lot say it's a heart attack on the plate, but they'll happily opt for the heart attack!' She laughed, and Kim did so with her. 'Will you be staying in Inverness long?'

'I don't know.'

'What brought you here?'

'I'm not really sure.' Kim paused.

'You hadn't planned it then?'

'Can't say I had.'

'Long way to come when you hadn't planned it.'

'I suppose. Opportunity arose. One thing led to another. You know how it is.'

'I see.' Liz, thinking opportunity might be a euphemism for something more animate, probed no further. 'Well, it's a lovely place for a wee holiday anyway. Beautiful.' She touched her hair in a wistful gesture as if she, too, would have liked to have been beautiful.

'It looks nice,' Kim told her. He could have been referring to the Highlands, or to her hairstyle, perhaps both. 'I don't think I'd call it a holiday exactly.'

'Oh, would you be looking to try and find a job? Cos I'm not sure you've come to the right place in that case. Jobs are hardly two a penny in this area. People normally leave here to go down south looking.'

'I already have a—' Kim began, then stopped. 'I hadn't thought about getting a job to be honest with you.'

'You're not staying that long then.' Liz sounded disappointed.

'No, no, I'd like to, I just hadn't thought about it. I haven't even had a chance yet to tell my wife where I am.'

'You sound as though you're dreading it.'

'A bit. I didn't mean to, but I've left it a bit long. I can't explain.'

'What did you say when you left?'

Kim didn't reply.

'It's always better to call,' Liz told him gently. 'She'll be worrying.'

'But what can I say to her now? I've left it too late.'

'Course you haven't! You only arrived yesterday. I think she'd appreciate a call to hear you're all right. I would. She's probably in a right state.'

'I can always tell her anything, you see, only I'm not sure about this. Nothing to tell. It just happened.' Kim stopped and looked Liz straight in the eye. 'I don't know why I'm telling you.'

'You needn't worry. I'm not saying a word to anyone.'

'She's hardly going to be very pleased whatever I say at this late stage.'

'Don't you be so sure,' Liz laughed. 'I bet she won't mind, long as she knows you're OK. Lot of women are relieved when their husbands are out the house a while; time to themselves. Course, it's unbearable now Nick's gone for good, but it was different when he went away short-term. I used to enjoy it. I'd not have to think about food, or apologise for watching some nonsense on the telly. Bit of peace and quiet. Which isn't to say I didn't like it when he got back. It was just a little time to be me. She might be pleased for a short while on her own.'

Kim had always been of the impression that Sylvie hated it when he went away. It was suddenly troubling, the thought she mightn't mind, might even relish being without him, just want to be left alone to get on with her own peace and quiet. He didn't like the idea but, to an extent, it let him off the hook. He said, solemnly, 'That could be true.'

'Sure it is!' Liz reassured him. 'Doesn't mean she doesn't love you, or that she's not waiting for you.' She was doubtless prompted by the grim expression on his face. 'Only that you're out of her hair for a while. How long you been married?'

'Nearly twenty-three years.'

'Well, there you are. I think, long as you ring her, you should stay up here a while. Do you both good.'

'You do?'

'Adventure.'

Her word was an extremely attractive one. It had all the hall-marks of the unknown, of excitement, spontaneity; something everybody thinks about, even craves a little, but rarely does. 'I'd like that. I've never been much of a one for taking chances.'

'Perhaps it was chance which brought you up here in the first place. Proves you're capable.'

'Possibly.'

'And she won't mind.' Liz looked the sort, Kim thought, to throw caution to the wind, take risks for the promise of chance. It was infecting.

'I'd need to find some casual work,' he said at length, surprising himself.

'Oh?' He had surprised her too. She put her hand in the

103

basket. 'Do you mind?' she asked, indicating she might like not to waste the last piece of toast.

'Please, you go ahead.'

'Only you don't look like the sort who'd be after casual work,' she said, spreading the butter and strawberry jam with an air now of what the hell. 'I hope you don't mind my saying that? But I suppose if you get something with changing shifts it could give you some daytimes off to explore. Castles, scenery. That way you can take some advantage of your adventure.'

'I could.'

'I can direct you to the Job Centre if you like. It's only in the High Street, next to John Menzies, but most of what's available is, how shall I say, very much the lower end of the market.'

'That's fine.'

'Construction sites, kitchen work, you know.'

'I'm not fussy. If I'm looking for anything, I guess that's the sort of thing.'

'Pity it's not summer, I would've been grateful for a bit of help myself then. It's too quiet, though, this time of year, for me to take anyone on. Apart from you, I've only got one other guest at the moment, that's why I can afford the time to join you for breakfast. I'm not exactly being rushed off my feet. There's a lot of casual hotel work in the town though. There might be something going at the Station Hotel. They've a lovely kitchen and need a lot of people to wash up. Though there's usually a bit of competition for placements.'

'I don't think I'd stand much of a chance there.'

'Why ever not? They should be pleased of someone like you. They get a lot of rough types applying. And a lot of sad blokes in their forties and fifties whose wives have left them. They usually only ever last about a week. They tend to like a little nip.'

'Perhaps it'd be better to go for a washing-up position in a small restaurant? Might be nicer, more personal.'

'That's an idea.'

'Or something else completely?'

'Could do. Do you have any qualifications at all, love?'

'Not any that'd be of any help to me here, I don't think.'

'You look like you're the type who might know a bit about computing. Would I be right?'

Kim touched his chin. 'Oh, God, is it the beard?' he asked.

'It's only stubble so far,' Liz said.

'I must buy myself a razor on my way to the Job Centre.' They smiled at each other.

'No offence intended,' Liz told him.

'None taken. I wish I was better with computers but they're more my son's department. He spends hours when he's not working playing around on his. Flirting with girls on the Internet, and having cyber-sex no doubt. My skills are much more basic.'

Liz laughed. 'You have a son? Lovely.'

Kim didn't respond. He didn't know how much he wanted to give away and had probably already said far too much. He just took a swig of his coffee, as if distracted because he liked Liz and it was important to him that he didn't appear discourteous.

'Redundancy, was it?'

Kim didn't exactly nod, but nor did he give any indication to the contrary.

'Terrible. My husband was in timber. Went in one day and they said they were no longer requiring his services. Just like that. Destroyed him, it did. And us, come to that.' She paused. 'What sort of line of work have you been in then? You say your qualifications wouldn't be much use up here. They're very specific to where you were then?'

'Not really. I just didn't think there'd be much call—' Kim stopped. He finished his coffee and unconsciously wiped his lips with his napkin in a way that suggested his mind was miles away. 'I worked in a hospital for a while,' he ventured after a minute's silence. He could hear the crunch of Liz's toast in her mouth. After she had swallowed it, she didn't start talking again immediately. He might have mistaken her for a chattery character, but was pleased that she was easy with silence. 'Belfast,' he added after another long pause.

'Well, we have Raigmore. Huge place. It's a trust hospital so they use short contracts. Might be something going there, you never know. You must have been in management, I would imagine?'

'Not really, in fact.'

'Male nurse, then?'

105

Kim shook his head, confused by Liz's friendly questions.

'Don't tell me you were portering?' Her laugh was one of surprise.

'That type of thing,' he said, being now more economical with the truth. 'I was a bit of a Jack of all trades, fetching, carrying, doing anything I was asked that no one else wanted to do.'

'Pardon, that sounds very rude of me. You just look – I don't know. Perhaps too young to be a hospital porter. My miserable dad used to be one, and he's ancient, so I always think of them as older men, but that's my prejudice.'

'Fair enough. I probably used to think the same.' Kim felt keen to put her at her ease. 'So did your dad work at Raigmore?'

'Oh no. It's a modern hospital, built in the last ten years or so, and he'd retired by then. Apparently it's a good place to work, and he would've liked to have had the chance. Not that I got that from the horse's mouth, you understand, he wasn't telling me. It's on the outskirts of the city. I can tell you which buses if you like.'

'Thanks. I expect I might just fare better there than at the station hotel.'

'Well, if you've already got experience in that line of work.' Liz was nodding. 'Makes sense. You might as well start with an advantage.'

'I think I'll go to the Job Centre first, just in case, then I'll go on to the hospital.' Kim extracted his legs from beneath the table. 'Might as well take the bull by the horns. Are they far from here?' He stood up and followed Liz into the hall where she gave him a map and detailed directions.

'Hey, d'you want to use the phone before you go?' she called after him. But he was halfway down the street and didn't turn round. Perhaps he hadn't heard.

The Job Centre on the High Street was not exactly effervescing with the tricks of its trade. Tricks, thought Kim, was the operative word, each insecure offering of work being as it was as poorly paid and unsentimental as a prostitute's encounter. He, along with various other men, stood about the place either peeping at or ogling the scant notices depending on their shame. Together, they were all silently weighing up in their minds the relative, necessarily fleeting merits of a no-kissing tryst with a local fish filleting processing plant, or a frenetic coupling with the more exotic-sounding Norbird Highland, a chipboard factory a few miles out of town. Or was neither actually alluring enough? Neither them, nor the other scrawny choices – office cleaning, hotel washing-up – worth the bother? Fuck it, wasn't the dole less hassle, an altogether more reliable, if nagging, partner?

Some of the men shrugged and left, the door banging stroppily behind them, and could be seen outside immediately lighting up, their cigarettes at a disillusioned tilt. Inside, one or two, seasoned job-seekers, greeted each other with the desultory, dead-end cheer of office party-goers. Others just stared and stared at the pink record cards dotted about at hopeless intervals on the display boards, returning to one or two of them again and again. It was as if they were willing it to be the case that their eyes had deceived them and the advertised jobs were in fact even halfway decently paid, remotely long-term, vaguely unexpected.

Kim was aware of his unshaven face, and the fact that he had somehow managed to shake off his professional status somewhere between leaving Oxford and reaching the corridors of Inverness's station hotel. But he felt, suddenly, a classic, foolish guilt about his middle-class trousers, and a consciousness of the possible whiff lingering about him still of the middle-class air he had acquired at some point on the road between Herefordshire and his general practice. He decided to dispense with it as best he could in the fresh Highland air, that which had made him sleep so deeply and feel so relaxed. Outside, he sighed and began to follow Liz's map and directions for the bus to the hospital. Though he no longer expected – or wished, perhaps – to be mistaken for a doctor, it would nevertheless be a more familiar environment than the one he had just left.

On the bus towards Old Perth Road Kim leant back heavily against his seat and crossed his arms. His stomach, distended by his full-on breakfast, pressed against the waist of his trousers. Surreptitiously he undid the top of his button flies. He was going to enjoy the journey.

He stared at the window rather than out of it. His eyes fixed on the glass. It was smudged with dried layers of grimy rain on the outside, and condensation on the inside which he didn't get round to wiping with his coat sleeve. He just sat still, thinking.

Well, somewhere along the line, he told himself, if he was heading off to try and get work, he had obviously made the decision to stay in Inverness awhile. He wasn't aware of there having, over the previous few hours, been any moment of revelation. The decision had just crept up on him and now, contemplating it formally, he realised he had no wish to change it.

And yet it was very leaky in parts. He was still unclear about why he had made it, or how it was best achieved and put into practice.

Until he had worked out a few basics, and for as long as he was putting off ringing Sylvie, he thought it wise, for the time being at least, to keep his identity under wraps. For all her common sense and humanity, Liz had not been able to persuade him to ring home. For the first time since leaving, Kim consciously acknowledged to himself at last that, for all the abominable cruelty it implied, the inclination to do so was not there yet. Until he found it – which he wished and hoped he would very shortly – and could tell Sylvie where he was and why, his name and circumstances were certainly nobody else's business.

The bus deposited him near the hospital. It was an ugly building made of huge blocks and what looked from the outside to be too few windows. The architect, thought Kim, as he stood glaring up at it, must have had a hangover. He made his way through the accommodating electric doors to Reception. He stopped short of the desk itself to stand for a few moments in the middle of the floor to take it all in. The concourse was huge, but it was the general, instantly familiar smell about the place which struck him first. Kim had long ago recognised this to be a standard feature of every hospital everywhere, and one of the things which those who hate hospitals invariably cite as a reason for their loathing. Over the years he had often tried to extricate the different elements within it the better precisely to define the whole. It was, he had decided, mainly the combination of lino polished to a frenzy by ardent chemicals, the surgical whiff of bandages newly released from sterile packaging, and the treacly odour of flesh being slowly liquidised by old age, illness, despair and death. Was there nothing to be done with this smell? All the flowers in the world, it seemed, were no contest for it. Did their fragrances collectively lose the will to live the moment they crossed a hospital's threshold?

The tremendous bustle in the vast white concourse was also the same as Kim had experienced elsewhere – uniforms striding importantly, geriatrics making agonising progress at the barres of their zimmer frames, disaffected children chasing each other with boredom. So, too, were the regulation NHS and charity appeal posters on the walls and noticeboards; that ubiquitous token stab at homeliness, a couple of dusty pot plants by the lifts; the last-minute florist with its forlorn display of guilt bouquets; the helpful little League of Friends shop, run by the same doddery old lady as in every other hospital, for Dairy Milk, Lil-lets, and *People's Friend*.

The scene before him was for Kim like the bell for Pavlov's dog. He instinctively felt busy, but he had nothing to do. He knew he was in a hurry, but he had all the time in the world. He automatically put his hand out to his waistband to feel for his bleeper – which if it hadn't just gone off, was surely about to – but there was no bleeper. For a moment he was out of sorts, disorientated, and he sat down on one of the chairs designed for waiting, and waited.

Waited till he had pulled himself together. When, after about ten minutes, his misplaced doctor's adrenaline had eventually subsided, he went over to the drinks and snacks dispenser (same sandwiches with same snarling expressions and same fluorescent innards of chicken tikka), for a can of Coke. It was only when he had taken the last swig that he felt courageous enough to present himself to the reception desk and ask the way to the personnel department.

In the lift two junior doctors were venting their perennial opinions of a senior registrar. Kim smiled in what they might have taken to be a patient's respect for their distinguished white coats, but was in fact blokey recognition. How many times, at Belfast City Hospital, had he and his peers railed against some despot consultant? When he stepped out of the lift, he was aware of being nervous. Would Personnel have any work going and if so, would they be likely to offer it to someone with no experience? He made his way slowly to the right office.

109

Personnel were not unduly surprised by someone presenting himself unannounced. When he told them he was after casual work one woman might have raised an eyebrow as if to say, 'There's a man who looks as if he's fallen on hard times,' but no one treated him discourteously. Someone telephoned the Portering Manager's extension to tell him that a gentleman was coming to see him about a job. Kim was given directions to his office, a smile, and a good luck. As he walked to another part of the hospital he was grateful not to have been stonewalled and turned away. After the incident the evening before in the station hotel he had had swiftly to prune his assumption, which he had probably held all his adult life, that people, superficially at least, would afford him automatic respect. As he had been falling asleep, he had stared up at the unfamiliar ceiling of Liz's favourite room with (not much of) a view, thinking about the status which the label, doctor, had for so long thrust upon him. He was cross with himself for having grown so used to it that he had arrogantly taken it for granted. 'I am a doctor!' he had spat to himself on the bollard in the hotel forecourt. So what? he asked himself angrily a few hours later, just as he was about to drop off. A pretty duet of letters before his name and a stethoscope round his neck was, he realised, meaningless. Either with, or bereft of them, he had no more or less right to respect than the next man.

Kim found himself some way off from the wards in a long corridor. Although it was made up entirely of offices, it still had that hospital smell. Each door, he noted, was painted the jarring blue of a fertiliser sack, the kind his father used to use on the farm. He reached room number twenty-three. The Portering Manager really was called Mr Kindness. It said so on his door. Kim was delighted. He hoped the name augured well, and he felt momentarily confident enough to give the purposeful knock of a professional, as opposed to the anxious tap of a man desperate for a job.

'Come in,' said a voice inside.

Kim opened the door. The office was very small and had headache heating. No window. Any normal person might have gasped in such stuffiness, but Kim was used to it.

Mr Kindness was sitting at a desk which was covered in papers and files like a mini city of precarious skyscrapers. He invited Kim to sit down but when Kim did so he had to move several piles onto the floor just in order to be able to see his visitor's face. This revealed parts of the desk's leather-look surface. It was a dull red plastic. Mr Kindness had a complexion to match, and a huge stomach straining behind a thin white shirt. It was the kind of belly which means a person can never get too close to a table. Kim fancied he could detect a small splat of egg yolk near Mr Kindness's collar and could see that he might well be a man who found it something of a struggle to eat neatly. Managing to swallow quantities of beer, on the other hand, had evidently proved to be a more certain business.

Mr Kindness had eyes like round pebbles in the face of a snowman. His huge nose was laced with big pores which, had they been on a woman's thighs, would have given rise to mortified fears of cellulite. It was a nice face he had, open and cheerful, even though it had clearly seen a thing or two. This, thought Kim, was just the sort of man, to the consternation and bemusement of other men, that women found attractive. Not for his looks – Mr Kindness was by no means handsome – but for his character, and the simple fact that his physiognomy, quite apart from his name, also spelt kindness.

'It's kind of you to see me without an appointment,' Kim began.

Mr Kindness laughed. His belly bounced. 'I've heard that one a few times,' he said.

'I didn't mean—'

'Aye, I know. It's only folk find it a name to play with. I've heard all the jokes, I've made them myself a few times. Enough of that, though. I believe you've come for some casual work, Mr . . .?'

'Yes, that's right. Have you got any going?'

'Depends what you're looking for?'

'I'm not all that bothered. I need the work.'

'Well, whatever it is, it's no more than £3.46 an hour for five days, or forty hours, a week, and a temporary contract.' As Mr Kindness spoke, he watched Kim carefully. Either Kim had sloughed off his middle-class air successfully, or the Portering Manager had seen it all before and wouldn't have raised an

111

eyebrow if an aristocrat had walked through his door after his paltry £3.46. Certainly he gave nothing away if he felt his visitor wasn't one of the normal run of applicants. 'There's various types of portering,' he began to explain breezily. 'There's out-patient porters who take patients from the ward to the scanners or theatre, and what have you. There's Casualty porters who take patients out of the ambulances, into Casualty, and maybe onto the wards. Then there's the general ones who shift doctors' furniture, work out the back pushing food trolleys, dirty linen, clinical waste, and, say it I must, cadavers. In fact, they shift anything that moves.' Mr Kindness stopped as if weighing up whether or not to repeat an old joke of his which might be deemed feeble by a man like his visitor, but which nevertheless made him laugh every time. A second or two passed and he decided to risk it. 'Or,' he added, 'doesn't move, as the case may be!'

After he said it, he fell about. Kim found his merriment infectious and laughed too.

'Now,' he continued, righting himself, and trying to appear a bit more official, 'you'll have to fill in one of these.' He opened a drawer and strained across the desk to hand Kim an application form and a biro.

Kim looked at it. Name, address, date of birth. Oh God, he thought, I hadn't reckoned on this. Marital status, nearest relative, employment history, most recent post, National Insurance number. It gets worse, he said to himself. The pen poised above the paper, he gulped and hesitated. He was frightened.

'If you can't read and wri—' Mr Kindness started, then corrected himself. 'If you have any literacy problems at all, I can read out the questions and fill in the answers for you.' His tone was not remotely patronising.

'Thank you, but I should be OK,' Kim said gently, not wishing to imply that Mr Kindness's suggestion had been impertinent. He continued to hold the biro above the form, trying to think quickly. Eventually, with a nervous hand, he wrote Tim White in the space for his name, and gave the address of the B&B. By marital status he put single, but not before his right hand had wavered indecisively between the options like someone trying randomly to choose their lottery numbers. His left he had swiftly hidden under the table so Mr Kindness wouldn't spot his

112

wedding ring. He had forgotten about that. After the meeting he would wrap it in tissue paper and put it safely in the zipped pocket of his wallet. At this point he didn't wish to give anyone any clues about himself. He might have felt sentimental about removing it, but refused to allow himself to see it as a symbolic gesture. It didn't mean he no longer loved Sylvie, or no longer wished to be seen as her husband. It was purely practical, and anyway only for the time being. Till he sorted out what he was about, which wouldn't take long. Nearest relative he left blank; and in the NI box he put a false number. He knew enough about these things to know that it would not be discovered until the Contributions Agency did their annual checks in May. If he was still portering six months hence which, despite having no immediate plans to ring home, he very much doubted, he would cross that bridge at the time.

'My employment history's a bit complicated,' he then told Mr Kindness.

'You've not been unemployed recently then?'

'No, more sort of self-employed. I wouldn't say I was in employment now, though, as such.'

'Can you put down your most recent post, Mr White,' Mr Kindness asked, glancing at the upside down name Kim had written, 'self-employed or otherwise?'

'I worked in a doctor's surgery down south.'

'Reception was it, sort of thing, or cleaning?'

'Bit of everything, you know, general dogsbody.'

'But self-employed?'

'In a manner of speaking, yes, I suppose.'

'That'll do.'

Kim almost thanked Mr Kindness for leaving it at that. Pushed any further he might have had to be more specific with the untruth. But Mr Kindness was a man of tact and understanding. Guiltily, Kim cast his eyes away from him and further down the page. When it came to whether or not he smoked or had a criminal record, he sighed with relief, and scored a strong tick in each box saying no. 'I haven't really got any qualifications for portering,' he then admitted honestly.

'It helps if you can put something down. Have you any skills, Mr White? It can be an O-level in Domestic Science, it can be painting and decorating, for all the difference it makes to portering. Just to get an idea.'

Kim didn't say anything.

'I mean,' Mr Kindness went on, 'the only qualifications you have to have is that you look clean and tidy and that you're healthy and strong. You look clean enough, although you could do with a shave, maybe. We tend to appreciate beards or clean-shaven, not the willy-nilly in between. Are you healthy? I'm not saying you have to be really fit, but it'd be better for all concerned if you weren't going to have a heart attack in the near future. We have enough of them already without our staff going in for the melodramatics as well.'

'No chance of that. I mean, in as much as we can ever be really sure. It's amazing the amount of people, non-smokers, not over-weight, exercise regularly, cholesterol just fine, who do succumb. The last ones you'd think sometimes.'

'Oh aye? You know a bit about heart attacks? Someone in your family?'

'No, no,' Kim said quickly, 'just one or two people I've come across, around the place, who may have had them unexpectedly. But I'm very healthy, I do know that. I'm not about to succumb.'

'Well, that's all right then. We do a medical anyway. Look, leave Qualifications empty if you wish.' Mr Kindness took a slow sip from his polystyrene cup of coffee, eyeing Kim as he did so. 'Can I ask you, Mr White, why you've decided to move up north?'

Coming from someone else, and so unexpectedly, it was a star-tling question. While Kim had managed to use his wits and slalom his way round the various obstacles on the form, he hadn't bargained for this particular line of interrogation. He moved to the edge of his hessian seat, all the while blinking his eyes as if he were in a room full of smoke. He opened his mouth, and closed it again without any words having come out.

'I'm not saying you have to tell me, I was just wondering.'

'Oh, you know,' he said when he could, 'this and that.' He didn't look at Mr Kindness but instead concentrated his gaze towards his fingers as they brushed a fuss of fluff from the breast of his coat.

'Nothing more specific than that you want to tell me about?'

'It seemed a good idea at the time?' Kim said with an inflection in his voice as if to say, will that do?

'Problems back home?'

'Oh, no, not that, not at all,' Kim insisted.

'You just like the Scottish air, Mr White, is that right?' Mr Kindness sat back in his chair and it squeaked in protest at his bulk. 'Fancied a wee break in the Highlands to clear the cobwebs.' He crossed his arms with a smile, and pushed his tongue round his teeth and the inside of his lips.

Kim nodded.

'Can't say I blame you. All right, mate; now, referees. We do like to have a few words from someone who can vouch for you, or is that a bit difficult?'

'It would be a bit, yes,' Kim replied.

'I understand. They're all down south and what with the post and that being what it is, it all might take a while?'

'Yes.' He was warming to Mr Kindness more and more for presenting him with these generous get-out clauses.

'And you'd like to start sooner rather than later? Well, we do occasionally make exceptions.'

'That's very kind, Mr—'

'There you are, at it again,' he laughed.

'I'm sorry.'

'Never worry. So we'll forget the references, then, shall we? You're a man, I see, who likes to keep his cards close to his chest. Well, just as long as you turn up for your shifts and you do your work, we don't ask a lot of questions. Reliable, neat and fit, that's all that matters. And, of course, no drugs or alcohol to be consumed anywhere near the premises. It's not a lot to ask, but you'd be surprised by the amount who can't fulfil even these modest expectations. We look for someone with common sense, and there's not a lot of them. We have a considerable turnover. There's not many, shall I say, who we could describe as indispensable. That's because it's low-paid work, and much of it's shite. But, in its favour, it's regular and above board. If you do it well, we can arrange a fixed-term contract after a fortnight. When would you like to start? Tomorrow?'

'Really?'

'Why not? I have a good instinct, Mr White, and you strike me as a man who has a head on his shoulders, someone who'd keep it if we were to put you in as a Casualty porter. We'll arrange for a quick medical and fit you out with a uniform and a security badge. And you must learn the fire regulations, then that's it. If we do all that in the morning, starting at nine – if tomorrow's good for you – then we can start you off on the afternoon shift, two pm till ten pm. All right?'

'I've no plans.'

'Well, then, if you'd be so good as to sign the form there,' Mr Kindness said, pointing out the relevant box, 'and also here for the initial two-week contract.' He had to manoeuvre himself awkwardly in order to bring out another piece of paper, from the drawer beneath his stomach.

Kim signed both it and the application form. On the first he wrote Kim but remembered just in time to turn the 'K' into a scribbled 'T', and to put White as opposed to Black. It was an alarming moment. He feared his signatures smacked of falsity. But when he passed them back across the desk his new employer just set them aside. He didn't so much as glance at them let alone scrutinise their every stroke and loop. Kim felt at last that he was well and truly off the hook. If he worked hard and kept his head down there would be no more questions asked. He shook Mr Kindness's hand and walked out of the hospital a satisfied man.

# 7

The lights on the ceiling of the bus back into town were the colour of chilled chicken breasts, but they were warm and made Kim feel drowsy. He closed his eyes. He thought about his new job, what on earth it would be like. For all his cheery banter with porters in the past, he had adhered to the strict hospital hierarchy – unattractive microcosm though it was of the British class system as a whole – and hadn't spent much time with them. It was an omission on his part that his famed interest in other people had never properly extended its hospitality to the hospital porter. He had always been polite to them, and friendly, but detached. He realised now, with frustration and shame, that he had never before wondered, or asked, what it was like actually to be one.

It was sociable work, he now imagined, but tough. While some members of the public were probably appreciative, the majority were more likely to be at best indifferent, at worst offensive. How would he fare?

He hadn't a clue. For a few moments his mind went empty and he was on the point of falling asleep. Then suddenly he remembered one of Mr Kindness's questions, and jolted in his seat as if he had missed his step in a dream.

Why had he decided to come up north?

When he had emerged from the artificial womb of the hospital, the rain had been dive-bombing the tarmac. The sky was pebble-dash grey. Going back along Old Perth Road, Kim did not look at the window as he had on the bus journey out. He looked instead at his own hands which clutched the metal rail across the top of the seat in front of him. Pale hands, few hairs, but not womanly, a decent mountain range of knuckles; protruding veins mapped over the back of them, the delta of those which ran down his milky forearms brazenly exposing something of his private, inner anatomy. Sometimes, in surgery, he had seen his familiar hands

117

and arms from another's point of view. When his sleeves were rolled up and he was, for example, busily prescribing methadone to someone trying to kick heroin, he had more than once caught the patient's eyes as they fell upon this rude display of his with the envy of one whose own veins had long ago lost the will and disappeared. During those moments he had stopped trying, for a second, to understand his patient, and had briefly allowed himself to speculate as to how he or she might see him.

Dr Black. Or just Doctor. Of the reliable hands; the soothingly mild and reassuring accent not quite within reach – 'Would that be West country, now, Doctor, or more Midlands with a touch of Irish thrown in, my father/mother/granny was Irish?' (whose wasn't?); the firm sympathy; the willingness in a more enlightened way (he hoped) humanely to treat those whose troubles might well be of their own making, but were still troubles all the same.

Everything about him, he thought, was so bloody wholesome. And yet now if you flicked him with the nub of your spoon, there was a danger he might disintegrate into a pile of muesli.

Doctor. A label groaning with the pretty weight of responsibility, like foolish blossoms on a cherry tree. Rarely was the word spoken without respect. But did it merit it, absolutely? Did he?

Before he qualified, Kim had always imagined that teachers and lawyers and architects were looked up to in the same way as doctors were, but after he had assumed the title he was not so sure. There was something almost embarrassing in the reverence people seemed to hold for him. He couldn't make it out. Why was knowledge of the workings and failings of the mind and body any more due for respect than knowledge, say, of structural engineering, or of how to make the Battle of Culloden come alive for a bunch of bubble-gum toting school kids? What right had doctors to such respect over and above that which was afforded to everyone else, professional or otherwise?

He had long ago decided that it must be something to do with the nature of the information the doctor was able to impart. While it undoubtedly required an impressive level of medical knowledge and experience, it was also confidential, and it was this, he felt, which was the key. Someone in the waiting room could look at his fellow patients for hours on end, and speculate

118

about their troubles to his heart's content, but only the doctor would ever learn what was the matter with them. It was a privileged position, to be the security guard of infinite numbers of personal, as well as medical, secrets.

Whatever the reason for it, it had at first made Kim supremely uncomfortable. For many years he had felt the white coat had bestowed upon him an unfair advantage which he didn't deserve. When he had joined the general practice in Cowley, he had asked his patients to dispense with his title and to call him by his first name. It didn't work. Even the young ones, for whom formality was a dirty if not downright alien word, insisted on calling him Doctor. Yes, Doctor; no, Doctor; three bags full, Doctor. Kim concluded that they wanted to look up to him. For their own confidence they needed to see him as their superior. It made more smooth the passing to and fro of potentially troublesome details.

It had taken some time for Kim to accept this because he had been fiercely brought up to believe that no one was better than anybody else, that everyone was entitled to the same degree of respect. His father had maintained that this was a simple fact, but unfortunately one that many, for whatever reason, found impossible to comprehend. David Black's philosophy, in an introverted farming community where petty snobberies and prejudices were as common as foot and mouth disease, was remarkably singular and therefore hugely affecting. As a young boy Kim had watched him doffing his cap to a cowman in the lane same as he would to the vicar. That this behaviour earned David a reputation for being something of an eccentric only fuelled Kim's pride, and cemented his own more democratic beliefs.

Even though Kim failed to persuade his patients to call him by his Christian name, they seemed to like his easy-going manner. He never wore a suit to work. He felt happier in jeans and a jersey. If GPs were looked upon as half-wits who couldn't make it in a hospital by the rest of the medical profession, at least – because they were effectively self-employed – they didn't have to toe some party line like consultants did. GPs were more autonomous. They had the freedom to choose their own hours, and had fewer restrictions regarding what they could wear. There was room for character, for nonconformism. Kim could have a nose ring if he so wished, and there would be nobody to sniff at him and tell him it wasn't quite the thing. But while he was not exactly of the exotic inclination of one of Jack's girlfriends, his was not the solemn disposition of a lofty specialist either. Except perhaps when he was so tired he was ready to keel over, he always had a sense of humour. Some of his patients found it disconcerting to come across a doctor who made dry remarks and told funny stories, but they soon got used to it.

Why had he decided to come up north? He might want to dodge the answer, but the question kept at him.

When Kim was a student, someone had advised him to become an anaesthetist. Because he had always been genuinely devoted to and riveted by people, it was a suggestion which did not go down well. 'What?' he had asked, incredulous, 'and choose to be with people who are *asleep*?'

Kim had never once regretted tossing that idea out of court so contemptuously because, from day one as a GP, he had been arrogant enough to realise that his patients thought of him as a good doctor. The ability to listen was ninety percent of it. He was acquainted with a surgeon who was a medical genius but perversely uninterested in people. This man was admired by his colleagues but considered by his patients to be useless. Surgeons were renowned for many skills, but listening was not one of them. The man should have been a vet. Surely, Kim thought, almost the whole point of being a doctor was communication with people. The fact that he listened to his patients sincerely meant he could have been a mediocre, even positively bad, medical man, and they would still have looked upon him as an excellent GP.

He had confidence in himself. He had never had ambitions to become a smart surgeon, grand consultant, or lauded specialist. If general practice was the raw end of the profession, then so be it. When he and his partners had advertised for a trainee, they had received just two replies. No one wanted to be a GP these days.

All the admin. Half the job was dictating letters of referral; was scrutinising and signing piles of repeat prescriptions; was filling out patients' medical history forms for mortgage and life insurance companies; was registering four or five new patients a day, reading a pack full of notes from their previous doctor; was keeping up with all the latest developments in the *British Medical Journal*, let alone all the other publications. The paperwork alone could cause any reasonable character to flail about like a ham actor putting his all into a Shakespearean death scene. But that was before the sheer practical logistics – quite apart from the onerous financial implications – of fulfilling immunisation and other like targets. It was before seeing a single real-life patient. Or once being forced awake at 4 am to go and attend to a man with no intention of waiting till morning, or of bothering to go to an all-night chemist to buy a bottle of Calpol for his crying child, but to jolly well make the doctor come to him, right that minute, with a free one. Why on earth would any sane souls kill themselves with that type of work when glamorous gynaecology or powerful paediatrics beckoned?

Kill themselves, literally, Kim said to himself and shifted in his seat. Doctors, as he was very well aware, were neck and neck with farmers when it came to committing suicide. He was on good, firm ground, then, he used to tell himself, with a wry smile, sometimes even a laugh.

For all its petty horrors from day to day, Kim loved his job. But now he asked himself to think back over the past few weeks. Had the inherent stress of it been gnawing away at him peculiarly? Had he had any untoward thoughts?

The bus was rolling towards the city centre, towards the more intense pollution of lights from street lamps and offices and shops which wantonly thrust themselves through the window. Kim wiped a porthole in the condensation and looked out into the squall. It was now early afternoon and almost dark. What he recognised to be his stop was approaching. He stood up wearily. It had been a curiously fraught morning. He was discovering that subterfuge, like sulking, used up a great deal of energy. It may not have been easy at times being Kim Black, but not being him was a whole lot more exhausting.

He pulled his coat collar up around his chin, and ran straight from the bus into a nearby pizza parlour.

The place smelt of hot, flavour-enhanced dough and warm, watered-down tomatoes. The lighting was in your face, the kind which demanded respect. In it, the various people dotted about, smoking, tucking in, had the skimmed milk complexions of pregnant women resignedly suffering eternal, custardy nausea. Kim squeezed in at one of the meanly spaced tables. He sat on a metal chair which was fixed to the ground. Was the management so paranoid that it honestly supposed people would be tempted to carry off its measly seats under their overcoats? There were various apocalyptic developments in modern life, and nailing down public furniture was one of them. It was up there, almost, with cloning.

A laminated menu illustrated with faded photographs of pizzas with pineapple pieces, and banana splits, was propped between his squat salt cellar and the steel dispenser which bulged with a protruding belly of paper napkins. Kim ordered a cup of coffee from a slapdash waitress with anchovy lips and caper eyes. As she sloped between the tables her lemon flip-flops were at odds with the stockinged feet of her exaggerated-flesh coloured tights. They appeared to bestow upon her every step a mild limp. Kim's coffee was not swift in coming, but why should it be, he wondered, when its heavenly messenger was on an approximation of £3.46 an hour? As far as time was concerned, he was in a seller's market. He was happy to wait patiently, indefinitely.

Untoward thoughts?

Not as far as he could remember. The past few weeks had been no different from normal. Tiring, of course. There again exhaustion was a basic for a doctor, like yellow was to jaundice. Kim had often thought that parents – including himself – must have some biological mechanism which, when they had a baby, automatically formed round their wide eyes a pair of metaphorical blinkers and turned them into people possessed. What else would enable them so wittingly to endure assault by mewling and crying and shitting; the mania of enforced insomnia; and, in general, the preposterous unsociability of children? Kim believed that he must have some sort of similar function in him which rendered him so passionate about his occupation that he was still able to throw himself into it despite the obvious drawbacks. Being a doctor was like having a kid: it often involved unreasonable hours; frequently squalor; and usually heartbreak. And, half the time, he was so transported by exhaustion that sleep seemed continually to beckon to him like an amoral temptress.

Sitting with his hands crocheted round his polystyrene cup, Kim fell to pondering the past, very typical, couple of months in which, he estimated, he had seen and seen to, the guts of probably eighteen hundred patients. The majority of these had come in for routine consultations – colds, flu, sports injuries, family planning matters, travel injections. Others had come for minor surgery. There was nothing Kim enjoyed more than freezing out verrucas, having a go at a little cyst or mole or skin tag. If ever there were illustration of his passion for his work then this must be it. Who else would fall upon another man's wart with such affectionate relish? But to him it represented a challenge, and beat writing out a prescription any day. Using his hands was always rewarding. Recently he had rewired the house and found that to be a satisfying task in the same sort of way. He saw beauty in his own needle-point accuracy, in achieving the smallest possible scar. It was the creative, perfectionist side of himself coming through, in its singular way.

Most of these patients, with their straightforward ailments, had been a delight. So had it been that the unhealthy aggression of healthy men demanding sick notes had got him down unduly? Hardly. Granted, one or two had called him a bastard when he hadn't complied. This was standard. He'd been called worse. All the names under the sun in fact. Alarming originally, but after seventeen years as a GP they now just slipped off him. Water off a duck's back.

The past few weeks, there had been the usual run of patients presenting themselves in his surgery with their home medical manuals under their arms. 'My voice is hoarse, Doctor, says here it's throat cancer.' He had once or twice wanted to hurl the volumes across the room, but this was an impulse he and his colleagues admitted to experiencing on average three times a week.

He had had his fair share of worried-well patients, of course. Mainly women, suffering mild stress, perhaps wanting to test him out. They always appeared equipped not with their own diagnoses but instead with a list of symptoms as long as their large intestines.

'It hurts,' said one, Peggy Treasure, fifties, mandarin-coloured eye shadow, 'if I press here, Doctor.' She duly pressed a point near her ankle and went, 'Ow!' Kim had asked her what would happen if she didn't press there. Predictable answer: 'Nothing.'

'So,' he had told her, mischievously, 'might I suggest, with respect, that you just refrain from pressing there and you'll be cured.'

It was a risky tack, but just sometimes it got them laughing, and it was the triumph of his afternoon.

There had been a lot like Peggy Treasure recently, Kim recalled. Their little twinges here and there, their little rashes, their little pains. These were actually only a psychosomatic manifestation of a little fatigue here, a little depression there; in fact, of course, just life. But how to tell them they were just life? How to help them let go of the idea that their symptoms spelt terminal Cancer?

'I promise there's nothing wrong,' he had told Peggy Treasure in his milkiest of Magnesia voices.

'Are you saying I'm making it up, Doctor? Are you saying I'm mad?'

Had 'just life' been getting progressively worse of late, he asked himself. Had more and more patients been presenting themselves with the symptoms of quiet despair, and had he himself been becoming respectively more pessimistic and despairing too?

Grown men, middle-aged men, company directors, had been sitting in his room and weeping. Then his role had not been far from that of a priest. Gordon Stannard had confessed to sexual infidelity, but loved his wife. He had cried in that way Mackenzie used to as a child, and which Kim had at first found so troubling; those racking sobs emanating like a series of earthquakes from the solar plexus. Kim recognised that he wouldn't be a reasonable man if he hadn't found the guilt and pain of Gordon Stannard and his perennial ilk affecting. But it was an occupational hazard and he was well equipped to deal with it. He had listened to him. Sure enough, after half an hour, Gordon had dried his eyes and walked to the door, if not exactly with a swing in his step, then a man relieved. Kim had told him to come back any time, and had smiled as he left believing it was a job well done.

Now, as he sipped his meek coffee, he remembered how he had been taught that often there was no prescription necessary, that a doctor's mere presence was the treatment itself. One or two of his fellow medical students had been sceptical at the time. While Kim had himself been well able to believe it, he had nonetheless been flabbergasted in the course of his subsequent career at the miraculous effects a little listening could achieve. He tore open a pink paper sachet and stirred a sprinkle of too fine, modern sugar into his modern cup, hoping it might give a little zest to the inadequate coffee. As he did so, he reflected that some folk are of the rather corny notion that talking's the thing. But as far as he was concerned, people could talk all they liked, in itself it wasn't enough. It seemed to him, perhaps even more cornily, that the all-important balm was having another person to listen. He had found that expectations in this respect were extraordinarily humble. Just to listen. People weren't so bold as to go for gold and hope for sympathy. All they wanted was one grade up from a cloth ear to hear them out. But, as he had discovered, in so many cases even this modest wish was not being accommodated. At such times it was his duty to cast aside his strict medical qualifications for a few moments, and step in as a fellow human being. There had to be someone prepared to give these unhappy men and women a little more than the time of day.

Naturally, in the past couple of months he had witnessed more than common or garden unhappiness. He had witnessed, too, common or garden tragedy; seen people fall apart after tragedy. Normal. There was the couple whose baby had died a cot death, who were simultaneously evicted from their flat for non-payment of rent. They were not coping. They had lost their baby, their home, their minds.

With them – the Roystons, they were called – and other patients besides, Kim had had to wear a number of hats at once – GP, priest, social worker, sort of friend. He had had to be on constant alert for any possible risk of suicide – filtering stray words, phrases, even gestures, with all the expertise of a psychiatrist, all the patience and thoroughness of a forensic scientist examining microscopic fibres.

Had the responsibility been too much? Perhaps all these troubles of the world had begun to weigh too heavily on his fallible shoulders? There again, wasn't he, as Jack was wont to put it in his inimitable way, trained for strain? Wasn't he used to it, wasn't it part and parcel of being a GP? It hadn't got to him in the past. He had long mastered the art of separating sympathy from empathy.

Yet he was not an unemotional man. Of course he felt for the likes of the Roystons, but keeping his own feelings about their miseries in check was what was demanded of him as a professional. This was something which hadn't come naturally to him, as it had to some doctors he had observed. It was something he had learnt. But he had never quite learnt to be privately unaffected.

A few times over the years, in the privacy of his home, and with Sylvie, he let off his chest months' worth of others' miseries which had built up inside him. A handful of times, if he hadn't actually broken down in floods, the tears had streamed down his face. He wasn't ashamed, never in front of Sylvie, who always understood. It was a necessary purging, an entirely reasonable replenishing of the reserves, and renewed his strength till the next time.

Thinking about it now, he felt the need again for some tears – for others, as far as he could work out, not for himself – but he was in public, and they wouldn't be as effective or good without Sylvie's help and support. His ability to resist made him realise that getting away from the burden of other people's problems and unhappiness had not been the reason he had come up north.

'Would you be wanting some more coffee, or to order something to eat now?' The waitress stood above him, steaming pot in one hand, other hand splayed out over a zealous hip. Her tone wasn't rude exactly, it merely betrayed a blowsy indifference to whatever answer Kim might be about to give. He wondered what in all the world he could possibly say which would surprise or delight her. She had an expression which looked as though it was in need of some good news or cheer. Kim could think of none. If he told her that she was pretty, which she was in a churlish sort of way, she would doubtless be affronted, and rightly so. He could hardly compliment her on her merry service. He decided it was easier to adopt a policy of omission.

'Just coffee for the moment, thank you,' he said.

She poured some more of the brown liquid, pale as a tinted mirror, into his cup. 'The Hawaiian's nice,' she urged unexpectedly. 'Pineapple. It's very popular. 10p off of every one goes to the Save the Polynesian Pig Fund.'

Kim had given money to many a good cause in his time but he

had to admit to himself that until that moment he had never thought of contributing to the welfare of an exotic, far-flung swine. 'I'll think about it,' he told the waitress and she flip-flopped away. The notion of pineapple on a pizza was as galling to his sense of taste as was the prospect of a nail down a black-board to another man's ears. He was not hungry. After his second cup of coffee he stood to leave. He paid at the counter. He left a tip plus 10p for the pigs. A pathetic sum, he said to himself, walking out of the door. He had always believed himself not to be a mean character. Parsimony was a trait he despised, having seen that side of his father manifest itself in so many unimaginably petty ways. Now Kim was on a financially challenged wage, he wondered if helping people out was going to remain on his agenda. Being able to act upon concern, he reflected, was some-thing of a luxury. Being able to go in for the odd gesture of generosity was easy on a secure salary. How complacent he had been. Take the GP's pay cheque away from him and maybe he was no better than his father? Mean as pig-shit.

As he made his way back to the B & B he thought about money. The following day, after work, he knew he was going to have to find a cheaper room. He had gone out of the house to buy ice-cream with just under a hundred quid in his wallet, having cashed it from a machine earlier that day. The coach journeys and various sundries had speedily whittled it down and left him with about £19. (He would blow that on another night at Liz Lawson's because the bed was comfortable and her breakfast irre-sistible.) There was also his cash card. He could take some money out of a wall.

A convenient service till was at the side of a bank near the pizza restaurant. No queue, for once, Kim thought, and he began immediately to walk towards it. Its illuminated green letters appeared to pulsate alluringly on its black screen. But just as he was about to take his card from his wallet, unthinking, he turned his back on the machine. Taking out money from such a Big Brother device would have been a rash move for someone toying with the idea of not alerting interested parties to his whereabouts. Without further ado, he simply started to stroll in the rain back to the place where he was staying. It was not a long walk and he took deep breaths of the wintry air.

The next morning Kim reported to Mr Kindness punctually at nine. He spent the following few hours being prepared for his first shift.

The fire regulations were not difficult to learn. The medical was fun; Kim felt like a spy. The doctor had a very different style from his own. Efficient to the point of being brusque. Non-existent sense of humour. When Kim supplied him with the exact dates of his last tetanus and hepatitis jabs and made a feeble joke about being rather anal about these things, the doctor, far from smiling with gratitude as Kim would have done (patients were so rarely that helpful and specific), just pursed his lips as if offended by what he considered to be coarse language. Kim thought such evident primness something of a disadvantage to a man of his profession.

'Do you have proof of these dates, Mr White?'

Kim carefully didn't blanch at the name. He was ready for it. 'No, sorry, I don't.'

'Well, in that case I shall have to give you the jabs anyway. I'm sure what you tell me is true but we can't be too careful. We've a lot of grown men through this door who'll say anything just because they don't like needles.'

Kim rolled up his sleeves and watched as the doctor prepared his syringes and administered the injections. There were no soothing comments along the lines that it wouldn't hurt or it'd be over in a jiffy. Kim felt the man had much to learn about patient relations.

He had to fill in a benign questionnaire. It was straightforward. No, he had never had TB or contracted malaria. The doctor read Kim's answers in silence. His verdict at the end of the fifteen-minute session was that Kim was healthy, which he knew already.

'Thank you, Doctor,' he said automatically, like a parody of one of his own respectful patients.

After the medical, it was time to return to Mr Kindness to be kitted out with the porter's uniform and security badge. His regulation shirt was of a particularly virulent blue, with a tie and jersey to match. There was not a natural fibre among them so under the hospital lights they almost appeared to glisten, rather glamorously, Kim thought. His grey trousers were a little itchy round the waistband but smarter than anything he ever wore to his surgery. He changed in a window-free room, not much bigger than a cupboard, a few doors along from Mr Kindness's office. There was a chair, a rail with a few metal hangers, one of those electric hand-dryers that makes a noise like a small aeroplane and still contrives to leave the hands damp, a sink the size of a cereal bowl with a transparent plastic box above it of lethal liquid soap, and a basic mirror studded to the wall.

Kim was feeling clammy. The claustrophobic air had been over-indulged by its heating, and his nerves were a-dither. He tried to make a respectable knot in his tie. He was out of practice.

When he glanced in the mirror he jolted with surprise. The man staring back at him was not himself or, rather, only an approximation of himself. The skin around his eyes looked puffier than usual, his eyelids greasy – as if someone had mois-turised them with Nivea. He realised he had the air about him of any number of middle-aged men – fatigued complexion, nudging stomach, hair starting to dust with grey, skin round the jaw-line becoming lazy. But it was his uniform that was most surprising. Although it was a regular one, its immodest brightness was alien to Kim, whose chosen style tended towards sartorial sobriety. As well as a hospital porter, he could be the man sweeping the litter and gob on a city's streets; the security guard in the night bowels of some eerie office block; the factory worker at Bird's Eye who coaxes thousands of bare fish fingers towards their breadcrumb sprinkler. His uniform was the same as other men's, and empha-sised the fact that so his face was too. It could look surly, it could smile; whether it wanted to or not, it could reveal its history of hardship, of pain, of disappointment. Without his doctorly acces-sories, chances were, the people who were soon to pass him in the hospital corridor as he wheeled his trolleys to and fro, would not notice him, for all the efforts of his hopeful uniform. Those few that might chance to do so, would see his usual face, and might linger upon it just long enough to detect in it the usual tales of either lack of physical affection as a child, or too much of it (the engraving on the brow's the same); the thwarted ambitions to make a mark on the world (whether as the owner of a little garage, a ground-breaking computer buff or, more likely, as the one who scores an historic goal in the FA cup final); probably a joyless marriage behind him, or two; a real but inarticulate love for his 2.4 kids, the regretful weight of being completely unable to communicate with them. In short, the commonplace disaffection and alienation of the majority of men over forty.

They'd be wrong, of course. Kim might look but he didn't feel like those men, far as he was aware. He was content enough, content as any fellow could hope to be. A childhood that was like most – wanting in many ways but not outright bad – was far enough behind him no longer, he presumed, to have any poignancy or significance. He had become a doctor, which was, in terms of his career, all he ever wanted. He had married a woman he loved. His relationship with his children was buoyant.

Kim shifted the knot of his tie deeper into his neck and left the cupboard to join Mr Kindness once more. Together they went to the staff canteen which echoed with the thud of wood-look trays and the china chink of thick plates. As in every hospital canteen throughout the land, there were behind the food counters aluminium coffins of baked beans and fried potatoes and an indeterminate slop consisting of counterfeit meat and gravy. Dinner ladies' grubby paper hats both billowy and sunken like the surface of a molar, bent low over their fare, complexions greased by the oily light, smiles smudged by steam.

Kim's boss allowed a magnanimous amount of lunch to be ladled onto his plate. Kim himself was more modest after another epic breakfast chez Liz Lawson. They sat at a Formica table, with a few crumpled paper napkins, and a nurse who had propped up against her bowl of trifle a novel with swirling silver letters on its cover. She did not notice the two of them, but carried on reading, her face full simultaneously of cynicism and hope.

Mr Kindness, bent on small talk, asked Kim one or two questions. Did he prefer a sandwich to a hot meal at dinnertime? Did he know Scotland at all? Had he been before on holiday? They were harmless enough but Kim was flustered by them.

'Not really,' he said. 'A couple of times, long ago. I went up Ben Nevis once.' This was not true. Kim had never been up a mountain in his life. He said it for fear that he was not being polite to Mr Kindness, who was trying hard. Kim was an open, easy-going type, never one to be constrained in conversation. Having to be secretive did not suit his nature. He was wary of lying but still he preferred to lie than to say nothing and appear rude and uncommunicative.

'Funny you should say that. We have a lot come off the hills, we have helicopters land here sometimes. I take it you made it up and down in one piece?'

'I did.'

'Wouldn't catch me up there. I've seen one too many with broken limbs, hypothermia, frostbite, you name it. Half them that go up there don't seem to know the difference between a mountain and a pleasure beach. You'll find that people come in with injuries after such stupid accidents. Not just the hills. You can't imagine what high jinks people'll get up to to get themselves hurt.'

Kim nodded. 'I can believe it.'

'No, I mean it, till you've worked in a hospital you cannot believe it. Some of the tales I tell my wife of what goes on here, she thinks I'm pulling her leg, honestly. One man was so fed up with his wife gassing on the phone he'd superglued the receiver to her ear to teach her a lesson. I'd laugh if I thought it was funny. You wait, some of the stuff folks come up with. Fancy a sweet?'

'No, thanks.'

'Because it's nearly two now and we'd best be getting you started.' Mr Kindness stood to stack his empty plate and tray on a tall trolley. Kim followed him upstairs to Casualty. He was shown the porters' locker room, a glass box which had an unpromising-looking cooker and smelt of hair oil and worked-upon shoes. There he was introduced to the deputy head porter on duty, Eck, and handed over to his charge.

'It's graft, you know that, don't you?' Eck asked him when Mr Kindness had left. 'But you'll get used to it. You might even enjoy it, you ne'er know.' His eyebrows, which were reminiscent of the bristles on two expensive paintbrushes, rose at the end of his sentence like facial punctuation. Kim noticed, sticking out above his collar and tie, hairs high on his neck, his Adam's apple embedded in them like a pale egg in a bird's nest. The backs of his hands were similarly hirsute but Kim could make out the letters CELT on the knuckles of one hand and IC on those of the other. It must have been frustrating for Eck that the number of his knuckles did not match the spelling of his team. Kim wondered if he had got over it in the tattoo parlour or if he was daily disappointed by the lack of symmetry with which he had had to make do.

Eck sallied into Casualty and Kim followed him up to the desk.

'Alan, our new porter, Tim White,' Eck told the man behind it. 'Is there anyone waiting?'

'Aye. Cubicle four. A Miss Robinson waiting to be taken to have her legs plastered.'

Eck showed Kim to the cubicle and gave him directions as to where he was to take the patient. 'You be polite, but don't ask too many questions. People don't like a nosy bastard.'

Kim went inside the cubicle to find a young woman, about twenty, it was hard to tell. She looked like a display on a market stall. Her bare arms had shiny blotches across them the size and colour of aubergines; her neck was bloodied with red crusts as rich as strawberries. Her face resembled an Ugli fruit. Tears bumped over the moguls of its swollen bruises, but she was silent. In Belfast she would have been the victim of a so-called punishment beating. In Inverness it was something rather different. Kim took Eck's advice and didn't ask. He wheeled her to the room where her legs were to be plastered. As he left her there she said thank you, in a whisper. Kim wanted so much to ask her who was responsible but he bit his lip, he no longer had the right to put personal questions to patients. He said goodbye and returned to Casualty.

The next eight hours were gruelling. While he was used to the haunting groans of people in severe pain which might have upset another novice with less experience of hospitals than himself, he wasn't used to having to push cumbersome trolleys for miles and miles, and at a lick. It was physically astonishing. He was now rediscovering, only too painfully, some of the more obscure muscles he hadn't revised since medical school. And he was also having to get used to orders being shouted at him by junior doctors, nurses, paramedics and receptionists, most of them half his age, and some full of loathsome superciliousness to boot. One man in particular angered him, a Dr Gordon, who couldn't have been much older than Jack. Kim wasn't able to observe much, rushing as he was to and fro with emergency charges, but he was able to glean that young Dr Gordon was incompetent as well as supercilious, an unforgiveable combination. Twice he had over-heard desperate nurses tactfully giving him instructions. In his early days, as he was willing to admit, Kim had displayed his own fair share of incompetence. But he now prayed to God he had never harboured at the same time such unwarranted arrogance.

When the shift was over, Kim changed back into his own stale clothes and slumped down on one of the benches in the locker room. He thought he knew exhaustion. Some of these neglected muscles of his appeared to quiver like the death throes of a suffo-cating fish. After a few minutes he forced himself up with a loaded sigh and went out to the bus stop. Only then did it occur to him that he had nowhere to go. It was ten fifteen. He counted the contents of his pockets. The grand total of £4.61. That morning he had risked paying Liz with a cheque which he had thought less traceable than Switch for some reason, but he could not do that again. As far as cash went, there was no question of another night at the comfortable B & B. Tomorrow he would find a cheap room to rent, for which he would pay when he got his first wage packet, but that didn't solve his immediate problem.

An almost empty bus drove up and Kim got on it, careless of its destination. There were two girls on the back seat with white mini-skirts, bare legs to match, and homes to go to. Flat neck-laces like a chain of silver fish slithered down their cleavages and snatches of their conversation filtered down the aisle. One said, 'Sod it, I don't care,' in a voice of gruel-like resignation.

Before reaching the centre of town, Kim spotted a pub out of the window and got off at its nearest stop. He preferred the idea of a pint of beer to having to think about where he was going to sleep. Easier.

It was a basic pub: plain green walls, peeling, scratched; a bar, bottles, tables, chairs; no pool table, not a fruit machine in sight. The only frivolities were the beer mats. The place was crowded and smoke-clogged enough to give a non-smoker the bends. Kim squeezed his way to the bar and ordered a Guinness. Then he stood in a humble corner to drink.

The older men about him had double chins forested with ash-coloured stubble. Few smiled. One, crude as the noon-day sun, openly clawed the cushion of a fat lady's bosom. The younger men had lawn-mower haircuts and, to make their conversational sallies more macho, studded their syllables with punches of the neck. Their girlfriends wore thick make-up and wary expressions. They were sexy in the real, raw way that airbrushed models, with their computer-elongated legs and image-manipulated irises, could never be. All their skirts were of the same parsimonious cut, their tops of equally high-pitched colours, but the girls themselves were startlingly alluring in their optimistic endeavour to attract the opposite sex, these pint-heavy men on whom subtle signals would have been lost at birth. Several laughed. When they did so their shoulders heaved roundly and in their eyes proper tears formed as a merry challenge to their unreliable mascara.

One woman, mid-thirties, in particular caught Kim's attention. She was sitting near his corner with an older friend, perhaps her mum, and was less brassily conspicuous than her slightly younger counterparts. She had fat, flawless cheeks, rounded glasses and clean hair. Her immodest stomach was tucked into tomato chutney-coloured jeans; her arms, undefined by muscles, were fleshily folded across her cream T-shirt torso. She didn't move like the other girls in the pub, whose gestures were meant to be innocuous but were in fact fearsome with the hovering ogre of wasted opportunity. Seeing her, this woman of quiet possibility, Kim felt the tweak of basic longing.

After a few minutes her companion gave her a kiss and made her way out. With a small lollop of her hand the woman indicated to Kim the empty seat beside her and invited him to sit down. He thanked her with a nod. Closer to her, he could smell Vicks Inhaler. He noticed, with a surreptitious sideways glance, that the bottom of her nose was red, probably from the chafing of too many paper handkerchiefs. There was something so comforting about this affecting woman having a common cold. They drank their pints next to each other in silence.

When she had finished hers, she stood to leave. A corner of her mackintosh was trapped under Kim's thigh. He made an apologetic move to free it and she smiled by way of a thank you. It was a smile which appeared to linger, as if she was on the cusp of wanting to say something. Kim waited during that transient moment, mildly on edge with hope, yet she didn't say a word. Instead, smiling at him still, she passed him and manoeuvred her way out from behind the table. He himself might have said something then – What was her name? Did she know of a place he could stay tonight? – but he hesitated too long, she was gone.

The landlord called time, and Kim was shaken seriously into addressing the fact he had nowhere to sleep. He finished his last spittle and slop of beer and sat holding his redundant glass, its insides obscured with a cream foam like lace curtains in the front-room windows of a nosy neighbourhood. He looked about him and saw that nobody else appeared to be alone. The whole pub, still, was populated with friends in animated groups of three or four or more, and couples within those groups, whether man and wife; a giddy pair whose night beckoned with sexual if not romantic possibility; or just two best mates, some keeping themselves to themselves, others together sizing up their chances of even unfulfilling encounters. A few gave him poor-lonely-bastard looks, looks which on principle he had never allowed himself to be floored by in the past, but which now, with the winning woman gone, and without a bed to go to, seemed all too poignant and excruciating.

He stood up and walked out into the empty night.

# 8

Yesterday a pigeon flew into my chest, just below the neck, with a thud against my breastbone like a clod of earth against the surface of a coffin.

It all happened so fast, its scaly claws frantically skid-marking my skin, its ghastly feathers wildly brushing my hair, its germy beak diseasing my cheek. I screamed, and fell to the ground. It was in the High Street outside a photographic shop on the corner of the narrow lane leading to Oriel Square. An elderly couple helped me up. They thought I had been mugged.

I can still hear the pigeon's flapping wings whispering their evil portents. I can still see the watery tapioca jelly of its jerking eye up close to mine. It floats on my retina, to and fro, like the ghost impression of a light bulb flashed on and off in the dark.

Stuff of nightmares.

It was the first time I had been out of the house since Kim had gone to buy ice-cream.

Jack and Dora had forced me. Four eternal days and nights, I had stayed in, after the policemen had left, crusted to the armchair in the lounge like lichen. The way I stared at the telephone, I might have been a girl, newly engaged, who can't keep her eyes off her new ring, inanimate node, miraculously imbued, pulsating, with the resonance of human emotion and myth.

During those four days I devoured the checklist of all possible emotions in the circumstances. Anger came, and went. But for a few hours there I was shouting at him in my head, all the things under the sun. How dare he just leave me like this? Us? Did all those years count for nothing? I swore at him like a woman being ground by the pains of labour. Was it all a fucking lie, all along? Was he so fucking, fucking selfish he could do to us what anyone in their right minds would think twice before doing to their worst enemy? I told him, in my head, that if he were to walk through that door, I'd tell him to fuck right off back again whence he came, he had destroyed this family, the thing which for all our years together he had purported to hold most sacred. If he thought I was ever going to fucking forgive him for this, he had another thought coming. Etcetera. I got a lot off my chest, in my head, as it were. I didn't mean it, of course. Or, rather, I did, very much so, at the time, but the time only lasted an hour or two. I despised myself a little for knowing that were he ever to come back through that door, I would welcome him, not turn him away. Feeling any others would have had more sense, and more strength, and secretly ashamed, I tried for about fifteen minutes, to hate him; failed, abjectly; gave up the idea as a lost cause. I couldn't be as wanton with our past, and my love for him, as self-protection might have advocated. So I sunk back to all the other emotions, less animate but more compelling: vain hope, lost love, mute despair.

I was tepid-sweating, and unwashed. Because I had barely moved, a muslin of dead skin still veiled my body, no means of sloughing off. Beginning to itch. Hair in clumps on the scalp. A mildew dankness behind the backs of my knees, underarm. Normally meticulous in my ablutions, then, I couldn't care less. For all their pleadings, my son and my best friend couldn't winkle me from my spot, except when I needed the toilet, but I was back there, afterwards, quick as a rat.

They told me, kindly, I wasn't doing myself any good, that adhering myself to the phone wasn't going to bring Kim home any sooner. They brought me my favourite tomato soup still bubbling thickly in the bowl like a foetus's kicks. Heightened senses, I could smell the vacuumed metal of the tin it had come from, and pushed it away in disgust. 'You must eat,' they both told me. One of those things people say, straight out of the stock of platitudes that roll at the first sign of illness or disaster. They were being concerned, good. I explained I'd rather be kicked in the breast with a hobnail boot than endure the weakest whiff of food.

After four days, Dora said that enough was enough. She came in before work as she did every morning following Kim's disappearance, and informed me plumply that I was not to let myself get like this, this wasn't the strong Sylvie she knew, I was to have a bath and some air, to start constructively to help the police find Kim, and to help myself.

She took me in hand, led me upstairs and ran me a bath with frivolous bubbles, washed me. The drops of water and the tears merged, same temperature. I couldn't be sure for a fact I was crying.

I agreed to go out only if Jack stayed behind for the phone. Not that it was exactly effervescing with calls. The police had telephoned once a day to say that they were continuing with their inquiries, doing their utmost. The only hard information they had come up with was that, when questioned, the man in Barnett's, a Mr Strachan, had answered that he had seen Dr Black on the relevant night. A regular customer, whom the shopkeeper could positively identify because Kim had bought his *Guardian* there for many years, he had hovered over the freezer cabinet, so far as he could recall, but had left empty-handed. Kim had been sitting on the wall outside when Strachan had closed up shop. Sitting on the wall. I said to the policeman, Whatever for? Whatever explanation could there be for that? There was no guessing. The witness said he had been friendly enough, apparently, they'd engaged in a little chat on the forecourt about nothing in particular – they'd agreed getting up in the night and early mornings was a struggle – and Kim hadn't seemed noticeably distracted, though of that Strachan couldn't be sure. Stupid man. Wasn't it an omission not to have put to Kim, out of downright courtesy if nothing else (basic curiosity for starters), what on earth he was doing there, on that wall, in such cold? Clearly not, for nor could he be sure, when he had parted from him, what the doctor had been intending to do, where he had been intending to go, he'd said nothing to that effect, and it hadn't occurred to him to ask. It was a cold night, he had imagined he couldn't have wanted to stay out for long. I don't give a fig for his imaginings.

When they rang yesterday the police reminded me to inform our bank manager that Kim had gone missing in order that he might alert me to any unusual transactions in unexpected places. Other than that, nothing. The telephone was bizarrely inert when I was staring at it so rigorously during those dragging hours – each one like another stretch on the rack. The news had obviously travelled round my colleagues and friends. People are bad enough if someone they know suffers a bereavement. I'm one of

138

them, I cover my cowardice and embarrassment and inability to call with the excuse that the person 'probably doesn't want to be disturbed at a time such as this', when actually I know fine well a friendly voice is all-important. And if someone's nearest and dearest goes missing! Then, it seems, a collective rigor mortis of articulation prevails, resulting in a dormant telephone, a marked lack of letters, and a redundant doorbell. Their moribund silence, it's the choppy icing on the chill cake of loneliness.

If his dad did ring while I was out, I told Jack, I wasn't going to have him getting the answering machine. I said I wanted to go for a walk on my own.

'Best if I stay with you, love,' Dora had said. I don't know if she thought I was going to throw myself under the bus to Blackbird Leys. I insisted I was OK, in fact I became quite cross.

We struck a bargain. She'd drive me into town, on her way to work, and I'd walk home alone.

The city was glistening with people: a businessman with a briefcase running as if under fire; a girl greeting a friend with that inimitable, teenage extravagance of gesture; a mother with a pushchair squashing her forehead against the hostile glass of a smart shop's window, defeat of hope betrayed in the very back-view set of her shoulders; the pinkish puff of an old lady's pet appearing to skim the pavement like a dustball; an elderly road-sweeper with a neat barrow trying with his harsh brush to smooth limp and sticky leaves along a sodden ground, his grubby neck brightened by the day-glo stripe of his uniform as if by a buttercup. These were the obvious city vignettes which I'd so craved when deprived of them during my melancholy nocturnal sojourn with Stephen. Now, though, I felt ambivalence towards their very banality. They were comforting, continuing as they did to persist despite my broken world; but they were depressing too because they brought into relief the very extremity of my own circumstances. Life must go on, I was saying to myself as I stared out of Dora's windscreen, of course it must, and thank God it does; and yet at the same time I was feeling a notional resentment that it was doing just that, despite me, and with an almost obscenely tactless disregard for my smarting sensibilities.

We parked some way from the centre and walked to Boots

together. Dora wanted to give me some non-prescription calming tablets, or what she called anxiety suppressors. I said the only anxiety suppressor that would do me any good was Kim's return. Anything other would be useless. She insisted that I at least try them, and I headed into the shop with her.

We passed the islands of shiny make-up and gilded lotions, outsize display bottles filled not with real scent but coloured water. Women behind the counters looked serious, their faces a volcanic landscape of foundation, powder and rouge. One tear and it would be as lava billowing down an ashy mountainside. These weren't the type of women who could afford an upset.

Dora led me through skincare and past feminine hygiene towards the pharmacy area. I had the impression people might be looking at me, accusingly, as if I had been the one to drive him away, but of course they were far too intent on which computer-generated conditioner to choose, and whether either a cream or a gel would be most officious in driving the piles from their bums.

Dora sat me down on the chair near the neat lay-out of her more basic wares and went into her drugged-up back room, with its trellis of shelves and piles of little boxes, each with a grown-up name and efficient expiry date but no clue as to its contents' confidential purpose. I had some minutes to take in the range of Nurofen, cough pastilles, and Germoline on offer out front. I couldn't help noticing that the gossamer condoms came in sizes extra large, jumbo, and mega-jumbo as opposed to a straight small, medium and large (a good marketing ploy – was there a man in the world who would willingly buy a condom labelled small?). I fell to wondering about sex with strangers, new lovers, perhaps potent with Aids; the circumstances, so removed from my own, where condoms, size immaterial, were not only on the agenda but were so apocalyptically essential. I asked myself if I was destined, condom or no condom, ever to have sex again. If it wasn't with my husband, it certainly wasn't to be with any other man. An untimely widowhood of lonely nights sprung out before me, fast unfurled under my eyes and nose like one of those paper coils which children blow from a whistle at parties: same screech, same drama. First time it hit me, there in Boots, five days after Kim closed the front door behind him: perhaps no more sex for the rest of my life. Up until that moment, between the brief

140

respites brought about by hope, and during every contraction of despair, it was the abstract absence I had mourned – the love, the companionship – which, were Kim himself never to walk back through that door, I knew I would never find again, wouldn't want to. Yet now, amongst the packets of Nicorettes, bottles of Pepto Bismol, and tubes of KY Jelly, the throb of certain sex went out like a lost aircraft on a radar screen. Since my experiences on all those dismal couches, since the very moment I met Kim, I have never had to worry about where my next bout of sex is coming from. I've never slept with another man since we met, never wanted to, and I couldn't imagine it now. In it there would be such paucity of comfort, such a cruel inversion of purpose. I shiver at the thought of an alien smell; alien fit; functional, disingenuous, alien love.

Rather no sex, than sex with anyone but Kim. Men suppose women to be scatty with their favours; they underestimate their capacity, single desire sometimes, to be Fort Knox faithful for ever, even after the horse has bolted. I was pondering this, sitting on the chair near the leaflets for a new method of contraception involving miniature traffic lights, when Dora returned in her white coat, not dissimilar to the one Kim used to wear as a junior doctor in Belfast. She handed me a small box of herbal pills. I thanked her and promised I would take a couple when I arrived home.

Outside, above the street, sagged a grey duvet of sky. People at bus stops were twitching in the cold, tapping blood-spent feet on ruthless pavements, heavy shopping bags forging welts across their freezing fingers. I scrutinised the crowds, the only consolation for chipping myself off from the telephone's side, perchance to spot his face amongst their faces. I hesitated my way towards the High Street, eyes as alert as an insect's with rapid, multi-faceted focusing. I must have glanced at hundreds of faces, determined not to let pass a single one before considering it, and rejecting it as not the one I wanted it to be. It was slow headway I made. But, truth be told, my eyes didn't alight upon a single figure who for a second caused my heartbeat to falter. The cliché is that one spots the back of someone's neck, with its unique fingerprinting of hair against collar, one bustles after it through the crowd, dodging strangers, stepping on toes, panting apolo-

141

gies, careless rushing, shouting the name, reaching the person at last, them turning, and finding their face is one distorted into an Elephant Man monstrosity, not because it is deformed, or even ugly, simply because it's not the person one thought it was, one wanted it to be, and its very physiognomy encapsulates the perversion of disappointment.

There were young blokes, I saw, with engorged biceps and defiance slashed across their whole bodies; there were old men with shocked spines and watery images of the War playing yet in the flickering of their hazard-light eyes; there were men in their thirties and forties, polished shoes, smacks of misguided after-shave stalking their every step, mortgage wrinkles just beginning to cut in deep, mid-life crises pending. There wasn't one man like my Kim.

Turning into the High Street, I pressed on with my task, mind taut with concentration. I passed an old-fashioned tobacconist and The Body Shop but was too preoccupied to be tickled by their emanating, conflicting smells, one sour, one sweet. I was watching not only the pedestrians, but also peering through the windows of cars chugging laboriously, devilishly, in the traffic. In an old Ford Fiesta, a dead-ringer for Sally Winston, but it couldn't have been her because she lost her licence. Further on, one of the magistrates who hears a lot of my cases was coming out of the NatWest Bank. He is imaginative in his judgements, but brusque to the point of rudeness. Shy, some say, which makes me see red, as if that excuses the behaviour of an adult of privilege and learning! I didn't fancy one of his grudging hellos, nor did I want to be made to feel stupid for the very fact of my unfortunate existence, so I quickly veered from his line of eye contact, a figment in the shop window nearest to me suddenly proving irre-sistible. When he had safely gone, I turned cautiously and started once more to survey strangers.

Rarely had I observed them so closely, except those easy times when I used to drive to collect Kim from the airport, pitch up way too early, and install myself in my own, personal viewing gallery. Not the balcony where people go to see planes taking off and landing, but the hall where their passengers would pass through, namely Heathrow's Arrivals – happiest spot in England.

About once or twice a year Kim would go – goes, (my callous-

142

ness with tenses reveals the little respect I have left for hope) – away for a three-day conference or on a week-long specialised medical course, (only occasions we were ever apart for more than a few hours). On the day he was travelling home I would go to Arrivals at least an hour before his plane was due to land. I'd buy myself a drink, never a paper; stand at the barrier, senses fizzing with the anticipation of his emerging from the baggage hall and customs, seeing him casting quick searching glances along the line of waiting crowds, spotting me, face lighting up, us hastening towards each other, hugging; his smell, the set of his body against mine as erotic as the first time I sampled it at that fortuitously over-populated party in Stranmillis. I'd build up to these valuable moments of greeting, of exaggerated togetherness, via the irresistible process of observing others enjoy theirs. What I'd do was keep an eye on the arrivals screens, gulping with enviable places and flashing facts – 'Paris AF 635; Expected 16.10; flash; Landed 16.05; flash; Baggage in Hall'. I'd try to guess not only from which flights those passengers streaming through the automatic doors came, but also which patient individual or group in the now familiar crowd each would pick out for his or her delectation. Travellers appeared either with a perplexingly large amount of luggage, piled high on wayward trolleys; or a sinisterly small amount, perhaps one bag just big enough to hold a murder weapon but nothing so humane as a roll-mop of pyjamas. There was virtually no guessing, and that was part of the fun of it, who would reserve their smiles, their screeches, and hold out their arms to whom. If the man of little luggage, possible murderer and loveless creature that he appeared to be, was, to my mind, almost certainly heading for the Brylcreemed chauffeur holding a hitch-hiker's sign saying Mr Cholmondeley, you could bet your bottom dollar I'd be wrong. He'd be the one laying claim to the fetching wife with see-through eyelashes, and the duet of Miss Pears daughters with happy poppies on their girly dresses, and an excruciatingly cute way of neighing, 'Daddy!' Very occasionally, like Pelmanism, I could match the pairs. The waiting girl with grubby knees, labourer's boots, and skirt made out of material reminiscent of dragonfly wings, was certain to single out and proffer a grungy kiss to the emerging youth, all Goa grime, tie-dye enthusiasms and dreadlocks as matted, as dense, as underlay;

143

and sure enough she would. But while the guessing game was part of the pleasure, the majority of it was in simply witnessing the joy of family and friends coming together. An old widow with salon-stiff hair, vivid complexion, and fingers gnarled as root-ginger, miraculously lifting young grandchildren who, in their excitement, are letting go of their Mighty Mice and smudging her dead-petal cheeks with kisses; a lover, whose nervous eyes while waiting had swivelled against improbable detection, suddenly, due to the ecstasy of spotting her married man, feeling temporarily unshackled, throwing caution to the wind, brazenly clawing him, marking the territory, fleetingly, as her own.

I feel almost ashamed to admit to the rapture these scenes would kindle in me. Such a pastime, completely free (except, perhaps an extra couple of pounds for the short-term car park), might seem inane in its innocence and sentimentality. And yet, I think it served as an uncomplicated counter to my work. On any given day I witness so much bluster and bombast, so much misery and hatred, it was always heartening to spend time awaiting Kim in Arrivals viewing the flip-side of despair, reminding myself it did exist. Of course, every night I came home, his affectionate and loving presence was proof enough. But to see others as happy as us was affirmation that we weren't alone, that I wasn't making it up, that there were people capable of loving each other, or at least managing to give the impression that they did so, after all.

So, anyway, in less benign circumstances, I was watching all the individuals on the High Street so intensely that, as far as pigeons were concerned, my eye was off the ball. I was nudging past Morris's Photographic, determined not to let go from my sight a single face, and a poisonous pigeon rammed into me with all the rubbery, cawing, brittle feathered menace of an horrific mythical creature.

I lay on the ground for a few seconds with my arms clutching my face to blank my eyes, hands cemented over my ears to numb the flustered sound of frightened flight. Every muscle in me was tense. The cold of the pavement permeated my hair and the back of my heavy scalp where it pressed the stone's hard surface was bandaged with an anti-halo of headache.

'Are you all right, dear?' It was an old man's voice which trem-

144

bled through to me. Tentatively I released my arms from my head, opened my eyes to a shot of harsh sky and the close-up of a kindly face the skin of which hung loosely from its skull as if about to drop away like colourless, gloopy cake mixture from the sides of an upturned bowl.

He and his wife helped me to sit upright. As I did so tears ran from my eyes without crying, like one of those dolls which can be made to weep drops of water when tipped a certain way but eerily makes no sound.

'Did they hurt you?' the woman asked. 'Looks like they scratched you on your neck.'

With their withered limbs the old couple helped me to my feet, and brushed wet pavement grit from my sweatshirt and jeans. Their concern made me feebler of mind than I might have been had they, along with everybody else in the street, just stared at my slumped figure, no more than a brief candle of curiosity flickering, given me a wide berth, and stepped by. But their unsolicited kindness in the dust of indifference was affecting. I wept on.

'The scoundrel who did this to you didn't snatch your handbag as well, did he?' the man asked, custard-creams on his breath. His old-fashioned term, and his hand, textured like Japanese rice paper, holding mine, could not calm me. I managed to tell him that I'd had no handbag and that I hadn't been mugged. I felt ashamed, as if, yearning any human kindness, I'd fooled them on purpose, tricked them with my devious ploy. And they were close to finding out the truth, turning their backs in exasperation. Another silly woman with nothing better to do but to toy with their venerable sympathies.

I told them, pathetically, it was a pigeon. The man, who had a flat cap and the musty air of a dank garden shed, might have been a pigeon-fancier, the type to nurture the homing kind in his back yard, to give them names like Petal and Charlotte, and to call them his ladies. Certainly, his expression was of pure puzzlement, as if unable to comprehend such a melodramatic reaction to a brief brush with one of God's creatures.

'Your handbag wasn't taken then,' he said, at a loss but not unsympathetically, 'that's one good thing.' His wife, whose pale mackintosh matched her blue-grey hair, nudged him and told him to hush. She uttered the dread word phobia, and said, 'There, there, poor dear, I quite understand, nasty, nasty things, like flying rats they are, a menace to us all. Your poor nerves. Can we take you across to the coffee shop for a bun?'

This was the difference between the generations, I thought. Forget the fact it was old people helping me in the first place; it was the notion of a bun – a bun as an effective tranquilliser, somehow, which at once annoyed and touched me. Annoyed me because it was so obviously grossly inadequate; touched me because the couple were speaking from a simpler era, perhaps, when a naive bun with a cartoon-character tongue of sugar-pink icing was just the ticket. While I was more in mind of a valium, I was at the same time imbued with a foolish nostalgia for a time when communities apparently functioned, and their sweet balm for all trauma was a nice, iced bun.

Jack was waiting for me with a bank statement which had arrived in the post while I was out. Don't ask me how I made my way home. It was addressed to Dr and Mrs Kim Black.

It is a joint account we have. Always has been. It started when we were in Belfast, at Ulsterbank. It seemed logical to pool our paltry weekly assets. Whoever had the money at the time could see us both through. When we got married, though we were earning, it seemed even more right that everything we each had should belong to the two of us. Dora and Ron have the same arrangement, but we have friends – married couples, live-in partners – who are completely separate financially. They go out for a meal and split the bill. Once we were in the Opium Den with the Dawsons. When the bill came Francis promised Pat if she paid his share that time he would remember to pay hers the next. I have to admit I found that shocking; there was something alien to me, couples owing money, being indebted to each other. Dora agrees with me, and together we marvel at other people's peculiarities. Of course, Mackenzie thinks I'm 'soft in the head', that I should keep my own money away from Kim's and to myself. 'I'm going to guard my financial independence from any man like I guard my life,' she declares. Behind all her shyness, Mackenzie is very forthright of opinion. I told her, if you love a man you might want to share everything with him, even money. Alien concept.

146

'Sorry to say this, Mum, but sometimes I'm ashamed to have you as my mother!'

'It's easier,' I insist (we have this conversation quite often). I'm not offended. Our disputes, for the most part, always retain a light-hearted tone.

'It's not about *easy*,' she counters. 'It's about principle.'

Thinking back yesterday to my conversations with Mackenzie, I felt uneasy. The days had passed and I still hadn't rung to tell her that Kim had never returned with the ice-cream. Every time it occurred to me or Jack to do so we had put it off. He kept saying to me that there was no point, his dad was sure to be back soon.

'We don't want to worry her unnecessarily,' he'd say. 'It'll disrupt her studies. He'll be home, and then it'd all've been for nothing.'

'So if he does come back, should she never know?' I'd asked him on one occasion, maybe yesterday, maybe the day before; I don't know. Time has lost its symmetrical and formal categorisation, which I always used to visualise neatly in my head as the pages of my desk diary and the face of my watch. It has become a dense, inscrutable mass, abstract and amorphous.

'Depends on why he went,' Jack had answered, and I realised my son was a wiser man than me. I realised, too, that I had no, no, no idea why, why my husband had gone. Why? That small word was torturing me like a nocturnal mosquito closing in on the ear with its relentless, ticklish zizz.

Jack sat me down at the kitchen table.

'D'you want me to open it for you?'

I shook my head appreciatively. It must have been the first time I was opening a bank statement and worrying about something other than the overdraft. The familiar sheet of NatWest pink paper slipped out. Jack was standing with his hand on my shoulder, staring at it as hard as I was. Together we glanced down the entries.

'Anything you don't recognise, anything at all?' he asked. I could feel his breath on my neck same as I had Kim's when he'd checked on the haddock the night he went out.

Marching across the statement were computerised facts and figures in boldest black – indisputable dates, cheque numbers,

Switch transactions (in various shops like Sainsbury's and Boots) – all testimonies to the ruthlessness of banal domestic spending. An inelegant pattern of letters, Toys R Us, sprung out at me, beside the date 4 Nov, and the figure £15.63. I remembered all too well what that was for. Some purple and grey plastic monster featuring a hunchback, boils, chicken claw feet, and eyes as brutal as sectarianism; so ugly I had carried it to the till with a kind of squeamish despair. Kim's nephew had put in a special request for it, for his birthday. I had bought it, in my lunch hour after the family conference with the Winstons. The day Kim left. I hadn't even had a chance to show him what he was giving little Gareth, when he went out for the ice-cream.

'Are you OK, Mum?'

I read some impersonal message from the bank at the bottom of the first page with the latest, astonishing, interest rates for borrowing. No inclination, even, for indignation. I turned over. Top of the second page: 4 Nov The Taj Mahal CP £13.75.

'What's that?' I asked. 'I don't recognise that.'

'It's the Indian in the Cowley Road. You know, near Tesco's.'

'Yes, I know and, well, they must've got it wrong. Bank's made a mistake. I haven't been to that place for weeks. Last time I went was with Dora when Dad was at that conference in Stockport, the summer some time, July or August.'

Jack sat down beside me, and opened a liver-spotted banana. He ate the lot in no more than three bites. It was either his youthful hunger, or his affection for his mother which made him devour it so rapidly. Either way, he laid aside the soft skin, flaccid as a spent condom, and put his hand back on my shoulder as if guilty of his self-indulgent interruption.

'The fourth's the day he left. Closest I got to the place that day was driving past it to and from work.'

'So Dad must've gone there then for lunch.'

'Indian food gives him indigestion, Jack, you know that. Whenever you or Mac suggest a takeaway, he usually goes for a chippy or a Chinese. Anyway, he doesn't go out for lunch, week-days, more than once in a blue moon.'

'Are you saying the bank's fucked up then? I mean, it's a bit of a coincidence, isn't it, a joint we all know in the Cowley Road? I bet you it's not a mistake. Has to have been Dad. If not at

148

lunchtime, then maybe in the evening.'

'Not possible. He was having supper here.'

'But he didn't, though, remember.' Jack's voice was very quiet, almost a whisper, as if he was reluctant to make the point.

'I was cooking it. Whole reason he went out was to buy ice-cream to round our supper off. He's hardly going to think, "Oh, I can't find any ice-cream for me and Sylvie, I think I'll go out for a solitary curry instead." It's not logical, Jack. Either the bank made a mistake, or someone stole his wallet and used it for a night out.'

'And spent just thirteen quid of someone else's money? I don't mean to be unkind, Mum, I love you to bits, but that's hardly the way of the world.'

'It's going to take more than that to convince me your dad had his dinner in the Taj Mahal that night.'

'Why don't we get the bank to check his signature, eh? Obviously, he was meeting someone. That's the most likely scenario. While he was out at the shops he suddenly forgot he had a plan to meet someone there for a meal.'

'What, and not called me? No. He never not calls me, love. The slightest thing. He calls to say even when he's only going to be five minutes late. He calls to say, "I'm ringing to say I've nothing to say, only wanted to hear the sound of your voice." Any excuse. Between patients, whenever he can catch a moment. You know that. Sometimes it's just to ask me how I am. Sometimes he rings to tell me he loves me. Other times he rings for no reason at all. A person who rings for no reason is hardly going to fail to ring when there's a thumping good one. Even if he had suddenly remembered he was meeting someone for a curry in the Taj Mahal, which is so unlikely I'd've put it down as virtually impossible, he'd have made it his business to phone me before he'd sat down.'

'It might've slipped his mind, Mum, just this once?'

'No, not even just this once. He wouldn't've been able to concentrate. I know Kim. It's the way he works. Thoughtful. He couldn't do a thing like that, just carry on the conversation, knowingly have me worrying myself out of my mind. That's the preserve of men who like psychologically to torture women. I've known those sort. Your father isn't one of them. You know that.'

149

As I spoke, Jack was kneading my shoulder. I stopped talking. He hugged me. Had I been a girl and the object of such sympathy, I would have longed for him. As his mother, I just ached with the love of my son. I hugged him back. 'Anyway, who?' I asked into his neck. Jack smelt of Kim, same personal smell, savoury otherwise indefinable, irresistible. 'We've rung round every friend we can think of. Who'd he've been meeting?'

'If I knew that, Mum—'

'It's so unlike him.' I paused. 'Even if it were a goddamn lover,' I added in a whisper of painful deliberation, judging my son well old enough to bear my bleakest thoughts, 'he'd have called me.'

Jack didn't respond, as if even he could now consider the possibility that his father was seeing another woman.

'It gets worse,' I told him. 'I didn't believe it could. Will you call the police again for me, love, I can't face talking to a living soul.'

The police acted swiftly yesterday. Within minutes, literally, of Jack telling them about the Taj Mahal entry on the bank statement, they were down there carrying out their investigations. Two of the waiters were able to confirm that a male customer had dined alone at the restaurant on the night of the fourth. One remembered the man particularly because he had looked so cold. The waiter had been prompted to recommend the hottest curry on the menu and, although the customer had politely declined, he had nonetheless started the meal with his coat around him. They were shown the photograph. Yes, the waiters said, that was definitely him.

My first reaction was that they had both got it wrong, they had mistaken Kim for somebody else. Obviously they were unreliable witnesses. They must have tens of customers a night and could not possibly be expected to remember every one who passed through their doors. People didn't come that observant.

Yet this morning the police rang to tell Jack before he went to work that they had traced several customers who had been at the restaurant that night. One woman had been able to recall a man giving up his table to her and her friend. She had noticed the man's nose was still red from the cold outside, which was quite something after a curry. In fact she had been rather embarrassed at how accurately she was able to describe him – black coat, soft black trousers, short brown hair with only a dash of grey, quite scruffy. She'd said it was both because she had hungrily watched him as he had finished his meal, hoping he wouldn't linger, and then her friend had told her that she found him rather attractive so she had looked at him again and scrutinised him even more closely. Together they had speculated whether or not he was a widower but decided he was too young and that he was probably from out of town. Anyway, the police had gathered enough evidence to inform me conclusively that it was Kim they had seen. I mightn't have believed them still – any number of men might have been wearing a black coat – but one of the woman's details confounded my scepticism. No one gets a red nose in the cold like Kim. His solitary curry was a fact, then.

So where do we go from here?

I am back in my armchair in the sitting room, bored of the carpet and mantelpiece; the dull set of the window, its limited patch of view (three houses, opposite, like ours; a tree, a street lamp, and a stream-line of indistinguishable cars). I've never looked at these things long enough in the past for them to bore me. But I have stared at the colours and shapes in – and just out of – this room so much these past few days, and so hard, it is as if they have been dry-mounted onto my retina like a photograph onto card. I feel boxed in by these lines – walls, ceiling, skirting board, shelves. Only I'm unable, unwilling to move. Soon, perhaps tonight, I will go out again, hunting. If I'm allowed.

Last night I made Jack baby-sit the phone and Dora take me to the Taj Mahal. Not to eat, of course, last thing on my mind. To sit, to watch, to wait, to clutch at straws. It was a disappointing sojourn. Two hours or so, I insisted, we stayed, although my place setting remained steadfastly empty throughout. Dora picked at a cochineal-coloured curry and eked out the minutes by eating, separately almost, every succulent grub of rice. How could she have been expected to enjoy her meal in the presence of such a desolate companion? Perhaps she, like me, was thinking of the last time we came, Kim not missing, when we had laughed away, and my mouth, like hers, had been watering at the sight of this food. Now its very smell, to me anyway, was powerfully

151

emetic. The only thing that prevented me from needing to rush to the lavatory was my more powerful obsession with keeping watch. As loyal Dora half-heartedly made her way through her supper, my dogged attention remained ten feet away. Entering the restaurant I had surveyed and dismissed everyone in the room – resentful of them not because of who they were, but because of who they weren't – before settling at our table. Then I had immediately focused on the door and fixed my eyes there, not even taking them from it to look at the waiter to tell him I wanted nothing. Each time it opened, the nylon camisole hanging over its window shimmered as if in some form of erotic response to its flirtatious bell. I shimmered, too, with currents of hopeless hopes sparked and extinguished. All sorts of people, but not one of them Kim. When Dora walked me home I was tempted to keep an eye on the passers-by but could only look at the pavement. I had binged on enough disappointment.

I was extremely upset when we arrived home. Dora and Jack hadn't wanted me to go in the first place, but for the time being they are scared, at least to some extent, not to indulge my despair. They don't know what I might do if they don't, and I am willing to exploit their fears. Today, I wish to wallow in it here in my armchair. Grant me this just a little bit longer.

Today is Day Five. It is a quarter to two in the afternoon. Although time seems to have merged into this waste-disposal mass, I could quote the very number of hours it is since Kim has gone, but will refrain.

All through last night, endless night, I was devising explanations for his lone dinner at the Taj Mahal. You cannot know what I came up with, so outlandish were some of them, but such is my desperation for answers.

You think you know someone.

Fuck it, sometimes we'd be sitting together in the car, in this room, wherever, it doesn't matter, and we hadn't either of us breathed a word for hours on end, watching telly, reading a book, or just easy silence. Then, all of a sudden, no prompting, at the same moment we'd both voice the very same thought. It'd happen even when we were apart, prompting each of us to phone at identical times. Perhaps there's nothing so unusual in that, but it was the frequency of it which seemed to preclude mere coincidence, and the fact that so often it wasn't just an obvious domestic matter. The children tease us in sing-song voices, they say we have this corny telepathy because we were so 'in lurrve'. It's fairly defeating me now. Connection seems to have gone completely dead.

In fact, one of the reasons I fell in love with Kim was that I was aware from the very beginning that he was someone I wanted properly to get to know, and almost certainly could.

I'm not saying that I believed I could ever read him like a book, or that I viewed him as some kind of pushover. He is a complex man. The challenge was to unravel and define those complexities. I'd say I came about as close as one human being can get to understanding another. Certainly, one of the most flattering things Kim ever said to me was that I was the very first person with whom he could be himself. Before he met me, he said, he hadn't believed there existed a man or woman alive with whom he could be himself. From a young age he found his own imperfect way of dealing with this.

At the farm he was the stupid one, according to his father and brothers, not because he had problems at school (he didn't, far from it), but because he was slow with a challenging piece of fencing and clod-handed with the manly workings of a tractor. They didn't interest him. He was better with the sheep (some of his earliest patients) – deft with shears, and a mild presence. The fact that he didn't frighten them was seen almost as a weakness. The more so that they seemed actively to respond to him. It stood to reason, as far as his father and brothers were concerned, that Kim, like the sheep, was a stupid bugger with wool for brains.

How they treated him sometimes, it's a joke, like something out of a melodramatic Victorian novel, or an exaggerated sample case study in a child welfare manual. Caricature textbook stuff, it was, on how families can best go about inflicting psychological damage on their kids. Of course, in many ways he had an idyllic childhood – countryside, freedom, never wanting for a meal on the table. In my line of business I've seen a lot who've had it worse than he did, but it upsets me to think of some of the stuff he went through. It wasn't relentless, he remembers happy times, periods – usually during summer when his father blossomed – of familial harmony. Still, it is a wonder Kim's turned out so well-balanced and sane. Perhaps he's his mother to thank for that. Faith was pretty ineffectual in a household containing a wilful husband and two headstrong older boys, but she was ever-loving. It was David's attitude to him, during his bleaker moods especially, that was so strange.

David's sheep were his livelihood and, deep down, he harboured a sort of grudging fondness for them. But outwardly he bestowed upon them a contempt which fell only just this side of cruelty, and just this side of how he occasionally behaved towards Kim. He felt threatened by a son who wasn't afraid to show his affection for the sheep. This meant that at times he revealed less respect for Kim than he did for his dogs which, even when hard at work herding, always maintained what David viewed as a decent decorum. His dogs weren't soppy animal-lovers like Kim: they kept a supercilious distance from their wretched charges.

Mark and Craig, prompted by their father's lead, also mocked Kim, but went further. When David was out of earshot they called their younger brother a sheep-shagger. Looking back now, Kim tends to see the funny side, but at the time it cut deep. Even that, though, he felt, wasn't as bad as being called stupid. All the names under the sun didn't get to him as much their calling him stupid.

He was forced to make the decision, as young as five or six, simply to keep his trap shut, not to say anything at all, that way it would reduce to a minimum the chances of his saying something that would invite ridicule. He's made up for it since, he's not remotely short of chat these days, but right till he left home, he barely spoke. I can barely believe it.

'Lost your tongue, son?' his father would ask. 'Lost your tongue, have you, lad?'

Except with his mother. As she worked in the house – doing the laundry, making up the fires, scrubbing the masculine splatters of sticky piss from the underside of the lavatory seat – he would follow her everywhere entertaining her like a portable radio, telling her his ideas, his hopes, his dreams. She was full of encouragement and stories. Sometimes, when the others were way out in the fields, she'd take a rest, and the two of them would lean on the kitchen table with big mugs of tea and lumps of cake and long conversations. I can just picture it. They'd stuff as much talk in as they could before being interrupted once more and retreating to silence, fairytale toys coming to life in the nursery when the coast is clear, rushing back to position at the first sound of footsteps outside. These snatched moments alone with Faith were vital to Kim's survival. He lived for them, their gentle but revelatory privacy. He might be stupid, but he felt he knew her better than any of them, even than her peculiarly devoted husband.

'Mummy's boy,' his brothers would say.

'Bollocks, of course,' Kim has told me. 'Just because I could talk to her and not to them. Trying to get a decent conversation out of Dad, especially in his wintry mood, was like trying to light a fire in the rain. And Mark's and Craig's language in those days consisted entirely of bullying and banter. An exchange of ideas or opinions – except opinionated insults – never crossed their lips.' He can laugh about it now.

But after he left home and went to Belfast it took a good year or two before he could talk to anyone else freely – could talk to anyone at all, pretty much. As far as women were concerned, if one tried to chat him up, he thought she was playing some kind of practical joke and that a whole lot of her friends were watching from the corner and laughing. He presumed that if he opened his mouth he would say something ridiculous and people would automatically assume he was a fool. When I met him, he was only just beginning to emerge from this terminal shyness born of his misplaced belief which had him down as thick. When he talked to me during those sessions at Smokey Joe's, I had no idea that he was opening up with me in a way that was unprecedented for him. During those precious, snatched moments with his mother, he came close, but he hadn't been able to be completely himself even then – there had never been enough time. His father and brothers had always been on the warpath, inhibiting him at every turn.

These days Kim is more sanguine than I am about their taunts of stupidity. He has the magnanimity of spirit to put his achievements as a doctor partly down to this early name-calling. He says it fuelled a natural ambition. 'It became my mission to prove them wrong,' he has told me, a thousand times. 'Were it not for

155

that, I mightn't have had the strength to get through medical school, to endure those infernal shifts as a junior doctor. So many times I thought, "I may love medicine but enough is enough, this is inhuman, I'm jacking this in." Then I'd hear the pages of the *Children's Medical Dictionary* Mum had given me for Christmas being ripped up by my brothers and their boyish cries of, "Kim wants to be a doctor but all he is is a thick-o"; them pinning me down on their bed and farting in my face to put me in my place. And I'd remember the hot metal feel of my adolescent face in the guts of a tractor engine and my father's steely voice, when I literally dropped the spanner in the works, telling me I was crap, I was thick, I was goodfornothing. I'd think, fuck them all, I'll show them, if it kills me. It kept me going, it's what got me through. Some ways, they did me a favour.'

We talk about the past a good deal. Kim is a great one for respecting its influence but not placing on it too great a significance.

'You can over-egg that pudding,' he says. 'As an adult you make your own choices.'

We argue this one for hours, so we do. I believe that our pasts shape us irrevocably, that almost everything we say or do is moulded by them, for the rest of our lives. They're the blueprint for who we are.

Kim, as he tells me often enough, reckons that's crap. He owns our pasts play a part but believes that as we grow older we should take responsibility for ourselves. 'You woolly social workers,' he tells me – it drives me mad when he says that, even if it is only teasing – 'you all reckon every bit of blame can be put upon everyone else but the individual concerned. Depression? I was brought up *in a cardboard box*. Oo-er, you were *lucky*, my step-dad beat me with a frying pan when I was three. We all have this stuff. The majority have the resources not to let it persist in the mind, to linger on and *on*. Waste of a life. We have to rise above it, let bygones be bygones. If I'm shy, it might have been triggered by how Dad and Mark and Craig treated me way back, but if I continue to be cripplingly so, then that's my problem here and now. As an adult, I should at least endeavour to find the ability, the resources, to deal with it and combat it. Water under the bridge.'

It doesn't matter how much I tell him of the irreparable harm I see some parents inflicting on their kids in the course of my work, how many screwed-up little characters I see in the making, Kim can't let go of the idea that, despite all the shit thrown at us, we nonetheless have a lot of choice in how we behave and in who we are. He's fought against experiences in his background, admirably, and come off OK. Well, he's privileged in a way. I tell him loads of people don't have the reserves of strength in themselves that he was able to find.

'That *you* enabled me to find, my love,' he reminds me. 'You were the one who helped me become the open book that I am today.' (Kim may be less reserved than he was, but he is no open book, believe me.) 'I admit there's not many have the same luck as I did in finding someone like you to encourage me along. There are good forces in our lives which are as influential as the bad. You in mine.'

He's shrewd enough, he always says something flattering like that which completely wrong-foots me and puts me off my argument. It always ends up with him having me laughing.

Still, it's forever struck me as a funny paradox, his lack of sympathy in respect of people who remain wholly motivated by the wrongs, real or perceived, that were done to them in their pasts; and his boundless compassion for people in general, warts and all.

There are various bemusing aspects, like this one, to Kim's character, but none so grave as they ever make me feel I don't know where I am with him. On the whole they're lovable. The way I see it, they comprise that priceless puzzle of his nature which is all him. His obsession with the news being a fine example.

'I like to know what's going on in the world,' is his rather boring explanation for it. Well, that might spawn a keen interest, but whence did the obsession spring?

'Does it matter?' he asks, and he's got a point. 'You're far more of a riddle, my angel. What about your blessed pigeons?'

I hear him saying those words now, clear as a digital recording, and it does my head in. It causes the repetitious requiem to strike up again inside me – Why, why, why? it goes.

The self-dubbed open book, it seems, has pulled off the greatest riddle of all.

# 9

The car was a shit-hole but it was a lift out of the middle of nowhere.

Even on the black stretch of road Kim had been able to make out its colour, a patchy mustard, except for one wing which had been painted orange with glossy brush-strokes. The whole body-work was covered in sores of raw metal. Half the front bumper was bent out of place and, as the car had slowed up by the verge beside him, it had appeared to idle along the tarmac. Kim had opened the door and climbed into the passenger seat.

A feeble light ebbed from a cloudy bulb above the rear-view mirror. On the floor he could now discern a couple of copies of the local paper grubbily boasting yesteryear's scoops and brittle with age. He squeezed his feet between them; an empty bottle of Lucozade; a confetti of confectionery wrappers; and a crumpled KFC box with a greasy splodge left behind by chicken nuggets, like the imprint in a bed of someone who's died.

'You heading for the city centre,' said the driver, a man of about fifty, more as a statement than a question, and Kim nodded by way of a thank you. 'That's Pat in the back, by the way, take no notice of her.' An ugly mongrel lay on the seat behind slobbering its rubbery chops round a punctured furry ball. The loaded smell of wet dog was hard to ignore. 'How long you'd been waiting?' His Scottish accent was very broad.

'Not long. Ten minutes, thereabouts.'

'Anywhere you want dropped? I'm just going to look in on a friend who lives near the station, and then I'm off home to Hilton.' He glanced at his chunky digital watch. The black hairs on his pudgy hands ran all the way down his fingers stopping only within striking distance of his nails. 'I'm not in any hurry, I suppose.'

'Anywhere'll do, thanks.'

'My wife might have different ideas, of course.' The driver made a tutting sound which was shorthand for, 'Need I say more, mate.' He shifted in his seat, which was covered in a supportive vest of wooden balls. His back appeared to be hurting him. 'You English?'

'Yes.'

'Right.' There was a barely perceptible pause. 'Where d'you stay then?'

'Belfast,' Kim lied.

'Rough place, is that? By the sounds of things. I've not been.'

'Yes, but there's a lot more to it than what's on the news. You never see the normal side of it. Many ways it's a great city.'

'How long've you stayed there then?'

'Since I was a nipper. My dad moved there to work.'

'What doing?' Inevitable question.

'He was what they call a competition winner announcer.' It was the first thing that came into Kim's mind, God knows from where. 'It was in the days before the lottery. Various companies who ran competitions employed him to go round Northern Ireland knocking on doors of people who'd won something, let them know.'

'Joking. Why didn't they tell them by post?'

'I think they appreciated the personal touch. It was a good thing my dad was there. Sometimes they used to faint. The women.'

'You're joking! My wife'll love that.'

'True. Often they needed someone to help them through the shock. They'd crack open the brandies. Always served it in the best glasses. It was a special occasion.'

'That's one happy job.' The driver shook his head in disbelief. His hair was covered in white flecks of paint which looked like fake snow in a Disney film. 'I've not heard of it before. Being the bearer of good news. He must be a very cheerful bloke, your dad. Or was he always pissed off he wasn't getting all this stuff himself? I'd've been. Though I expect a few nice things found their way into your house, didn't they?'

'No, in fact, though I wished—'

'Bet you did!' The man laughed heavily, but then stopped abruptly because of a jab of pain in his back. He took one hand off the wheel to give it a good rub.

'You all right?'

'Agh, it's a fucking pain in the arse. Ignore me. It's been on and off for twenty years, I can't be bothered to think about it any longer. So, your dad, that line of business, he must've got something good when he retired then?'

'A lousy ballpoint pen, if I remember rightly. Can you believe it? But he was over the moon. You were right, they don't come much more cheerful than my dad. He loved meeting all sorts of people, giving them things.'

The man's thoughts were very visibly racing onwards; Kim could see the pleasure in his amiable face. 'What sort of stuff,' he asked, 'cars and TVs?'

'Everything. Dishwashers, foreign travel. Houses, sometimes.' Kim was on a roll. He could make up anything. 'Easy Homes and Persil used to do one, you'd pick up a leaflet alongside the washing machines in Electricity showrooms. All you had to do was answer three simple questions, finish off a sentence, and there was the chance you'd win ten grand for a new house. A lot of money then.'

In one slow movement the driver puffed out his chest and straightened his back for a few seconds. His face squeezed itself, the wrinkles round his eyes momentarily deepening. Then, he bent back into his more natural, deportmentally unsound position. At the same time his lips formed an 'O' from which he puffed a sharp sigh. He was trying to pass it off as an expression of amazement, as opposed to a temporary relief from pain.

'You should get that seen to,' Kim, not taken in, suggested quietly.

The driver realised there was no use pretending anymore. 'Oh, believe you me I have. Plenty. Not that it did me a bleeding ounce of good.'

'No? It should have.'

The driver shook his head. 'Well, it didn't. I've done with doctors, useless buggers the lot of them. Hours I spent in frigging waiting rooms. Then in, out, wham, bam, thank you, ma'am, and I'm still no better off than before I went in. Waste of fucking time, I can tell you.'

'Perhaps you should try a new doctor. They can't all be bad, can they?'

'Oh yes, they can. I tried every doctor there was going. All

160

crap. Quacks. I'm not seeing another ever again, mate. I gave that lark up a long while ago.'

'Where's it hurt?'

'Bottom of my spine. I know what caused it. Painting someone's ceiling and falling off a step-ladder. Years ago. Course, none of the doctors could come up with any kind of cure that worked. I believe there is one, they're just not telling me it. Fuck 'em.'

Kim was on the point of making a suggestion, telling him the kind of person he should try to get to see, but bit his tongue. 'Fair enough,' was all he said.

'Better things to do with my time. Unless one of them wants to suggest my having a beautiful woman walk all over my back in her wee bare feet!'

Kim laughed. 'What about your wife?'

'Are you joking me? Ten Ton Tessie'd polish my spine off for good, and me too very probably.' He laughed. 'What's your name, by the way?' he asked.

The question, so out of the blue, caught Kim off-guard. 'Tim,' he said after a few seconds.

'Nice to meet you, Tim. I'm John. How long you over here for then?'

'I've got some work, hospital portering at Raigmore. See how it goes.'

'Missing them back home though, so you must be. You can't live with them, eh, you can't live without them.' Big grin.

Kim smiled.

'Kids?'

'Six.'

'Aw, three's enough for me,' John told him. 'I had them tie a knot in it. You should try it, mate! I only hope the knot lot are less crap than the spine lot! No wonder you wanted to get away for a bit.'

'No, they're good kids. I lost my job.'

John nodded, and didn't ask the obvious question. 'Here we go, city centre,' he said instead, as if he thought he had already been too inquisitive.

Kim was touched by John's tact. John was a big man, with a rough face and heavy hands. He didn't appear to have the appro-

161

priate physiognomy for tact, the kind of tact which has it on instinct that if a man says he has lost his job you say no more.

'I'll drop you off here, all right?' John pulled up outside the main post office. The street and the nearby square were cold, dark and deserted. 'Will this be any good? Are you close?'

'This'll be fine. Thanks a lot.'

'No problem. I enjoyed talking to you.'

'You too.' Kim smiled and tried the handle. The car door wouldn't open.

'It's a bit stiff from the inside, I'm afraid,' John said. 'Give it a strong shove.'

Kim pushed against it with his arm. No good. And again.

'Harder, mate,' John urged. 'Bloody thing's getting worse.'

His passenger threw his whole upper body against it. At once it flew open, and Kim went with it. He fell out of the car and onto the pavement.

'Christ, mate, I'm sorry,' John said, leaping out himself and rushing round to help pick him up. 'Are you all right?'

'I'm fine,' Kim said, standing up. Although he had always been a fastidious man, it didn't occur to him on this occasion to brush the grit from his coat. 'Absolutely fine.'

'Agh, that's terrible. Well, I suppose I shall have to get my wife to start entering a few competitions. Then maybe a colleague of your dad's'll come visiting with a new car!'

Kim smiled and patted John on the shoulder. His donkey jacket was so thick Kim was anxious he might not feel his friendly gesture. Just in case, he said, 'Safe home.'

'Safe home,' John replied, getting back into the car. As he drove away, out of the window he waved his hairy hand.

Later that night, deep in the night, Kim was skewered by guilt.

After John had driven off, Kim had meandered about the streets of Inverness hoping to hit upon an all-night café where he could stay with a cup of tea till morning. No such luck. Every shop, pub, bar, restaurant, coffee house, and takeaway joint had been locked and barred, the window of each one as black as a coal face. There had been barely any cars – he had seen two, perhaps three, in over half an hour – let alone pedestrians. Even the proverbial stray cat was missing from the scene, failing to make its spooky, glint-eyed progress round the city's bins.

Eventually, in some black back street he had spotted over a small door a bright yellow bulb and a light-box saying, 'A1 Mini-Cabs'. Life. He approached it, circumnavigating the funereal ribbons of piss on the pavement. He bent his head beneath the low threshold and went inside. The stench of stale cigarette smoke wrestled in his nostrils, but was marginally less bitter than that of the layer upon layer of dried-up urine outside. The room was short and narrow, its brick walls yellowed by nicotine, and maddened by biro doodles and graffiti. Running down its length, on the right-hand side, was a plywood counter; opposite it a bench upholstered in brown plastic. Over the door was a tinny box with a grille which vibrated and splurged out almost visible clouds of heat. And that was all, except for a young man with a book of puzzles, a can of Boddingtons, and a jaw like a blood-hound.

'Where do you want to go?' he asked, looking up from his puzzles.

'Nowhere,' Kim replied. 'Do you mind if I just sit here?'

'You don't want a cab?'

'No.'

'You mean you don't want a cab?'

Kim shook his head.

'So fuck off wi'ya then.'

Kim stayed put.

'What did you say you want?'

'Just to sit here a while?'

'I heard the first time.'

'It's freezing out there.'

'You can get a cab home or, as I told you, you can fuck off,' the man said peremptorily, and bent back over his puzzles.

Kim didn't move. After a few moments, the man looked up again. 'Did you not hear what I said? Did I not make it plain enough?' His fingers scrabbled into his packet of cigarettes and pulled one out. While he lit it, he kept his eyes firmly on Kim who continued to linger. 'Are you drunk?' he asked.

'I locked myself out,' Kim explained.

The man kept on staring at him as if trying to puzzle him out. At length he said, 'Fuck it, sit there then, I don't give a shit what you do, long as you don't barf all over my floor.'

Kim sat down silently, grateful for the man's excrement of hospitality. As Tim White, who had nobody, his expectations were modest. Brief friends, like Liz, John, and Mr Kindness, were all that he could hope for. In his increasingly stale clothes, and roughly unshaven, he was hardly an attractive prospect. He was beginning to smell on himself that greased grime smell he had often encountered among his homeless patients, and those from the most dispossessed estates he served, of human being, unwashed and dejected. He sniffed his wrists and thought, it doesn't take long.

For a few minutes he viewed the crude drawings and potted philosophies scrawled on the wall behind him, but they didn't hold his attention for more than a couple of minutes. He started thinking about his lift with his brief friend John. Then it was that he began to experience an uncomfortable guilt. He had wantonly hoodwinked a kind man with some cock and bull story. For no apparent reason.

It didn't, after all, appear to be the case that anyone was looking for him, far as he was aware. He'd been keeping a vague eye out in the papers, but had noticed no reports concerning his disappearance. If no one was looking, which surprised him a little it had to be said, then he had no real need to hide. And yet he was finding himself becoming more and more careful, more and more inclined not to be found. Anonymity was a novelty he was warming to. It was a release from the constricting clothes of identity and responsibility. These were not things he had ever resented – far from it, he had always found them rather appealing – but, finding himself without them prompted that same sort of almost bodily pleasure of swimming naked in the clear green water of a warm, natural pool. The drawbacks were obvious – loneliness, and an awareness of his own cruelty to name but two – yet, for the moment, in a perverse kind of way, he must have been enjoying not being him, not carrying all the clobber he had accumulated over the years. If this was not the case, why then wasn't he able to tell a trusty if casual passer-by his real name, place he lived, and circumstances? He was wanting to prolong the weird pleasure, even if it did mean cruelty to those he loved, unique loneliness, and conning a kindly stranger.

He was too overwhelmed by the extent of his own cruelty to address it now. He neither wanted to, nor could, acknowledge it properly at this point. Not feeling proud of the conning of a stranger was enough to be going on with. In fact, he felt ashamed, as it was, that this had come so naturally. It was a low thing to do, if irresistible. Worse, because John had believed it all – poor bloke had no reason not to – he had been diminished in Kim's eyes. He had taken him for a gullible man. Perhaps even despised him a little for entertaining such bullshit.

Sitting there in A1 Cabs, Kim decided that his motivation had been twofold: this unexpected relish of anonymity which he had so recently and perplexingly discovered, and the sheer audacity of story-telling, seeing if he could get away with it. As a young child he had made up stories with which to amuse his mother as she laboured through her day. Fantasies about the things he had got up to the night before, when the family had gone to sleep. He used to tell her of the places he had gone – the Arabian Desert; Troy; Bethlehem; Culloden; Blackpool. Those he had met and hung out with – King Arthur's knights; Bomber Harris; mermaids and dinosaurs; Alexander Fleming; and Rachel from Form B. His mother had not only believed every word, she had asked for more. In those days, unworldly still, he had loved her vehemently for going along with his outlandish tales. It had made him feel alive.

Three days and four nights in, for all the pleasure of not being Kim, and the novelty of taking on a new identity, it was at the same time pretty lonely being Tim White, a man who did officially exist – he had the Raigmore security card to prove it – but who, having no past and no personality, only did so to a degree. For nobody to know him, not even him himself, was the very kernel of loneliness.

When Kim Black had gone about his business, outwardly he was respectable – if rarely a suit, then usually clean clothes, clean-shaven, confident poise – indicating to the stranger in the street that he was probably a professional man of modest but certain means – if not a doctor, then a don, maybe, or (God forbid) a bank manager. And the flash of a subdued gold ring on his finger proclaimed to the observant world that in his life there lurked, somewhere at least, a wife and, in all probability, a smattering of kids. To back up this sure-fire impression, in his pockets, there had always been a litter of paperwork, documents, and plastic: driving licence; passport; cheque book; electricity bill; and several credit cards. And whenever Kim had opened his mouth, he had family to speak of, and patients and friends; several diverting anecdotes; questions to ask, and information to impart. He had emotions – some of which he could hide, some of which he couldn't, some he hated, others he embraced. He had beliefs – in God, abortion, the merits of one drug over another; and likes and dislikes – he loved porridge and T.S. Eliot, loathed Thatcherism and Victorian architecture; as well as opinions – about history, medicine, literature, any number of subjects. All of which arose from a lifetime of education, observation and experience. But, using a new name, that was all gone. Since the journey from Oxford he had become somebody else. Was it a wonder that he had wanted to start to sketch, even if only in rough, at least something across Tim White's new blank canvas? That he tried to answer those questions which people asked?

The telephone behind the counter rang and was answered gruffly by the controller who had slumped asleep over his book of puzzles. It was the first call in almost an hour and gave both of them a fright. Kim looked at his watch. It was nearly four o'clock. Not yet dawn. He shivered and pulled his collar more tightly round his neck and chest. After the man had dealt with the call, he switched the kettle on and stunned Kim by offering him some tea, but it wasn't a conversation opener. Milk? Sugar? was as far as it went. Kim stood up, took the cup gratefully, and returned to his seat.

As he drank in the silence, a whole set of questions seeped into his mind just as the hot tea slowly appeared to seep into all the corners of his still chilled body. He looked at his watch again. Ten past four. He looked at the stricken walls and the stricken figure of the man behind the counter whose very bearing seemed to be at odds with the world.

'Tim White,' he said to himself. 'Where did he come from?'

Up until that moment, Kim had not examined closely what had prompted him to take on a new name. He had merely harboured the vague notion that it was best not to be known as himself before he had spoken to Sylvie, and that to try for an unskilled job with the title of Doctor might have caused some sort of trouble, raised eyebrows. It had been an instinctive thing, in Mr Kindness's office, to dissemble. But now, in the HQ of A1 Cabs, he wondered what it was he had feared so about calling Sylvie; about eyebrows raised. And, more to the point, why the hell he had gone for a job at all. Why the hell had he gone away from home in the first place?

It wasn't, after all, just that he was on an incidental little trip to the Highlands without having quite got round to telling his wife that he would be home soon. Because this was how he had looked upon it up until then, an innocent anomaly, while he enjoyed a temporary little blip of freedom and anonymity. Only now did he acknowledge to himself that this was patent bollocks. He was running away. Must have been. Really wasn't wanting to be traced. A man doesn't, he thought to himself, just piss off without telling anyone and fail to ring home because he feels a tad too exhausted, doesn't have a 10p coin handy, and anyway someone's occupying the phone. He doesn't just happen to get himself a whole new identity, and a whole new job – which is manifestly less secure and more humble than the one he already has – simply for the fun of it. And yet, as illogical as that might seem, for the life of him, Kim could not remember ever having felt the need, even the desire, actually to go AWOL, to be someone else; nor did he have any recollection of at any time having planned to do so.

Oh, he had casually fantasised about it, of course. Who hadn't? It was the oldest cliché in the book. Man (or woman), happily married, good kids, good job, comfortable home; sitting in a traffic jam, perhaps; having yet another row about the rubbish; even doing something pleasurable like enjoying comfortable marital sex of a comfortable Tuesday evening. He (or she) daydreams about letting go of his normal, boring, predictable self, throwing to the wind the status quo, the responsibilities, every safe thing he knows, in order to join a protest group in a tunnel under the site of a new runway; take shitloads of drugs renowned for their hallucinogenic properties; travel barefoot to Bali; take up weaving in Shetland; embark on a series of passionate, preposterous, pointless affairs. To reach out to where the grass is greener, and never to go back.

Before he met Sylvie, for all his reasonable life, Kim had wanted to become a doctor and to fall in love with and marry an intelligent, beautiful woman. Basic stuff. He did not congratulate himself on the originality of his ambition. A successful working and family life was something most men aspired to in their youth, and beyond, even if it turned out for many to be easier hoped for than accomplished. But for Kim things couldn't have worked out more perfectly. While in the very process of training to be a doctor, in Belfast, he had met a woman who more than fulfilled that commonplace but elusive dream. She was everything, and she loved him. What could have been more straightforward?

And yet, fulfilment staring him in the face, he had prevaricated. The moment he met Sylvie, at some sweaty party and a while later over a deliciously sweaty breakfast, he had been in no doubt that she was the one for him. She had an incisive mind and at the same time was calm, thoughtful, gentle. A winning combination. She drew him out of himself like no one else. Had a way with people. Telling her things was irresistible. Such warmth of reception! Her looks were not remarkable, and all the more alluring for that. Kim did not admire gratuitous beauty. His eye beheld beauty in the plain.

But it had been over two years after those initial meetings with her before he'd walked in to that throw-back jeweller's shop on Royal Avenue in the autumn of 1974. It wasn't prudence which had dictated he wait for a proper length of time while they got to know each other, it was fear. Sylvie was perfect, but he'd been terrified that more perfect might yet come along. Even if it didn't, being married, out went the shameful prospect of fun with the imperfect. It was hardly a laudable fear, but it was a compelling one.

The issue had been forced when Sylvie became pregnant with Jack. Kim remembered the lovely night she had told him. They were in his cheerless, empty digs in an area behind Queens with biblical street names called Holy Land. The brown and orange curtains were closed, his single bed with greying sheets was unmade, and the tap was dripping as usual into the basin, water deeper forging its yellowing path across the etiolated pink surface towards a rusty plughole. He sat on the poorly carpet; she, beside him, shivering on the cream tiles of the fireplace, practically in the flames, burning her eyes into the coals. Her trousers, which had been handed down to her from her brother, were baggy and thin, a nonsense against the cold. Patches of their threadbare brown corduroy and her dense, misshapen jersey, began to scorch her skin. She moved about on her bum, gently as a sea anemone, to distribute the scorches, but would not leave her place of intimacy with the fire.

On the floor near them was a second-hand toaster, a bag of white sliced bread, and in crumpled, greasy paper some butter with a pebble-dash facade of burnt crumbs. They were eating piles of toast. The sound was of crunching, of the spit and pop of the fire, and of some fellow students in the next room. They commented on their rhythmic thumping and groaning. The hollow noise of the semi-detached sex of strangers, distorted by brick and indifference, was disturbing somehow, like the cries and knocks of victims trapped under rubble.

They drank cheap beer and were happy. He loved her so much that he was a loopy, light-headed exaggeration of his normal self. He had been planning to propose to her in the Botanic Gardens for some weeks, at that point not so self-confident that he could believe she would hang round waiting for him for ever. He had the place, the speech, all worked out, only not the time. He was still holding on, idiotically, for nothing, for some notional possibility. On their sixth round of toast she told him she was pregnant, and that released him. He pulled her to him, squeezed her so hard she laughed. Her dark hair in his face, he even remembered the shampoo-taste of strands across his tongue, he asked her to marry him there and then, in that glume of a room. It wasn't the ideal setting, but he instantly knew he'd made the best decision of his life. Naturally enough, the very moment he'd voiced those three straightforward words, all those months of procrastination revealed themselves for what they were, a senseless torment. All these things are so bloody obvious in retrospect, Kim told himself, his bum now aching from sitting so pensively, and so long, in one position. When at last he'd acted on his greatest desire, all his young man's terrors of marriage had of course just fallen off him like morals off a mercenary.

'Oi, it's six-thirty,' the controller barked suddenly, hewing

169

Kim away from his thoughts. 'My shift's nearly over. Things'll be getting busy soon. Time you buggered off.'

Kim stood up quickly, and with his two dead legs felt slightly wobbly on his feet. He grunted at the man by way of an equalising thank you, and pushed through the heavy door to go in search of a local paper and an early-morning café. The dawn streets were still as dark as night, but a few pedestrians had emerged and could be seen, lurking or dashing.

It was so cold. He hastened towards the livelier streets where there were more shops and cars and people. Round the side of Marks & Spencer he spotted two policemen looming, and automatically bolted his eyes to the pavement. As they drew closer, he quickly turned his head away, pretending to cough in order to hide his face. They passed by, uninterested, and Kim felt an icy twinge of regret for his ready-warm wife, his ready-warm bed. If he hadn't planned to leave them, what was his reason for being in this unknown place, not wanting to be discovered?

He paused outside a newsagent. For a moment he pondered upon the idea that he might be suffering from amnesia, but the moment passed. People with severe memory loss cannot retrieve from their minds their name or address, or even the simplest facts about themselves; cannot list the names of their family and friends; and certainly don't have a clue about their past. Not only was Kim able to do all of these things, he was also in full possession of his medical knowledge. To make sure, he even tested himself, there and then, on the hostile pavement beneath a plastic purple and white awning saying Cadbury's. He made himself name various diseases; remember management guidelines for asthma and high blood pressure; the dosage regimens of the drugs required for various conditions; and the telephone numbers of his local hospitals. He was happy to find that he could recall them all.

When he was quite finished he went in to buy a paper and then entered a nearby café which echoed to the sounds of morning – bacon frying, groggy men hacking. The place had about it a heated smell of steamed milk, and mops, and beans. Already he felt less dejected. Sitting down, he ordered a cup of coffee and was able to compose a mental list: illness or amnesia; being discovered guilty of misconduct at work; redundancy; debts;

170

alcoholism; stress or depression; domestic dispute or marital breakdown; psychological/sexual/violent abuse; abduction. This was, he thought, a pretty comprehensive breakdown of the reasons people might have to run away. Then he went through each one to see if he could apply any of them to himself.

Amnesia, and redundancy: no. Debts: a few unpaid credit card bills, all in all to the tune of less than three thousand pounds. A worry, for sure, but not one so onerous as to force him to flee a loving and beloved home. Abduction: obviously not, unless he could count that by the Oxford to London coach, which had seemed somehow to swallow him up before he knew what he was doing. Abuse: alas nothing so exciting as to make him of the remotest interest to a psychologist. He'd had no more than the normal teasing by his father, and bullying by his brothers. As far as abuse went, that was about the best he could come up with.

He was on the point of addressing alcoholism, depression, and marital breakdown – he wished to be systematic about his soul-searching – when the waitress brought him his coffee.

'Anything else?' she asked.

'That's fine, thanks,' he told her, spreading out his paper. 'Just, can you tell me if I'm looking in the right place to rent a room?'

'That's the one. Section at the back.'

'I've got to find something by twelve,' he said, turning the pages with sudden urgency. His shift was starting at two.

'That shouldn't be a problem. Their classifieds are very good.' The woman leant over and helped him find the relevant page.

Five hours later, Kim had made thirteen telephone calls from the payphone outside the café, walked seven miles or more, and seen five rooms. The first two had been too expensive. The third, halfway along the Moray Firth to Beauly, too far out of town. The fourth had had a landlord with a cosy face like everyone's favourite grandfather who sweetly offered him a cup of tea and enquired if he liked to fuck young boys. It hadn't been entirely clear if the key to his room lay in a definite no answer, or a definite yes. Either way, Kim made his excuses and left.

He leapt straight onto a bus back into the city centre and, feeling footsore and forlorn, stopped off for a quick half pint in a dark pub. Naturally, he was longing to tell Sylvie about the horrible places and grisly landlords he had seen, but she would have asked the inevitable – why was he looking for a room? He was unkeen to ring if it wasn't to tell her about his morning, but the thought that he ought to did still keep pecking away at him. Perhaps now was the moment.

He spotted the payphone. It was sticking out of the wall between the black door to the Gents and the juddering fruit machine with its attention-seeking pings and coloured lights. He sighed, mustering up the courage, conscience telling him he really must ring at long last, however reluctant he still was to do so. He stood up and walked across the wooden floor, glass in hand. There were only half a dozen or so other customers, all men, each one at a respectable distance from the other, either on a stool at the bar or a low chair by a window, with only a smoke or pork crackling crisp for company. This, thought Kim, is the way of day-time drinking, it's not to do with being sociable, but to do with necessity. It exists as an easier way to accommodate pervading joblessness, despondency and dispossession. As he lifted the brown plastic receiver, he fancied they were keen to listen in on the novelty of a conversation, to hear what he might have to say. The man nearest him wasn't being very subtle about it. His head was cocked in his direction the better to hear. Or so Kim thought. Perhaps he was just imagining it, and it was simply a pose fashioned by regret. Kim turned his back to the room and cupped his hand over the mouthpiece. He braced himself and tapped out the number. He waited, and there came the tell-tale pause before the click-start of the answering machine's outgoing message.

His stomach suddenly felt as though it had a lining of liquid metal. He hastily replaced the receiver before waiting to listen to Sylvie's taped voice or leave a message. His explanations, whatever they may have turned out on the spur of the moment to be, were going to sound hollow enough as it was, without being stammered onto an unforgiving machine. For all his cowardice, if he was going to contact home at all, he wanted to speak to Sylvie herself.

He stood by the phone for a moment, at a loss. Then he downed the remains of his beer and hastened into the street. The bright sky instantly slapped a headache across his brow. He looked at his watch and began walking very fast in the direction of the next place, his sixth, that he was due to see.

Fifteen minutes later he approached the street he wanted, sweating. No. 43 was a 1920s villa which had a cat-litter facade and a thick timber porch against which was leaning a brace of ferruginous bicycles. The garden was a neglect of tangled weeds. Its borders were blooming not with flowers but with old bottles and cans, plastic bags, the odd glove, and ill-disposed nappies. Inside, the hall, an indeterminate colour, had all the brightness and atmosphere of a stagnant pond. The landlady, Mrs Blake, was its only saviour from complete gloom with her sartorial flourish of turquoise dress, thin white belt, pink shoes, and her vivacious, if severe, expression.

'You've come to see about the room, I suppose?' she trilled as she showed him into what she optimistically called her parlour. 'Well, I don't usually take in gentlemen, as I said on the phone, but I have been known to make exceptions.'

'What would they be?'

'I don't know, Mr White – it is Mr White, isn't it?' she asked, looking him up and down. 'It's a matter of feeling, in here.' Keeping her eyes firmly on him, she pressed her hands into her chest so fervently that the womanly flesh under her thin dress material bulged between her fingers. 'I don't like any alcohol on the premises,' she told him, mouthing each word with slow deliberation as if exciting herself with the anticipation of his reaction.

'Doesn't bother me.' He spoke without a trace of hesitation. He liked a drink, socially on the whole, but the lack of it had never unduly troubled him. He had seen some wretched, wretched patients suffering from alcoholism whose obsession wasn't merely with drinking itself. They had a habit, in the dry surroundings of his surgery, of steering the conversation round to drink, however an outlandish non-sequitur it might be. It was as if, in the absence of actual booze, the very mention of it lent some kind of temporary relief. He had always felt for people for whom drink or drugs was their all. He himself had many shortcomings, but had been blessed with a nature which was not addictive. So it was he was indifferent to Mrs Blake's house rule. Personally he needn't worry about alcoholism; he could at least check that one off his list.

173

She asked Kim a few more basic questions. He told her the truth because, as he had trudged round between viewings earlier that morning, he had made a decision. He would stick with his false name – used as a necessary means of getting his portering job – because a provincial city was a small world. But otherwise there was no need to lie about detail. Fun though it might be trying to create a whole new persona, it made him feel guilty, confused and disloyal, as had been proved after his lift with John. There was no real reason to deny he was married. It was not only pointless but also insulting to Sylvie and to their past. And to say he had six children, for example, made him wonder if deep down he felt his two were inadequate, which was far from the case. For all the double-edged freedom it might have represented, his conscience couldn't do it. Whatever his reasons for running away – which he was yet to find out – there was no need to become another person. If Sylvie and the police were trying to catch up with him, and their job was made easier with him giving all his real details to people except for two, then so be it. From now on his real name, and the fact that he was a GP, were the only things he needed to conceal, for the sake of his job. He would remain Kim Black in all but name and occupation.

Mrs Blake led him up the dark stairs and along a corridor with a patterned carpet and vast old-fashioned radiators. From behind one of the doors along the corridor's length some feeble pop music could be heard.

'I have one or two young ones,' she explained quickly. 'That's Laurie's room.' Hushed voice. 'New Zealand. She's out most of the day. The others are mainly maturer ladies, some single, some divorced. It's a good mix.'

They looked into the shared bathroom which was cold and smelt of dank bath mats and seedy towels. The basin was covered in the matt splatters of dried toothpaste swill, and the bath itself, with its pus-like scar from tap to plughole and the weeping bottles of shampoos and shower gels running along its ledge, was not inviting. He didn't mind it, he wasn't a squeamish man, but it did go a little against the more surgically-minded instincts of someone with a training in hygiene.

Mrs Blake unlocked a small door at the end of the passage. The bedsit – one of thirteen, she told him proudly, which she'd managed to fashion out of a not substantial family home – was somewhat wanting in instant appeal. It was small and dingy and had the air of a place which had never witnessed, let alone been infected by, happiness. A dark climbing plant covering the outside of the window obscured the brick wall view of the house next door, and scuppered the chances of invasion by even a minimal amount of light. The walls and ceiling had perhaps been white once, but they looked as though they had last been painted around about the time the house was built. They were now the colour of a newly excavated skull. The carpet had the look about it of having for decades welcomed and preserved amongst its scant fibres insect-wing layers of dead skin deposited by the mouldy feet of former occupants. A harsh bulb hung from the ceiling, no shade to quell its aggression. There was one picture on the wall, a photographic enlargement of a Constable landscape reproduced on a plastic canvas of exaggerated weave and bordered by a thin, too-gilt frame. On a shelf beside a sink only large enough for a pair of hands and a tea-cup, stood a scaly kettle, a toaster, and one of the very first microwave ovens. It was the sort of idyllic setting a person might have been overjoyed to find were he bent on killing himself. When Mrs Blake asked Kim if he wanted to take it, he was too tired even to hesitate. She handed him a key and left him alone 'to settle'. After she'd gone he sat on the narrow bed and clutched the sulky green counter-pane, his rough and dirty hands snagging on the nylon quilting. He trembled with the thought that suicide might have been his subconscious intention when he'd agreed to her terms and said yes.

And yet as far as he knew he was not even depressed, let alone suicidal. Many of his patients had spoken eloquently of their desire to top themselves. A few had attempted it. Kim thanked God that fewer had succeeded (on the whole those who had, tended to be the ones who hadn't taken the precaution of giving anyone due warning beforehand). Always, he had felt sympathetic to people who said they were so depressed they saw no other way out but to end it all. But his sympathy had never once graduated to empathy. Never once in his life had Kim felt so bloated with despair that he had been tempted himself. He had too much to be thankful for, he had a good life. Even if he had suffered from clinical depression (which he didn't), he would have had enough experience of suicide to put him off the idea for good. It had been on the increase of late. Unlike nurses in Casualty, he had admittedly not often in the course of his career found himself confronted with the dubious opportunity of watching and hearing the undignified, agonising process of a stomach being pumped. Nor, unlike police officers and forensic pathologists, had he actually seen, desecrated by high-speed trains and scattered over railway tracks, human bodies which had been reduced to dead-ringers for the prosaic, crusty remains of cold, discarded pizzas. But he had, all too often, had to witness the almost uniquely unbearable grief and ruin of families left behind by the suicide of a loved one. It was levelling indeed, and had proved a more effective deterrent than any anti-depressant of which he was aware. After dealing with such incidents, he would go home, hug his wife a little harder, and thank God for his own wonderful life.

By the time Kim left his room, locked the door, and said goodbye to Mrs Blake on his way out to work, he was feeling relieved that he had been able ceremoniously to dismiss both alcoholism and depression. And though it meant he was going off none the wiser, at least he had a room to go back to, the very existence of which gave him more strength to face the gruelling shift ahead.

At the end of his first forty-hour week as a hospital porter Kim had come to know physical exhaustion in its purest form, entirely unfettered by its intellectual counterpart; the unique chill of Mrs Blake's communal bathroom; and the names and – very personal – circumstances of a number of his fellow inhabitants at no. 43.

For a modest extra sum over and above the rent, Mrs Blake had offered him evening meals in her strip-lit basement kitchen. He didn't much fancy more company after his heavily populated day at Raigmore, but he had no inclination to shop and cook for himself, and did not earn enough to squander his wages in cafés and pizza joints, so he had accepted. On the nights when he wasn't on the late shift, he had tea at six-thirty with Mrs Blake and those of her other lodgers who didn't fancy a dejected, microwaved pastie alone in their rooms. One of these was an elderly man, simply known as W., whom the rest of them – usually about four or five women – patted on the shoulder when handing him his bowl of Heinz tomato soup or glass of water, but otherwise ignored. He had a troublesome drip on the end of his nose but didn't speak, and his presence served as no restraining order on the conversation.

On his second day chez Mrs Blake Kim had done a morning shift. So in the evening he was able to share an anaemic but large cottage pie in the kitchen with his fellow lodgers as they doled out to him more facts about themselves than he'd have felt entitled to even with his GP's hat on. And throughout the rest of the week it was more of the same.

Yolande Jacobson, whose very eyes and stomach were concave with disillusion, dexterously breast-fed her child, dallied with her cabbage, and revealed how she had recently left her husband because she'd discovered that the unusual but very pretty name he had suggested for their baby was the very same as that of the Japanese woman he'd been screwing throughout her pregnancy.

Norma, forty-three, topped Yolande's story with one of her own. A week before her wedding she had discovered her husband was having an affair with a neighbour. He vowed he'd get rid of her, and the wedding went ahead. 'I was nineteen and in love with him,' she explained, 'and all my life I'd dreamed of my big day. So fool me, I went with it, and guess who we bumped into on the beach in Miami? He'd booked her on the same flight, and when I asked him why she had come on our honeymoon, he said the tickets hadn't been refundable.'

Another woman about Norma's age, Jackie, was busy organising Scotland's Stress-Incontinence Day because she herself had suffered that particular affliction since the age of twenty-two. He was given a lecture on the importance of pelvic floor exercises.

Bulimic Karen in Room 9, he didn't meet because she didn't like to eat in public, but he heard about her. She was the source of any strange nocturnal noises he might have noticed, and the bathroom's perennial smell of vomit. But if ever he had a chocolate craving, she was his woman, apparently, because under her bed was a suitcase with more Milky Bars and Malteser packets in it than in any all-night garage, and Karen was very giving.

It was now Friday night. Kim and W. were eating macaroni

177

cheese with Mrs Blake; Yolande and baby Lynne (formerly known as Hatsumomo); Norma; Jackie; and another two women whom he hadn't met before that evening. Susan was a quiet, unmarried teacher in her mid-thirties with a Yorkshire accent and a white blouse buttoned up to her chin. Laurie, one of Mrs Blake's younger lodgers, was about twenty-nine; an abseiler from New Zealand who was in Inverness to join a team painting the Moray Firth bridge. She was late and arrived in full abseiling gear – bright orange dungarees and jacket jingling with ropes and pulleys, scratched white hard hat under her arm, big boots splashed all over with bright yellow primer. A well-built, strong-looking type, she made an entrance when she burst in, washed her hands with liquid soap over the kitchen sink, and joined them at the table. Mrs Blake looked somewhat put out but dished up some warm macaroni for her all the same. Kim was amused by Laurie but it was Susan who made a greater impression on him.

'I'm not very hungry,' Laurie said. 'Rory caught a fish and fried it up for lunch in the bothy. It was a twenty-five mile per hour wind so we had to give up, we were cooped up inside most the day.' She took a mouthful of food and looked at Kim. 'Are you the new lodger or Mrs B's new boyfriend?' she asked.

Mrs Blake looked up sharply but appeared, despite herself, to enjoy the frisson caused by the question. W. carried on eating regardless but Jackie's eyes instantly darted into the creamy mush on her plate and stayed staring at it with almost as much embarrassment as the stress-incontinence had afforded her over the years. Susan looked at Kim. Her sensitive expression appeared to say, 'Don't mind her, it's her sense of humour, she means no harm.'

'The new lodger,' Kim replied.

Laurie went on to ask him his name, where he was from, what he was doing in Scotland. All the while the others quietly listened. On the previous nights they had spoken about themselves. Kim hadn't volunteered any information about himself and they had asked him little, perhaps waiting for him to do so in his own time. Laurie had no such reticence. Her line of questioning, though straightforward enough, had a tone about it which Kim couldn't pin down at first. She stared at him penetratingly. She made Kim feel paranoid. He worried that she could see through him, that she knew that really he wasn't a hospital porter.

'Are you married, Tim?'

'I am.'

'Don't you miss your wife, I mean, what with you being up here and her in Oxford? Must be hard.'

'I haven't been up here very long.'

'What does she think about it?'

'I don't know,' he told her, and looked away, stared at his tense hand round his glass of water. He knew everybody's eyes were upon him, could sense them hovering there, like insects treading air, waiting for the answer to their unspoken question, 'How come?'

Eleven days had gone by and Kim still had not spoken to Sylvie. He fooled himself that this, in part at least, was due to his conversation over breakfast with Liz a few days before. She had put into his mind the notion that, though Sylvie was sure to be worried, she probably did not mind that he had gone. This, though well-meant, had come as a shock, a brutal one at that. He might have scoffed, but Liz's detail had been so convincing. She had said how a woman likes not to have to think about food once in a while, which had a definite ring of truth. And how it was something of a relief not to be mocked for her choice of television programme. Certainly, Sylvie had complained more than once that he turned his nose up at the things she occasionally liked to watch (usually documentaries about one woman's struggle to overcome ovarian cancer, so mawkishly made that they stretched even his famed curiosity about his fellow men). Liz had said that Sylvie was actually enjoying his absence. This had knocked the confidence of a man who had always taken it as read that, though he and his wife were both perfectly capable of getting on with their lives when not together, they didn't take active pleasure in being apart. There were plenty of indicators to prove this. Whenever he came home after being away for a few days, Sylvie would always turn up at the airport a good hour or two before his flight was due to land. She said it was because she so loved to watch people greeting each other in the Arrivals hall, and he adored her for that. But he felt sure that that wasn't her only reason. Going early heightened the anticipation of his home-coming. I mean, he told himself, when I'm leaving for somewhere and she drops me off at Departures, she goes straight home, it's not as if she makes a special diversion to Arrivals after I've gone.

Sylvie, he went on in his mind, had always been an extremely loyal and devoted wife. Over the years she had spoilt him. Ever since she had accepted his proposal back in his unprepossessing digs near Queens, she had given him to believe he need never doubt her constancy even when the circumstances, especially during the early part of their marriage – impoverished and over-worked in Belfast – had been far from easy.

Just to think for one moment about the marriages he had observed or heard about – those of his patients, colleagues, friends; those Sylvie had encountered during the course of her career – made him thank God for his. The scope for human unhappiness, broadened to the width of a black hole when two people joined together, had never ceased to astonish him. Every day in his surgery he had been freshly intrigued by yet another unique spin on marital misery. It appeared to be infinite in its variety and, conversely, to marginalise the scope for happiness almost to extinction. He had recognised that as a GP he was probably the last person who would get to hear about marriages that were good. It was his own which hinted to him that others must also exist, and which prevented in him apocalyptic despair.

He only had to look at the two women in front of him, Yolande and Norma, for proof. So predictably singular were their anec-dotes of unhappiness. Mrs Blake, no ring on her finger but full of references to Mr Blake, clearly also had her own story to tell. And W., too, whom Kim could see out of the corner of his eye, wrestling stiffly with his macaroni, scratching the tormenting eczema which had seeped across the backs of his empurpled hands like a red wine stain textured and weakened by an urgent sprinkling of salt. The women of the house treated him with special delicacy. They seemed to know instinctively what W. had quietly hinted to Kim in the passage outside their rooms a couple of nights before, that he had suffered at the hands of a very bad advertisement for their sex. Under this roof alone, Kim thought, flourished a cornucopia of miserable memories.

But, if he was the exception, what was he doing here? Perhaps, deep down, he knew Liz had touched on a truth and Sylvie wanted to be shot of him, so he was in fact doing her a favour by walking out? Could that possibly be true, with all evidence, in her consistently loving behaviour, to the contrary? Yet else why hadn't he rung her so that he had an accurate answer to Laurie's simple question – what did she think about him being gone?

Kim and Sylvie married in the registry office at Belfast's City Hall in mid-December 1974. The colours of that day still shone in his mind as brightly as those in a children's cartoon. The sun in a cornflower sky had bleached the building's stone to the same off-white as Sylvie's knee-length dress. She clutched an untamed bunch of pinks and in the breeze her dark brown hair wisped into the pale red lipstick of her wide, wide smile.

Sylvie had got her degree the June before and was a few weeks into the first term of her two-year postgraduate course in social work, also at Queens. Conveniently, the baby was due the following summer, but she was busy in the meantime. Kim, having completed his three pre-clinical years that June, was in his fourth year, after which he would have another two clinical years to complete. He was both studying, and doing time in Belfast's various hospitals. There hadn't been the freedom, money or inclination for a so-called proper wedding. There was no family, only a handful of friends who had been with them at Queens; none over from England.

Kim's best man was Conor Hughes, a fellow junior doctor, now a GP living with his family in Newcastle-under-Lyme. He was married to his childhood sweetheart, Mary, who grew up in the very same street as himself in West Belfast. She was a funeral director with a popular parlour in Runcorn and the kind of big red-rimmed glasses not normally associated with someone of her profession. Kim had met Conor a few days after he arrived in Belfast from Herefordshire. At eighteen, Conor had been already stout and balding, and looked as though youth had not so much passed him by, as never even come close. Kim had been drawn to him precisely because of this, and the fact that Conor had the merriest disposition of anyone he had ever come across. His dry jokes had sustained him, like coffee or amphetamines, throughout their gruelling training together. Just as Mary's friendship and support had later sustained Sylvie when he was working so hard

181

during the early months of marriage, especially after Jack was born. Some years later, in 1979, when they all moved to England at about the same time, they still kept in touch but only managed to see each other rarely. Geography, Kim reflected, not the passing of time, was the great leveller which came between them.

The reception, such as it was, took place in a pub near the university. A dozen or so of them ordered endless pints of beer and sat at three tables pushed together under a window. The wedding breakfast consisted of plates of fish and chips piled high as molehills. Kim could still picture confetti landing on them, everyone laughing and fussing at the paper petals, pushing them aside with their forks before they could take any mouthfuls.

No time or money for a honeymoon. Just a weekend trip on the bus to stay in a Portrush guesthouse. The owners a middle-aged couple who shouted at them, albeit very politely, because they were so unused to guests under seventy, guests who were easy-of-hearing. From day one, Kim relished, in his own voice, the virgin juxtaposition of the words 'my' and 'wife'. On their wedding night he and Sylvie made love in a bed which, seeming to moan at their every move, had long lost its own sense of purpose, but couldn't deflect them from their mutual exuberance. Next day, rough jerseys itching their chins, they walked along the Giant's Causeway taking in great gulps of fresh air and in such a wind as to give them both earache. Afterwards, a lukewarm Sunday roast in a suicide hotel in Port Stewart. It jutted into a fearsome sea and, so Kim thought he had heard somewhere, had since been closed down for demolition. They loved every minute of their weekend.

Then back to the tiny rented flat they had found off the Lisburn Road in exchange for their respective digs. It was round the corner from where Sylvie had lived with Jodie and Siobhan. The old stove stank of gas, the seams of the windows were as draughty as mouth organs, and every night it took until about two in the morning before they managed, huddled together, to shiver the edge off the viral damp which infected the sheets. When Jack was born in July 1975, a wizened old man with the fresh smell of warm milk, he slept between them. Sylvie had a few weeks' maternity leave or, more accurately, summer holiday, before the start of her second year of her postgraduate course.

How they survived physically and financially he will never know. Money was almost non-existent. Kim, about to start his fifth year, was working like a crazy fellow. By day he was taking blood, taking patients' histories, examining them, putting in drips, giving intravenous injections, assisting in theatre, and seeing patients in Casualty. He was also being either ignored by consultants, or being grilled by them on ward rounds about the management of his patients. (Their attitude, and his determination never to become like them, as well as the inhuman hours young hospital doctors were expected to work, all contributed to his desire to become a GP.) By night, his beloved son could scream heavy metal in his ear, and he was so fast asleep he didn't even realise the little creature was there.

He barely saw his new wife that first year of Jack's life. He worked every evening and weekend, and tried in between, for a few sorely needed extra pennies here and there, to do odd jobs – bar work in the doctors' bar at City Hospital and the East Wing Bar at the Royal, whatever scrap he could lay his hands on for a few spare (usually unearthly) hours. This made his life almost untenable. During his rare times off when he could stop himself from luxuriating in sleep; refrain from talking about the work which he had lived and breathed for the previous thirty-two hours; or – if they did ever go out to eat – manage not to fall asleep with his face in his food, then they were sustained by elated glimpses at strange hours of the day and night. Glimpses in which they developed a fast-forward, shorthand language for catching-up, swapping news; in which they clamped themselves to each other, as a device does to a battery charger. He saw more of Conor, of heartless surgeons, even of fleeting patients, than he did of Sylvie and their boy. It could be said, those early days, while he loved her, he barely knew her, only saw her, as Conor used to jest, through his glasses tiredly. But he could imagine her, during his days, going about hers as she brought up their child, and responded to his nuclear smiles, all on her own.

Typically, Jack's awe-inspiring lungs – physiological phenomenon, at no more volume than half a litre each, that they were – would wake her at dawn. Kim's alarm would go off a while later, and he would open his eyes to find Sylvie sitting up beside him, head lolling against the tapioca wallpaper, breast-feeding, the pair of them harmonious. (He could even remember feeling a little left out, wistful that he had to leave them, jealous of Jack's undiluted hours with her, almost as threatening in their way as was the prospect of those she might spend with an adult lover.) After he had gone, he could see her in his mind, getting up, throwing on her own clothes with barely a thought, the quicker to attend to Jack, carefully to dress him. He could hear the stress of the kettle, the tingle of teaspoon in her cup of coffee; the intimate, impenetrable, irresistible dialogue between mother and son. He could visualise her in one of her long flowing skirts and her sheepskin coat going with the rickety pram to the shops along the Lisburn Road; nipping into the bakery where the women behind the counter whose names she surely knew never failed to inspire her with an, 'Isn't he beautiful!'; same in the butcher's and grocer's, only not over loaves and doughnuts and soda farls, but over mince and sausages, carrots and beans. Emerging, a wary glance outside the fortress police station at a blinking soldier from Solihull or Seaham dressed in the colours of a dappled glade but equipped only on the outside for untimely death, yet not within. Perhaps a visit to friends, like Jodie and Mary, with places nearby and kids of their own. Cups of tea, telly, and chocolate bourbon biscuits – the backdrop to conversation about other people, children, bombs, figures, the dread and yearning to get back to work. Afternoons, using Jack's sleeping time to catch up on some studying, clean the bath, catch up on a text about court welfare, snatch a precious nap herself on their unmade bed; waking to Jack's latest cries and, across the small, evening-lit window, a muslin of condensation formed by a combination of deathly dank and their lovely breath. Bath-time, followed by more breast, more age-of-reason solitude. The tenacious rhythm of maternal days.

Kim knew from the start that Sylvie didn't like birds. Whenever they were in the street together she would make loops round the pigeons. He could understand it, he wasn't over-keen on them himself. But whereas he might have been maddened by her neurosis, instead he loved her all the more for her eccentricity. The extent of her fear and loathing fascinated him. Sometimes a simple stroll to the post office would take twice as long as it otherwise might. All those sideways steps of hers, stops, and false starts. It was like a sort of contemporary formation dance, and she didn't finish doing it till the offenders had arrogantly strutted away, diverted by stray crumbs beneath the hem of pretend grass round the stall outside the grocer's or spilt rubbish in the gutter. Occasionally, Kim remembered, when one flew up in front of her, she would duck quick as a shot and bury her head in his side, or let out a cry and crouch to the ground, hands over her head, just like people near bombs. She was ashamed of herself, in the streets of Belfast, not a city for phobias. She hated herself for reacting so foolishly to a stupid pigeon in a way that would have only been sensible had it been to a stupid explosion. People looked at her, sometimes frightened themselves, and he would reassure them with a smile and a gesture, or even a comment about his wife having a terror of beaks, and claws, feathers and flapping. People were always interested, sympathetic, sometimes knew something of the same fear themselves, but were, amazingly, never angry for the false alarm she might have caused.

In Oxford there were more pigeons than in Belfast, or so it seemed. Oxford was for pigeons what Las Vegas was for gamblers. Perhaps they fancied the bright lights of tourists, great gaggles of them on the streets, who left in their wake winning droppings of sandwiches and chips and buns. No tourists in Belfast's city centre, and few citizens who did anything other than hasten from A to B, let alone linger, so little litter on which to binge. Even pigeons spurned the dusty, throat-choking rubble left by bombs and favoured instead the myth of dreaming spires. They were happy there, carefree, and sated in numbers.

But the people in Oxford were crosser than their Belfast counterparts, with less to be cross about. When Sylvie did her public dancing, they looked askance, impatient, sneering. Pensioners never seemed to mind, but occasionally middle-aged men or women gave her a wide berth, just as she was giving one to a pigeon. And if she ducked or yelped a student or teenager would invariably look at her with the unflinching stare of an unformed child. The people of Oxford made her feel more embarrassed than when she'd been in Belfast and had had good reason to feel embarrassed. They made Kim mad with anger. Let them think what they will, he thought and, unlike in Belfast, he didn't feel inclined to give them the benefit of an explanation.

185

Kim and Sylvie moved back to England after he had done his finals in the summer of 1977, completed his houseman's year in July 1978, and taken a six-month senior house officer's job in obstetrics and gynaecology (or 'Obs and Gobs' as they used to call it). It was a coincidence that he landed himself another temporary SHO post, in paediatrics, at a hospital in her home town. She was reluctant to go back at first but, the more she thought about it, the more being close to her father and sister and old friends began to appeal.

They bought their house in Divinity Road with a vast mortgage. It was about a mile out of town, away from the tourists and the worst pigeon ghettos. Sylvie started working for the Oxford Social Services, in a generic social work team. Her ability to deal with people and their miasma of problems impressed Kim from the very beginning. Whatever her job threw at her, she always showed that admirable combination of pragmatism, common sense, sincerity, compassion. She always rose to the challenge of her work and became absorbed by it. Liked to bring it home with her. That was not a criticism. She used to discuss it in such a way that meant she wasn't banging on about her work exclusively, but was prompting the pair of them to examine the stuff of human nature. Her eagerness to talk to him about her cases, and to hear about those he had happed upon during his day, meant that their married life effervesced with conversation. Of an evening, they could analyse for hours the behaviour and conundrums of their respective clients or patients, and in turn this might set them off on the subject of their own families and friends. The most mundane referral could keep them going till late into the night. A woman in her nineties battling with a daughter determined to make her go into day-care. A simple enough scenario in many of her colleagues' minds, but to Sylvie in fact bristling, fizzing, fusing with the universal, circuit-board complexities of the mother-daughter relationship.

He had been frightened, after Mackenzie was born, that Sylvie might become too tired and preoccupied with the children for their nightly discussions. Men's anxieties about having children, aside from the financial ones, were largely selfish, to do with them losing their wives or partners as they crystallised into mothers. But his fears were groundless. For all her intimacy with Jack and

186

Mackenzie, Sylvie never left him. They talked on. She could be breast-feeding or changing nappies and not be deterred. Adoring and loving mother that she was, she was not so child-fixated that she lost interest in him and his work, and the outside world. And even though she was on maternity leave – and therefore deprived of the conveyor-belt diet of ready-made topics provided by her clients – this did not mean that she was suddenly short of subjects. Her boundless fascination with life didn't stop only at those problems which the Social Services considered grave enough for their professional attention. Minutiae enthralled her and she was miraculous at inspiring the unconverted with her enthusiasm for it – a chance remark or exchange overheard in the street, banal revelation, snatches, juxtapositions, non-sequiturs, she could recall accurately, repeat, and so tellingly bring alive. Non-sequiturs were her favourite, the loopy splatterings of people's thoughts seemingly thrown together by no more than the chaos of irresistible chance. He and she would bring them home to each other, ones they'd picked up on during their respective days – Sylvie's were always much better than his – and they'd have a game whereby they'd try to make up the unconscious connections between the two parts. But detailed physical observations of friends and strangers at parties, in the street, in shops and pubs and parks, also jump-started her imagination; their gestures, ticks, clothes, expressions. For all her speculation as to what a man here might have had for breakfast, or a woman there loathed about her brother-in-law, she was intrigued by how wrong outward impressions could be, how quickly and how often people were misguided by them. She frequently asked Kim his opinion on the connection between clothes and character, for example, or physiognomy and emotion. She always cited an observation she had made at a friend's – Jodie's – wedding, which might seem trifling to others, but which had had a profound effect on her for many years following the event. A man who had been in love with the bride for a decade had sat in one of the front pews, probably the better to view her marrying some other man less constant than himself, the better to languish in his own sense of lost opportunity. Such poignancy of positioning, Sylvie had mused from her spot a few feet away. Several times during the service she had glanced at his face and it was, she believed, daubed with the graffiti of suffocated hope. The feeble smile was fixed, but at the same time the lips seemed downtrodden: his mouth was like a rich, expressive silk which changes colour at every barely perceptible adjustment of light. How unhappy she had thought him at that moment. And yet, later, at the reception, the man had greeted Sylvie merrily, introduced his new love who wore a hat brimming with velvet bluebells, and spoken of his pleasure for Jodie's new happiness in a voice weighted with sincerity, not a note of regret. Where did the truth lie? With a facial expression so seemingly reliable as to appear definitive in its revelation, or with a tone of voice that was, apparently, infallible in its ingenuousness? Was neither to be trusted, after all, or both?

Sylvie had never forgotten this, nor many more, similar examples. The infinite opportunity for getting it wrong, for misreading people's signals, haunted her. In her work, in her home life, it meant she always questioned her assumptions with an assiduousness which didn't occur to others. If a client had what anyone else in their right mind would have taken to be an aggressive sneer, Sylvie was more open to other interpretations. She refused to judge him till she had got to know him and, sure enough, the so-called sneer would turn out to be this character's singular smile, his own way of conveying pure, natural, wanton benevolence. If one of the children was 'looking' unhappy, this was not for Sylvie evidence enough that in fact he or she was so. Other indicators – lack of appetite, say, or general grumpiness – would have to come into play before she was convinced. She hated to pick up false leads, and was ever admirably, exhaustively, thorough in her pursuit of the truth.

To Kim's mind this meant that Sylvie was never bored, or boring. As well as insight, she had astonishing energy. Even with two children, and back at work, she always found time for Kim, not only in terms of conversation and moral support, but also on a more manifest level – cooking his favourite food, providing a constant source of clean socks and shirts, working as his memory (telephone numbers, times and dates of crucial appointments, names of acquaintances they bumped into in the street or at parties). Her attention to domestic detail appeared so effortless that, had he not been an appreciative man, he might have started to take it for granted. He couldn't believe that she enjoyed making the bed every day, and she only convinced him that she did when she admitted that she never bothered doing it when he was away. It wasn't the act itself which gave her pleasure, she said, but the almost sensuous joy she gained from puffing up pillows and straightening sheets that were still warm from his body which had left them a while before.

Sylvie was the perfect wife. Yet, he asked himself, did a man want a perfect wife?

Perhaps he did, more than an imperfect one, anyway. The question was, did he want a wife at all?

# 10

The bulb hanging from the ceiling above his bed shone directly onto Kim so that when he turned it out two identical images of it remained in both eyes, like two persistent comets, and blinded him in the darkness. He became irritably determined to buy a bedside lamp.

He was in an irritable mood. Laurie had got to him earlier at supper with her questions, and more besides. After she'd asked what Sylvie felt about him being away, his hesitant, 'I don't know,' and his failure to expand, hadn't succeeded in shutting her up. The opposite, in fact. She'd wanted to know more and more. Did Sylvie work? Doing what? How old was she? Was she a good mother? In his view, did they get on well together?

'Yes,' he had snapped to that last one. 'Of course we do.'

'Why of course? A lot of married people don't.'

The others had looked embarrassed. 'I'm not sure it's really any of our business,' Susan had told Laurie gently but firmly. Susan had a tact and warmth and kindness about her. Kim appreciated that she was the sort of woman men fell in love with, quietly. No sudden coup, as was to be expected with more obvious and blowsy types. If you spent time with Susan – walks in the Highlands, trips to the library, conversations in coffee houses – you would wake up one day and suddenly realise that your ill-defined appreciation of all her sweet qualities had reduced, like a sauce, to an intense and valuable love.

He wanted to have sex with Laurie.

Pain in the arse that she was. Too bloody pleased with herself, too cheeky. An overt type if ever there was one. It was a gutsy sexuality she had, only it hung about her as languid as a foxy stole. She had wrong-footed him with her nonchalant flirtatiousness, with her body which, even beneath the climbing gear, was sinewy, and sexy in an annoyingly predictable sort of way. No wonder, as he lay in his rented bed, thinking about her in the next-door room, perhaps even hearing her footsteps as she padded about, he was out of sorts. He went over the evening in his mind. She had used that antipodean intonation – reaching a higher pitch towards the end of sentences so that even statements sound like questions – to which he was indifferent in others but which, in her, was combined with an over-inflated confidence, and so had grated on him like a dry finger over the surface of a birthday balloon. He had bristled every time she'd opened her mouth. Yet there had been a base desire – nothing to do with the heart or mind, more like the lurching pull for nicotine – to unknot all her ridiculous ropes, get inside those endless zips, and feel the ping-tautness of her abseiling skin.

On average, Kim had slept with about six people a day since the age of thirteen. Each for a fraction of a spectral second. It began with the girls in Ludlow. A glimpse of one or other of them on market day, out shopping with their mothers; the stand-offish curve of a calf, the hint of a tentatively emerging breast; his pulsating longing, followed by consummation, wholly fanciful and fleeting and faithless, before moving in his mind on to the next voluptuous diversion. Later, the Belfast girls, in a class of their own, white as tulips, warm as treacle pudding, and whose laughter, even, effervesced with that horny Northern Irish accent. During the course of his seven and a half years in the city, he had managed it so that a number of the longings had materialised into reality. By the time he met Sylvie, he had happed upon not a few passing ships. Most of them disappointing – not the girls them-selves usually, but the experience itself, of unfounded sex, so rent with disillusion. Nature of the beast. How many times had he told himself that anticipation alone was not to be underestimated, and yet how many times in those days had he fallen into the same trap? The desultory lack of appeal, Kim recalled, of morning-after detail when it didn't belong to a woman he loved but instead to a night-before stranger: skin bleached stranger by sunrise, foreign threads of hair on his pillow, the inscrutable eyes of a girl with no name. Almost every time it was the same, and every time it left him feeling no fuller than empty.

Of course, he had had a handful of proper girlfriends, two or three of whom he had loved. But he had soon come to realise that the steadier relationships, as good as they might have been, did

191

not preclude the scope for fantastic figments. Even after he had married, the desire for other women hadn't gone away, nor had he really expected it to. He had battled with the longings, but always fought them off efficiently. The sums of infidelity just didn't add up. The risk of throwing away everything, for nothing. In very nearly twenty-three years of marriage he had never slept with anyone else; hadn't wanted to, really. Once or twice he had come close. Who hadn't? When those moments in the company of an amiable woman – friend of a friend at a party, maybe, or a cheerful acquaintance in a pub – had unaccountably graduated, one second to the next, from idle flirtation to malignant possibility.

He couldn't have gone ahead, he thought to himself as he lay in the dark. The comets having eventually faded, it was the same pitch black whether his eyes were open or closed. The notion of hurting Sylvie was far more painful than the notion of hurting himself. He could guess her eyes if she ever found out, it wasn't hard. The image of them, which he always automatically conjured up in his mind whenever he was sailing close to the rockiness of unchartered sex, were as a lighthouse against the temptation of further action.

He hadn't seen those eyes earlier that evening with Laurie.

He closed his, now, and wondered why. Perhaps because, with Laurie, he wasn't Kim Black but Tim White. And perhaps Tim White, being only a sort of husband to Sylvie, had less of a conscience, and could justify, more, a certain openness within his marriage, a certain freedom of movement.

The next day, Saturday, Kim was working the afternoon shift. He woke up at ten o'clock. Mrs Blake did not approve of breakfast so late, but allowed him to make himself some toast in her kitchen. As he was leaving the house, he met Laurie in the porch putting her newspaper into the basket of her bicycle. She was wearing a long brown skirt with a pattern of cream flowers. Made of light viscose, it flowed round her legs in the Christmassy wind. It was her weekend off, and she was looking unexpectedly feminine, though the abseiler's sexuality was still coaxingly evident beneath the folds of her soft coat.

'Where are you off to?' he asked.

'Meet a friend,' she nodded. 'Pub in the centre.'

To his annoyance, Kim found himself perturbingly curious to know the sex of this friend.

'You?'

'I've to buy a bedside lamp,' he told her. 'Mrs B's lighting is somewhat wanting in subtlety.' Laurie smiled in recognition. She had phenomenal teeth over which her lips had to stretch like rubber bands, and which looked as though they had been whitened with a special pearly agent, the better to kiss with. 'Then work. Shift starts at two.'

'We're both in good time?' she stated as a question. 'I don't have to meet my friend till one? Where're you going to buy your lamp?'

'Hadn't thought.'

'There's a nice shop I can show you in the centre for that sort of thing?'

Laurie left her bike in the drive and the two of them started walking towards the city centre. As they did so, she told him about all the wonderful things New Zealand had going for it, and his mind drifted on to all the risible things he might say to her later to lure her into his bed.

In the shop he picked out the simplest lamp he could find. It cost £26. He had nothing like that amount on him in cash and, diverted by Laurie's company, he paid for it with the Switch card in his wallet which went by the name of Dr Kim Black. She didn't even look as he signed, let alone read the name. She was too busy sighing over a cushion in the shape of the Loch Ness monster.

'Fancy a coffee?' she asked as they stepped outside.

Kim looked at his watch. 'Won't you be late for your friend?'

'Oh, he's always late for me.'

Kim thought for a moment. 'I'd like to,' he said, 'but I'd better get moving myself. Bus takes ages.'

Laurie didn't flicker. 'Oh, all right,' she said casually. 'See you later then.'

'Will you be in this evening?'

'Will you?'

'No plans.' He transferred the strong paper bag with the lamp from one hand to the other.

'Me neither?' she said.

'Perhaps we could . . .?'

'There's a nice pub near us,' she declared with formidable confidence, not a mote of hesitation, of delicacy.

'Drink then.' If he thought about Jack's girlfriends and some of his younger women patients for one moment, the startling things they let drop about their modern methods of seducing men, he should not have been surprised by Laurie's assertiveness.

'That'd be great?'

'Shift finishes at ten. If I'm lucky I should be back in time for last orders.'

'Well, no worries if you don't. I've some Bourbon in my room?'

Her last statement, with its questioning intonation, sounded like an invitation which was meant to be interpreted loosely. Kim didn't want to make assumptions, but believed that he might be able to spare himself the indignity of saying all those ridiculous things he had lined up to cajole her into his bed. Feeling encouraged by the prospect of Bourbon, and its horizon, he wanted to touch her before they went their separate ways, perhaps tap her shoulder or kiss her on the cheek, first step on the foothill. But, before he could work out quite how to set about it, she did it for him. Leant forward and kissed his lips, just like that.

'I want to fuck you?' she whispered into his ear.

So the impression he had got had not been entirely presumptuous. By way of confirmation, he cupped the back of her head in his hand, pressed her face to his, and kissed her hard. Her tongue was thick and wide, filled up his mouth, and tasted of tired chewing gum recently discarded. Without disengaging from her lips, he put his bag on the ground and with his free hand squeezed her supple waist. They stayed like that for a minute or two. When they parted Kim still felt warm as he made his way to the bus stop in the freezing air.

A while later, after a tiresome bus ride, he arrived at the hospital. He was in good time and a good mood. He felt that sensation of sweet anticipation, like melting chocolate, for his night ahead. He headed for the locker room, changed into his uniform, and then went to check in with Eck, the deputy head porter on duty.

Although it was still only the early afternoon, the casualty department was already hotting up for its prime-time Saturday evening slot. The waiting room was a microcosm of contemporary ills. In it sat various young children who'd harmed themselves doing cartwheels or glue. An anorexic teenager, thin as a banshee, propped up by a middle-aged couple who must have been her parents; all three of them quietly groaning with the pain of hunger, whether literal, spiritual, or both. Several Black & Decker fall-outs – men who had slipped off ladders, hammered their thumbs, sliced their fingers with saws. Joyriders who'd started early and come to an abrupt halt before the nocturnal fun had really begun. The round-the-clock smokers coughing up samples of their molasses-rich lungs. And those who hadn't been able to hold out for the tarpaulin of dusk before untimely overdosing on whisky, barbiturates, heroin, crack, paraquat, or strange inner voices, to name but a few.

Kim steeled himself for his starter's orders, and before long was pushing trolleys in and out of the lifts, along polished corridors, through swing doors, into wards and theatres. The hard rubber wheels which rattled over the minor bumps in the lino floor trembled his arms, and the familiar hospital bustle pummelled his adrenaline.

It was a strange picture he had of strange photofit faces. His fleeting charges were all upside down, chins as foreheads as in an either-way portrait, and cut off at the neck by the tight tuck of blankets. A few did their level best to offend him with insults and spittle, cursed any member of staff who passed, cursed life, cursed themselves. Some had their eyes closed and weren't able to speak. Others cried with frustration or pain. Most made touching small-talk, in whispers, brave as could be.

The nursing staff and the handful of doctors on duty were swept off their feet. Kim watched them with a keen eye. They seemed to be coping well enough, with the exception of Dr Gordon, the houseman who had a sneering way with all the nurses (he ignored the porters almost completely) but whose career, because of his appalling incompetence and inability to function well under pressure, relied almost wholly on their very level-headed support and expertise. He was a self-important and mean-spirited man, with a braying voice and nostrils which twitched like those of the loftiest specimen at a dog show. He had the air of someone who felt that respect was his right, and yet neither his title, his white coat, nor his crucial responsibility were adequate enough to fool those whom he treated as inferiors into believing he deserved it.

Kim was relieved to be free of the worrying, life-giving responsibility which Dr Gordon was so ineptly failing to live up to; and at the same time nostalgic for the understandable buzz he remembered it had given him from his early experiences of it during his clinical years in Belfast, and his six-month SHO job in Oxford – following the paediatrics one – in Accident and Emergency. He thought back now to the month-long stints, as well as the voluntary evenings and weekends, he had spent at Belfast's Royal Victoria and Mater Hospitals. It had been, as he had guessed before applying to read medicine at Queens, a prime time to be in the city's casualty departments. People like him, from England, weren't the only ones who chose to train there. The course had also been very popular with students from as far away as Malaysia and Norway.

At the Royal, which backs onto the Falls, there had been an inspirational consultant with whom many of them had come into contact called Mr Sutherland. He was unusual amongst his peers in that he occasionally used to venture on to the scene of a bombing or shooting himself because he felt it important once in a while to do the vital, hands-on work alongside the paramedics. Kim had been privileged enough on a few occasions to go out with him in the ambulance. It was on location, as it were, that for the first time he had seen – and had urgently had to deal with – hands and arms and legs and faces and brains in such states as God had never devised for them.

Kim was a natural medic but under Mr Sutherland had become particularly practised at making pin-point diagnoses, whether in hospital or out in the field, and in acting quickly and efficiently after having done so. Presumably Dr Gordon had had the benefit of no such enlightened mentor. Certainly, he had no such innate flair for the job. It was galling for Kim to witness the extent to which he leant on the nurses. While this was an unspoken tradition amongst young doctors with little experience (and they – usually – expressed enormous gratitude for their

196

help), it was only so up to a point. Kim also watched as Gordon treated the nurses as no more than handmaidens and took advantage of their good natures and greater competence. He left used sharps lying around, and everything else behind him in a mess for them to clear up, and never even grunted a please or thank you. Occasionally he had relied on the more experienced nurses for correct diagnoses and dosages.

More than once during Kim's several shifts since working at Raigmore he had been tempted to intervene but had had to bite his tongue. He still felt strongly the doctor's instinct to preserve life at – almost – all costs. But in his capacity as Tim White, hospital porter, he was not entitled to Dr Black's white-coat responsibilities, opinions and experience. He knew he was sailing very close to the wind. There had been an occasion, a couple of days before, when he had been with Dr Gordon and a student nurse in a cubicle with a pregnant woman. The fledgling nurse, who could not have been expected to know otherwise, hadn't said anything as she saw him about to put a drip up on the patient. Typical of a junior doctor, Gordon had over-estimated the seriousness of her condition, and failed to realise that her low blood pressure wasn't due to shock, but was in fact perfectly normal in pregnancy. Fortunately his colleague, a young Dr Birch who had rings under her eyes but who never missed a trick, had stepped in by chance to tell Gordon that he was needed elsewhere. She had immediately spotted the mistake and prevented the woman being needlessly admitted in the nick of time.

Unfortunately, just as the early Saturday evening drunks were beginning to turn up and throw up in their droves, Kim found himself in another compromising situation with Gordon.

At about six o'clock a thin man of about twenty-one came in following a minor car crash. He wore Adidas trainers and had the white sliced pallor and undeveloped look common amongst his urban peers of someone who had lived all his life underground sustained by only the artificial, untrustworthy light of a television. He limped up to the desk slowly and gave his name, Rory Hamilton, just as Kim happened to be at Reception taking an instruction from Eck. He noticed Rory because he had one of those winning faces. Far from beautiful, it was essentially plain, gawky even, and not without its fair share of bullying spots. Yet there was an openness and sweetness about it which prompted Kim to give him a friendly and reassuring smile. Rory smiled back and then moved cautiously, as if in some discomfort, towards the nearest empty chair and settled down in preparation for the long wait ahead of him. A while later, when Kim was next passing through Reception, he glanced at him again. Unlike many of those around him, Rory was neither shouting angrily, complaining loudly, nor even frowning crossly. He was just sitting quietly with a patience which struck Kim as unassuming and admirable.

There was no blood on Rory to give him that dramatic edge over the next man, nor did he have so much as a visible cut or bruise to his name. He did not look ill and, even though not looking ill remained an inexact science, he was kept waiting for what Kim estimated to be two and a quarter hours before being called to a curtained cubicle ostensibly to be seen by a doctor, but actually to be told to wait for what turned out to be another thirty-five minutes. Kim walked past him more than once. He had changed into a gown and was lying semi-recumbent on the trolley. There wasn't a picture on the wall, a decade-old magazine to flip through, even a puzzle to play with, just the trolley, a plastic chair, and another, smaller trolley with drawers, a glass top, and a tray of instruments. Rory looked so bored that he appeared to be trying to work out the ugly yellow pattern splashed across the grey curtains, but still his patience didn't appear to have worn out.

Kim might not have spoken two words to Rory were it not for the fact that a woman whom he had taken up to one of the wards had left her coat in the cubicle he was now occupying. Kim returned to fetch it for her just when Dr Gordon had finally gone in to examine Rory and question him about his medical history.

'Does this hurt?' Dr Gordon asked, moving to the end of the trolley to check Rory's lower leg and yank his ankle. He lifted up the hem of the patient's long gown to reveal a swelling under which the sharpness of the bone had sunk to extinction, like an island beneath a global warming sea.

'Yeah, bad, and it hurts a little when I breathe,' Rory told him.

Dr Gordon stayed by the ankle for a while, pressing and rotating it. Rory flinched as imperceptibly as he could and

198

rounded his lips but didn't go so far as to say, 'Ow.'

'Nothing to worry about,' Dr Gordon said cockily. 'Though an X-ray wouldn't go amiss. Let's just have a listen to your chest first.' He asked the boy to slip his gown down over his shoulders. Under the strip lights his thin skin looked as white as Tipp-Ex and fragile shadows sheltered between the downs of his ribs. There was a bruised area, a fresh, pulpy pink, purple and blue colour. Dr Gordon either overlooked it or decided it was insignificant. Certainly, he didn't ask after it. 'Chest sounds OK,' he told him.

'That's some bruise you've got there,' Kim ventured to point out as casually as he could while extracting the coat he had come to collect from the shoulders of the chair. It was the most diplomatic way he could think of to bring it to the inattentive doctor's attention.

Dr Gordon turned to him with the sort of expression a self-important bus driver might give a passenger who distracted him while he was driving. 'Take this lad to have his ankle X-rayed,' he told him curtly, before instructing Rory to stay lying down. 'I'll see you again afterwards, Mr Hamilton,' he added. He then whipped open the cubicle curtains so that their hooks made a harsh metallic swish round the rail. He disappeared with the flourish of a spear-bearing actor who, only on stage for one scene and without so much as two words to say, is determined that the very thing going to get him noticed is the exquisite drama of his exit.

Kim released the brake and was about to manoeuvre the bed out of the cubicle to take Rory to be X-rayed as he had been told, but he was too anxious. Without thinking, he asked if, in the crash, Rory had suffered any blow to the chest.

'It hit the steering wheel,' came the slow, and now slightly breathless reply.

Kim was worried by the breathlessness. He knew from it that Rory's condition was far more serious than Dr Gordon – who had failed to ask him the simple but vital question about his chest – had presumed. Kim wondered if, in the impact, Rory had broken a rib which in turn had pierced the covering of the lung. If so, it meant the air he was breathing in, with nowhere to escape, was leaking into the pleural cavity which was increasing in size with every inspiration. During the few seconds that he was contemplating this, he noticed that Rory's breathing was becoming shallower and more rapid. This prompted Kim to suspect he had sustained a tension pneumothorax which, if untreated, would cause a cardio-respiratory arrest and death.

Kim quickly glanced out into the corridor alongside the row of cubicles. There were people everywhere – nurses, doctors and his fellow porters, all rushing to and fro with concentrated, dedicated expressions. He tried to catch the attention of some of them, but they were too intent on their immediate business. A drunk, oblivious to the fact that he was peeing into his trousers, was at the same time verbally abusing a nurse who was looking increasingly afraid. It was one of the porter's duties to help with such breaches of security and to protect the staff, but the situation didn't yet look drastic and Kim knew he must not leave Rory. Other nurses were helping Dr Birch deal with an emergency, shooting by with a patient on a trolley festooned with drips. Dr Gordon ran past and Kim tried to appeal to him to take another look at Rory. 'I thought I told you to take Mr Hamilton to X-ray,' he half-shouted, not stopping. 'Can't you see I'm busy?' Kim became desperate. Looking carefully to see that nobody was watching, he could hold out no longer. He quickly shut the curtains. He noticed that the veins in Rory's neck had become distended and were beginning to stand out like those of a straining weightlifter. Rory's breathing was worsening, and his lips steadily taking on the hue of a frosted blueberry.

Kim immediately went into action so instinctive that anyone trying to stop him would have had to have pinned him down. He delicately but swiftly slipped Rory's gown from his shoulders again and noticed the bruised and puffy area on his chest had the consistency of a wet sponge: a sure sign of surgical emphysema. Then he felt for Rory's trachea and placed his index and middle finger either side of it. It had moved across his neck. He instantly began to percuss his chest. Rory was too scared by his lack of breath to look startled about the fact that someone in a porter's uniform was performing these doctorly tasks.

Kim was listening intently to the sounds his practised fingers were making across Rory's upper torso. On one side only, they were worryingly hollow and deep. This fact definitively confirmed Kim's diagnosis of tension pneumothorax. His worst fear.

Wasting no more time, he leapt aside hastily to open the curtains and was about to shout for someone when he heard Rory struggling more and more for breath. There was no time to shout and wait for an on-duty doctor, no time even to close the curtains again. Feeling sick to his stomach both with fear of what he was going to have to do, and with that of being detected, but without a second's hesitation, Kim turned to the trolley of laid out instruments. On it, among other things – neatly arranged boxes graded by size, alongside cotton wool, bandages, swabs, needles, tape, KY jelly, and a variety of rubber gloves – lay several of the objects he was looking for, called venflons. Each was about ten centimetres long and had a plastic casing with a needle inside. Their caps came in a variety of colours to denote their different sizes.

By now, just as a soldier in danger is trained to kill, the doctor in Kim went on automatic pilot to do the opposite. He immediately picked out the grey venflon which he knew to be the thickest. Then he felt about, with the tip of his finger, for the optimum site on Rory's chest needed for his purposes. All the while Rory's breath was becoming increasingly desperate. He was starting to struggle for every last ounce of oxygen, unaware that the more air he tried to take in, the more it was compressing his lung, and so the less able the lung was to inflate. Kim knew he had only a matter of moments.

'Don't worry,' he told him urgently, gripping his shoulder with his free hand. 'I promise I know what I'm doing, promise.' But he wasn't so sure. Tension pneumothorax was a rare condition. He hadn't had to deal with an actual case for many a moon. He remembered what to do in theory. In practice, though, it was another matter. He still felt sick.

He found what he was looking for, namely the mid-clavicular line in the second intercostal space which, in layman's terms, was a spot between the two ribs a couple of inches or so below his collarbone, and three inches above his right nipple. Then, regardless of anyone in the corridor who might see him, he tore open the venflon's sterile packaging and pulled away its outer plastic casing. With not a moment to waste in giving explanations as to what he was about to do, he reassured Rory with some comforting words and locked eye contact. 'It's all under control,' he said, knowing he was employing every acting skill at his disposal. He was terrified,

201

almost excited, himself, and was forcing his hands not to tremble. 'You're going to be fine.' He hoped these small clichés might at least convey some medical authority and expertise – despite all sartorial appearances to the contrary – and, perhaps even more importantly, fill Rory with confidence and inspire him to trust him. At the same time, he aimed the venflon at the spot he had so carefully pinpointed, and stood for a suspended millisecond with a pose which a non-medically-minded onlooker might have mistaken for a knifeman intent on murder.

'Just what the hell do you think you are doing?' A voice suddenly bellowed so close to his ear that Kim could feel its owner's clammy breath on his neck. 'Get out of the fucking way!'

Dr Gordon had been passing the cubicle and seen that the porter whose name he didn't know had still not carried out his instruction to take Mr Hamilton to have his ankle X-rayed. He had looked in and was on the point of giving him an earful when he had clocked the unimaginable – a madman in porter's uniform about to stab a patient in the breast with a venflon. In some ways Kim didn't blame Dr Gordon for his anger, even when he tried to elbow him aside, and yet it wasn't the moment to explain. He could not allow the most incompetent houseman imaginable to take over, and watch as he faffed about trying to match symptoms to practical procedure. He couldn't trust such a man to perform so skilled and critical a task.

Dr Gordon's shove was so aggressive that Kim stumbled. His adversary leant over the patient, looked completely nonplussed for a second, opened Rory's lips with his thumbs and forefingers, bent low over his mouth, and took a deep breath in preparation for a kiss of life.

'Stop! You can't do that,' Kim shouted. 'It's tension pneumothorax, you fool.'

'What?' hissed Dr Gordon, looking up, the veins in his neck nearly as bloated as those of the patient. 'What the fuck do you know?'

Kim watched in horror as Rory was beginning to lose consciousness.

Unceremoniously, he shoved the young doctor against the back wall. Then, instantly locating the right place in Rory's chest again, he forcefully plunged the venflon two inches into him.

Then he deftly removed the needle but left the hollow inner plastic tubing in place, sticking out of Rory's jittery flesh, in order that the rest of the trapped air could eventually find its way out. As he did so, a hiss of beachball air was released and Rory let out a startled gasp more of breath and surprise than of pain. Almost immediately his breathing improved. He was not out of the woods, Kim told himself in that over-used doctor's phrase, but his life had been saved.

'What he needs now is a CXR,' he icily informed Dr Gordon who was leaning against the back wall in shock at what he had just seen, 'to see if the lung has re-expanded,' he went on, spelling it out, 'so that a chest drain with an underwater seal can be put in.'

'I'm going to call Security,' Dr Gordon said, 'and you'll be dealt with immediately by the appropriate authorities. You know that passing yourself off as a doctor is a criminal offence.'

'I said, what this man needs now is a CXR. Now!'

'You don't need to tell me.'

'Of course not,' Kim muttered so politely that the sarcasm was lost on Dr Gordon who was now fussing over Rory proprietorially as if it was this very fussing which had brought him back from the brink.

Kim glanced at Rory whose lips were beginning to return to a reasonable colour, whose veins in his neck had subsided, and whose sweet face was slowly regaining some of its vivacity. He squeezed his hand, and made his way silently out and along the still-bustling corridor.

'Come back here!' he could hear Dr Gordon calling after him. 'Come back here!'

Kim could rely on the fact that, having so manifestly failed his patient the first time, Dr Gordon wouldn't dare to leave him a second time, even if he didn't believe Rory had ever been in any real danger, and even if it was to chase after an excruciating imposter.

Nonetheless, he stepped up his pace and went to the locker room where he grabbed his clothes, and his lamp, before rushing for the exit. He might have saved someone's life but it meant that he was now, officially, on the run.

*

Kim did not have sex with Laurie that night. He would have liked the reason to have been last-minute restraint in the face of a *fait accompli*, but no such self-congratulation was in order. Circumstances intervened, nothing more noble. The fact was, there was no time to hang about. He fled from Inverness without going back to Mrs Blake's. There were only two things there to lose: a toothbrush, and the consummation of some desire which was worthless.

It was about ten o'clock and the night air challenged Kim's lungs. He blew on his hands and scampered along the main road away from the hospital to keep warm as he tried to hitch a lift. He climbed in with the first person to stop, a lorry driver who was on his way to Perth with a load of shoes. After the man, Colin, had given Kim an inventory of all the different types he was carrying – black ones, brown ones, suede ones, leather ones, lace-ups and slip-ons, the list went on – neither of them felt particularly inclined to talk and broke into silence.

Although the well-equipped cab was dark except for the glowing lights of the controls and the clock behind the huge steering-wheel, it felt homely. Into each door was set a fold-up holder for two cans of drinks. There were trinkets, postcards and family photographs stuck onto the dashboard with Blu-tac. The framed smiles of a woman and two girls who Kim took to be the driver's wife and daughters brightened with the passing of each orange street lamp. A dog-haired rug and furry cushions were ranged neatly along the three-person seat. Between Kim and the driver sat a tartan thermos filled with tea and a Tupperware box with chocolate wafers and squashed fly biscuits. The heating was on full blast and a local radio station was playing an earnest song which turned out to be by Tom Jones in full throttle.

It was a slow journey along the A9. They drove through Aviemore with its filing-cabinet hotels, its overpriced ski shops, and its faux-chalet bars. Every one of its neon fast-food joints seemed to have in its forecourt a huge, ketchup-coloured dragon, dinosaur or reindeer by way of a cynical ploy to lure children inside. Each outsize animal had an overly friendly grin of vast white teeth, and was wearing skis, an orange bobble hat and a stripy scarf which fixedly flowed out behind it. Kim felt dispirited by the ugliness of them, and thought that had Dr Gordon had a thread of medical know-how, he might, this moment, have been sipping Bourbon with Laurie in her room while she assertively seduced him, instead of contemplating the tackiness of fibreglass monsters and heading into the unknown.

The unknown wasn't without its attractions, of course. There was something exciting about not having a clue what time they would arrive in Perth and, when they did, where he would go.

But the novelty of not knowing which bed he was going to be sleeping in was diluted slightly in the face of not knowing if he was going to be able to find one to sleep in at all. He might have the choice of a number of B & Bs and guesthouses or, depending on the late hour of their arrival, none at all. At once, he regretted not being on the bed he had glimpsed a couple of times through Laurie's open door, narrow but inviting in a horny sort of way – tossed sheets and grubby pillows with the promise of grungy, bedsit sex – listening to her trashy music while grappling with her forceful tongue, her abseiling breasts. There again, he had escaped the dull ache of disillusion which would have invariably followed, and the dead weight arising from the knowledge of having committed adultery for the first time, the no going back, the something altered for good.

Even so, perhaps what he was after was the uncertainty of strange beds, with or without the presence of strangers. So alluring in all their variety, so anonymous and meaningless, such absence of association, so free. So damn bleak.

He thought about his steady bed at home with its white, old-fashioned iron frame, its worn antique sheets (picked up for a few quid by Sylvie in junk shops), its squashy feather pillows, the several squeaking springs in its put-upon mattress. It was inviting also, but in a way entirely different from Laurie's: clean, warm, familiar, intimate, private; symbol of all his and Sylvie's off-limits activities – drunken fucks after parties, lazy love-making when too tired to move, energetic passion suddenly overtaking them, conception of their daughter, twenty or so years of marital sex in all its forms. Symbol, too, of their shared past – reading favourite books out loud to each other, screaming rows, telly suppers, flu, pre-dawn breast-feeding, painful middle of the night extrication (when on call), Christmas stockings, one miscarriage (before Mackenzie, mattress still stained with blood), sleep.

While having these thoughts, Kim was staring out of the wide windscreen watching each marking on the black road as it was sucked under the front of the lorry. A green sign indicated twelve miles to Perth. In the fug of the cab, he was feeling so tired his eyelids were yanking themselves downwards and he couldn't stop yawning.

He was asleep when they arrived in the town. The driver parked. Kim was vaguely aware of the jerky, spluttering halt of the engine but didn't wake up until Colin nudged him and told him he was stopping to get some rest in his cubbyhole above. Kim asked if he knew of a B & B which might take him in.

'No, can't say I do,' the driver replied. 'I suppose you could sleep in here, but I'll be leaving early in the morning.'

'Thanks. Where're you going?'

'Carrying on south. Newcastle, Middlesbrough. You?'

'Wherever.'

'Well, if you're not bothered, you can come as far as you like.'

'I need to.'

'Oh yes?' The driver looked at him askance, but obviously decided he wasn't a violent criminal. 'Well, it's nice to have a bit of company. Now, if you don't mind, I'm going to turn in.' So saying, he opened his door, leapt out, and made his way up through a latch behind the cab into the tiny space above it which was fitted with a short bed, a shelf, and two small windows. Left alone, Kim, with his coat still on, lay across the seat with the rug over him, a cushion against the passenger door for a pillow, and fell instantly asleep.

He woke to an intense cold, which had stiffened his entire body, and the metallic stretch and roar of the engine. The driver was already beside him starting up. A taped voice could be heard again and again repeating in a nasal tone the words, 'Beware – vehicle reversing. Beware – vehicle reversing.' Kim opened his eyes and sat up creakily wondering about the hapless Equity member who had auditioned for, and won, that particular voiceover.

The clock said six fifteen and it was pitch black outside. There was condensation on all the windows. The driver wiped them with the back of his weary gloves. Kim could see their smokey

206

breath on the air and that his own fingers had turned the yellow-white of raw beef-fat.

The journey was long and slow, and together, while listening to the corny jingles of Radio 2 and saying nothing, Kim and Colin watched the Prussian blue of the emerging autumn dawn.

They stopped off at two truck-stops on the way, one for breakfast, one for lunch. They were both brightly lit canteens with plastic tables and chairs and identical menus consisting of different combinations of chips and sausages and eggs. Burly men with donkey jackets eyed the plump teenage girls who were serving the slurry of beans or mince from the canal-lock pans behind the counter. Once they had been given their food, the lorry drivers nodded at each other. Having clocked up years on the road and an eternity of truck-stop meals, they all knew, or at least recognised one another. Some sat together, slurping tea, smoking, gossiping as delectably as any group of women, putting off the moment of having to return to the lonely fug of their cabs with only the monotony of motorway and the tinny frazzle of CB radio for company.

Kim paid for his lunch and joined Colin at a table by the window overlooking the dual carriageway. He had no idea where they were. It was as if the truck-stop was a landmark in itself, a functional but anonymous point on every driver's journey towards his final far-off destination in the south, or Europe, or beyond. It was unsettling, Kim thought, having no sense of place, like holding a conversation with someone whose age or sex is unfathomable.

A man with a plate of food piled as high as a rubbish tip greeted Colin and sat down beside him. His shirtsleeves were rolled up to reveal forearms as wide as hams and branded with tattoos. Eric 4 Lindsay; Eric 4 Mary; Eric 4 Emma; Eric 4 Katie; Eric 4 Deborah; and so on, totalling a tally of eight different names. Eric was evidently a man who embraced the freedom of the road.

But he had the air of someone who had gorged on self-indulgence, become fat on self-gratification, yet remained disgruntled and dissatisfied. He told some questionable anecdote about a woman he referred to as Truck-Stop Lil, of whom Colin had clearly heard, and who, Kim gathered, was apparently based at

Watford Gap and worked the M1 single-handedly. Otherwise Eric's conversation was full of complaint – complaint about the road, the traffic, his bosses, about his bad back, about crap women drivers, about eight women, about getting eight times the grief. Colin and Kim remained quiet as they listened to Eric's litany.

'He's got twenty-three kids by these eight different women,' was all Colin said to Kim as the two of them left the canteen and walked back across the oil-rich tarmac to his lorry-load of shoes. It was hard to distinguish from his tone whether Colin was impressed or disgusted. Probably both.

A few hours later, on the outskirts of Newcastle, Kim parted from taciturn Colin, and checked into a bungalow B & B. It was a dump. No sheets or pillowcases, only careworn blankets with inhospitable stains, overflowing lavatory, broken furniture, torn curtains, dysfunctional storage heaters, wallpaper flocked with mildew. The very air seemed to be infected with tuberculosis. He only stayed one night, and left the next morning with no destination in mind.

And so began a country-wide, month-long stint of hitching lifts, taking Green-line buses; walking in the alien towns and the obscure villages of England. He passed through housing developments and industrial wastelands; along railway lines; over streams and brooks babbling with chemical sputum; and across inorganic fields of barren grass littered with plastic bottles, burnt-out cars, harsh twisted steel and fragile twisted condoms.

Wherever he could, he'd find casual work and do day- sometimes week-long, shifts. He was on a building site outside Gateshead, he shunted trolleys round a supermarket car park in Darlington, he looked after dogs in a kennel near Pickering, and sold candyfloss at a funfair in Whitby. Everywhere he was paid cash, no questions asked.

All the while he was staying in different beds, being thrown out of squalid establishments, being taken in by kindly farmers, loners or matriarchs, for free. In Worksop a pensioner let him sleep on his settee because he thought the breath of another human being might help nudge the chill from his perishing bedsit. In Leek a widow, with eyes the pigment of which looked

208

as though it had been washed away by tears, gave him for the night both a bed and the oral biography of her late husband's long, long life. The next morning, she praised him for being such a good listener and told him he should have been a doctor. In the same town, a glazed youth found the necessary resources to punch and kick him in return for the sixty-three pence he had left in his pocket and which he had earmarked for his dinner. His eyes were opened here, and here, by magnanimity and compassion, by aggression and cruelty.

In all these places, and in Rotherham and Glossop, Congleton and Keele, Swansea and Dawlish, and while washing dishes in hotel kitchens for a pittance, helping out on farms (fixing fences, slopping out cow sheds) in exchange for a free meal, sweeping people's driveways, he thought about Sylvie.

She hadn't wanted to address her phobia but, very soon after they moved to Oxford, Kim had suggested to her that she should.

She'd had more than a fright with an old man who lived alone in a basement room from which he was being evicted. Her department had sent her along to see him. What they had overlooked to tell her was the fact that he didn't live entirely alone. In fact he shared his bedsit with thirty-nine pigeons.

Kim would never forget her description of that day. She'd found the house off the Abingdon Road quite easily. It wasn't particularly inviting, she recalled, with its cracked black window frames and its pitch-burnt brick, but the canary-yellow colour of the man's basement front-door was unexpectedly bright and made her wonder if it reflected its owner's sunny disposition. She mentioned the ruffled sound she heard as she stood in the single-bulb alley waiting for him to open up. It came from within and she took it to be sheets being shaken straight for folding. She shivered, not knowing why. When he eventually did open the door to her, it wasn't just the putrid smell, and the eerie sound of portent flapping and requiem cooing which overwhelmed her but, everywhere, on every surface – the red and grey patterned carpet, the tiled mantelpiece, the bowl of old Weetabix on the rotten wooden table, in the folds of the net curtains, in the very fleck of the old man's cardigan, and on the pate of his bald head – was splattered the snotty, watery concoction of curdled sour milk and olive-green algae. Kim could remember someone telling him that we should feel sorry for birds, they're all incontinent, no sphincters, so merciless shit falls through them with nothing to stop it. He did not feel sorry for them, and the recollection of the incident brought even him out in a fresh shudder of squeamishness. Anyone would have found the scene horrific, but for Sylvie it was something more, so profound a shock. Even though it was nobody's fault, he still felt angry that his wife had been exposed to it. A week later she had a miscarriage. Who knew if the two unspeakable dramas were related.

It was after this that Kim had persuaded her to see someone for a course of cognitive therapy. She had been reluctant, terrified, at the very prospect but he had accompanied her to her first three sessions at the local psychiatric hospital and in the event she had displayed nothing but admirable, characteristic courage.

In the first session she had been told to try painting a large picture of a pigeon and to stroke it. To sit in on her fear had been a sobering experience. Even to mix the grey powder paint and form it on paper into the nightmarish outline of her greatest enemy, was a trial. Kim could still visualise the tension of her blue veins as they pulsated round the delicate, pale wrist which held the brush; the reluctance in her hesitant, blinking eyes. In the second session, she had had to hold a stuffed toy pigeon made of felt, and handle a feather duster. Because the duster's feathers had been dyed scarlet and therefore were as removed from the real thing as a supermarket chicken is from a live and clucking hen, this she had managed, but the real pheasants' feathers of session three had defeated her, made her cry.

Before meeting Sylvie, Kim had come across many patients in the course of his training with odd phobias, obsessions and fears, who had easy panic attacks. While sympathetic, he had perhaps underestimated how debilitating and disruptive they were to their lives. Looking back, he chided himself for his lack of imagination and thanked his wife for opening his eyes to a medical, psychological, emotional phenomenon which, until she enlightened him, he hadn't really studied thoroughly enough.

Kim had been advised that Sylvie should attend the following sessions alone. When she had told him about the fourth one, she had laughed with relief, and the absurdity of her phobia and the situation she found herself in because of it. (Another reason that he loved her: never taking herself seriously, not even her greatest fears.) Session four had taken place in a long room which had a small cage at the very end of it containing a fluorescent green budgerigar. The therapist had encouraged her slowly to approach the cage, and she had embarked on a sort of alternative version of Grandmother's Footsteps, slowly and quietly advancing, seeing how close she could get before beginning to hyperventilate. She had been extremely pleased with herself for having managed to stop within five feet of the cage. She still had a long way to go, she told him, but she was getting there and he was proud of her. Over supper they'd joked that she'd soon be allowing him to set up a bird table for Jack in the garden.

The day after the session with the budgerigar, she'd discovered she was pregnant with Mackenzie, and they decided that it was probably best if she didn't continue with the cognitive therapy – which promised ultimately to have her exposing herself to the close-up flapping of real pigeons as nonchalantly as any tourist in Trafalgar Square. They were worried that, in the course of getting to that point, she might suffer a fright again which might put the foetus at risk.

So the phobia cure was put on hold and the pregnancy continued apace. Mackenzie was born a few months later, an angelic child whose repertoire, which consisted either of sleeping or smiling, was modest but winning. Unlike her brother's, which included shouting and jumping and fighting and competing and showing off. He was boisterous, demanding, challenging, and, despite Sylvie's best efforts to sensitise him in terms of culture and emotion, showed a fascination for cars and engines and tractors and aeroplanes which was visceral and seemed, in the early years at least, to belie many of her good intentions. Mackenzie soon began to show an interest in clothes, and emotionally analytical conversation, almost entirely lacking in her sibling. As they watched their son and daughter grow up, Kim and Sylvie's progressive views on gender-stereotyping were, in the form of their own flesh and blood, turned on their heads.

Jack had, in the end, turned out to be a compassionate and considerate character – despite the very hot-blooded turnover of girlfriends which, genuinely, wasn't so much machismo for the sake of braggadocio but, more, the combination of youthful opportunity, experimentation, natural curiosity, and zest for life. Perhaps, as his father, Kim's opinion of him in this matter was indulgent. Yet even his mother and sister owned that Jack was never the insensitive bastard. He did not flinch from the kind of in-depth discussions Sylvie and Mackenzie so relished, about the relationships between people – family and school friends, Sylvie's clients, Kim's patients, their colleagues and families, lovers and children. This was a testimony to Sylvie's thoughtful upbringing. So, too, was the fact that Mackenzie was hard-working, ambitious and confident in a world which was geared to producing genera- tions of girls irrationally obsessed with their own beauty or – more commonly – their perceived lack of it. Her shyness was caused not by low self-esteem but, rather, by appropriate humility in the face of above average intelligence and good looks.

Kim was proud of his children, loved them to distraction, but was not completely blind to their faults. From him they had both inherited a selfishness which teetered only just this side of accept- able. He had a theory about selfishness. Thirty percent selfish was about as low as it got in a human being, and was perhaps the basic minimum necessary for survival.

Forty to fifty percent was fair to average, would occasionally prompt eyebrows to rise or comments such as, 'Can you *believe* how someone can be that selfish?' and 'Selfish bastard!' but was pretty damn commonplace, never really that surprising. Sylvie came across it all the time – people wrangling over residence and contact of their children with scant regard for the hapless pawns themselves, let alone each other.

Anything above fifty or sixty percent was troubling indeed. Alas, Sylvie had become accustomed even to this higher plain of self-interest and egocentricity. In her line of work it was not exceptional. There were plenty of cases when parents wanted to keep their children not because they gave a toss about them, but because they themselves wanted to be seen as good parents, to be seen, apparently, to love them. He remembered Sylvie coming home one evening and describing a woman she had visited at home that day who – true quote, true story – had told her unashamedly, 'I don't enjoy the company of my kids, they're noisy and I'd rather watch the telly and have sex with my new boyfriend without being interrupted, and frankly I'd be much better off without them, but I don't want my ex to have them because I don't want the neighbours to think he loves them more than I do and to see me as the callous bitch I am.' Over the years, Sylvie had accordingly lowered the threshold of what she regarded to be the norm in terms of selfishness.

Kim himself had seen some of his severely depressed patients veer from virtual catatonia to a form of high that was characterised by a seismic, hundred percent selfishness which was even more astonishing to witness than the unusual level seen in those involved in custody battles (and the occasional mid-life crisiser). Such undiluted selfishness did not allow the person to function in society without becoming a figure of resentment, suspicion, terror, hatred. The gratuitous, blatant, almost pervertedly sexual pleasure in the subjects' dark declarations – and the behaviour that went with them – concerning not giving a fuck for anyone but themselves, was, Kim had come to believe, a definite manifestation of madness. He had seen reasonable, touching souls afflicted by the emergence of an exaggerated selfishness, an exaggerated distortion of their former selves, as if their characters were being reflected as monstrous figures in fun-fair mirrors of mania.

Jack and Mackenzie's selfishness was the middling kind, temporarily enhanced by dint of their youth (hogging the phone, not turning up for a meal when expected, loud music, all of which added up to a not inconsiderable percentage). He felt sure it would, like with most well-balanced people by the time they hit thirty-five, level out to the commonplace average. He couldn't condemn them. They had probably learnt it from him. Certainly not from their mother, who was nearer the saintly mark.

As Kim journeyed on country buses (in every one, perplexingly, an empty soft drink can lolling on the floor from seat to seat, and a gob of old chewing gum stuck to the window ledge), as he walked footsore along infinite roads, and as he sat in stark or doily B & B rooms whiling away dreary afternoons between a few hours' work here and there, he pondered his own selfishness over the years.

A passion for his work had been necessary to sustain him through his training and the rigours of general practice (there was little else to keep a doctor going) but, over and above that, he had been obsessive about it, putting in extra long hours when he might have been with the family. Yet he felt he was always there for them if they needed him, and vice versa. His passion for Sylvie and the children was every bit as great, greater, than that for his job. They were together at home every night (even if he happened to be toiling away in another room), and they could flourish regardless of his actual presence. They knew he loved them, that was never in doubt. Meanwhile, his work demanded practical application – patients to be seen to, journals to be read, paperwork to be dealt with, and so forth. It was endless. Sylvie, ever uncomplaining and accommodating, had taken care of the domestic side of life even though she had her own much-loved career. She had dug a great hole of opportunity for him to throw himself into his work and, however deep she dug, he had always filled it to capacity.

Other areas of selfishness? Plenty. Too numerous to mention, but mainly in the behavioural patterns and the petty decisions of day-to-day. Watching the news four times a night. A good example.

It was a week or so before Christmas and Kim was in Stoke, a pottery town of kilns and smoke and kidney-red brick. He had taken on a couple of late shifts in a fish and chip shop. Perhaps he felt it was better than shunting trolleys round a supermarket car park because he got to wear a white coat. The place was warm, at least, almost too warm as he shook the great sieve of chips above the cauldron of hell-hot fat. And cheerful enough. The owner had pinned up some paper-chains, the orange links of which matched the fish batter. There weren't many customers, but they were friendlier than the grumpy housewives trying to park outside Tesco's in fuck-off cars, practically mowing him down. A young couple came in in clubbing colours and with ecstatic eyes, smiling at each other, at him, at the world.

'Plaice or cod?' he asked, wondering if he had been on some self-destructive bent, testing Sylvie all those years to see how much she would tolerate, how far he could go before she would snap so he'd lose everything that was most dear to him.

Was it possible that his improbable journey was his ultimate screwy test for her, devised as a means of discovering if she would be there, still, the perfect wife, waiting patiently and forgiving, when or if ever he decided to go back?

Or was it, less laudable still, the selfishness of self-pity: I'll go and work in anonymous towns in anonymous jobs, sleeping in anonymous beds, away from all I know and love, because they're better off without me?

He laid the couple's fish into the week-old newspaper, half expecting, almost hoping, to glimpse a column inch or two reporting him missing. Instead, he dropped the dripping chips onto the reams of text accompanying the court-drawing picture of an eighteen-year-old au pair girl with long blonde hair who had allegedly shaken to death the baby in her charge. Whatever his story, in terms of news (and he was something of an expert on the subject), it just didn't compare.

# 11

Kim is still alive, I do know that much. Precious little else, except for the fact that a month or so ago he bought something in a home decorating shop in Inverness, and more recently there were four Switch transactions, all for under twenty pounds, at, respectively, a guesthouse in Newcastle, a grocer's in Whitby, a chemist in Rotherham, and Safeways in Swansea. The police have done their checks. The owner of the guesthouse confirmed that the man who had stayed the night of Sunday 16 November fitted my husband's description. Kim has also been caught on the Safeways close circuit television camera coming out of the store at 15.04 on the date he spent his £7.23 there. I have watched that three-second footage a hundred times to determine for sure it is him. He is little more than a Fuzzy Felt silhouette, blurred and ill-defined, and his face, with its video-blank skin and foetal black eyes, is impossible accurately to identify, yet I fancy I can recognise the set of his shoulders, the indistinct line of his jaw. He is alone. The image is disturbing by association. It carries all the haunting resonance of other such contemporary images seen so commonly and memorably on his precious news – a teenage girl leaving a nightclub in Bristol, a toddler with a trusting hand being led away by a pre-pubescent abductor, both subsequently to suffer very detailed deaths. Heart-rending icons for our time.

It is 22 December. Kim has been missing for precisely forty-nine days. I am counting, as scrupulously as I did in pregnancy, only I cannot rely on coming to term. The kids and I had been hoping, assuming even, he might telephone on his and my twenty-third anniversary last week. How could he not? He must know how important it is to me. But no. Perhaps Christmas Day will bear fruit. A call from him, wherever he is, is the only present I am after.

I am back at work, and have been for a few weeks now. Dora and the children persuaded me that deflection of the mind is an efficacious balm. I am doing my job, but every lunch hour I talk to Suzie at the Missing Persons Helpline for a good fifteen minutes. Her capacity to listen is that rare thing, and reminds me of his.

I tell her those thoughts I am now wary of repeating to my friends for fear I may lose them to boredom and exasperation. Every day Suzie reassures me that they are still in close contact with the police, and are doing everything they can to generate publicity, and I trust her tenacity. She hasn't said as much, but I know her job is harder because Kim is not a blossoming young woman with fanciful tits or a cherubic boy with cute must-have curls. The papers are spectacularly uninterested in the loss of a middle-aged man. What constitutes news is a bit like the point system for residency in Australia, only the things which score most are physical attributes as opposed to strong family connections. I had thought that being a doctor might go in his favour but, while someone with a professional status might be in with a chance when applying for citizenship in another country, those crucial points don't pull rank when trying to gain the respect and attention of the British media. Kim is not sexy or rich enough to make the news. So it is the news has let its most loyal fan down.

I tell Suzie that I want to get in my car right now and drive to Newcastle and Whitby, Rotherham and Darlington, searching. I ask her what he is *doing* in these unexpected places, and we speculate together. At best, I sometimes imagine he just wants to get some fresh air, clear the cobwebs for a while; at worst, I suspect he has lost his mind. I try to re-live the past few weeks, months, for any clues but however many times I press the replay button in my head I cannot find a single hint of what was to come. We were having a lovely time together. No shortage of our usual curiosity about each other's work, ideas, opinions and thoughts; no sudden want of communication; still plenty of fun, jokes. Or am I so very blind?

Speculation with Suzie, Dora and the children (Mackenzie is home for the holidays, thank God, and is being as strong as can be expected), takes up a lot of my time. Another woman – other women – cross my mind in all their various incarnations, but not as persistently or compellingly as his temporary (with any luck) need for solitude, or mental breakdown. Suzie tells me that the chances of his coursing the country with a mistress are unlikely.

217

In all her years working at the charity, she has only come across two such cases. I was amazed when she told me this. She and her colleagues don't know why it is, she said, but they have a theory. 'Women,' she told me, 'tend to have an instinct if their partner has disappeared with a lover, and know deep down that that is the case, so they don't bother to ring us. Combination, must be, of not wanting to waste our time, and humiliation.' I've searched and searched myself but, to be honest, I don't have that instinct. Though of course, as I keep reminding myself, the wife is always the last to know.

The work does deflect my mind from Kim's absence, but so does Kim's absence deflect my mind from the work. Given the choice, I suspect I would sit at home, give all my time over to speculation. I could while away the rest of my life that way, grow mouldy waiting, a sort of latter-day Miss Haversham. Still, I am stronger than I was and am somehow managing to function, to give my cases the care and attention they deserve. I don't think the conclusions I reach are any less considered and reasonable than they used to be, despite my no longer being able to discuss them with Kim. Perhaps they are more so.

I am not saying that there isn't some logical explanation for Kim's disappearance. But if I have been taken in by him, he was deeply depressed, say, and never let on; if I was so damn oblivious to nuance, to the feelings of the man I have known, devoted myself to, and loved for over twenty-five years, then I am all the more determined to unclog the wool from my eyes henceforth, and burn it. I have become more sceptical about the client of mine, the parent, who on the surface is the most convincing. I no longer wish to be taken in. If you think you know your own marriage so well, but that, very possibly, has turned out not to be the case, you have to be all the more scrupulous in your judgement of other people's. Especially, as in my case, when your job is to dictate the very circumstances, the very place and length of time a person is allowed to spend with their child.

I think of one of the families whom I am dealing with at the moment. I met the Lewises, Samuel and Kathy, and their two children, about nine months ago.

The couple had just got divorced. Kathy had moved out of the family home in Abingdon, and Samuel's new girlfriend, Judy, had moved in. Ostensibly for practical reasons – Kathy's new place was a one-bedroom flat in Oxford – the children had stayed with their father. Kathy wanted her contact with them to be stepped up from two hours every Wednesday afternoon, and alternate weekends, to something more equal.

During the eight weeks that I was writing the report, I believed Kathy to be a dazzling mum. She apparently managed to maintain a very affectionate relationship with her kids as well as keep up a demanding job in sportswear PR. She convinced me that though she had made mistakes with the older child in the past, she was fully aware of them and anxious never to repeat them. To my mind, she presented as a totally rational, thoughtful and child-centred individual.

Her ex-husband, on the other hand, seemed extremely anxious to get on with his life without her. Intelligent and articulate though he was, my instant reaction was that this was unreasonable. He employed not a little of his wedding photographer's charm to cajole me, as if trying to encourage an unhappy bride to smile, to his point of view. When I still didn't go along with it, he became angry and said that I was being hoodwinked by Kathy. But, as far as I saw it, he was the smooth one.

I remember discussing the Lewises with Kim. He agreed with me, that the mother's case sounded totally plausible. I recommended to the judge that she should have a generous amount of contact, and his ruling, back in July, reflected as much.

In due course a letter arrived from Mr Lewis questioning my judgement and partiality. In all my years working for the Social Services and the Probation Service nobody has ever sent in a complaint about me. He wished to have the original order set aside and for it to be substituted with another stating that there be no direct contact between Kathy Lewis and her children. Just before I came back to work, an updated welfare report was ordered by one of the judges at Oxford County Court.

Since then I have had various meetings with the Lewises and extensive written and fax correspondence from Samuel. He is becoming increasingly desperate due to his ex-wife's inappropriate behaviour towards the children. It seems that she is more concerned about her own feelings than she is about theirs, and has twice kept them on longer at her home than the limitations of contact allowed. Once she returned them to him a full two days after the given time, regardless of their physical and emotional needs.

I have spent many hours with her and the girls at the Family Centre, watching closely, and her manner with them seems to bear out his view.

The Family Centre is grotty with its chipped radiators and lino curling at the edges like Kraft cheese slices too long unwrapped, but it is warm. There are small separate rooms with venerable chairs, bright toys and children's colourful paintings of the sun and trees, two up two down houses and grinning families. Orange squash so strong it dyes the lips, is served in paper cups, and the doughy smell of Playdo seeps from the old presentation biscuit tins in which it is kept. The three permanent members of staff have well-meaning smiles which aim to belie the fact that where they work is the setting for such sadness, and that the centre's inimitable atmosphere of cheery control is the only place where some hapless, helpless parents are permitted to see their own flesh and blood.

On the first occasion, Kathy asked little Isobel several times if she could have a sip of her juice. Four times the child said no, but her mother picked up her cup and drank some all the same. Once Meg told her mother to stop tickling her and added, 'I don't like that kiss.' Kathy carried on. These are two small examples of many in which she refuses to allow Meg or Isobel to control their own – not unreasonable – desires.

I am slowly coming to see how right Samuel was when he told me that Kathy had hoodwinked me. She has developed a distorted view of reality. Yesterday she told me that she doesn't believe she has done anything to create the difficulties which have been so distressing to him and so, indirectly, to the children and herself.

Having to write a second report is proving a levelling experience indeed. My original opinion has been completely turned on its head. Last time, I failed to pick up on the full extent of Kathy's selfishness. Even if I had, knowing me, I would have tried to find the reasons for it, tried to forgive, and strived to help her see it for herself and do something about it. But now I feel it is unpalatable, unacceptable, and that there is not the time to waste, dilly-dallying, while she sorts out her personality. A kindly man and his two vulnerable young daughters are suffering, hurt by her refusal to understand how they see things.

I now feel certain that the only proper course of action is to recommend that her regular contact with the children should be reduced to indirect contact, meaning telephone calls and letters only, before more damage is done. Something of a volte-face, I know, but I believe it is right.

Before the case goes to court again, Kathy Lewis will be allowed to see the girls for an hour on Christmas Day, again in the controlled environment of the Family Centre. As I tell her this news in my office today, I wonder if my own children will get to see their father on Christmas Day. Surely Kim must realise that we have high hopes, and he cannot be so selfish as to let us down.

We have never been a family of the fashionable view that Christmas is bunk. Even in their more adolescent phases, Jack and Mackenzie could not disguise the pleasure they gained from it. If ever I tried to fudge the family traditions, I was promptly put in my place. One year I suggested we spend it away from home, perhaps in a hotel, only to be greeted by vehement opposition. If Kim doesn't reappear this year, tradition will have been overturned in a way that none of us could ever have contemplated.

On Christmas Eve we daren't leave the house to go to Midnight Mass. I miss 'In the Bleak Midwinter', the icy cold of the candlelit church, the regular mince pies out of a festive packet, the lukewarm mulled wine. I would miss, more, Kim's home-coming, were it to materialise.

Instead the three of us sit, rather desolate, in the hot front room, watching telly with the volume a few notches louder than necessary in order to drown out any sounds in the street which might give rise to false hope. Approaching footsteps have us all holding our breaths, only then to recede, and disappoint. Better that we don't hear them in the first place.

All the accoutrements of the family Christmas are in place. The turkey, already buttered and stuffed, is in the fridge. The tree twinkles with its tasteless, irresistible, coloured fairy-lights.

The presents under it include ones for Kim too. We each bought him something of our own accord, there was no general agreement that we would. Careful thought went into the choosing and wrapping, as if to carry on as if he had never gone might, illogically, hasten his return. None of us could bear the notion that he might allow our Christmas to pass by without him.

At 12.30 the doorbell rings. Mackenzie jerks her head away from the television in expectation.

'It's Dora, isn't it, Mum?' Jack says, putting his bottle of beer on the carpet and extracting himself from the squash of the sofa. 'Didn't you say she was coming round after the service? I'll get it.' As he pads to the door, his fat socks slip over his heels and the loose toes nearly trip him up.

'Dropping off her presents,' I announce lightly.

I can hear Dora stepping in from the night, hugging and kissing Jack in the corridor, and him muttering, 'Cool.' She comes wobbling through the door swaddled in a thick coat, scarf and gloves, and with a chunky wool hat on her head. 'Bloody hell, it's freezing out there,' she tells us. 'You're best off not going out.'

'No plans to,' I tell her. 'Not budging.'

'Very sensible. Look, I brought you this. I thought you could probably all do with some.' From a large plastic bag patterned with ugly reindeer, she brings out a bottle of brandy and plonks it on the coffee table. 'It's lovely and warm in here, mind.' She sits down on the sofa and unbuttons her coat. 'No call, I take it.' Dora knows us well enough to bring up the subject uppermost in our minds.

'We didn't really expect it today,' Mackenzie says, turning the television down. 'Tomorrow's when we'll hear from him. He'll most likely turn up, just like that, in time for lunch. He's a sucker for chestnut stuffing.'

Dora stays for half an hour or so. Before she leaves she wishes us luck. 'I won't ring you,' she says thoughtfully, 'because I don't want you thinking I might be him, but if he does step back through that door, I expect you to ring me as soon as you can, all right?'

After she has gone, I go straight to bed, knowing that sleep will not come. Jack and Mackenzie stay up to watch some more television, smoke a joint, trying to mist the mind so as not to compare this Christmas Eve with others, more complete.

Christmas Day itself is full of diversions which fail to divert. Jack makes us all petrol-strong coffee for a late breakfast. We debate when to put the turkey on and one after the other each have a lingering bath.

The telephone goes a few times, and we studiedly do not get excited. It is one of the policemen, and Suzie at Missing Persons, various members of our family, all wishing us a Happy Christmas, and each time I am tempted to ask them how they feel that might be possible.

My brother-in-law, Craig, has Kim's voice (less the Belfast inflection), but I am ready for it. Not for a split second do I mistake it for his.

At three o'clock, we decide to start lunch without him. We have the works – turkey, roast potatoes and parsnips, sprouts, carrots, bread sauce, gravy – which we've all made religiously, regardless of the fact that our appetites are more in the market for an apple or a boiled egg. Normal Christmas Days we eat till we groan from the pain of our self-indulgence and distended stomachs. Mackenzie usually has to lie on the sofa to recover but cannot resist several chocolates all the same.

Jack makes a hearty go of his food, but Mackenzie and I just cannot manage it. I can see it's going to be turkey rissoles till Twelfth Night. We push our plates aside and try to find the spirit to pull the half-dozen or so cheap crackers which decorate the kitchen table. I tell them that they are welcome to go and visit their friends.

'Joking me,' Jack says. 'He still might turn up yet. Anyway, we're not leaving you alone.'

After lunch, we sit in the front room and open socks and soaps, paperbacks and bubble bath, and hug each other harder than usual.

Kim does not come home. Nor does he telephone. I blow out the candles after supper in the kitchen, and go to bed early. The sheets are cold as metal, and I shiver between them contemplating another interminable night.

# 12

A kitchen porter job was going at the Patio Restaurant in Birmingham and three men were up for it. Kim was one of them.

It was 22 December. In the morning, the chip shop owner in Stoke had laid him off because the Christmas trade had not been what he had anticipated. He had seemed genuinely sorry and had rung his friend, the manager at the Patio, to see if they needed an extra pair of hands.

'No promises,' he'd told Kim as he put down the phone, 'but it's worth a try. I said you were a good worker; clean.'

Kim hitched a lift on a slip road to the M6, and was in Birmingham by lunchtime. The Patio was in a concrete street in the centre of the city. It had a burgundy facade with gold sign-writing. In either side of the dark window Kim could see a bunch of nicotine-lace curtain tied back with gingham ribbons, and a menu boasting 'French-style Cuisine' which included chickpea and aubergine log with provençal tomato coulis, coq au vin, and tarte tatin. When he opened the door a cowbell sounded, the overhead heater ruffled his hair, and the smell of garlic warmed his nostrils. The paint on the walls was a deep terracotta, and the lighting was low, so it felt like night-time even though groups of office workers with glasses of red wine and dedicated shoppers with rolls of wrapping paper sticking out of their bags were having a Christmassy lunch. Kim went up to the bar, hesitant.

'Excuse me,' he asked the waitress behind it who was pouring out some drinks, 'is Paul about?'

'Who wants him?' Her manner was proprietorial but not unfriendly. She had a beauty spot to the left side of her upper lip. In the semi-darkness Kim couldn't tell if it was real or pencilled.

'I've come about the washing-up job. Stanley Newley sent me. I think Paul's expecting—'

'Hang on a minute and I'll take you downstairs.' She emerged from behind the bar with a tray of drinks which she took to a table in the corner. When she came back, she wiped her hands on her mini-skirt, clomped in her ill-advised stilettos down the narrow lino stairs and through the swing doors to the kitchen.

The kitchen's bright lights dazzled Kim and for a second a related headache flashed inside his forehead. It was a steamy, medium-sized basement room with stainless steel units and pans, ladles and knives. It smelt of cooked tomatoes, melted butter and sizzling meat. A thin man with a goatee beard wearing a chef's uniform was at the vast stove tasting a glutinous-looking soup. There were two other chefs working with him, one chopping vegetables, the other mixing a cake in a deafening machine. A fourth man stood at the sink. His head was inside a deep pot, but Kim could tell from his pin legs and trainers that he couldn't have been more than about seventeen. The hem of his apron idly jigged as he scrubbed.

Kim followed the waitress to the other side of the floor where another man, with dyed blond hair and a black shirt, was sitting in a back office the size of a cupboard. His door into the kitchen was wide open and he was speaking loudly on the telephone to compensate for the steamy echoes of crashes and bangs being made by his employees.

'He won't be long,' she said, and left Kim standing beside him feeling foolish.

'Right,' Paul said when he hung up, 'you must be Tim.' He stayed sitting on his stool and with his eyes gave Kim a thorough going-over. He was as unflinching about it as a beady mother meeting her prospective son-in-law for the first time. 'We'll have to get you to do a trial, you know, see if you're a hard worker, reliable. There's a lot of them think it's a doddle, and that's no good to me. I've one vacancy. It's between you, Stephen over there,' he said, indicating with his head the figure bent double over the sink, 'and some old codger who's coming in tonight. Have you a place to stay yet?'

'No.'

'Well, you better find somewhere, and be back here by four-thirty so you can be shown the ropes before the start of tonight's shift. Report to Chef.'

'Can you recommend a place?'

Paul gave him a long look before answering. It was as if he was trying to puzzle Kim out, but he didn't ask him his story. Instead he told him the name and address of a pub with cheap rooms and the number of the bus which would take him there.

'Don't be late back,' Paul warned as he left. 'I can't stand people who are late.'

By now Kim was so used to dismal rooms that the one he checked into above the pub did not surprise him. It was in the attic. The beams were painted with an old black gloss and the walls were darkened by damp. It had the deadened air of a deep cave eschewed even by bats. He lay down on the bed, his head against a pillow stuffed with unyielding foam, and closed his eyes. Exhausted. He had an hour or so before he had to return to the restaurant. He fell asleep but even though he still had his coat on and he was curled up into a ball, he shivered with a cold which penetrated his very marrow-bone.

When he woke up, it was pitch dark in the room. For a moment he had no idea where he was, but this sensation was so common, now, that it no longer had the power to catch his attention. So often, recently, he had woken up and for a full five minutes had been unable to determine what town he was in, let alone which B & B or bed. He had told himself that this was part of the fun but, when he'd tried to define that fun, he had not been so sure. Sometimes he had thought he was back at home and that the only reason the room looked different was because he was still inside the tail-end of a dream. When he realised he was in fact alone in a strange bed in a strange town, he hadn't quite been able to work out whether what he felt had been mild pleasure or gentle disappointment.

But there was little mistaking the unlived-in air of his latest room, and he was not disorientated for more than a second or two. He was frightened he had overslept and would have lost his chance of a job in the warmth, a job at all. He hastily felt about on the wall above the headboard and turned on the bulb. His watch said a quarter to four. He was all right. If he hurried he would be in good time.

The bus went at a very relaxed pace but he managed to arrive at the Patio at twenty past four. The main entrance was locked but he found his way through the basement back door. In the kitchen two junior chefs were already preparing for the evening rush. They were chatting loudly and appeared to be enjoying the

226

fact that they were going about their business with such abandon, the fact that the mess they were making was not going to be their lookout. A man of about sixty with a grey beard, thin face, and bulging eyes was keenly cleaning up around them. None of them seemed to notice Kim who, glad of the steamy warmth, lingered by the door, watching.

A few minutes later the head chef turned up and asked his juniors what the old man was doing.

'We thought we'd get him started straight away,' one of them said anxiously.

'You did, did you?' Chef said, raising an eyebrow. He had a brutal expression on his face, but his voice was soft. 'Harold, is it?' he asked the old man. 'Did they show you how the machine works?'

Harold hesitated for a moment before nodding quickly. It was obvious to Kim that they had done no such thing, but Chef said, 'Right, I suppose you might as well get on with it then. We open at six, and I want it spotless before the first dirty plate comes down.' Without wasting a moment, Harold picked up a huge pan, placed it in the sink and turned on full blast the boiling hot tap. Chef turned to Kim.

'Into the manager's office.'

In the cupboard which passed as an office the two of them were forced to stand rather more closely together than they might have done given a choice. Chef shut the door and pressed his back against it.

'I take it you're Tim?'

'Yes,' Kim said, feeling the edge of the tiny desk pressing into his legs.

'Have you done any kitchen work before?'

'No.'

'It's all about speed and efficiency, you know, how quickly you can get those plates clean. You've got to keep on top of those plates. It's hard.' The chef eyed him carefully.

'I think I can manage.'

'We'll see. You won't be paid for the trial shift, but if you get the job it's £1.80 an hour.'

'That's well below the minimum—'

'Have you a lot of other jobs lined up, Tim?'

227

'No.'

'Well then. Now, it was between you and Harold and the young bloke who was here at lunchtime, but he was crap, so it's just the two of you up for it. Harold'll be working through till eight-thirty, then you'll be taking over for the rest of the evening. But I'll want you back by half six so Warren or Paddy can show you how to work the dishwasher and that.'

'Can I wait here?'

'Here? If you like, as long as you don't get under our feet.' He opened the door, stepped back into his kitchen, and started giving orders to the two junior chefs, and to Harold who was being served a steady stream of dirty saucepans and mixing bowls.

Kim sat in the office reading an old paper, drifting off to sleep for a few minutes here and there, waking and watching the activities in front of him.

There was a slow build-up of plates. The first six came down at just before seven o'clock. Kim could see Harold scraping the leftovers into the large bin to his right and placing the plates into the dishwasher. Just as he finished the first set, three more arrived, and just as he was dealing with them, the waitresses piled willy-nilly another six, another three, and another eight, either side of him. Meanwhile, Warren and Paddy were sending more pans and cauldrons his way, crashing them into his sink, carelessly splashing water over his trousers and shoes as they did so and creating puddles at his feet. Even through the steam Kim could see the set of Harold's face, rigid with concentration, absolutely determined to keep abreast of the impossible.

As the piles of plates grew higher and higher and Harold was getting into serious difficulties, Kim was tempted to step in and help him. But he knew that to do so would be to ruin Harold's chances of getting the job. He wondered if he had just come out of prison, or some kind of institution, and he was trying, solitarily and against the odds, to rehabilitate himself. He noticed his eyes blinking desperately, his unsteady hands. He obviously needed the job so badly and was trying his optimum best, and failing. Kim's heart went out to him, but he realised there was nothing he could do.

He watched as Harold took a loaded tray of clean plates out of the dishwasher and put another lot of dirty ones in. The trays

228

were heavy and awkward. As he lifted them, and tried to take their weight against his stomach, he wobbled on the slippery floor and the plates clanked against each other. He puffed and strained. The waitresses feigned not to notice and just carried on sashaying to and fro, adding to the piles all around him. Warren nudged Paddy and the two of them smirked cruelly as they witnessed the old man's wretched struggles. But he managed to change the trays without mishap and, almost disappointed, the two junior chefs turned back to their cooking.

Harold began scraping more bones, limp lettuce, congealed coulis, and old fingers of steak fat into the bin. The leftovers began to rise worryingly high. Harold held his breath, lifted the splitting black bag out and hastened with it to the back door evidently praying its contents wouldn't begin to ooze and drip from the scar. He succeeded in negotiating the puddles on the floor without slipping. His relief when he returned to the sink safely swiftly turned to despair as he discovered that, in the few seconds he had been away with the rubbish, half a dozen more impossible piles had been left for him. The taps were running, the machine noisily churning. Water was sloshing over his shoes and his clothes were soaked. It was as if he was drowning.

The drying-up cloth in his withered hand was wet through. Tentatively he asked one of the junior chefs where he might find another. His voice betrayed the fact that he was out of breath.

'In that cupboard over there,' Warren told him grudgingly.

Knowing he couldn't afford to waste another second or else the plates might engulf him, Harold began to move away from the sink, but he did so too quickly. Kim ran towards him but it was too late. He had slipped on the waterlogged tiles and fallen flat on his ear. The sound of his skull on the ground was hollow and haunting. He lay there for a few moments, in the greasy puddle, silent and still, all dignity got clean away, like a dying man's last breath. Kim knelt down beside him, held his crinkly wet hands, and slowly helped him to sit up. He whispered one or two questions to him to find out if he was all right, and paused for a moment to observe his pupils as well as to see if he seemed puzzled and confused but, physically at least, he had somehow suffered no damage. It was humiliation which was daubed across his face and was evidently giving him the most pain. Pink tears glistened in his reddened eyes. Kim wanted to hug him.

Meanwhile, Warren and Paddy were pissing themselves laughing.

'We told you you were meant to keep the floor dry,' one of them told him.

'That's enough,' said Chef, walking over to Harold. 'You all right, mate?'

Harold closed his eyes.

'He's OK,' Kim said for him.

'It's not quite eight-thirty, but I think you better take over,' Chef told Kim. 'All right, Harold,' he shouted, not unpleasantly, but as if the old man were deaf, 'now, could you give your apron to Tim here? It won't hurt too much getting it off?'

Harold forced himself to open his eyes again. He blinked at Kim, as if taking in his younger and stronger frame for the first time. His mouth fell apart like the splitting open of a rotten piece of fruit. How could he possibly compete? Kim had never seen a man look so defeated. Even his terminally ill patients had seemed to have had more hope. There was nothing he could say.

'All right, Harold?' Chef shouted again. 'Will I help you with the apron? Only Tim here's got work to do.' Chef gave Harold a hand so he could get to his feet, and he carefully lifted the apron ribbon over his head. 'Are you hungry?' he bellowed.

Harold shook his head.

'Oi, Warren, give him something to eat before he goes. Looks like he could do with a square meal, poor thing. Quite a shock. Do you like chicken and pommes frites, Harold?' he asked, leading him away.

Kim watched as the stooped figure made slow progress across the kitchen floor and was made to sit down on the stool in the office to await a plate of food he didn't want. He put on the soaking apron, rolled up his sleeves and, in the claustrophobic steam, began swiftly but desultorily to scrape from the various skyscrapers of filthy plates globules of greasy remains into Harold's emptied bin.

Blood and guts, pus and skin diseases, growths and sores, all manner of medical horrors, could not bring out the squeamish in Kim. If these were the things the very mention of which could

230

cause others to cringe and squirm, they had no effect on him.

In the course of his training and career he had come across every permutation of human effluence. On many a home visit he had encountered astonishing squalor – urine-soaked carpets, shit smeared everywhere, you name it. He had never forgotten how he had once upset one old lady's chamber pot which was filled to the brim with months-old fag butts and phlegm. Its contents had flowed over his shoes and socks, and given even him something of a turn. He had also seen his fair share of corpses in grisly guises in his time. What unsettled him, more, was the abject misery of the lonely alcoholic or the person with Alzheimer's and without a soul in the world. What upset him most was the pain and loss surrounding afflictions and death, not the afflictions and the dead bodies themselves. So it was that he felt quietly unsympathetic towards those who were affected by the mere sight of blood. Until he landed the washing-up job at the Patio, Kim had always considered himself to be the non-squeamish type, and the squeamish types to be rather wet.

As early as later on the same evening, following Harold's untimely departure, Kim discovered squeamishness for the very first time. He attacked the piles of plates left behind by his predecessor, and many more which kept coming. The waitresses cared little for neat stacking. They just squashed one plate onto another, so that fatty rinds and grease, abandoned tomatoes and fishbones, snotty paper napkins and soggy fag-ends, chicken pie crusts, microwaved potato skins and spat-out gristle, cemented them all together. It was Kim's job to prize the plates apart, and scrape their detritus into the stinking bin before placing them in the dishwasher. The soft and slimy textures against his gloveless hands, and the pervading stench, prompted his stomach to churn. But during his sojourn at the restaurant he came across plenty of other duties which were just as bad, and sometimes worse.

Clearing out the refrigerated area, which he was prevailed upon to do about once a week, was Hell's work. He had to sort out the rotten vegetables and green-patina meat from their fresh counterparts, and wash down the shelves. It didn't make him feel squeamish, but he damn near froze to death.

Squeamish was what he felt every night when the plates were all clean, everyone else had finished and gone home, and he was

231

left alone to scrub out the sauce boats. The Patio was proud of its sauces, particularly the pepper sauce which was new to the menu and which was spooned over the steaks in a self-consciously sophisticated drizzle. Every night Warren and Paddy made the same seven sauces for the various different meat and fish dishes in several different stainless steel pots. Over the course of the evening they simmered on the stove and visibly formed a wrinkled skin on their top and, invisibly, a centimetre-thick burnt crust on their bottom. In the early hours and alone, Kim had to slop out the remains, dig for the crust, and go at it with a series of instruments including a steel brush and a chisel. Sometimes all seven pots took two and a half hours to clean and caused him to retch on average every three minutes. As he scoured and heaved, he felt he was a lesser man for not being able to rise above it. And as the days went by, he decided the only way to tackle his revulsion was to practise mind over matter.

This he managed to achieve, to a certain extent, as he became more used to the feel of sopping food in the plughole and the stink of the bin. Christmas Day was something of a turning point. He was working so hard he did not have time to consider other Christmases, let alone contemplate the grisly detail of his own. On the early-morning bus into work, of course, he wondered about Sylvie, Jack and Mackenzie, not yet awake. But he quickly quashed the thought that he might be with them. The fact that he wasn't, and that he was instead going to be spending his day Brillo-ing encrusted bread sauce off china and steel, was entirely of his own doing. It didn't occur to him to telephone them. Perhaps he knew that Happy Christmas, coming from him, might for the first time have a hollow ring. Or, worse, that theirs was just as happy as ever, despite his absence. Anyway, he arrived early, started work immediately, and was on his feet non-stop till past midnight. There were various parties in for lunch and dinner and the kitchen was busier than ever. But the chefs were full of festive banter and Paul, infected by the Christmas spirit, opened a complimentary bottle of red plonk or two for the staff to drink while they worked. A few glasses helped Kim face the sink, the bin, and their contents. The mind was warmed, and so the edge taken off his disgust. Even the leftover stuffings, like the contents of a postmortem stomach, couldn't phase him. Only the hangover the next day brought the stirrings of nostalgia and regret. Lying in his pub pit, day off, eyes to the ceiling, tears rolled into his ears, tickling their insides.

But he stuck it out in Birmingham. It was a strangely anonymous town, its heart having been ripped out in the sixties to make way for the arteries of motorway, car in the community. Kim felt that the grey pallor of his basement-kitchen complexion was well camouflaged against the cityscape of dank concrete and tarmac. He stuck to the stinking pub room and the stinking job. The Patio's manager, Paul, was an arrogant bastard, with his (perplexingly) successful restaurant, cocky hairdo and stiletto heel of a wife, but not subhuman. (More than once when Kim was skint Paul slipped him the week's rent for his room.) Unlike his city, Paul had a heart, somewhere in there.

Chef was surly most of the time but there were flashes of civility. The norm in other men, coming from him, Kim felt this civility to be an uplifting, exciting thing, a bonus. If Chef ever said thank you, held the door open to him, asked him how he was or – miracle (it only happened once) – whether he needed a hand, Kim's day was made. Even Warren and Paddy, for all their coarseness, made Kim laugh, their ridiculous chat and litany of hideous jokes. Their cruelty to Harold, unforgivable though it had been, of course had its roots, as Kim discovered over the weeks. As they mixed their sauces or rolled out their pastry, they jabbered away, their banter littered with hints and details, references and anecdotes, all of which drip drip revealed backgrounds and experiences straight out of one of Sylvie's textbooks. They were fighting for survival. Quietly Kim became fond of them, smiled against his better nature at their tales of (their own, exaggerated) football heroism, boozing and shagging.

The waitresses, for all their nonchalance when it came to stacking plates, were warm and kind, gave Warren and Paddy as good as they got. Sometimes they cried from throbbing bunions; from sheer fatigue; at the hands of fleeting men who only purported to love them as a means to a sexually functional end; or out of marital despair. Annie, the one with the questionable beauty spot and unquestioned magnanimity, discovered her husband had a whole other wife and family in Frodsham. For twelve years. Annie had only been married herself thirteen. The level of deception, Kim thought as he witnessed her solar plexus howl of distress one afternoon in Paul's office, was a horror story at the same time utterly unimaginable, and predictably pedestrian. Later, she confided in Kim, told him that she could talk to and trust him. He liked that. It gave him something of the same satisfaction and pleasure he felt when helping his patients.

For all the stinking tasks he had to perform, Kim did enjoy the camaraderie of the Patio's brutal, crude, noisy, volatile, unruly, fallible team. Having become used to the devil he was rapidly getting to know, and having contained his distaste for the regurgitations of his new trade, he remained at the Patio for several weeks.

But one Monday afternoon towards the end of February, squeamishness rose up to overwhelm him very graphically once again. There were few customers upstairs and, seeing that Kim was temporarily under-employed, Chef ordered him into the back yard to clean out the very bottom of the rubbish skip. Seeing as it was filled and emptied regularly, it was as pointless a job as it was possible to conceive. But Kim knew Chef was only asking him to do it because he felt that Paul should be getting his £1.80's worth. There was no deflecting him. It wasn't one of his days for a flash of civility.

So Kim did Chef's bidding, went outside into the chill wind. Under the darkening sky and surrounded on three sides by a grim brick wall, the small back yard was almost pitch black. But he knew it well and managed to avoid all those things which had been abandoned there – the rusting bicycle, broken fridge, redundant radiator. He turned on a cobwebbed bulb and climbed inside the skip. The light shone directly down into it. There was a slippery squelching under his feet. He dutifully began to shovel up the contents beneath him, trying not to focus too closely on the colours and shapes and smells of the compacted leftovers which had accumulated and formed a seeping crust at the bottom. He unfocused his eyes so that all beneath him was an undetailed blur, like flesh on an X-ray. But he couldn't help noticing troubling movement. He looked down automatically, and found that his eyes adjusted all too readily and sharply, and landed on a huge ball of maggots. He reasoned that he had occasionally come across such creatures before, sometimes in wounds and bodies no less, and he had dealt with them efficiently and responsibly. But there was no reason in his new-found squeamishness which had, amazingly, lain dormant for some weeks now. No longer. It suddenly grabbed him by the throat like the nightmare seduction by an old hag. Clearing out a heaving, stinking skip, he told himself, was very different from trying to cure an infested human being, something which had about it the beauty of pain relief, good intention, and deed.

# 13

All of a sudden, maggots wriggling over the crevices of his soaking shoes, Kim was struck by the scant appeal of the kitchen porter job. He stared down at his cheerless feet and looked at the muck clinging to the hems of his trousers. He felt very sick and shivery. His hands were so cold that when he moved his fingers it seemed as though the bones in them were creaking. How, he asked himself, had he ended up in such a condition?

For the whole four months that he had been away from home, Kim had not managed to fathom why he had gone. On all his travels; in every field, town, and job, that he had passed through, he had carried his mental checklist of possible reasons. He had longed for it to have been something so predictable but intriguing as a mid-life crisis, for example, but however much he willed it to be the case, he knew that it was not so.

Now it was no longer agreeable to ask himself what the hell he was doing and not to come up with any answers. He realised that he had to try to get to the bottom of what he had turned his back on, and why. Until that moment his stint on the road had been an adventure, even the gloomy rooms and back-breaking work. But suddenly the physical reality of communing with maggots in a skip in the back yard of Birmingham's Patio Restaurant could not compare with that of being on his giving sofa by the fire in his warm sitting room, cup of tea or shot of whisky in hand, the woody smell of smoking logs, the feel of his feet almost burning in his socks, spot of news on the television, the company of his beloved family.

Cold, disgusted and despondent, Kim told himself to sit down at the bottom of the skip and not to get out again until he had an explanation for himself. He could feel the damp, rotting food seep through the pants of his trousers, making his bum so cold he could barely feel it, and he could hear the slippery squirming of the rice-pudding maggots all around him but, even so, he placed the heavy shovel across his knees by way of barring his own escape. Grimy B & Bs, desultory towns, waste landscapes had all failed successfully to force the issue. At last, he realised that he must resort to the discipline of desperate measures.

First, he cast his mind back to the night he had left home.

It had been a rainy evening, and in the traffic he had become impatient to get back to the bosom of his house. He had been tired but in a good mood. There had been some nonsense play on the car radio which had made him all the more look forward to an evening with Sylvie: intelligent conversation, physical warmth, watching some programme together, the cosiness of easy familiarity. It had always struck him that, after so many years of marriage, the thought of reuniting with his wife, following only a few hours apart, was something which he looked forward to every time. Cosy familiarity, after all, was more often than not looked upon with contempt, a vitriolic contempt at that, the kind normally reserved for weightier, more deserving and loathsome matters, like cruelty to children, or far right politics. Perhaps people sneered at cosy familiarity because it shared the same lack of imagination, and therefore those who aspired to it were necessarily blinkered. But if it had about it a certain smugness and complacency, and was somehow threatening in its quiet way, it was not obscene. Kim had never been able to get as worked up about it as some. He felt that to bestow upon it all these extremes of interpretation was a form of aggrandisement that was unwarranted. Cosy familiarity continued to give him, at least, a pleasure that he couldn't regard as anything but innocent enough.

Early on in his marriage, he had imagined that Sylvie's physical presence might not go on delighting him in the way it had then, that he might, over time, at best grow accustomed to it, at worst uninterested. He also presumed that a day might have come when the two of them would have been able to anticipate most of what the other was going to say, and so become, if not bored, then at least not as riveted by each other as ever. And he had expected that at some point down the line he would probably start taking her for granted – and she him, for God's sake. It was the way of marriage, surely, and he was prepared for it to such a degree that he wasn't dreading it. It might have its compensations, even, such predictable familiarity. But it hadn't happened. And when he walked out to buy ice-cream that November night,

237

it still hadn't happened. He loved her as passionately as ever, the lateral take she had on people and life, the way she made him look at things from a fresher and quirkier point of view, her boundless vitality, the cock of her neck, the smell of her vanilla scent combined with the smell of just her. He relished her intellectual and physical presence as much as he had ever done, since those erstwhile days in Belfast.

Of course, he had not planned to go that night. Try as he might, he could discover no recollection of even a minnow of a thought along those lines. So it was spontaneous, but what had fuelled such improbable spontaneity?

Up until his sojourn in the skip, Kim had been of the belief that the reason for walking away had to have been big, important, significant, the stuff of movies and melodramas. It had to be good. The drastic step of bowing out of a fulfilling marriage and job, leaving his children and all that he had ever dreamed of, couldn't possibly have arisen from anything much short of cataclysmic. Initially, when he couldn't find it, he supposed that he must have been too close up to it to see it for himself. So he opened his eyes wider, delved as deep as he could. Yet search as he might, the splish-splash reason had still eluded him.

In the depths of the skip, he recognised for the first time that it did not exist. If it had taken so long to reach this conclusion, it must have been because he had so hoped that the explanation would be startling and fascinating, complex and enormous; worthy of all the fuss it had possibly caused. All the previous weeks he was praying that it was sufficient to justify the unique drama of clean disappearence. But he couldn't lay claim to a glamorous thriller twist, the spectacular demise of a twenty-year affair with his wife, the love of his life, even a common or garden nervous breakdown. None of them. With the shovel pressing into his knees and his bum now completely numb, he knew that to reach the truth he was going to have to lower his sights.

So, once again, he returned to that November night. He had walked along to the shop. No ice-cream or, anyway, not the sort he was looking for. This had led to petty confusion and indecision, the kind too boring to voice to anyone else but which, Kim guessed, if other people were anything like him, they indifferently faced every day – which pair of socks to put on, black or blue? Bath/drink now, or in fifteen minutes' time? Which street to walk down to get from A to B, same distance, just one with trees, one without? Should he buy the ice-cream he knew she didn't particularly like, or pursue her favourite brand elsewhere?

Pondering this, the opportunity for a pointless game of guessing cars' headlights had modestly presented itself, a mild diversion from a mild dilemma. Then, seeing an Indian restaurant in the distance, the stomach had experienced the sudden yearning, not to be ignored, for the spiciness of curry. (He had always been bemused by the power of food, physiological or other, which could catch out the best of them when it wanted to.) Then, later, stepping out into the freezing night, the lure of warmth posed by a passing coach. Exhaustion, and seduction by the prospect of a long, long journey; undisturbed sleep. All these, the patter of little circumstances, conspiring. He might ask himself why he had been unable simply to resist each one, to do the done thing, to find – or not to find – Sylvie's ice-cream, and return home to carry on life as relished and expected.

Individually, these trifling temptations might have been easy enough to ignore, but a number of them seemed to have dawdled in front of him that night, one after the other. Together, they perhaps comprised the fateful, hidden twist in the unsuspecting cocktail, the primary ingredients of which were aspects of his own character.

His overwhelming natural curiosity, for one.

Kim had always structured his life in such a way as best to satisfy this curiosity as pragmatically as possible. He had become a GP because it was a means of combining a certain medical proficiency with a stunning inquisitiveness. Of the two, the stunning inquisitiveness was probably the driving force of his ambition, more so than biology, physiology, pathology, and all the other compelling constituents of medicine. Being a doctor meant that every day of his working life, and several times a day at that, he had the extraordinary privilege of being allowed such insight into people's lives, of being able to support them medically and emotionally often at the most difficult times. His profession demanded that he ask them intimate questions about their bodies and, by natural extension, he learnt about their minds, experiences, thoughts, emotions, anxieties, loves and hates. He could offer remedies – if sometimes only in a limited capacity – and so his position therefore granted him the pleasure of a daily diet of stories unfolding. Each and every one of his patients' unique situations was, to him, a metaphorical page-turner.

And he had married a woman who every night provided another rich source of unputdownable narratives. He had also expertly organised his leisure time to take into account this particular trait of his. Evenings off, and weekends, he watched the news obsessively, read all the papers and journals he could lay his hands on, had time for. He would take twice as long as Sylvie to do the shopping, deflected from the task in hand by the contents of other people's baskets, and an involving conversation with the person at the checkout. Sometimes, awake at night, or to pass an idle moment in a post office queue, he enjoyed speculating about what would happen if he just walked out of his life, not because his world was falling in on him, but purely for the sake of freewheeling. Who didn't? But they were fleeting thoughts only, insignificant, and the stuff of common, not even extraordinary, curiosity. Everyone had them. Over the years countless patients had said to him, 'Sometimes, Doctor, I just wonder what it would be like if I were to walk away from everything,' but they never did. The sentiments were common enough but – pretty well – everyone dismissed them pretty damn quick, for the simple reason that they were also impractical, sad, impossible and, in matter of fact, completely devoid of appeal.

Over the years, he had always found that this natural curiosity of his had been reasonably contained, in as much as it had never crossed over the boundaries and become an impossible force in his life, and in that of those around him. One symptom of mania was a loss of the appreciation of the normal social constraints which he viewed, to some extent, as a form of curiosity run riot. Kim had patients who'd had to be sectioned because, among other inappropriate and seemingly aggressive behaviour, they had got themselves into the socially vulnerable habit of going into the street, or pub, or park, and firing unacceptably intrusive questions at astonished strangers.

Of course, his curiosity, while obsessive, had never been manic. It had always been respectable; never got out of hand. But maybe the petty temptations which came his way the night he went AWOL, had tripped it into a different league. What must have driven him, over and above the mere desire for curry and warmth, were the questions, subconsciously posed to himself (he spent most of his time putting questions to other people): What if I just go with this? What if I just let go? See where it takes me? Where will I go? Who will I meet? What'll happen to me? What's it like to have barely any money, to be alone, to have no one, and no respect afforded automatically? Why not hold out my arms by my sides and, dandelion-like, see where the wanton wind decides to posit me? Free myself up to Fate? Can I not just indulge, awhile, in the tremulous promise of chance?

So, in the face of a fragile paper-chain of opportunity, and defences perhaps not what they might have been (due to the unromantic, fleshly basics of hunger, cold, and fatigue), had it just been a case of the natural curiosity in him having inconspicuously bubbled up and overflowed from within the limits of polite and responsible convention?

As Kim asked himself this question, he gripped the steely shovel all the more tightly against his knees. He was shaking, but couldn't tell in the cold if there were tears. More than merely shaking, he was sobbing.

It appeared, then, the degree of his self-indulgence was as unacceptable as the maniac's pure form of selfishness which at least had the excuse of being the fallout of serious chemical imbalance.

He had put off and put off and put off ringing Sylvie, a procrastination which was no less than inhumane. In his extreme curiosity, about himself, he had omitted to be curious about others. In the course of the four months, he had never seriously considered how she and Jack and Mackenzie were feeling, the level of their suffering. He had suppressed curiosity about that wonderfully, as a convenient means of enabling his own selfishness to thrive, uninhibited. He had known all along that, if he had rung them, they would, with one word, have persuaded him home. But his curiosity had been at full throttle and he hadn't been ready. He'd kept saying to himself, 'Just a little while longer.'

Such capacity for cruelty was a troubling side-effect of this newly uncontrolled curiosity of his. Did it, by extension, mean

241

that the curiosity itself had a more sinister provenance? But what?

Dissatisfaction with his humdrum life, perhaps? Try as he might, he did not believe this. At no point before or during his journey had he ever doubted that he was happy at home. Of course, there was a certain repetitiveness about doing the same job, and living in the same house with the same wife for many years, but even that repetitiveness was limited. New things to see and learn and talk about with Sylvie and the children every day; new patients with new illnesses and problems several times a day. Anyway, repetitiveness wasn't something he despised. He was the sort of character, rather, to find comfort in its constraints, if constraints they were.

If not the humdrum of repetitiveness, then that of responsibility, maybe? To have done what he did must have meant that his relationship with responsibility had been sorely strained to breaking point. And yet, even that was not the case. He had been as irresponsible as it was possible to be, but not because he was fed up with or frightened of responsibility. The opposite, in fact. He believed in and liked it, saw that which he bore for his family, friends, colleagues and patients not as a trial at all, but as a life-giving force. For all his fears before marriage and fatherhood, he had discovered a constant and definite pride in looking after his family. For all his patients' neediness, he had found sure satisfaction in making them well again. Other men had often talked about this 'burden' of responsibility, but Kim had always known that to slough it off was only, in its stead, to invite the weight of freedom.

So, then, no, a disgruntled shaking off of laborious repetitiveness and gritted responsibility was too pat an answer, too neat.

His extraordinary hunger for the world beyond the familiar was a more probable one, maybe. As simple as that. There didn't have to be the Great Reason. Just a sudden, circumstantial infection of man's eternal quest for novelty, adventure. No darstardly hidden agenda against his family, his job, his life, except in its unfortunate ripple effect – that of enabling him for the first time ever to throw his cherished responsibility to them all out of the window, and to display such cruelty.

He had never supposed himself to be a cruel man. He had often thought that to be callous and cruel was a lazy and easy way of going about life. People found all sorts of excuses for it, and some had no desire to fight against their own weakness. He had had cruel thoughts, of course, plenty of times. Sometimes, angry with Sylvie, he had wanted to strike her with sharp words just where he knew it would hurt. On the whole he bit his tongue, but sometimes he couldn't stop himself. It wasn't laudable, but nor was it unforgivable, especially if, as he had always ensured, any cruel observations or remarks he was wont to make were followed up by swift apologies and evident remorse. Certainly, she had never accused him of cruelty. She could now, just as she could easily – dread thought – turn him away when he went home and never forgive him. He would deserve it and she'd have every right – his recent eruption of cruelty had been fast and furious and unforgiveable. Whence had it come? What had made it possible?

Now, against his better nature, he looked back at his past. At his most suggestible, that November night, had he been able to sustain such cruelty having learned it long ago from his father, having copied it deep down from his brothers? Had it always been lying dormant, waiting for an outlet? Those remorseless winter moods when his father distanced himself so brazenly from his mother. His brothers' capacity to taunt even one for whom they couldn't help but feel a deep, unspoken familial love? Some wanky pop psychologist might say Kim had way back been branded, by association, with this pattern of behaviour. Repulsed by it though he might have been, and determined to live by another set of rules with his own family, it was bound to reveal itself, show itself willing, given the right opportunity, in the end. The very thought made him feel more sick than any amount of heaving detritus.

As these different thoughts, possible answers, and the probable truth dawned, he shifted uncomfortably in his 'seat'. Something was digging into his thigh. He pulled it out from beneath him. A chicken drumstick draped with a soggy tutu of goosepimpled, chiffony fat. He threw it aside, and wiped his greasy fingers, which he could not feel, on his greasy trousers. Ah, see, he said to himself, what capricious Chance, with all her seductive promise, has managed to proffer!

As he heard the drumstick plop a few feet away from him into the slimy sludge of disintegrating lettuce leaves and brown broccoli gloop, he knew that he had gone missing, and was in that skip, because of no more than the watery ingredients of whimsical opportunity, egotistical curiosity, and diversion by the unedifying notion that chance might just turn up a little *amuse-gueule* to tickle his fancy. These were not reasons enough to have caused the untold despair anyone with half a brain should have realised such an act would have inflicted upon his family.

To his shame, there was no good reason for having gone, just unremarkable and pathetic fallibility. He thus felt himself to be more culpable than any other man who had ever gone missing from his family. Other men went because of redundancy, debt, disillusion, grand failure, self-loathing, breakdown, amnesia, emasculation, terminal illness, abduction, depression, hate, extra-marital passion.

And his reason, as someone who had an idyllic life and who could lay claim to none of those things? The urge for a chicken tikka, and the frivolous, unworthy desire for a little flutter, a little paddle in the pool of novelty and chance.

'Hey, Tim, you're taking your time out there,' Chef suddenly called from the kitchen. 'Are you nearly done?'

'Coming now,' Kim replied. He stood up, put his frozen hand on the frozen side of the skip, leapt onto the concrete, and went inside.

Seeing Kim's filthy clothes and his shivering figure, Chef looked at him sympathetically. Perhaps he felt guilty having given him quite such a revolting job. He suggested he wash his hands and place them for a few moments on the stove, which Kim did willingly.

'I'm afraid I'm going to have to hand in my notice,' he told him as he went to stand against it. Chef was stirring a large pan of soup over a low blue flame. 'I'm moving on,' he added.

Chef stopped what he was doing. 'Is it because I asked you to clean out the skip?' he asked.

'No.'

'I know it's horrible, but it must be done occasionally. It won't need to be again for ages. You're a good worker. I'd rather not let you go. You saw the usual sort of applicants we get. Shite.'

'I'm sorry, but I've made up my mind.'

'Nothing to persuade you? Paul was talking of putting you up to £2.30?' The tone of his voice betrayed the fact that he knew the scrawny carrot hardly constituted an irresistible incentive. 'We can't really afford—'

''Fraid not. I'm sorry.'

'I didn't think so. Where're you moving on to then?'

'Oxford.'

'Got a job waiting for you there?'

'Possibly.'

Chef nodded. 'Fair enough.'

It was agreed that he would stay on for the rest of that evening. Chef said he needn't stay to work out his notice. He knew someone who could replace him temporarily, till they found a more permanent person.

After they closed up, he said his goodbyes. Annie, the waitress with the questionable beauty spot and questionable husband, gave him a kiss on the cheek. It showed a certain dedication, he thought, coming so close to him in his particular sartorial state. He was pleased. Paul and the chefs shook him by the hand, and left him to scrub out the sauce boats for the last time. For all their differences, they had worked long and hard together, and they parted on good terms. Chef wished him luck. Paul even urged him to visit for a meal sometime, and made some joke about avoiding any of the dishes which came with a sauce.

When Kim had finished his final duties, he locked up and hid the keys under an upturned saucer on the outside ledge of the grimy window in the back yard. He took the night bus back to the pub. His room was as cold as ever, the sheets so icy it was almost painful to get inside them. Even so, he fell instantly asleep.

It was early afternoon when he woke the following day. He felt warm beneath the blankets, but his face was exposed, and his nose slightly damp and red in the freezing air of the room. He didn't feel inclined to brave getting up. Putting off the evil moment, he lay completely still, looking up at the peeling ceiling, brooding on the nature of chance.

So, he discovered, he had wanted to give chance a go, and what a peculiar thing it had turned out to be. It had buoyed him along from Oxford to Inverness, from Inverness, via all manner of places, to Birmingham. He had met people along the way he would never have met, taken jobs he could never have imagined himself taking, and stayed in towns and villages, guesthouses and beds, he might otherwise never have known existed. But had this chance, to which he had given himself up for a whole four months, fulfilled his unconscious expectations? Had it been good to him?

This quest for novelty was a double-edged thing. On the one hand it was behind the glories of exploration, technological revolution, literary and artistic endeavour, outlandish invention, eternal innovation. On the other, it was a destructive force, it prompted sane and stable men as himself to unseemly experimentation, to drop everything that was most precious and important to them in order to sample the shock of the new. And shock it was, but to what end?

Certainly, in the conventional sense, to have downsized from a loving home to a series of solitary bedsits and rooms, and to have regressed from professional status to blue-collar anonymity, might have been said to have been something of a misfortune. And yet, he did not feel that, for the greater part of his journey at least, chance had been in any way bad to him. Its offerings had been humble, but he hadn't knowingly been asking for anything more. Perhaps, Kim thought, if a person's expectations were low, chance didn't bother to put itself out too much. Only if someone's expectations were high, and that someone persistently encouraged chance to perform on his behalf – a little bribe here, a flutter of the eyelashes there – did it then come into its own. Perhaps chance, like a vain man or spoilt woman, rarely rewards those who don't make the effort to court it first, with hard toil, for example, or faith. After all, the playwright must fill the blank pages before he makes it into the West End, the lottery winner must first stake his pound before landing his millions, a lonely soul must leave the front door, if he or she is ever to find love; and all of them must do these things in a spirit of hope.

When he had set out, Kim had not asked for anything, as far as he was aware, except food, warmth and rest. When he came to discover new places, and new people who were more likely to give him the time of day than rob or beat him; and when he had found the means to earn just enough for a bed at night and food in his belly, he had considered himself pretty lucky. If chance hadn't exactly done him proud, then it had not left him out on a wintry night, nor put him in the path of characters with knives in their hands and malice on their minds. He couldn't complain. On the whole it had served him pretty well.

And yet, somehow he had ended up disappointed. The full force of this had only dawned on him the day before. When chance chose to posit him at the bottom of the stinking skip, he had been shocked by how strongly he believed it had let him down, how resentful he felt. He had asked nothing of chance, as far as he knew, but deep inside, he must have harboured powerful hopes for quite a lot more than he got. To have left behind all that he loved most, he had to have had, hidden away all those four months, the inkling of a notion that chance might just turn up something even better than he already had. Quite what it might turn out to be, he had presumably been leaving up to chance alone. Perhaps he had wanted it to come up with something spontaneously, something which he himself couldn't possibly have imagined because what he already had was as good as anything he could consciously or unconsciously conceive. So he had sat back idly, secretly hoping chance would not only do the work for him, but also surprise him with a new perfection. What astonishing conceit!

Because while, yes, turning his back on his wife and kids, and patients, and self, chance had put him in contact with a number of nice characters, temporary acquaintances from Liz Lawson to Laurie and Annie, to John, Mr Kindness and Paul; and while it had taken him to Inverness and Gateshead, Stoke and Leek, Pickering and Darlington, among others, and introduced him to the underbelly – B & Bs, truck-stops, motorways, and dispossession – of a country he thought he knew, it had presented him with no such alternative perfection to the one he loved. Anyway, if it had bestowed him with perfection once, why the hell, when many people's lives were so way off anything anywhere near perfect, did he, Kim Black, ever hope, even without realising it, that he could be the deserving beneficiary of another novel dose? And what, precisely, had he unwittingly supposed that alternative perfection to be?

Chance had an infinite number of things at its fingertips, and it might have thrown him any one of them, according to its whim. But even if it had felt disposed to single him out again for another idyllic life, he did not believe it could come up with anything to match that which he already knew. His was a journey which had been fuelled not only by unadulterated selfishness, but also by arrogance and egoism in the extreme. It had been characterised by the limp orgasm of flaccid and pointless anonymity, mixed with the dubious throb of loneliness and disillusion, the long suspected but nonetheless startling burden of freedom. And was he any the wiser, happier, more enlightened? No, none of those things. His eyes had been opened to three things only – namely, guilt and regret, and his own unbearable capacity for cruelty – all of which he would have been better off without.

He had always thought of himself as such an ordinary type and was now discovering such guilt and shame and callousness in himself as he prayed no normal man would ever have to feel. His only hope and prayer was that when he went home he might, against all reason, be forgiven. But for the moment, he pulled the covers over his cold head. For a little longer, he couldn't face the day.

# 14

Jack and I are in the kitchen eating scrambled eggs on toast, laughing. He has fallen in love with a girl called Josephine who wears long skirts, neat pumps, and a little Wedgwood brooch at the neck of her blouse. After all the pierced navels, you have to laugh. He laughs himself. 'Who'd've thought it, Mum?' he says to me. He met her at the college where he works. She was the guest at a wedding reception there. She couldn't find the Ladies, went into the kitchen by mistake, and asked him to direct her. When he'd done so, she thanked him, and shyly asked if he was responsible for the vanilla ice-cream they had just served for pudding. He was. She told him she loved the minuscule black speckles in it, and they launched into a conversation about the wonderful properties of vanilla. It's so unlike Jack. Perhaps I underestimate him, but his usual chat-up line is more along the lines of, 'Have you heard the new Verve album?'

It's a blustery February night outside, and although it's only Tuesday I'm already looking forward to the weekend. It's been very busy at work of late. The season of goodwill well and truly over, and summer not yet anywhere near, it must be the prime time of year for strife. February seems to be the month of few solutions. Couples dig in their wintry heels, more implacable than ever.

It's nice to be sitting here with my son, forgetting it all for a while as he confides in me about the gorgeous Josephine. He is so animated in his excitement that it's about ten minutes he's taking between each mouthful. The scrambled egg he's left to eat now has about it a distinctly chilly air.

He's telling me about last night's date, their third. He took her to the cinema in George Street and on to a Chinese near the coach station. He's repeating exactly what her views were on the film they saw (with which he agreed completely, surprise, surprise), and telling me in incredible detail, down to the last little dish of noodles, what they ate. The toast and scrambled egg are beginning to cement themselves to his plate but I haven't the heart to point this out to him. He's in full flow, now, about what Josephine told him of her background and work. Nothing about what she looks like, which is something of a departure for Jack. His normal enthusiasms – much to Mackenzie's horror – are more along the lines of, 'Great legs,' or 'Great tits.' Not this time. I'm learning more about Josephine than any of her fleeting predecessors put together. Her dad's the foreman of a factory making mattress covers and fleecy blankets outside Bedford, where she was brought up; her mum's a part-time librarian and part-time child minder. She's two brothers, Jason and Toby; unemployed, and trainee accountant respectively. She herself moved to Oxford two years ago when she was twenty-one, and lives in digs on the Iffley Road with her friend Elaine. Josephine is a salesgirl at Blackwells, 'so she's more than the usual puréed turnip between her ears,' is how Jack puts it. (I think how Mackenzie would balk at that one, but she'd have to concede it was an improvement on 'Fantastic pins,' or 'Tits to get lost in.') Distracted by his descriptions of her and her family, Jack pushes his plate to one side. He's sparkling, and has no appetite, a sure sign indeed of devotion.

'Mackenzie'll be amazed,' I say at last, when I can get a word in edgeways.

'Mum, I promise you she'll really like her. She couldn't not.'

'I'm going to ring her in a minute, even manage to get to speak to her if her college phone is mended.' I stand up and take his plate away to the sink. I feel like spoiling him tonight, waiting on him hand and foot. He's a good lad. 'Can I tell her?'

'Course you can. Oi, sit down will you, I'm talking to you. Haven't finished telling you about last night.'

Jack is usually so much more reticent about his private life. He's been known to confide, but only up to a point, not like this. Immediately I do his bidding. I don't want to let the moment pass. The dishes can wait indefinitely, for as long as he wants my full attention. This intimacy with my son is all-important. Particularly with Mackenzie away. We've a very close mother-daughter relationship, even more so now, with Kim gone, but in her term time our regular contact is only via an unsatisfactory payphone. So I prize Jack's presence about the house. I don't

250

know how I'd've survived without him. He's angry at his father, which has, I think, made him more protective and more appreciative of me. He's more open than he ever was.

'We just talked and talked, like really talked. Deep shit, not just the superficial shit. We were the last in the restaurant to leave. Didn't notice the waiters hovering, poor sods, longing to get home. When a couple comes in like us, me and Josephine, they must look at each other and go, like, 'Oh, God, here we go, in for a late one with these two.' Thinking of it now, I feel a bit bad. But we were that involved, we didn't care. I'd say we were really getting to know each other, you know, before—'

I nod.

'It's all new to me, but it's the best way round, you reckon?'

'Almost invariably.'

'I mean, it's normally a few drinks, or a couple of E's or what have you, and, well, same old story. Give yourself a pat on the back if you can remember her name in the morning. If you can remember it! Chances are you never even heard it. And all you can think about is getting out quick, before she starts giving you any head destruction. Most times, you can't get out too soon.'

I smile.

'I mean, what happened with you and Dad? Not that I'm being nosy or anything.'

'We waited awhile. Not all that long, mind.'

'No, I don't intend to wait all that long. I get the impression she . . . A decent, what, couple of weeks or so? I don't want for her to get bored waiting. I mean, it's got to be an improvement on the usual couple of hours, and yet not so long she'll go off the boil. I don't think she will, mind. You get an instinct about these things, don't you? What d'you think? I've got it all worked out, Mum. I'm going to save up and take her out for a really decent meal; maybe London. Then a nice hotel. Not some shit-hole. Something a bit classy, a bit special. What d'you think?'

'Sounds great,' I say. I'm tempted to slip him twenty or thirty quid towards it.

'You can help me choose, maybe, sort of thing she might appreciate.'

'I'd be pleased to,' I tell him, thinking he's finished for the evening, he's probably done enough confiding for one night. I stand up, empty cup of tea in hand, with every impression of being someone about to do the washing-up.

'Why not right now? Sit down, eh? You've nothing planned, have you? Washing the dishes doesn't count.'

'No.'

'Well then. I could use your advice.'

I sit next to him again, arms resting comfortably on the familiar knots and grooves of the kitchen table. I admit to him I'm not a great aficionado of restaurants and hotels, but Jack insists I tell him the kind of thing a girl like Josephine might like. Together we come up with a few suggestions, discuss their relative merits. Jack is responding well to how seriously I am taking him. Of course I am. It's a privileged mother who is party to her son's romantic plots.

We are deep in conversation, even trying to second-guess the type of food she enjoys. Jack reckons that, while not exactly a vegetarian, she's probably not a big, fat, juicy steak type. So I suggest a fish restaurant. He thinks that might be too limiting. We debate on. I am touched by the trouble he is taking. It swells my heart. I only hope to God she won't break his, but by all accounts, it seems unlikely. Josephine is inspiring Jack's romantic side like no one else. A woman couldn't do that who didn't feel anything for him. For all the passion he feels for her, I have the distinct impression it may just be reciprocated.

The doorbell is ringing. It is only when it does so for the third time that Jack and I hear it and realise it has sounded twice before.

'Dora?' he asks.

'Must be.' Dora's the only person who drops in of an evening. She's never unwelcome. Only tonight I don't want anyone. I don't want to interrupt this valuable time I'm having with Jack. I sigh.

'What's up?' he asks.

'Didn't fancy a visitor. Tired.'

'We don't have to answer the door.'

'No, she knows we're in. Anyway I couldn't do that to her. I was having a nice time, that's all. Things to sort out. Restaurants.'

'Never mind, plenty of time,' he says, smiling, genuinely not put out. He knows how important Dora's friendship has been to me over the past four months. Apart from Suzie at the helpline, she's the one person who I feel I can talk to about Kim, ad infinitum, even more so than with my children. They have their own feelings to contend with. It's essential that I listen to them, and not over-burden them with mine. Dora's ear is astonishing, it's like a bottomless well, with a capacity to listen and hear that knows no bounds. One day, as I drone on to her with more theories about Kim's disappearence, and voice yet again my melancholy hopes, I feel the words will have to hit a rock sooner or later, but they never do. She responds sensibly and compassionately right on cue. All the more remarkable for the fact that all these theories and hopes of mine are built on the most marshy of speculations. Because there is no hard evidence, still, and nothing more for the police to go on. They, poor souls, have gone cool on the case. Nothing more to be done. Nothing to say a man can't bow out of one life and embrace another. What's illegal in that? I am just haunted by a fact which I can't help repeating over and over again to Dora: I thought I knew my Kim, every last millimetre of him, and I knew shit. You get on with life, but this is something which never goes. The speculation as to the whys and the wherefores, I know, will outlive even the misery. It'll be there still, years hence, and in my dotage, the who was he after all, the man I thought I knew and loved more than anyone, and why did he go? Am I living in some alternative reality that my judgement of character can have been so awry? Questions that are more tenacious in their own, menacing way, than any amount of missing.

Jack pushes the chair out from underneath him and it makes a harsh scrape on the floor. He goes to the front door. I get up and shovel the leftover food on his plate into the bin. Before I turn on the tap I hear the door opening but no greetings in the corridor. I assume Jack's just given Dora a quiet kiss on the cheek and is following her back in here. I spurt some globules of washing-up liquid, colour of toy emeralds, over the dishes in the sink, and start going at them with a scouring pad. 'Hang on a sec,' I say cheerfully without turning round. 'This scrambled egg's a bugger to get off.'

I am fully aware of their presence behind me, but they're not

253

saying anything. Suddenly it occurs to me that something's wrong. In a split second I wonder if something's happened to Dora's husband, Roy. Accident. Lover. I'm more edgy since Kim's gone. My instinct is to expect the worst for the slimmest of reasons, and immediately, not to wait for an hour or two to do so. I let go of the plate in the water and turn round.

Not Dora.

Kim.

I'm standing here, I glance at him, and all I'm thinking is that my hands are wet. I need to find a cloth before I touch him. When we were saying our wedding vows, I heard us voicing these incredible words but I couldn't help wondering if the tear in my eye was causing my mascara to run, would people notice it beneath my veil as I was walking back along the aisle? The mundanest of thoughts have a habit of gate-crashing the grandest of moments.

Can't see a cloth. Don't want to wipe my hands on my skirt because it's made of this pretend velvety material which is lovely and warm for winter but which goes funny, kind of clumpy, if you get water on it. So I stand still, looking all about the place. I might be nodding.

'Your hair's got very long,' I remark, still rooted to my spot because I've nothing with which to dry my hands. 'What's the time?'

Kim says nothing. I notice he has not sat down. There is silence.

Jack moves close to me, protective. I vaguely take in the expression on his face. It is not one of pleasure. In fact, his cheeks are red and puffed up like a trumpeter's. I can tell he is very, very angry. I am not, and I think I worry that he is about to blast his father. It frightens me, confrontation, and the thought that Kim might, slightest provocation, just walk straight out of that door again without any explanation. I take Jack's hand, perhaps to calm him. Then again I ask the time. Again, no answer.

I look at my watch. Ten past eight. The date says the 24th. I try to think quickly. His birthday? My birthday? Our twenty-third wedding anniversary? Hardly. He missed that, spectacu-larly. Valentine's Day? No. What's the significance of 24th February? Not even Leap Year. Shrove Tuesday, isn't it? Am I right? Fucking Pancake Day. We've not celebrated it since the kids were about ten, and then only when we remembered. I always imagined if he came back, it might be Christmas Day, or our twenty-third, or something special. Or at least four o'clock in the morning, a bang on the door! A sort of dramatic entrance. It never occurred to me he'd come back on, for us, a normal, boring Tuesday evening on a moveable feast day in February. I couldn't ever have imagined that. You wouldn't.

'You've missed the seven o'clock news, and supper, I'm afraid. In time for the nine though. Are you hungry at all? We had scrambled eggs. They were really good, weren't they, Jack, my love? I could make you some scrambled eggs, toast?' Waiting for the answer to my question, I look at Kim properly for the first time. Up until now my eyes have been darting everywhere but haven't, somehow, fixed on him for more than a split second here and there. He has lost weight. Neck's gone a bit scrawny. His clean-shaven face cannot disguise his exhaustion, and his clothes look as though they have been washed or, rather, dabbed at in patches with a soapy towel, but they're ragged as hell. Same ones as he left in, only a different shirt, like a school uniform sort of shirt. He can't take his eyes off me. It's as if they are pleading.

'Mum, sit down, eh?' Jack says, stepping even closer to me, his hand still in mine.

'No, love, I'm fine. Your father looks as though he could do with something to eat.' I start rinsing the saucepan.

'Sylvie—'

His voice. I have heard it day and night in my head, and now it's really back in my kitchen. The way he says my name, it has an inflection like nobody else's. I've always thought it his way of imbuing those two syllables with as much love as they could possibly contain, till they were fit to bursting with it.

'Sylvie—'

It hasn't changed. I drop the saucepan in the water, and rush to him. But just as I am about to give him a hug, something stops me with a jolt, inches from him. Elation tinged with an unknown quantity. Restraint? He puts out his arms. Slowly, I hold first his hands, same firm grip as ever. Then his elbows, bonier than before. Then him. My Kim. Home.

*

An onlooker might have been surprised by my initial reaction, so deadpan. An onlooker might have said that it would have been more in keeping with events if I had turned round and, on seeing him, either screamed and whooped for joy, devoured him with limpet kisses, and clung onto him for dear life; or screamed and shouted with the voice of Hell's Furies, and pummelled him with my fists till he was a crochet of bruises.

Yet I had been thinking, naturally, of that moment, his home-coming, several times a day for four months. Focusing on it obsessively. I had devised my words and very face down to the last detail. I'd rehearsed my lines, my look, judged them to perfection: elation, of course, joy, happiness, affection and, yes, forgiveness, whatever the circumstances, really. I'd done anger. The reason for his going would have had to have been a good one, so I would have to forgive him, despite the pain that reason caused me. Even that of another woman – if it was an affair, I probably wasn't entirely blameless. These things often take two. Yet, of course, alongside the elation, I'd be sure to portray in there somewhere just the right amount of cautious restraint.

Just in order to show him that he had some work to do before we could be back exactly where we were before 4 November. He couldn't just walk out, come back, and pick up where we left off without some explanation. I was going to demand answers, however much it made him wriggle. If all was forgiven, then that, at least, was my due.

Of course, when that well-scrutinised moment did actually materialise, I wasn't quite as I had hoped I might be. I was stopped in my tracks by an almost comical shock. Cliché, I'm afraid, was responsible for scuppering all my carefully laid plans. Another woman might have been more able to control it. I'm the type, *in extremis*, whose emotions tend to arm-lock me. I'm up for grabs.

So it was some minutes, all that faffing, thinking about my wet hands for God's sake, before I could move and before I hugged him. When I felt him up against me, same breath as that over the dish of haddock the night he went away, I disintegrated into tears.

All night I held onto him, embossed to his body, so warm, crying. In the dark, the room looked pretty well normal again, everything back in place. We didn't talk much. Case of too much to say. Where to begin?

The following morning we sat in the sitting room, by ourselves, still not saying a lot, just readjusting to one another's presence. Later that day, and the following one too, was a flurry of ringing and celebration. We rang Mackenzie first. I said, 'Guess what?'

'Dad's home,' she said, without hesitation, and I put him on the line. We were all bloody blubbing. She was on the next plane.

We called Dora, my colleagues, the police, and Suzie at Missing Persons. We called all the family and friends we could think of. Those hours had the same spirit as those just after we announced our engagement. Kim and I collected Mackenzie from the airport. The scene. Such elation, beyond the norm. Raised eyebrows in Arrivals.

We called the surgery to see if Kim's job was still open for him. When he went missing, Kim's partners were so kind to me, and as helpful as they could be in the circumstances. For a few days, overworked though they were, they managed just the three of them. But after the first fortnight with no news, one of them, Abigail, rang me, and as gently and tactfully as the situation would allow, told me they were going to have to take on a locum. She said they all hoped I wouldn't mind. It was a painful moment for me, but I completely understood. They could not cope as a depleted team indefinitely. Nor could it reasonably be expected that his salary could go on being paid into our account in his absence. It stopped when the locum arrived, at the end of November, something which hasn't been easy for me emotionally, as well as financially. I didn't ask whether or not, if and when Kim ever did come home, his job would be open to him once more. It was too early days. But as the weeks passed I worried desperately that it would not. Luckily, when the time came, it was, and Kim, probably rather sensibly, was back at work almost immediately.

Mackenzie stayed, bless her, so magnanimous in the forgiveness of her beloved father, for three days before having to return to Northern Ireland and her studies. The four of us in the house once more. The spirit was good, only Jack cut a darker presence. His pleasure at seeing his father was tempered.

'I saw what he did to you, Mum,' he told me after Mackenzie had gone. 'You might be able to forgive, but I cannot forget.'

From the moment I set eyes on Kim again, I was given five days' grace; five days of undiluted euphoria, bugger any restraint, any notion of letting him make a little payment for what he had done. But on the sixth day, Kim affectionate and loving as ever if not more so, shaven and clean now, and back to work, no trace of his recent adventure about him but a more chiselled profile than before, and the disappearance of his modest double chin; and Jack's words chafing in my ears, common sense and reality began to set in.

Why should I forgive him? Over the last couple of weeks he has talked of circumstance and chance, novelty, curiosity and opportunity, and these words all seem very abstract to me. At one point, long before he came home, during one of my many conversations with Suzie, we systematically went through the list the Missing Persons Helpline has compiled of all the different, and, let's face it, not very unfathomable, reasons that people go missing. There was debt and redundancy on that list, stress, depression, abuse, mental illness, abduction, and we went through them all. I ruled some of them out completely, and wondered and tortured myself about the outside possibility of others. The only one I didn't even consider was the last – 'just because they feel like it'. Didn't give it a moment's thought. Inconceivable. More so than hidden debt, or inconspicuous depression. Not my steady, reliable, responsible, trustworthy, loving Kim, not just because he felt like it.

What a fatal oversight that dismissal seems now. For apparently undefined temptation happed his way, and he thought why not, for once? Of course, I am mortified with hurt and anger, and I don't understand, and yet I've been trying here to kind of see what he's saying. It's in the nature of my training, after all. But I can't help believing it's feeble, feeble stuff, really. Because, also, why? Why don't we all just go along with our caprice, fuck responsibility, and all other things besides? It's not as if we haven't all thought about embracing the excitements of the unknown, but we don't do it. For most of us responsibility and love are not just trifles, flies to wanton boys. They are part of the system which is society. The run-down places he saw, and some of the run-down, lonely, desperate people he met on his travels and whom tells me about, are the very victims of the kind of lack of responsibility and disregard for love which he welcomed so readily that rainy night. The fabric of community and family is broken down when these crucial elements are toyed with so carelessly. Unforgivable.

Unforgivable, too, has been the lack of any real explanation for how he could have been so contemptuous of our feelings. This is what haunts me more than anything. He speaks vaguely of his past, something he has not only never resorted to before, but has always dismissed as insignificant. It's come in handy now. Only not in my book. Almost any cause for his abandoning us so cruelly I could forgive – mental breakdown, true stress, depression, illness, whatever – but not this, not this wishy-washy concoction of circumstance and novelty and dubious reference to his perhaps having inherited or copied his father's wintry detachment. It's not enough. I am craving powerful stuff to forgive, not a fleeting moment of eye off the ball; distraction. That is pathetic, and cannot inspire me for all my good intentions before he came home, to forgive him, nor again to trust him.

You can't fix trust. It's not like a plate, just squirt on the Superglue. Once broken, never mended. Every time his wretched stomach rumbles or his toes feel a little chilly, I shall be wondering if he's plotting on hopping onto the nearest bus as a way of tickling his wearisome fancy. It is not a way to live, that constant worry. For all the loaded conviction in his mouth, and my God he is the master of conviction and probably means every word, I do not believe a syllable of it. He begs and pleads my forgiveness, and makes love to me with the passion of a lover straight out of a nineteenth-century epic novel.

I have chosen not to give myself the grief of intolerable and eternal anxiety; not for the rest of my life to be a slave to my watch as I ask myself, is he coming home? The way I have done this is by deciding not to forgive him. In fact I haven't just decided, I couldn't if I wanted to – and I certainly cannot come up on cue with the words or gestures to reassure him that it's all going to be all right, given time. I don't know. I do still love Kim. After all, he has same voice, same physique, same face, same lovingness but, in this altered light of recent anomaly, I cannot love him as I did before. I love him for our past, and it is because of that, that I don't want to lose him and have no intention of separating from or divorcing him. We will stay together, but it is from now on a distant marriage we will have.

I walk around him now, not to him. I no longer bother to make the bed, because the warmth of the sheets from his body no longer gives rise to delight. We eat out of packets: I feel, why cook when I wouldn't bother if I were alone? He tells me about his patients, desperate to resume that old intimacy of confiding. I have thrown myself into my work with new enthusiasm, but his encouragement doesn't spur me into wanting to reveal anything of those clients of mine who populate my day. I nod, but that is all.

Far as I see it, we've lost everything but our past, and even that I can't be sure of since he was able so nonchalantly to toy with it. I find, these past three weeks since Pancake Day, that I've not much time, or inclination, for the future. The very thought of it makes me feel slothful. I think I'll just let it, of its own accord, bleed on.

# 15

Her pigeon phobia had gone. This, Kim learnt a month or so after having returned home. She happened to mention it, by chance. They had made a trip into the centre of Oxford to do some chores and were walking along the pavement together. In the Broad they found themselves approaching a dither of pigeons. Automatically, for her sake, Kim started to walk round them, but Sylvie didn't appear to notice, just carried straight on through them. Not only didn't she do her elaborate avoidance dance, but when they flapped up all around her, she even failed to duck. Just walked on, oblivious as someone who enjoys a stroll across Trafalgar Square. Kim was amazed, stopped her there and then, outside the window of the Paperback Shop, and asked how it was so. She told him, briefly, that one day, soon after Christmas, she'd been on her way to work and a pigeon had been strutting along in front of her for several minutes, hadn't got out of her path. She had made a decision. To look at it properly, to focus on its beak and feathers and claws, in a way she had always refused to do before, and to force herself no longer to be afraid. She had had, she said, more important things to be frightened about, very real things which shadowed her every waking, sleeping moment. Why waste her energy any longer being terrified of bloody pigeons?

Of course, Kim was delighted that she had shaken off her debilitating phobia at long last. A freedom of sorts. Yet he couldn't fail to get the reference.

'I'm sorry,' he said, outside the Paperback Shop.

'The pigeon phobia was rather easier to deal with,' she told him, matter-of-factly, not bitterly. Even managed a semi-smile.

Things, Kim mused, had not been the same since he got back.

The very foundations of their marriage had shifted.

First few days, especially when Mackenzie was home, Sylvie had displayed euphoria. But it did not last. It gave way, gradually, to a sort of wary detachment in her which, try as he might to divert, he could not. They talked, a bit, to start with. There was perhaps too much for her to take on board: the fact that there was so little. That he had gone for no reason. Once, she said, if there had been a nervous breakdown, then there would have been something now for them to work on together, to solve, and remedy. If there had been another woman, then at least there would have been something the thought of which she could have got her claws into, to hate. But curiosity and chance? They were so abstract, so unmanifest. There was nothing concrete on which to focus her anger and resentment.

Jack, on the other hand, didn't need something to be angry about, he was just angry. Could barely bring himself to look at his father, let alone speak to him with anything but fury.

At the beginning of March, he took some girl, whom he wouldn't let Kim meet, away to London for the night. The following evening Kim found him and Sylvie in the kitchen. She was a little tearful, but smiling. Jack announced that he was leaving home, going to move into a place in the Iffley Road. He didn't expand, and took a bag before supper. Hugged his mother. Gave a peremptory nod to his father. Only later, over a quiet lasagne, just the two of them, did Kim learn from Sylvie that he had moved in with his new girlfriend, and that she was called Josephine. Silently, Kim wondered how long it might be before his son and he could resume that easy relationship they had enjoyed for twenty-two years. His disappearence had unravelled in four short months two decades' worth of loving familiarity, acceptance, and affection. Why hadn't he thought of that before he sat down to his curry at the Taj Mahal?

After Jack had gone, Kim felt terrible sadness and regret about this flailing relationship with his son, and tried to forget about it as best as he could when he was working. Ever since his decision in the skip to return home to a normal life, he had not only been terrified that Sylvie might have not wanted him back, but had also been very concerned that, after his inpromptu sabbatical, his job at the surgery might have been lost to him for ever. The thought had weighed on him that his partners might not want him either. Posts in general practice, even though he was experienced, and even if it wasn't the most popular area of medicine, weren't two-a-penny. Presumably Sam and co. had made other arrangements in his absence.

Meanwhile, at home, Sylvie's wary detachment gave way to low-burn alienation. While she was pleased for Jack that he had found someone whom he loved, she could not forgive Kim for precipitating their son's leaving home sooner than he might otherwise have done. She had told Jack that perhaps it was not wise to move in with Josephine quite so early on. He had said, 'That may be so, and in a perfect world I might have left it a little longer, but I do know it's right, and I'm not sticking round here.'

Try as he might, Kim could not claw back the happy family atmosphere that had once existed so naturally in the house. Sylvie couldn't talk in the way she once had. If he asked her questions about her day, about the children, she answered with the caution of someone who can never quite relax. When he pressed her, she never once talked of parting, but revealed to him indirectly, that she could no longer trust him. One evening she did open up, temporarily. 'I never thought,' she said, 'you were so lacking in imagination.' Did he not, she asked, once consider what she and Jack and Mackenzie might have been going through? He hadn't answered, so then she proceeded to tell him. She described the horror and pain of not knowing, enlikening it to the suicide of a loved one, but assuring him that it was worse. At least suicide usually had the benefit of a note, and a body. In his singular absence, she and the kids had been denied such luxuries. The process of healing had never been able to begin. So it was a protracted agony they endured. She reeled off a list of what this consisted of: hurt, anger, betrayal, possible unrequited love, despair, the vagaries of hope. The list went on. Did he wonder, she asked, that she could no longer trust him? The legacy of his having gone, his reason for having done so never entirely clear, meant that every time he went out of the house, to buy a paper, to go to work, she could not be sure he would ever come back. No amount of promising could convince her. Married trust, built up so securely that they had always deemed it to be infallible, had been profoundly shaken.

But from time to time, catching her unawares, Kim found an expression on Sylvie's face that indicated something more profound than forgiveness. Of course, as she herself had often insisted in the past, people should be sceptical of such an unreliable indicator of truth as what was supposedly writ on someone's face. But, even so, whenever he glimpsed this passing expression of hers, he was sure he could see something in it, something which, against the odds, gave him a small reason for hope.